1 - Carter an S↑
We met... was it
long time ago?...
lot to share, time and separating
cannot change that ...

News from
The Republic of Letters
14 & 15

Chantal

News from
THE REPUBLIC OF LETTERS

EDITOR:
Keith Botsford

FOUNDING EDITOR:
Saul Bellow

CONTRIBUTING EDITORS:
Michael Hulse
James Wood

SENIOR EDITORS:
Sassan Tabatabai
Chris Walsh

ASSISTANT EDITORS
Zachary Bos
Joseph Jerome
Louisa Mandarino
Adam Webb

PROOFREADER:
Emma Hawes

PUBLISHER:
The Toby Press LLC

COORDINATING EDITOR:
Aloma Halter

CORRESPONDENCE:
For Submissions & Editorial:
The Republic of Letters
120 Cushing Avenue
Boston MA 02125, USA
rangoni@bu.edu
www.bu.edu/trl

FOR SUBSCRIPTIONS:
The Toby Press LLC
POB 8531, New Milford,
CT 06776-8531
Attn: trol@tobypress.com

News from The Republic of Letters
is published biannually. Individual
copies are $9.95, and subscriptions
are $35.00 for four issues. Please add
$12 for foreign deliveries.

Retailers may purchase copies of
News from The Republic of Letters at

Ingram, Baker & Taylor and all other
fine distributors, or from *The* Toby
Press LLC.

Some back issues are available. Please
see inside back page for more details.

For more information, please visit
these websites:
News from the Republic of Letters:
www.bu.edu/trl
The Toby Press: **www.tobypress.com**

Typeset in Garamond
by Jerusalem Typesetting

Printed and bound in the United
States by Thomson-Shore Inc.,
Michigan

Issue 14 & 15, 2005:
ISBN 1592640362

Contents

ARIAS

Peter Coleman: The Novelist and the Secret Policeman, *3*

Herbert Gold: Bewitched, Bothered, and Begoogled, *11*

LIVES

François Bondy and Melvin J. Lasky: 19

Romain Gary: Goliarde, *33*

Sophie Wilkins, Saul Bellow, Dylan Thomas: Letters, *41*

TEXTS

Chantal Hunt: Antoinette, *59*

Melvin J. Lasky: The Eminence Rouge, *95*

Henryk Skwarczyński: Polly Maggoo, *185*

Yuri Buida: Chemitch, *209*

Conall Ryan: Hostivar, *217*

ARCHIVES

R.B. Cunninghame Graham: The Gold Fish, *235*

POEMS

John Randolf Carter: Someone Comes Knocking, *247*

THE READER

The Reader: Andrew Saltarelli's Book
Against Forgetting, *251*

New Fiction, *269*

Pierre Bayle's Notebook: 281

Arias

Peter Coleman

The Novelist and the Secret Policeman

I may be able to add a footnote to the controversy threatening the reputation of the great Italian writer Ignazio Silone. The scandal arose out of the devastating allegation that, at the very time he was running the Communist underground in Italy in the 1920s, Silone was also an informer for the fascist political police. The controversy shows no sign of sputtering out, and even Silone's widow, Darina, at the time of her death, was unsure of the truth of the matter.

Silone's reputation depended on three achievements: his novels of peasant life in Mussolini's Italy; his political essays; and an almost saintly integrity. In my student youth, dog-eared editions of his early novels—now re-issued as *The Abruzzo Trilogy* with a perceptive and *simpatico* foreword by Alexander Stille—were handed around like dispatches from the anti-fascist front-line. (They had an added cachet of being forbidden fruit: the Stalinists did not approve.) His essays—at once anti-fascist and anti-communist—were never as revered as the novels, but they were still earnestly read. His reputation for adamantine integrity ensured that. He was as close as Italy has come to a Solzhenitsyn.

But some five years ago, two Italian historians began publicizing in the late Renzo de Felice's revisionist journal *Nuova Storia Contemporanea*, their research in the archives of the fascist political police. It documented, they claimed, Silone's work as a police informer. In the ensuing uproar, amid charges and counter-charges of misinterpretation, ignorance and forgery, some critics were totally disenchanted and changed sides, while others found new depths in Silone's work." At the very least, established opinions had to be reconsidered.

I never met Silone (who died in 1978) but I interviewed Darina in the course of my research for *The Liberal Conspiracy*, an appraisal of the Congress for Cultural Freedom (CCF). It was in 1984 in Geneva in a private hospital where she was to have a foot operation. She was a vivacious Dubliner, auburn-haired, tall and handsome. She told me about an article she had written on Silone's last hours, how to her surprise his dying words were in French (*"C'est fini. Je meurs."*) and how she had recited the Lord's Prayer over his corpse. (They had been married thirty-four years. There were no children; it was said to be *un mariage blanc*.) "There is no single truth about Silone," she said, "only many truths. He was a little crazed."

But a passing remark leads to my footnote. I asked her about one of her 1951 letters that I had found in the Congress for Cultural Freedom archives in Chicago. In it she had outlined to the Executive Committee, in Paris, Silone's success in encouraging the defection of intellectuals from the Communist Party of Italy. She had no memory of this letter, she told me. Then she added, as if in an aside: "Silone was not above getting me to sign his letters." I put this down as a Silonian idiosyncrasy and thought little about it.

But it kept coming back and sometimes coloured my research. Was there something cagey about the great man? Soon afterwards, when I was browsing the Arthur Koestler papers in London, I came across a note which the militant anti-communist Koestler had scribbled to a companion in Berlin in 1950 at the founding conference of the Congress for Cultural Freedom. It was the very moment of the outbreak of the Korean War. Silone, an uncompromising anti-Stalinist long before Koestler, was delivering a mild and conciliatory speech. "I always wondered," Koestler scrawled, "whether basically Silone is honest or not. Now I know he is not."

But the pugnacious Koestler was never an easy man to work with. (Sidney Hook said he couldn't read from a telephone book without enraging somebody.) Silone—suspecting him, and the Berlin Conference, of being part of a "State Department operation"—may have simply wanted to keep some distance. Koestler's note was not a final judgement, merely an expression of his well-known impatience.

Later in Austin, Texas, in the archives of Nicolas Nabokov, the CCF Secretary-General, I found a letter from Nabokov complaining of the impossibility of dealing frankly with the implacably anti-Vatican Silone. Nabokov suggested that Jacques Maritain explain to the Vatican that the CCF, although liberal, did not eat the Pope for breakfast. He wanted "a show-down" with Silone, although he had little hope that anything would come of it because you could never pin him down. But we already knew how elusive Silone was without Nabokov's help: he always was, for example, "the socialist without a party", "the Christian without a church."

Later still in Paris, the philosopher Raymond Aron told me of his anger with Silone in 1956 for having organized, without consultation with Aron, a CCF conference in Zurich of editors and writers to which he had invited several "voguish Parisian leftists" and "Frenchmen of the third order" (he meant Roland Barthes and Georges Bataille) to discuss and promote cultural exchanges with some philistine apparatchiks from the Soviet Union. Aron threatened to resign from the CCF. Most of the CCF colleagues thought he made too much of *une chose silonienne*, and the dispute fizzled out in the explosion of the Hungarian Revolution.

Not all Silone's colleagues had these edgy reservations about him. In 1969, when the CCF collapsed amid "revelations" of its CIA funding, its inspirational leader Michael Josselson suffered two strokes. One of the few to visit the stricken man in Geneva was Silone, who kissed him on both cheeks and addressed him as 'tu.' "It was," wrote Josselson in a note I found among his papers in Texas, "one of the most moving moments of my life."

These footnotes of scraps of gossip do little more than suggest that Silone was a hard man to label. Was he an impossibly fanatical anti-communist, as the Welsh politician Leo Abse wrote in London the other day? Or a drug addict of anti-fascism and anti-clericalism, as Nabokov believed? Or the exemplar of the age, as David Pryce-Jones sensed? Was he forever playing a double or triple game, or was he, as François Fejto thought, not Machiavellian enough for the circles he moved in? Was he indeed a police informer?

When the first reports of Silone the informer appeared, I dismissed them as incredible. I was not quite as certain as the journalist Indro Montanelli who said: "I would not accept the truth of these documents even if Silone rose from the tomb and confirmed them." But I believed (and wrote) that they were akin to the zealous defamation of such liberal anti-communists as George Orwell ("spy"), Arthur Koestler ("rapist") or James McAuley ("sex maniac," "mad murderer," heavy smoker" or whatever you fancy).

Their unforgivable offence was that they had all been right about communism and the Cold War, as Mikhail Gorbachev confirmed. But as arguments over Silone developed, and evidence and counter-evidence accumulated, I was one of those, like Darina, forced to reconsider my understanding of him, including the sketch I had written in *The Liberal Conspiracy*. I also recalled my earlier, seeming trifles of research.

What are the allegations? The historians Dario Biocca and Mauro Canali turned up in the fascist police archives a sensational correspondence between Silone and secret police official Guido Bellone, a much older man who had befriended him in his youth in southern Italy—perhaps at the time when Silone was first under investigation for storming a police station during a peasant riot. The story of the correspondence between the novelist and his police "handler" is outlined in their book *L'Informatore* (*The Informer*) and in Canali's long essay "Ignazio Silone and the Fascist Political Police" in the *Journal of Modern Italian Studies* (Spring 2000).

It began in 1919 (before there was either a communist party or a fascist party in Italy). It continued throughout the 1920s with Silone, by now a top communist, giving Bellone information about the underground Communist Party's activists and factions. It ended in 1930 with a striking letter from Silone breaking the association with Bellone at the same time he broke with the Communist Party:

> *My health is terrible but the cause is moral. A sense of mortality now overwhelms me completely; it does not permit me to sleep, eat or have a minute's rest. I am at a crossroads in my life and there is only one way out: I must abandon militant politics completely. The only other solution is death. First I will eliminate from my life all falsity, doubleness, ambiguity and mystery; second, I will start a new life, on a new basis, in order to repair the evil that I have done, to redeem myself...*

Many challenged Biocca and Canali, notably the leftist historian Giuseppe Tamburrano. In his painstaking book *Processo a Silone* (*Silone on Trial*), he dismissed their work as a travesty of scholarship riddled with errors. But there is no denying the authenticity of at least some of the archival documents.

Silone's supporters argue that throughout the correspondence he only provided information that was either innocuous or already known to Bellone from other sources. They also suspect that he was acting in the full (and carefully undocumented) knowledge of the Communist Party with the intention of probing what the fascists actually knew about the communist underground. In the later years of the correspondence, there was another major factor: his younger brother was arrested in 1928 for attempted regicide. Silone looked to Bellone for help. Did Bellone agree to help—at a price? (The brother died in prison in 1932.)

The controversy has not yet run its course. Meanwhile it has provoked a comprehensive re-reading of Silone's books and the discovery of new dimensions, especially in the novels of *The Abruzzo Trilogy*. It is not just a matter of playing the problematic game of teasing out details of Silone's biography from the novels, seeing, for example, a self-portrait in Silone's sketch of the tormented informer Luigi Murica in *Bread and Wine*.

Could it be that for the past seventy years we have misunderstood *The Abruzzo Trilogy*? We have read the novels as classics of anti-fascism. (In 1944 the Allies distributed copies to liberated Italians.) Perhaps this is a misreading. Perhaps they should be read as anti-communist?

The English historian, Martin Clark, recently considered this suggestion in the *London Review of Books* but he did not develop the idea. The current controversy gives it resonance. Silone was one of those who in 1921, with Gramsci, Togliatti and others then more important, founded the Communist Party of Italy. His disenchantment was swift. In his several visits to Moscow in the 1920's, he found a thickening smog of terror and lies (see his essay "Emergency Exit"). The only way you could remain a communist, he said later, was by deadening your conscience, by inducing an moral narcosis. Despairing of Stalinism (which he dubbed Red Fascism), he saw no hope at all in Trotsky or Bukharin. By 1930 he could no longer live with it. His expulsion from the Communist Party was his "emergency exit."

It was at this point that he adopted the name Silone and began writing his novels. Is it conceivable that so seasoned and intense an anti-Stalinist could keep his anti-communism out of his contemporary political stories? The novels were admired, or attacked, for decades as anti-fascist or communist propaganda, yet fascism is barely mentioned in *Fontamara* and the revolutionary figure offering hope to the oppressed Abruzzo peasants is a vague Liberator called the Mystery Man, more Franciscan than Marxist. The oppressive dictatorship that is the background to these fables might be communist as much as fascist—and in some cases more likely to be communist. *Fontamara*, for example, culminates in a Government massacre of a village of rebellious Abruzzo peasants: there was no such massacre in Mussolini's Italy, but there were many in Stalin's Soviet Union which Silone was well aware of.

Could it be that when Silone wrote to Bellone in 1931 about "the evil I have done," he meant the evil of communism whose servant he had been and which he had come to abominate? Are his famous novels, as Martin Clark wondered, a continuation of his work as an informer?

The Age of Ideology produced few artists as anguished as Silone. Desmond O'Grady, who knew him well, was one of many who found him a damaged man, "moody and often apathetic." The translator William Weaver found "a haunted man, a man of sorrows." The biographer Iris Origo said "he carried within him wounds which he knew to be unhealable." We may never find answers to the questions which *il caso Silone* raises. But it adds depth as well as darkness to *The Abruzzo Trilogy*, still among the greatest novels of the totalitarian years.

Herbert Gold

Bewitched, Bothered, and Begoogled

I just admire your writings so much," murmured the voice on the other end of the line. "Is it okay to say that? Is that the right word?"

Laboring under a yearning to gush, my caller seemed to sense that gush might lack appropriate dignity; yet, in a delicate balancing act, he figured that a light sprinkle could get the desired result from the consumer. I was the designated consumer, an "author."

He was the son-in-law of a woman I like. It was my duty to hear him out. "So tell me," he continued, "how do you get editors to publish your *oo-ver*?" He had read the word *oeuvre* someplace and understood that it was the polite way to refer to a writer's work.

Dissonant emotions stirred. I wished to answer: Oh, I pay editors and critics. I send cases of champagne to their home addresses. A rumble of disagreeableness began to roil my soul, making a music like the concluding storm of "A Night on Bald Mountain." But instead of surrendering, I reminded myself of my friend, his mother-in-law, and said with the practiced eloquence of a person who has lived by words, especially active verbs, for many years now: "Ummm…"

"I know, I know, you don't have to tell me," he said. "They know you from before. You're tried and true, like a name brand, I fully understand." Perhaps he didn't realize that I was probably published once for the first time. I had been an unknown entity and still haven't met most of my editors. For me, God invented mail; and in due course the children of the Lord invented the telephone, fax, and e-mail, not to mention couriers on ponies. Back in history, for example, 'Betty Crocker' was an unknown brand name. My name will never be that famous.

"Tell me," I inquired, seeking to express mild curiosity, a step on the path toward helping me help him by understanding how I fit into his life's plan. "What have you read of mine?"

"So you've been writing forever, gradually built yourself up through the years?" he asked.

"*Tell me.*"

He sighed. He was patient with artistic temperament, since he had one of his own. I waited, letting my breath sound into the telephone; not plagiarizing his sigh, but emitting a soupçon of pushiness. He said: "Haven't actually read anything of yours personally, but I've Googled you."

"Pardon?"

"On my computer. I search-engined you up. That Google is a terrific service—" My entire *oo-ver* was at his command with a few hits of the keys and wiggles of the mouse. "—and I see you're well-respected and, and, and you must be…" What were the additional concepts he was groping for? "Respected…make a good living…work from home and you don't have to go to an office. That's what I want to do with my *oo-ver.* Just today I came home from listening to my boss telling me what to do, but now I'm my own boss, I write and write until I feel too sleepy or my wife, Bonnie, complains I'm not listening to her when all I want to be is a distinguished American literary figure like, you know…"

"Yes, yes, thanks."

All through history, writers, editors, and teachers have criticized, stimulated, and therefore encouraged younger ones. Saul Bellow, reading early stories of mine, sometimes said, "Put it through the loom again," meaning revise and expand and contract, or: "Your characters are still in Immigration," meaning that not all of the necessary forms had been filled out, go back to work. Both the jolt of criticism and the resulting thought were marvellous gifts.

Perhaps there was a wise actor who said to Shakespeare, "To be" is a nice optimistic remark, but how about if you darken it a bit, because life is difficult, and add: "...or not to be." Or there was a geriatric bard who waved his invisible arms at poor blind Homer, suggesting that Apollo was a strong character who needed to be fleshed out: "Make it '*Far-flying* Apollo,' babe."

The contemporary term for this process is mentoring. I owe a debt in memory of those who helped me. I hitch-hiked thousands of miles when I was a runaway pre-beatnik lad; now I pick up the occasional hitch-hiker although it turns out that some of them are hitch-hookers or outpatients—very few future novelists. I concentrated my mind on my friend of fond memory, the Googler's mother-in-law. "Okay, let's talk," I said.

We met. It's the duty of an older professional in the mentoring posture to pay for the coffee; this didn't cut too deeply into my children's inheritance because we met at a sincere artist's retro-beatnik funky hangout, not Starbuck's. In preparation, he had scrambled his hair (an artist with his head in the clouds) and carried with him a portfolio stuffed with printout. He had beseeching eyes. I was ready to mentor, but not yet ready to let him slide the portfolio toward me.

"Since we spoke on the phone last week," I inquired with the kind of curiosity that never dies, especially in an *author*, "have you refreshed your sense that you and I might be"—I searched for the right language, but tumbled helplessly into pomposity—"on the same page?"

"I'm a very busy man," he said. "My day job, plus all my spare time writing." He cast another fond but beseeching glance toward the overflowing portfolio, which seemed to be inching its way across the table by some inner power of its own.

I tapped it back by some outer power of my right arm, firmed up by regular morning callisthenics. "So I guess you haven't read one of my actual texts."

"Not personally. Like I explained, I've got a lot on my plate these days."

That was okay with me; or at least okay enough while, like the gathering clouds of the thunderstorms of my Midwestern boyhood, rage accumulated in my vengeful heart—this is the typical inept poetic strophe of a confirmed author who doesn't need precision anymore because he has already arrived in the marketplace.

The hunger for encouragement never dies unless an artist sinks into megalomania; some do, of course, and I omit examples because anonymous insults hurt less. I have friends who give me good counsel: we give each other counsel. But the hunger for help which intends to target success through magic contact—no, no, no. My new friend figured he could save time by punching his keys, performing the act of Google, working the telephone—by efficient, post-modern basking. Sometimes I fear the capacity for malice has diminished in me, but evidently this isn't a serious problem. Now I fear that the capacity for compassion may be failing.

I tried to explain, commanding myself in sentence fragments: Cold world out there…all here together for a brief time on earth… Ramp up the empathy!

Minor discomforts are easily forgiven. For example, most writers don't refer to themselves as "author," just as no one but a newly-hatched lawyer, the yolk still sticking to his feathers, would refer to himself as an "attorney-at-law." I hope and pray my local politicians don't refer to themselves as "statesmen" or "statespersons." (It feels okay to say "writer," "poet," "novelist," "journalist"—there are many available choices.) I was willing to educate my Googler on tasteful lingo.

Oh, I explained so much. I received eager nods of agreement. He appreciated my pedantry.

The next day, my Googler wrote me a letter asking for forgiveness, dipping his quill into the pool of abjectness (another excessive metaphor, dear reader). He stated that his greatest desire and, indeed, newest goal in life was to read one of his favorite author's *oo-vers*.

Which would I recommend? Remembering, of course, that he's a very busy man. So which was the best?

I suggested by phone that he not ask a parent which of his children is the best. My Googler was growing wiser by the minute. Byte by byte, he was learning about metaphor and other tricks of the literary trade. "You mean, like a book is your child and you want all of them to have the best things in life, like a best-seller and an interview on Terry Gross?"

Something like that. I wondered if he used Terry Gross on National Public Radio as his example instead of Oprah because, due to my pedagogy, he was heading upscale, elite-wise.

Whatever.

"So when do we meet again?" he asked. "This time, the coffee's on me. Unless you want to have lunch?"

Isn't that what authors do?

Herbert Gold's writing, or at least his name, book titles, and miscellaneous data, can be viewed in Googleland. For those who are interested in actual reading, bound copies may be found in libraries, used book stores, and at fine garage sales. Some malls contain a bookstore, located between the Victoria's Secret and the T.G.I. Friday's. Go ahead, be brave, break the cobwebs on its front door and enter.

Lives

Melvin J. Lasky, 1978

François Bondy and Melvin J. Lasky

In those days when we shared our education together amidst the political turbulence of 1930s New York, Mel appeared as a very vocal poseur, anxious to become a fashionable critic like Edmund Wilson... What never altered was his sardonic half-sneer and nasal whine.

(Andrew Roth in the *Guardian*)

In 1958, Mel Lasky replaced [Irving] Kristol as American editor [of Encounter]... Was Lasky, at this stage, a serving CIA agent? It is not a question that could (with legal impunity) have been asked in print during his lifetime, but the answer is almost certainly yes, he was. More specifically, he was an agent—not a 'sleeper' or a passively co-ideological sympathizer. He had a CIA-mandated task to fulfil. And he did.

(John Sutherland in *Financial Times Weekend Edition*)

...In Paris, [Nicolas] Nabokov played a major part in launching the Congress's first magazine, Preuves*...Finding an editor who enjoyed enough stature to lure those* 'compagnons de route' *into a more centrist* arrondissement *proved to be difficult...Having failed to attract a French editor, the Executive Committee decided to give the job to François Bondy,*

a Swiss journalist of German mother-tongue who had been a communist party activist until the Hitler-Stalin Pact of 1939. A key appointment to the Congress Secretariat in 1950 (as Director of Publications), Bondy had collaborated with Melvin Lasky, who called him 'the editorial adviser of our time par excellence'. Preuves was unmistakably the house organ of the Congress.

(Frances Stonor Saunders in 'The Cultural Cold War')

If you're of the generation that Lasky and Bondy belonged to, both now gone, you would take the collective whine above as the plaint of lovers of the God that Failed. Andrew Roth is an unrepentant Stalinist (and it is typical of the *Guardian* to choose such a man to write Lasky's obituary), John Sutherland's 'almost certainly' reflects his dedication as Stephen Spender's 'authorized' biographer to the poet's 'innocence' of any ties to the Evil Empire of America, while the TV journalist Frances Stonor Saunders' book starts with a premise—that to be of the left is virtuous—and sticks to it.[1]

The anti anti-communist left still flourishes; Stalinists (Like José Saramago) are still reputed, laureled and lauded; the intellectual Cold War between the Left and the Center (no one has ever accused the Congress for Cultural Freedom or Lasky or Bondy of being rightists, only of being 'virulent' anti-communists) is still being fought. Younger readers think of the CIA as being a collective failure, and some of us,

---

1. THE CONGRESS FOR CULTURAL FREEDOM WAS COVERTLY FUNDED BY THE CIA THROUGH A VARIETY OF FOUNDATIONS. The only acknowledged CIA employees in the Congress were Mike Josselson, its Director, and John Hunt, the novelist, who was its Secretary. Some knew of the CIA's underwriting of the Congress and, given the importance of having a counterpart to Soviet infiltration of the intelligentsia around the world, were perfectly happy with the connection; many surmised that it was; some preferred not to know; and some didn't bother to ask. The Congress ran many artistic and intellectual activities, funding travel, exhibitions, concerts, international conferences and the like. Its greatest resonance, however, was achieved with its magazines: *Encounter, Der Monat, Preuves, Tempo Presente, Cuadernos, Cadernos brasileiros*, etc. The accusation is made that the CIA 'interfered' with their operations. I was involved with two of them, and knew well the editors of the others, and I know this was not so. The composer Nicolas Nabokov was President of the Congress. Irving Kristol was the first American co-editor of *Encounter*.

François Bondy

myself included, think that—in creating the Congress for Cultural Freedom (Would that we had founded such an organization ten or fifteen years earlier!)—it did much good and succeeded in creating the new world in which we live now, a world in which ideology-driven totalitarianism is pretty much a dead letter.

What kinds of men made this possible? What sorts of lives did they live? Arthur Koestler, Victor Serge, George Orwell, Ignazio Silone—we know about them. Lasky and Bondy are representatives of my generation's struggle against false gods. What sorts of men were they? How did they come to be what they were? Regardless of whether or not they were part of a 'cultural Cold War' (Saunders) or a 'liberal conspiracy' (Peter Coleman) it is human lives that count. We are more what we are than what we did.

*

A young man asked me at Mel Lasky's funeral in June if I did not find his career astonishing. A much older friend, around the same time, asked me whether the death of François Bondy, a year earlier, had been noted in English or American papers. I answered 'no' to both questions. Bondy was not 'noticeable' in the way Lasky was. He was no less a writer or editor but he was a much more private one. And Lasky's life, improbable and genial as it was, did not astonish because in so many ways it was typical, distinguished mainly by the man's courage.

What struck me as I stood in Berlin on the lush flowery slopes of that cemetery, the Walfriedhof, on a bright summer day, myself revisiting old haunts, was how much the two men had in common, and how—with their deaths—a kind of political writing, educated, civilized, acute, fascinated by every passing phenomenon of language or behaviour, had vanished along with the generation, that of Hitler and Stalin, which was their particular study and their battleground.

The heart of the matter for both men was that they were men of the pre-war Left abandoned, like so many others, by the gods of their youth. They had to, and did, make new lives for themselves, but not without cost. I knew both men and am probably the youngest of their pre-war generation. I *know* the times we grew up in were hard and cruel, disillusioning times.

François Bondy's Prague-born father, N.O. Scarpi, was a writer, a feuilletonist and a translator (of, among other works, Orwell's *Animal Farm*). When François was born in Berlin, on the first day of 1915, his father was working in the theater with Max Reinhardt. With that *mitteleuropäische* background, languages were a necessity. François spoke German to his father, French to his step-mother and Italian in his high school, while reading widely in English. He didn't just speak these languages, he wrote in them and thought in them with total fluency. So much so that when teased as to what his *real* language was, Bondy hesitated. Well, what language did he dream in? Bondy still hesitated. What language did he count in? Ah, Bondy said: in German. He was that much of a linguist.

Bondy went to school in Lugano and Nice before studying at the Sorbonne and in Zürich, which was to become his home.

Mel was born five years later in the Bronx, where his strict and remote Talmudist Polish grandfather still spoke only Yiddish and his successful father brought up his family to have independent American minds. Lasky therefore came from what the sweet and viperish Stephen Spender, his future co-editor at *Encounter,* disparagingly

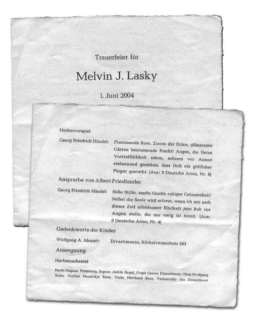

Memorial program for Melvin Lasky, Berlin, June 2004

called 'the Bronx box'. I doubt that Spender, who was part-Jewish, meant that in any anti-semitic way; he meant that Lasky was an upstart; *that* Stephen found unsettling.

Upstarts no, but super-achievers yes. The Jewish immigration of the turn of the century had ideas, energy and a fresh vernacular that was, via Delmore Schwartz and Saul Bellow, to transform our American language. Mel was part of a brilliant generation. He graduated from CCNY at nineteen in 1939 and went on to do a Master's degree in history at the University of Michigan. History stayed with him, and I remain much struck by what he once wrote about his CCNY mentor in history, Benjamin Nelson, whose informal discussion of current events Mel called 'gossip', writing on 'the visible surface of things.' That, of course, was to become Mel's art. Human histories derive from larger ideas, he thought, but they are in action in the here and now. He doted on the immediate, then and later. Bondy's European 'remove' served him equally well; Mel's immediacy was bound to be polemical.

While Lasky was still in his 'teens, François had briefly joined the French communist party, leaving in disgust with the signing of the Ribbentrop-Molotov treaty between Nazi Germany and Stalin's Soviet Union, in the fateful year of 1939. Lasky, who had been (like Saul Bellow and many others) an independent intellectual Trotskyist, lost his faith at twenty-two. In an unfinished memoir he has left a vivid picture of what he called the 'God that Failed phenomenon' meant to him. If you belonged to the 'Left', how did you reconcile the brute facts of Stalinism with the ideals of communism?

In decisive cases the great break could be a little diabolical twist, one of those famous Quantity-into-Quality changes, say from what the Old Trotskyites elaborated as 'Defensism' and 'Defeatism'. Can you possibly defend—morally, ideologically—the USSR when it is a repressive and degenerated (Stalinist) Workers State? [...] On our way to the Finland Station—with Baron Mannerheim's defense of Finland and Robert Sherwood's rousing Broadway play and Trotsky's stubborn apology for defending the Soviet invasion in 1940—there was much jejune confusion and, I suspect, hypocrisy; also repressed remorse. The most shameful, embarrassed, masochistic moment of all came, at least for me, in the late summer of 1941 [Lasky was then twenty-one]. Arguing in Lewisohn Stadium (we all attended the outdoor concerts in CCNY's backyard) I was suddenly paralyzed with outrage when I noted the general glee in most of our Trotskyite circles that the German army was cutting through the Soviet Russian resistance. All they could think of was how they had taken the *correct* position on Stalin's purges. [...] Who devoted a single thought to the onset of all the mass murders of East-European Jewry?

That one has to pay for recanting an orthodoxy is obvious. By the time of that luxurious summer burial, the zombies of that Left had, as we have seen, re-emerged from the distant past to howl 'Treason!' Of which, more later.

François had to pay his dues almost immediately with the German invasion of France. As a Jew and an ex-communist Bondy's position was much the more vulnerable and perilous. Arrested in France in 1940, he was interned for three months in Le Vernet and might easily have been deported to Germany and almost certain death. Fortunately, as his family had moved from Austria and Germany to Switzerland and become naturalized Swiss citizens, the French authorities gave him a pass to the Swiss border.

As Bondy settled down in a series of journalistic jobs—on Zürich's *Weltwoche* and *Neue Züricher Zeitung*—in New York Lasky joined the fiercely anti-Stalinist weekly, the *New Leader*, the official weekly organ of the Social-Democratic Federation. It was then an influential, if skimpy, magazine—as widely read among the political intelligentsia as was, later, the *Nation*. Its editor was the fiery and savvy Sol Levitas. As Mel wrote, every Friday 'we thought we were changing the world…and doing one's bit to win the war against Hitler…We became the conscience-stricken organ of 'the Homeless Left'. At twenty-two, Lasky and his 'managing editor', Dan Bell, were still engrossed with arguments about just how capitalism would fail. They were young, and as Levitas said to them, 'If things are getting so bad, why are they getting so much better?'

The *New Leader* was really Lasky's proving ground: not just politically, but also in terms of a direction to his extraordinary energy—Would *Der Monat* and *Encounter*, the outstanding magazines Lasky was to edit for many decades, have been what they were without that experience? Would Bondy's *Preuves*, had Bondy not served a long apprenticeship as a literary and political essayist and editor on Switzerland's best newspapers, and in a time when lies abounded?

Both men had wars that could be described as marginal; they neither fired a shot nor were shot at. Bondy was safe in neutral Switzerland. His qualities as a journalist were evident early: his versatility, his command of languages and literatures, his high seriousness, but also what Iso Camartin called his *phronesis*, a useful Greek term that implies thinking, understanding, practical judgment and perhaps what we would call today 'common sense'. Compared to Lasky's career, Bondy's was stable and sober, as befitted his nature, which was ever modestly ironical and self-deprecating.

Lasky was drafted in 1942 and de-mobilized in 1946, having appropriately served as a combat historian with the Seventh Army, where no doubt he made the connections that were to enable him to stay in Berlin when the war ended. Their lives, which had run on parallel lines, now began to converge.

*

If the war was a turning point, the post-war years, widely known as the 'Cold War', were decisive and defining. The war was thankfully over, one totalitarianism had been defeated, only for us to discover the full horrors of the Nazi regime and its destruction of not just the Jews, but Gypsies, Poles, prisoners-of-war, the mentally deficient or disabled, homosexuals and opponents of the regime. Another totalitarianism had taken its place.

While François was tackling the issues with his pen, the ever-restless Mel was, on demobilization, to take up his moral sword. And here, as in all our lives, circumstances were going to play a role in his life. He—as I had, only more briefly—had seen the evils of the time first hand, 'live' as we would say today. He had been to the camps in the East; he was fluent in German; he had seen the Russian occupation of Berlin with his own eyes. When he was de-mobilized in 1946, he decided to remain in Berlin. The place fascinated him and, as the chapter from his unfinished memoirs which we publish in this issue shows, he felt he had a role to play, as did François and a goodly number of other intellectuals in America and Europe.

What sort of a role, and why?

We had been slow to recognize—despite ample warnings—what was going on inside the Third Reich. We were as slow, or reluctant, to understand, though we had even greater warning, that equal monstrosities had taken place under the communist regime. In the five years between 1945 and 1950 a good part of our generation caught up to the truth which some—Silone, Koestler, Victor Serge, Orwell and company—had been telling us about. The moral position seemed clear. Like Victor Kravchenko (one of the earliest 'defectors') we 'Chose Freedom.' But in the joy of victory (with our 'gallant Soviet allies'), in the chaos of the post-war, of the migration of populations, of occupation, with the loss of all eastern Europe to the Soviet Union, how would we combat the huge machinery of the

Communist parties in the West and their intellectual allies and sympathizers, the Sartres, the Picassos, the Brechts, the Bertrand Russells, amongst our intellectuals? The answer was going to come with the Congress for Cultural Freedom, in which both men played leading roles, Lasky's being the more prominent. If a part of the press saw fit to limit Lasky to its favorite tag, 'Cold Warrior', it was because, as a mere twenty-seven-year-old, his definitive moment came when he challenged the Soviet cultural juggernaut on its own ground.

His account of that fateful meeting and his challenge, in fact its accidental, spontaneous and explosive nature, is in this issue. As when David Rousset stood up to a howling mob in Paris to denounce the Gulag and all its works, as Solzhenitsin did inside the Soviet Union, all it takes to challenge orthodoxy is one brave man armed with the truth. Lasky's view—as was to be Bondy's view in France—was that if freedom were to defeat totalitarian mass-culture, it would not be with guns but with an awareness that what was at stake was nothing less than free and objective thought. He thought the western powers then occupying Berlin were far too craven in yielding the cultural battlefield to communist orthodoxy. He was up against a packed house; he prevailed. As an example of sheer *chutzpah* it ranks high (that the reader can decide for himself). General Lucius Clay came close to expelling Lasky from Berlin for his outspokenness. He didn't, and in the aftermath the Congress for Cultural Freedom was launched with, as it turned out, the covert backing of the CIA.

What would such a project require? Secrecy, obviously. Also someone—in the event Mike Josselson (no ninny intellectually)—to mind the store. But above all, a hands-off appreciation of intellectual freedom and independence. What would have been the point of creating a U.S. 'apparatus' to match the Soviet Union's? The crisis was serious, the need urgent, the strategy high-risk. But it worked. The gravely-underestimated Josselson was no apparatchik. He kept the Congress independent. And within that context, both Lasky and Bondy could, and did, work freely. Neither of them was suitable as Agency 'employees'.

A way was found and the CIA funded it. But it was not, as alleged, 'responsible' for the creation of the Congress. The need for what one could call 'engaged resistance' to totalitarian infiltration of the world of the arts was not only plain in 1950. It had been plain since the 1934 meeting presided over by Romain Rolland. Koestler, Silone, Srerber, Serge and countless others had long seen the need, and come to such an idea from their independent and personal convictions. They knew what Willi Münzenberg was up to on the 'other' side. They'd been there on the Left and done that. The CIA did not lead; it followed. It did what it was created to do.

*

Both men went on to create and edit long-lived and vital magazines: Mel edited *Der Monat* (founded in October, 1948) and *Encounter* (which he took over from Irving Kristol as Co-Editor with Stephen Spender in 1958), and François, *Preuves* (whose first issue appeared in March 1951). François' cast of mind was more widely 'cultural', Mel's centered on politics and the Zeitgeist. These flagships of the Congress's publications (to which one could add *Tempo presente*, edited by Ignazio Silone and Nicola Chiaromonte) engaged in meaningful dialogue with their readers; it is the readership that made them different from one another in both content and style. Bondy's, like Silone's, was engaged with an audience to whom fellow-traveling was as much a habit and a need as digestion.[2] England and Germany were more receptive to the kind of lively commentary on current events and

---

2. It has to be said that both *Der Monat* and *Preuves* also had extraordinarily gifted co- and deputy-editors. Hellmut Jaesrich in Berlin had one of the most cultivated and discerning minds I've ever known. Utterly selfless, he was responsible not only for his own illuminating commentary, but for giving *Der Monat* authenticity as a journal in and of Berlin, then the front line of the struggle for a free culture. The same feat was performed in France by the sophisticated and gifted René Tavernier. Tavernier was a stern resistant and was part of the editorial committee of the clandestine *Les Lettres Françaises,* the most important rallying-point for French intellectuals during the Occupation. Nor should one forget the extraordinary K.A. Jelenski. He was virtually co-editor with Bondy while also acting as the magician at the great Polish emigré magazine, *Kultura.* Similarly, at *Encounter*, a distinguished sequence of English co-editors—among them Stephen Spender, Nigel Dennis and Goronwy Rees—brought culture as well as *Zeitgeschichte*, contemporary history, into the magazine.

issues that *Der Monat* and *Encounter* provided. *Preuves* was a slender defiance to the hegemony of Jean-Paul Sartre; *Der Monat* was on the front line, in Berlin, and had to withstand both the terrorism of the Rote Armee Fraktion (about which Lasky wrote remarkably) and a barrage of propaganda from East Germany. To that battle, Lasky brought remarkable gifts. He was a first-rate intellectual historian, a superb journalist and a polemicist of the first order—that is, one who backed up his arguments with hard fact and an immense knowledge of politics. At *Encounter,* he added another passion, one for the uses to which language is put, which finally led to his witty and discursive survey of journalistic practice, *The Language of Journalism*.

The 'line' followed by the Congress's magazines is clearly set out in an editorial François Bondy wrote for the eighth issue of *Preuves*, when it was still little more than a chap-book:

> If the word 'revolution' has such resonance, 'totalitarian-ism', the newest and most destructive phenomenon of our times [is far less examined.] The books which have examined the subject is detail, like Hannah Arendt's, are still rare…Few people and no political party in Weimar Germany thought of Hitlerism as anything more than a 'mask worn by capitalism'. Likewise, many people refuse to see that Stalinism goes well beyond the classical categorizations of left and right, progress and reaction, capitalism and socialism, while it is those very categories that require it to be re-examined in the light of a new reality.

Preuves had a difficult life in France. It survived, and eventually flourished, thanks to the Central-European who edited it. It was a deeply *European* magazine and much more open to new writers and artists than the NRF or *Esprit* or Sartre's *Les Temps Modernes*. The opposition to it was, and remains, purely political. What brought it into the mainstream was a political event, the Hungarian anti-totalitarian Revolution of 1956. That caused widespread defection from the communist ranks in France and elsewhere, and together with revisionist movements in Poland and central Europe, made possible the careful but constant inclusion of writers from those countries.

Hostile commentary—from Saunders to obituarists like Roth—make it seem that these magazines, which were must reading for people of my generation, were mere flim-flam, some ancillary part of a plot to force-feed passive intellectuals in the West with CIA and State Department pap. The magazines themselves give the lie to that. They might still be publishing today had not the Congress—to the joy of the anti anti-communists—been blown out of the water. Was Tom Braden, a former CIA executive officer himself, acting independently when he wrote in the *Saturday Evening Post* that the Congress was no more than a CIA 'front'? Thus betraying his oath of secrecy and the trust which had been placed in him? Or had the Agency itself decided to rid itself of the Congress, and Braden became simply the means at hand? If the latter supposition, why did the CIA so decide? Was it because the Congress, administered by two of its own and watched over by a jolly crew in Langley, was insufficiently malleable? Because of internal power struggles in the Agency? Because American objectives had shifted? Because the Agency knew the other side was about to expose its involvement with the Congress? Or was it just part of the general fall-out from Viet Nam, one every bit as relevant today as it was back then?

If Braden acted on his own (his shiftiest and most dangerous propagandist was Conor Cruise O'Brien, the Mother Teresa of the Left), then that represents—for we are now in the mid-Sixties—the first great triumph of gab, a foretaste of the loss of honor, discretion and modesty with which we are now familiar. The people who talked to Saunders largely belong to the same tattle club. For some reason America since the Sixties seems to find it impossible to shut up when faced by journalists. What need has the Bush administration of Bob Woodward, he of meaningless speech dressed up as significance? Public gab, like Braden's, is an over-statement of one's own importance. It's self-inflation. John Aubrey went round the great men of his century, the seventeenth, with slate in hand instead of a tape-recorder. He regarded it as important that so-and-so had passed a stone or had trouble making water. That was human information.

He didn't ask who his interlocutor's friends were at court and what they'd said to him.

I have my own view on the Congress, since I was happy to support it, for the same reasons that Mel and François and countless others did, and am not in the least abashed that it was sustained financially by the CIA. I know well only one avowed ex-CIA man, and I know *his* oath of secrecy was one he took seriously. It is only very recently that he avowed (I mean 'avowed', not 'confessed', as though membership were as dirty a secret as, say, joining Skull & Bones definitely is) what I had long suspected and he had often denied. 'Why did you lie to me?' I asked. 'Are we not friends of fifty-five years' standing?' He answered, 'If I had told you, you would have felt obliged to lie to others. I preferred to lie myself rather than you have to lie on my behalf.' I say handsome is as handsome does.

I will end, Aubrey-like, by conveying my 'feel' of Mel and François, what I felt to learn of their deaths.

Lasky was the more difficult of the two. I liked him a great deal and I like to think we often had fun together, when I dragged him off to his first real football game, chatted with him in his office during visits from South America to London, always being prodded to 'look into' this or that, when we ate together in London or Berlin or wherever (he was a considerable *Feinschmecker*), but I will not say that friendship with Mel came easily. He was both cocky and fiercely energetic, so that you felt—as I felt when meeting his wife, Brigitte, dressed like a pert little cossack in high red boots of polished and supple leather—you were being carried along in his wake. Both Lasky and Bondy were a kind of pre-computer Internet, so that one really never lost touch with either of them. Like all Congress people, they had stuffed briefcases and huge files of clippings which were sent hither and yon and which demanded reading and reaction. All that Mel sent over the years I have kept, together with the hurried scrawled notes that accompanied them. Nothing, absolutely nothing, was alien to his devouring curiosity, his remorseless tracking down of corroboration for facts.

Both men were terrific editors in every sense of the word: they prompted texts, stole texts, re-wrote texts, argued, pushed and got they wanted. But they were also placable, well-founded, intelligent men who were always eager to wise one up. Physically, of course, they were poles apart. Mel was stocky and brief and bearded: a strange irony gave him a remarkable resemblance to Lenin, as Dan Bell often reminded me of Molotov. I have no idea if this was a private joke of theirs. Bondy, on the other hand, while tall and beaky was relaxed and a much better listener than Mel.

I cannot say if they had happy lives. At home, in their familiar places, they radiated a kind of domestic harmony. At work they were somehow different. Their work always seemed urgent, and the time to do it in too short. They knew everyone and were open to anyone of talent. But politics is a taint on human life. It is a different kind of happiness which they saw as they outlived their youths and watched the collapse of the Berlin wall, Berlin being their spiritual home.

If you sense a hint of reservation in my feeling for Mel, it is the European part of me speaking. That I could share with a lighter heart with Bondy—we could be two Italians, or French, or Poles together. And Bondy's heart, to tell the truth, was, like mine, more in literature. Our talk was consequently of a different kind. Both *Der Monat* and *Encounter*, I thought, suffered from a similar deformation, a kind of hostility to the arts and especially to younger artists. They were *reportorial* in nature. Bondy read very widely, Mel not so much for pleasure but to find what he needed. This led to a number of arguments between us and, I think, leads me to a real tragedy in his life. Bondy had no need to write up his life: he was present in everything he wrote. The last time I saw François he was already stooped over and weakened. Time lay heavy on his hands. But it must be for twenty years at least that I have been hearing about Mel's 'memoirs'. I know that he did everything in his power to avoid writing them until it was too late. We were corresponding about those very memoirs when he died. And they remain incomplete.

—K.B.

Romain Gary

Goliarde

Among the many generous gifts—reviews, comments, advice—which Bondy gave literature, was this eliciting from his childhood friend, Romain Gary, of a kind of spoken autobiography. The masterpiece of this genre of good deed is Czeslaw Miłosz's re-invention of Alexander Wat in *My Century*. Writers, being beleaguered and very self-concerned, are not known for their generosity. All of us know of colleagues who will praise your work to your face but find themselves unable to do so publicly—lest they be wrong. But here it's clear that Bondy, the more reticent of the two, was fascinated by the enigmatic Gary, who fittingly led a multiplicity of public and private lives: aviator, resistant, diplomat and novelist under two names, neither of them his own, each winners of the Prix Goncourt, lover, star and fleeting connoisseur of the great. The book appeared in 1974 and seems to have been promptly forgotten. We have chosen a passage which leads, appropriately, from de Gaulle to America, and as the tone is throughout colloquial, begins *in medias res.* —K.B.

RG: Total amnesia. Ah, wait a moment, yes…A phone call from de Gaulle, at the time of a big steel strike. The TV shows a journalist interviewing a striking worker. De Gaulle rings up: 'What kind of business is this? By what right does a journalist use the familiar *tu* to a working man? They went to school together?' And then he hung up.

FB: But your relations with de Gaulle himself? Did you ever put him to the test with irony? I don't suppose you're going to deny you revered the man?

RG: Yes. No. I don't revere, I respect. Allow me to quote myself. I don't need to remind you how important his place in history was to de Gaulle. In Tulip, which was reissued in 1970—you'll recall it's a story set in the distant future—I wrote: *Resistance: the German movement which opposed the invader between 1940 and 1945 when the French occupied Germany under the commander of a tribal leader called Charles de Gaulle. The latter had finally been defeated by the Chinese at Stalingrad and committed suicide with his mistress Eva Braun in the ruins of Paris.* At which I got a fiery letter from de Gaulle [...] asking me if I intended to spend the rest of my life oscillating between idealism and cynicism. The old boy handled satire very well. I remember a dinner at the Elysée palace where a minister's wife protested so that the King was sure to hear her the way a well-known singer of the day imitated him. 'But Madame,' de Gaulle said, 'He's very good at it; and besides, on a poor day, I sometimes imitate him myself.' The way the great Charles has been sanctified, mummified, scrutinized and corrected calls for pity. And I can't think of anything more afflicting than the way in which his ideas and his thought are subject to endless exegesis. I hate relics. In my view all relics, whether those of Marx, Lenin, Freud or Charles de Gaulle, are nefarious. [...]

Besides, as far as de Gaulle is concerned, the surest way to betray a purely ethical heritage, is to seek to make it an object of current political consumption. When I once said on TV that my relations with de Gaulle derived more from metaphysics than ideology, the media sneered and smiled: the vertical smile of jerks, as first defined by the American novelist Richard

34

Condon. What I'd meant was that what drew me to de Gaulle and bound me to him was his sense of those things which are immortal and those that aren't, for the old man believed in the everlasting nature of humanistic values which today are dead, and which sooner or later the world will rediscover: as the French Revolution had rediscovered the old Polis and the Renaissance has rediscovered Antiquity.

FB: Why do you think so few writers and artists supported de Gaulle when he came back to power in 1958?

RG: Because instinct in writers and artists requires them to have neither respect nor sympathy for leaders, for chiefs and bosses and great statesmen, for providential men, for those who save their country and so on. If writers and artists all aligned themselves with established power we would despair of the world. Anyway, in the world of ideologies, no sooner do you pronounce the word 'great man' than you think of power, of Hitler and Stalin. These days, due to abundance, shit is in a state of confusion. The world seems to have no choice: the brain gets either stuffed or washed. Add to the above the individualism of the French when speaking of 'great men' in politics, and the average Frenchman feels personally diminished, as though he'd been robbed of something. I know a very distinguished gentleman who hasn't voted once in his whole life because to vote for someone other than himself enrages him. That's a lot more frequent than people realize. Look at the history of the twentieth century. You'll see that for all the votes de Gaulle got, he still paid for the Kaiser, for Hitler, for Mussolini and for Petain. [...]

FB: So what is Gaullism to you?

RG: A memory. There was a moment in history, an encounter, a spirit that passed over the French people. Now it's all gone well, and that is also good. There will be other moments, other men, other encounters, further spirits. It wasn't the last. It was a living thing and what is living cannot be preserved, embalmed; it wasn't once and for all. It arrived well and left well. I am happy to have been alive at the time. Today, eighty percent of the young in France do not know what a 'Companion of the Liberation' is, and that's all right too. If there is one thing that de Gaulle demands, it is originality; that means an end to the reliquary. There is a lesson to be learned from the way he refused to organize his succession, don't you think? He didn't want to be continued. He always spoke of renewal, and that does not mean marching toward the future backwards with our eyes fixed on a holy image. In the Soviet Union they embalmed Lenin under glass and exhibit him, look what that offered: an embalmed, straw-stuffed Lenin, a wax figure, a thing once and forever, forbidden to change anything...

FB: I seem to remember that at some point de Gaulle had suggested you might take up a political career?

RG: Twice. Both times with irony and scorn, as if to say I didn't deserve anything better. Well, he didn't exactly tell me to go to hell—that wasn't his way—but there was a lofty disdain in his suggestion. The first time was at the start of his 'crossing the desert', before I left for Bern; the second [...] was at the apogee of the R.P.F. when he was surrounded by eager young future marshals. Each time with an ironical smile that said, 'You too!' [...] I was thinking of leaving the Foreign Office altogether, to start up a projected literary-satirical weekly. Luckily, the project came to nothing, and I went to see de Gaulle, rue la Pérouse, less to ask his advice but just informally, to keep in touch. He offered no advice at all, but he did question me for a quarter-hour...about Malraux! Malraux gave him huge fun—Madame de Gaulle called him, 'That devil!'

FB: You finally took up your post at the French Embassy in Bern, and you stayed there eighteen months. Careful what you say, I am Helvetian...

RG: Don't worry: I have no memory of the place at all...An eighteen-month hole in my memory. I vaguely remember a clock with little men striking the hours or something like that. It seems I did some stupid things there. I'm told I went down into the bear-pit, the Bärengraben, perhaps hoping that something would finally happen. Nothing happened at all. The bears didn't budge.

They were Bernese bears. The fire-brigade came and pulled me out two hours later. [...] The effect Bern can have on people is bizarre. It's certainly one of the most mysterious places on earth, a sort of Atlantis that hasn't been found yet. The sort of place, you know, where everything takes place elsewhere. I finally sent Bidault a personal telegram: in code, Top Priority: 'I have the honor to inform you that at one in the afternoon it snowed for twenty minutes in Bern. It must be noted that this snowfall was not forecast by the Swiss meteorological service and I leave it to Your Excellency to draw the appropriate conclusion.' Bidault's conclusion was sharpish. He told his personnel director, Bousquet, 'Send him off among the madmen.' That was how I was appointed spokesman to the French delegation to the United Nations in New York. Before leaving I was allowed a few weeks' leave for reasons of stress—stress in Bern!

I spent them at the Hôtel des Théâtres on the Avenue Montaigne, then much frequented by the most beautiful models in the world: Dorian Leigh, Assia, Maxine de la Falaise, Bettina of course, Nina de Voght and Suzy Parker among others. The hotel had a tiny elevator and when you had the good fortune to go up with one of those goddesses you were taken straight up to heaven. Unfortunately, also there was also the celebrated Marquis de Portago, who killed himself later at the Twenty-Four Hour race at Le Mans. He had a stable of fantastic cars; I had just the elevator. [...] Also resident there were Capa, the famous *Life* photographer, who had covered the Normandy landings and would later be blown up by a land-mine in Indochina, Irwin Shaw, Peter Viertel, Ali Khan. What went on in those rooms must have been marvelous, things such as I can only imagine, for reasons of morality and inexperience. I was entitled to no more than a rapid glance, and only when one of those extraordinary creatures opened the wrong door. The door would open, one had to work fast, with just one's nose, to catch a few whiffs of paradise; then the door would shut. They were visions; I was visited, in the mythical sense of the word.

FB: Okay. Pure poetry, huh?

RG: I sometimes go back to the bar at the Hôtel des Théâtres, and I think what my life might have been if I had any initiative.

FB: All right. So after this crisis of humility, if you've recovered, let's leave for New York and your first contact with America.

RG: It's just about impossible to have a first contact with America. It's probably the only country that is really like what you thought it was like before you went there. The first thing you note on arrival is that American film is the truest in the world. Even the worst American film is truthful. That makes discovering America very difficult. All you get is a long series of confirmations. Every frame of an American film, whatever its inanity and the inverisimilitude of the whole, is freighted with authenticity. America is a film. It's a country which *is* cinema. That has a deeper meaning than the usual relationship between film and reality. It means that American reality is so overwhelming that it wipes everything else out, so that all means of artistic impression in America, theater, painting, music, etc., are specifically American. For thirty years, like the whole western world, France lives in an American civilization. And the authenticity of that way of life is fashioned in America. So that in part we face the threat of playing a purely imitative role. The French part always looked to the eighteenth and nineteenth century, whereas French life today requires American vitality. [...] I think Europe can only rediscover its reality and its vitality by returning to its real origins, the Italian cities, the French provinces, the German principalities, by a form of super-nationalism that can only be created through its roots. Otherwise, Europe will be no better than a failed America.

Never in the history of the world has there been a form of popular expression more representative of and symbiotic with a civilization than the American cinema. Every little psychological, political, ethical or ethnic frisson in the nation is immediately reflected on film.

[...] When I arrived in New York all I felt was a sense of

déjà vu. Every silhouette, every street corner, every slice of daily life was like those out-takes of film that spill onto the floor.

[…] The strongest and most ingrained American myth is the division of mankind into 'winners' and 'losers'. […] That is the basis of machismo, of the American dream of 'success' which causes such ravages in the American psyche, which destroyed Jack London and Fitzgerald, which pushed Hemingway to suicide. It's the one thing that never changes. […When I was in a gambling room in a New Orleans motel] the feel was of a family, no whores around, just men, *real* men. That's what I hate most: pure balls, nothing but balls, a comic-strip mentality.

[…] For some seventy-five years America has swung—on the 'Who am I?' level—between Captain Ahab and his white whale and Jack London's hobos. He was, at his beginnings, the first hippy. […] San Francisco holds the American record for alcoholism and suicide. Why? I think it's because life is much slower there. People have time to think. And to come to a conclusion.

"Goliarde" is an extract from It's Going to be a Quiet Night. *Romain Gary was born in Moscow in 1914. He moved to France at the age of fourteen and would later a pilot for the French Air Force. During World War II he fled to England and served under Charles de Gaulle in the Free French Forces. He was one of the most prolific and popular writers in France and is the only writer to be awarded the Prix Goncourt twice (Emile Ajar was given the award before it was revealed to be a pseudonym of Gary's). He died on December 2, 1980 of a self-inflicted gunshot wound.*

Sophie Wilkins

Sophie Wilkins

It must have happened to many people, to know Sophie before meeting her. Because one knew what she did by way of selfless translation Saul Bellow had talked about her long before we got in touch: with love and a note of sorrow at her troubles in her later days. He said, "You must get something out of her, quelle vie!"

I think of her as the greatest Responder I have ever known. She read with passion and always seemed to know what one was trying to do. In this way she was utterly unselfish. She wrote to me about *The Republic of Letters* when it was at its beginning (she sent a check for $500 which Saul and I stolidly refused to accept), and about my books when they were in their early stages. Always in terms of dazzlement that people were still producing (she kindly said) what she thought 'real' literature was about: rich fodder for the omnivore. I have treasured her letters, beaten out on an old machine and edited and xxx'd out and glossed with additional knowledge.

It became necessary one day that I meet her, for I could not imagine such a perfect responder. I knew much of her history by then, and had been encouraging her to put it down on paper. If I had a

mental picture at all, it had to do with age and fatigue and piles of paper and manuscripts.

We made a date, I traveled uptown, rang her bell. This sassy, dolled-up, sparkling woman?! We talked in a rush, catching up on sixty-plus years of whom we had known and what we had read. Having envisaged frailty, I wondered where, uptown, we might find a decent place to lunch. Ha! She whisked me off in a taxi to midtown to a place she liked and knew. Grandes dames don't allow even gentlemen to pay. She'd always paid for the life she had but it was worth it to her, to know and to love. And she said to her grandson, "Everything is learning, even dying."

—K.B.

Sophie Wilkins to Elga Duval

17 × 71

Dear Elga Duval:

Yes, I met Dylan Thomas, just barely. It must have been one of his first poetry readings in New York, in the spring of 1952 I think, but you can check that date in Brinnin, probably. McMillin, Columbia's largest auditorium, was filled to the last standing space, mostly by scuttlebutt and grapevine, and there I sat listening to that bardic voice rolling like tidal waves over the audience, sheer immensities of powerful rhythms all coming from that cherub-faced man in front of the big velvet-blue curtain that gave one the sense of being packed with the others inside a padded jewel box. Afterwards, at the cookies-and-punch reception that follows these university occasions, I came upon him standing alone, after that oceanic performance, with a space around him as though he were taboo. And there stood I, in the skirt and ski-sweater I wore in graduate school, staring, unable to move away without saying something because I had caught his eye, though I had nothing knowledgeable to say, guilty of not having read very much of him, trapped as I was in my specialty, the original German and English Romantics: a graduate school illiterate face-to-face with a Living Poet who at that moment threatened to be an exam I was about to flunk.

So I said, to those round, gentle, candidly wondering brown eyes, "Thank you for demonstrating that a poet in our time doesn't *have* to be a hollow man." And he said: "Do you really mean that?" By then others had closed in like so many magnetized iron filings and in due course we bore one sacred human trophy away from that non-alcoholic punch bowl to the West End Bar on Broadway and 113th or so. Where eight of us jammed ourselves, four facing four, onto the two benches of a booth, and ordered mostly beer. Beer was all Dylan had, by the way, three at most slim goblets of it, very ascetic drinking for the length of time we spent there, till close to three A.M. Not that I was counting, for the whole time I sat there between him and Oscar Williams we hardly exchanged a word, he being turned mostly toward the only other woman of the party, in the corner seat on his other side, who happened to be Roslyn Tureck, and I was listening to Oscar Williams entertaining the four men opposite with dirty limericks. Of those four, the one sitting opposite Dylan and participating in the coversation at that end, who may therefore have more to tell you about that evening at least, was David Markson, at the time a prophet of Malcolm Lowrie to whom he had made a pilgrimage in THE BALLAD OF DINGUS MAGEE (made into a film with Sinatra, I think). A student came around in the course of the evening to take pictures of the group. One of those snapshots, showing Dylan in quarter profile—that is, back to the camera—faced by an earnestly listening Roslyn always reminds me of David's story that he overheard the following exchange, Dylan having suggested that Roslyn spend the night with him: She: I don't do such things. He: The hell you don't. This bit of hearsay is all I know to uphold Dylan's reputation as a womanizer, as those few beers are all I saw of him as a drinker. All I ever saw or sensed was an extremely gentle, vulnerable man, whose wit did not wound; wide open to people, impressions, generous, threatened by the hard edges of things.

When it was time to break up we all seemed to crowd into one taxi, I think I sat on somebody's knee next to Dylan, and they dropped me off with Oscar Williams and Rod McManigle, a student

Thursday

Dear Sophie,

I'm terribly, terribly sorry — and so is Caitlin, who sends her regards — that I can't come along tonight as I very much wanted to & looked forward to. I've been sick as hell all day, really physically sick in the most obvious & unpleasant way, & could only just get through a reading at the NYU. Now the reading is over, & I'm going back to bed, hotwater bottle, & sleeping draught.

A great many apologies, & I hope, alas, to see you soon. (We'll be in the White Horse, on Hudson & 11th Street, & would like to see you & apologise in person — if you'll excuse the phrase)

Fondly,

Dylan Thomas

who later became an expatriate at Oxford, at my place on East 82nd Street. It was then that Oscar Williams cased my two-room apartment and declared it was just the place to give a party for Dylan in—I agreed so as to get rid of the two men who showed signs of wanting to settle in for what was left of the night; I was tired, unsociable, and developing a dislike for Oscar Williams.

Next day at Columbia I invited Maurice Valency, whose memorable lectures on Renaissance literature I'd been attending to the party for Dylan, and he agreed to come. Lionel Trilling—I was in his doctoral seminar, conducted with Jacques Barzun that semester—said thanks, but no thanks: he had seen Dylan Thomas at a party trying to throw another guest out the window.

Apropos of this Roaring Boy aspect of Dylan, I particularly appreciated what Richard Burton had to say in his review of Constantine Fitzgibbon's book on Dylan Thomas when it appeared, in 1965, in the TIMES Book Review, debunking all that and the womanizing legend as well, with a wit and charm that makes one wish he weren't too rich, too lazy, and possibly too depressed, to write instead of act, if he couldn't do both. (Babette Deutsch was moved to write him an appreciative note on that review.) Now that's a man to tap for memories of Dylan Thomas! But if you cannot reach him, you could probably glean something worthwhile from that review, it was front page and long, and lively.

In the following week or so I saw Dylan and Caitlin at another student party, and invited them personally, and Dylan assured me he would come, the following Saturday night, I think. Maurice Valency didn't show, but my fellow seminarists did, including Robert Brustein, now Dean of the Yale Drama School and author of several well-known books on theater, and Karl Kroeber, the son of the great Alfred and Theodora, now a Columbia Professor of English, and Roslyn Tureck came with Maury Green, a young psychoanalyst we both knew. The party was such a success that Karl Kroeber excused himself around midnight with the proviso that he might come back, with his sister, who turned out to be a beauty. And that despite the fact that the guest of honor never came—what came was a messenger with a note, signed "Fondly, Dylan" saying that he'd taken sick (with fever and vomiting, as Gene Derwood later told me) after a reading he'd had to give that night at the New School, and was sorry he had to take to his bed. I read the note to the assembled guests, who were of course disappointed but sympathetic; only Rosalyn Tureck left, with Maury.

I should have gone to see Dylan and Caitlin, as he asked in the note, the next day at the White Horse Inn; as I realized when Gene Derwood, Oscar William's wife, phoned a week later to tell me how sick he had been, and how troubled by the idea that I was angry at him. My anger, such as it was, was directed against Oscar Williams, for having maneuvered me into a detestable position—that of the lion-hunting hostess. It was him I didn't want to encounter again, and since in those days he was always with Dylan my instinct was to keep away. And that is all there is to my story.

Now quite all, though, for me, if it is for other: I must try to convey to you, if only between ourselves, a certain transcendent aspect of the experience that keeps it so vivid and fresh to me. Dylan's reading at Columbia happened to be the second of three similarly memorable occasions, and I must briefly describe the other two in relation to it. The first was Martin Buber, giving a talk on the Relationship between Religion and Philosophy, he made that distinction in terms of such pyramidal simplicity that to this day I buttonhole special people to recite it to them it remains a steady light in my thinking. With his silver hair and beard and silver-gray suit Buber looked very much the Father.

A year later there was Dylan Thomas, with his plangent cry to his "Father" not to go gentle into that good night; a boy of summer in his ruin: The Son. Even as Jesus rode into Jerusalem on a donkey, so Dylan came to Columbia under humble auspices, that of an obscure Institute of Arts and Sciences without academic standing or influence, consisting chiefly of Russell Potter who managed ably with probably minimal support and especially financing from the university. The contrast between the welcome from Columbia to Dylan Thomas and that for T.S. Eliot some years after Dylan was in his grave is instructive, if not edifying. It was a red carpet occasion, in '56, and had the full P.R. treatment. I was working on campus and received a

near-hysterical phone call from Carson McCullers for a last minute ticket. Though I went to McMillin early myself, I landed high up in the back row of the balcony, so crowded was it. From this vantage point I saw the same rich blue curtain parting, this time, to reveal The Poet, in an earth-colored greenish-brown suit, flanked by two equally stiff figures in elegant undertaker black-tie: Jacques Barzun and Lionel Trilling, no less, Columbia's most "representative" figures. Lionel Trilling must have given a graceful introduction, it was hard to hear where I sat. Then the centerpiece of the triptych moved forward to the lectern and read, in a creaky voice without inflection or modulation, intoned, ground out, line after line of those works students had known by heart since my high-school days, all the T.S. Eliot clichés, without a single grace note of something unfamiliar, something just for this audience, without a look, without a comment. The last line read, the venerable monument to himself allowed the applause to wash up, waited immobile for the curtain to close. It did not open again. Poor Carson McCullers, who had managed to get a front seat in the orchestra—I had done better for her than for myself—and had dressed in a spectacular black evening gown, had hoped in vain for an introduction to Him. The Holy Ghost.

It was, taken all together, a kind of religious experience for me. Or perhaps just an illustration of the way the old religious metaphors and archetypes retain life and validity despite the translations they undergo at the hands of history. I don't mean to be cruel to T.S. Eliot, or downgrade him as a poet by comparison with Dylan. It is only that, thinking of Dylan Thomas's life and his end, a lament rises into one's throat, that the gift of life which he was should have been marked for the ancient sacrifice, the blood of the lamb, life's scapegoat, however one wants to put it. The way life has of dealing that ace of spades to its own love child. But never mind all this maudlin self-indulgence—please pardon and overlook it, my story is done.

With Best Regards,
Sophie Wilkins

Sophie Wilkins to John Updike

24 V 2000

D ear John:

My idea was to go, both of us, like the Collier brothers, the piles of papers and books etc, bills etc. were doing just fine, but the doctors maneuvered Karl into the hospital, after a week of his not being able to hear at all, and so many things I couldn't do for him, and not being able to keep home help because he simply didn't like being handled by strange men, Polish or Black, who stopped showing up because he fought them tongue and fists, and the Dr. said he would be able to get an earman in the hospital to fix the one good ear, but never did. Instead the hospital gave him pneumonia and antibiotics and an offer of surgery which he was in no condition to survive (abdominal, intestinal) else he would die any minute. Then the Dr. returned from her weekend and said, "Your husband is a surprising man, he didn't die, so I can't keep him in the hospital he must go to a long-term-care place," and this is how Karl came to die in the Jewish Home for the Aged across the street, after less than two weeks (April 29–May 14) away from home. Sorry to be so heavy again, this is still the phase of wondering if he'd still be alive if I hadn't let him go to the Hospital which we both dreaded and would have done anything to avoid. But they did give him morphine and he slipped away on Sunday afternoon, a Sunday child to the end. The day before, the last time I saw him, he smiled at my apparently amusing efforts to make him hear me when he couldn't. He was so entirely himself to the end! We had a game, after dinner, of his asking for a cookie, having pushed his dinner away, especially the veggies I was sworn to feed him, and hungering only for those soft. digestible Pepperidge chocolate chip cookies. We'd sit in front of the TV which he couldn't really see or hear, and I'd hear him saying very softly "cookie" (slyly, subliminally, boring into my subconscious!) and again "cookie" and "cookie" having learned that if he spoke up he'd only get my set speech about not being allowed to give him sweets (both diabetic, etc.) and taking longer to get me to give in, so he spoke sotto voce, as if merely to himself, and of course I gave him his cookie, which was gone in a flash, whereupon "cookie" was heard again a minute or so later. He never complained, when I pleaded with him to tell me something he wanted he said, looking at me steadily, "I want what I've got" and when I told this to Saul Bellow, he said "I can see he's still with us." Also he had the most beautiful knees and feet which I kissed frequently out of uncontrollable admiration, such an elegant bone structure and soul structure, I felt like a peasant beside him but the nobles and the peasantry always understood each other, it's the middle classes with their progress and sci-tech etc who have ruined everything but then, it's the only class left, the triumph of social evolution, Creator and Destroyer, Ohm…Karl loved you because you are a rare kind, isn't it so? and deeply appreciated your friendship and all you did to show it, and I must add a *few* words (I hope a few only) on my own behalf because you seem uneasy with my praises of your writing and I can't leave you feeling that, as Charles Simmons said when I told him once too often how much I loved his work as indeed I do, I'm a good flatterer, which is excruciatingly unfair if you know the facts of how I got that way:

I am the other kind of American, the one who wasn't born here. I was conceived in June 1914 in Poland and born in Vienna in February 1915, having in the womb started life as a refugee, *viz.*

Wilkins and husband Karl Shapiro

my father had to leave in a hurry before the Russians shot him as a deserter, my mother had to seal the house etc and then took to the road on foot, in winter, with an 8-year old and a 12-year old daughter at either hand a big belly between, the undersigned, not knowing where their father was, heading for Budapest, but in a refugee camp someone said, "Prombaum? He's not in Budapest, he's in Vienna," and that's how I came to be born in Vienna, by the skin of my babygums. In Vienna we were raised on Hebrew because father was a Hebrew teacher, he had built a gymnasium (secondary school) where all the subjects were taught in Hebrew in a small Polish town Domina which may not have existed for a long time now. We were stateless refugees, and I was raised on tea and saccharine (sugar on the black market) and father went to Amerika in 1922 a few months before my brother (the rabbi in Chicago) was born, so I wrote in a school composition that my father went to Amerika and some time later my mother became pregnant (gave birth is what I should have said) but the whole school got a great kick out of my essay with illustration, I still have it somewhere, but I am digressing! Alas! At school the Hebrew quickly gave way to German so by the time I landed in new York from Vienna when father had his papers and we arrived as citizens, if you please, without any English, aged twelve, English then became my third language and, to make it shorter—I ended up translating not into my mother tongue, long-lost Hebrew, but from my second language into my third which should be illegal, yet I got awards for my translations of Bernhard and Musil which means that if the books don't sell it's not because of a bad translation, doesn't it? SO NOW CAN YOU SEE, by the end of this epistle, how my admiration which is boundless for exquisitely written English grows right out of my despair at bumping at every turn of a translation of masterpieces in the original, bumping against my limitations, my deeply felt blind spots etc, in the language to which I came so late? The enviousness would have given me cancer if I hadn't instinctively turned it into enjoyable admiration, even worshipfulness, but of course I express it like a peasant, like Yeats's 'the worst [who] are full of passionate intensity' but if you add a drop of Marx to your Yeats and translate, you get the *best-off* can afford to keep silence, like the omerta of successful gangsters, while the worst-off can't help yowling and throwing bombs, in good time, Basta. Hey man, that was such a beautiful letter, yours, I thank you, I treasure it, Iufsky.

Sophie Wilkins

Brattleboro, VT 05301

Aug 15, '84

Dear Sophie:

It isn't hard nowadays to count one's blessings, they're well under the number of toes and fingers. It's the scope of those blessings I do enjoy that I'm gratefully aware of. In this day and age, bringing out a small book or two and hearing from you and from Karl about one and the other makes me singularly lucky. I'm hardly conscious of anything resembling a "literary life", but as a writer I'm still well above the poverty line. How "my readers" keep their purity and sanity is a profound mystery, given what they have to absorb in the way of literary journalism and the general schlamerei of "educated" opinion. To a large sector of that opinion, the heavily ideologized one, I am something of an ogre-reactionary. Besides I am one of the old-guy heavies who have to be kept in their place. No question but that Karl has to put up with this being kept in place. No exceptions are made.

Members of our own dwindling generation who will see the picture as only those who have lived as we have, graduates of the same street-academies, veterans of the same wars, released from the same errors and prejudices, breathers of the vanishing atmospheres of the Thirties, Forties, Fifties are our best judges. When I read, or rather study, one of your letters I remember the conversation of old friends—the tone of those better days and the style of thinking and comment of Greenwich Village gatherings. Friends now dead also come back to enlighten and comfort me and to remind me that we—the living remnant—are along now, or all but. The survivors for the most part are silenter and silenter, reluctant, some of them, to say a single word. Of those still here a few have become dim, or too cranky to wish to make themselves intelligible. So you seem to me extraordinarily magnanimous. I send you a mere booklet and you answer with a *personal letter,* a really valuable communication in the old style. I sometimes think I write books in lieu of letters and that real letters have more kindness in them, addressed as they are to *one* friend. In pleasing you and Karl I have my reward. When you tell me I am more or less on track.

Yours as ever,
Saul

Texts

Chantal Hunt

Antoinette

Beauty is our family's prerogative."

My mother wore a slightly scornful smile when she described the man who made that fatuous claim, my great-grandfather, my grandmother Antoinette's father.

"Quite a handsome man," she would say. "But vain and weak."

When I had studied the photographs heaped up in a drawer of my grandmother's desk, my own verdict was that he was old and lacked judgment. It is true that he had a finely shaped nose, big light eyes, ample cheeks and just enough of a jaw...Yes, one could say, despite his frightened expression and the incompleteness of his face, that he was handsome...Indeed, as are nearly all those gentlemen with brown or prematurely grey hair under their képis or bowler hats: my great-grandfather, grandfather and uncles, all of them dead before I was born...On the other hand, my mother apart, the women of the family were not beautiful.

"It's the women who run things among us" was another of his sallies.

By the time my mother got to know him, he had already suffered two heart attacks and was rolling at a good clip toward an elusive death: in the wheelchair that my grandmother pushed indefatigably, and she, yes, had certainly run their lives.

My grandmother Antoinette must have been the exception that proved the rule...She lived quite alone and apart from all adult hurly-burly; she gave of her time and her energy to amuse us. Her nose was somewhat large and bent, and I never saw eyes, short of shade from her lashes, with other than a dullish sea-green expression. Yet her contemporaries, those who knew her in her provincial prime, spoke of her "wonderful eyes". Legend has it that a young man had killed himself for those wonderful eyes...As far back as I can search my memory, Grandmother was always an old lady. On the Brittany beaches where she helped me make sand-cakes and castles, the hem of her long dress was often wet from the tide. In those days fashion had brought skirts to knee-high. In the tea-shops to which she took us to stuff ourselves with ice-creams and pastries, she was one-of-a-kind. It happened that I might reach for my napkin under the little round marble table and find it alongside the tip of her tiny ankle-boot, itself half hidden under that sort of tent, her vast and only black skirt. All around us were silk-sheathed legs that were crossed and showed knees round, knees square or pointy, and some fleshy and dimpled with indentions on either flank...I could always recognize the thin legs, the drooping stockings, and the shapeless oversized shoes of the very old...but of Grandmother I saw but the slender black ankle-boot with its worn-down heel...

She wore hat and veil, both always black, and was never hatless until she had reached home. "She was a flaming redhead," those same people say who knew her young and splendid, when men died for her.

For at least the last twenty years I've seen Grandmother adjusting the same wig on her brow, a sort of grey fringe yellowed with age that clashes with the silvery white of the hair at the nape of her neck...Her hats, of straw in summer and felt in winter, are of an age with that fringe which they displace. In season she might deck her straw hat with a brand-new ribbon of the Lyon silk known as *gros grain;* a flower in black organdy tied with a piece of jet-glass would do for the felt one. Her dresses were of the same sort: they dated from the dark ages. Antoinette was gracious enough to us to be unchangeable and therefore eternal.

"How old is Grandmother?" I asked her daughter, my mother, recently.

My still lovely young mother answered, "Hold on, let me think. Seventy, I think."

So twenty years ago, on the beach at Croisic, she would have been fifty. Only ten years older than my mother today…

It has to be said that despite her cumbersome clothes she ran like a gazelle. Playing hide-and-seek only rarely could we escape her…She was indefatigable. After hide-and-seek came hunt-the-slipper, then "rough seas", then croquet which she and her team always won, since she was unbeatable…It was at croquet that I discovered that her ankle-boot concealed a thin, nervy foot, tough as steel. At every opportunity she would line up her opponent's ball and her own, hold hers down with the tip of her toes and then—quietly, as though it were nothing at all—whack! a master-stroke of the mallet against her ball and her opponent's went right off the pitch…She played *for real*; she wasn't into making life easy for us. She liked us to believe it was as much fun for her as for us; but if we should beat her, that was a real victory, a trophy we weren't likely to forget.

When we'd get dead tired, she'd read us Perrault stories, Uncle Tom's Cabin, Croc-Blanc, The Jungle Book, whatever, always in a clear calm voice…Never even remotely breathless. Sometimes she'd tell us bits of her childhood or youth…Such adventures she must have had, how many suppressed fits of giggles; the best were saved for children sitting rigidly on their chairs, prisoners of grown-up talk! We died to hear them…Of course she'd had a privileged life…At our family table we no longer ran into a man with elephant ears in which grew such tufts of hair that one day a wasp took to nestling there…He shook his head as a horse does clouded with flies, but the underbrush had to be trimmed with the grape-scissors, right there, at table, during dessert!…Nor was there in our lives an aged single-toothed basset hound to leap from his master's lap and attack stranger's calves with his incisor! Antoinette had been fifteen back then, and dying of boredom at the dinner table to which her father had dragged her to replace her mother who had a cold. Someone had unthinkingly opened the door to the room where the dog had been sequestered. Between soup and roast the entire company stood on chairs while the animal growled and bared his single tooth, attacking each chair and trying to hoist his aged body up, deaf to the commands and supplications of his master. Grandmother made out that she alone knew how to address the beast and, thanks to a bit of bread dipped in the soup, had led him back to his basket…

And then there was the elderly lady ventriloquist who, very calmly from the depths of her chair on the master of the house's right, reserved for her by her advanced years, mouth shut and face impassive, imitated the troating of the stag. The act apparently never failed for all present would rush out of doors hoping to see the beast or its antlers rising above the heather…She spoke to us of people whose names we never tired of hearing: a certain Monsieur Cuiscuisse de Lenfoutras de Kergorlax Tamore, who had taken her to the garrison ball in Poitiers, or the nut-and-bolt factory belonging to Lenus Desfesses *&* Co., who so proudly emblazoned his juridical status in big black letters across the street from her nursery window…Such extravagant names quite overshadowed the names of our class-mates, though she didn't like our making fun of them. "Pansu?" she said. "Velu, Pupied? Perfectly common. Known hundreds of them in my day." And then her gifts would overwhelm us with the sudden invention, just like that of the great scientist Cosine, the "Mnelectricupedaliwindbreakshakeparanailcycle".

At times she would stop entertaining us, sit down in an armchair and read…These were often old books, leather-bound and worn white with use. She would often laugh all by herself, a silent laugh. At such times her face showed a sort of slightly scornful jubilation, and that we adored. "It's so utterly stupid," she would mumble, still reading, inviting us to bear witness: the Princess Palatine did not muffle her words, her memoirs were full of scatological detail…What could be more irresistible than to hear that from our mother's mother?

Of course, as soon as he heard us burst into laughter, our father would interrupt indignantly: "Really, mother, such matters are not for children!"

She said nothing, pretended to shut the book and, as soon as his back was turned, returned to her reading.

Hers was a mocking nature, which was why we liked her so much. She refused to bow down to the rules set down—arbitrarily, she thought—by men...She would terrify us by going swimming even when right in the middle of the beach the red flag, indicating danger, flew...In her black woolen bathing costume, a copy of the one she had worn in 1910—billowing trouser-legs down to below her knees, turquoise sailor-shirt collar flapping behind—she would set out with steady calm strokes into the turbulent water...and would always come back as slowly, smiling, to be greeted by the Life Guard's angry admonitions, which she took without flinching.

It seems to me she got many such warnings: from her son-in-law, our father, in particular... He thought the ingenious treats she offered us "unreasonable", and he hesitated not at all to let her know his displeasure. He never showed the slightest regard for her womanliness, nor for her twenty years of greater experience...

She had two great passions: sweets and antiques. She knew how to pass them on to us, pastries and sweets she proffered non-stop, my dolls were provided with Empire or Louis-Philippe-style four-poster mahogany beds and dressers. My father never thanked her for her generosity, talked of waste and predicted years of dental torment to any who yielded to her sweets.

In the family house where we spent our holidays, Grandmother laid no claim to be the head of the household. Her daughter, my mother, presided over meals and my father, seated opposite her, patiently managed their functioning. Grandmother had chosen to sit unimportantly at the foot of the table, a place where her old dog could settle up against her skirt without bothering anyone. As soon as her son-in-law was distracted or elsewhere she stealthily laid her plate down on the floor up against her boot, though the lapping immediately engaged the pitiless attention of my father. "Mother," he would say indignantly, "kindly do not allow *our* plates to be licked clean by your sick old dog. It's disgusting, it's dangerous."

She replied calmly, with a pitying smile towards a man who so little understood the affection she bore to her companion of many years, "My dog is not sick," and when the next course came around, and this time openly, she once again put her plate under the table.

My father, with a glance at the barely visible frown on my mother's brow, managed to contain himself. "Oh come on, Antoine," she said, recalling him to order.

Storm had passed; we were all relieved…We did not dare think our father wrong…Still, we couldn't help siding with Grandmother. "We" consisted of my brother, Louis, and myself, Maia, plus the boy and girl cousins who paraded before us during the holidays.

Louis was the oldest, and also Grandmother's favorite. We all knew that and were resigned to the fact. He was two years older than we were. For several years I had tried to make my grandmother like me as much as she did him. He was of a stormy nature and rarely showed any affection…while I showered my grandmother with kisses, picked flowers and made bouquets for her, drew her houses, angels, dogs and cats. She always thanked me with a warm smile; my drawings were propped up on the mantel piece in her room up against her mirror, she held me tight and said if I kept it up I might—who knows—become a great painter.

But she did not need me as she needed Louis.

As soon as she came into a room she would ask where he was, and if she didn't see his curly mop of hair somewhere, her face would grow anxious, even panicked.

"He must be in his room," my mother would say calmly.

And we heard him climbing the stairs on all fours.

More than once I tried to be late for dinner. In vain I awaited a trumpet-call from my grandmother, her face anguished at the thought of losing me, then her smile and her arms held out to the joy of finding me again…every time, my father's voice rose from the stairwell to tell me to come down without further delay. No one had believed in my disappearance. One night, just at dinner-time, my mother had been through the whole house. She had come back to the drawing-room pale and trembling.

"I can't find Louis anywhere,' she had said, falling into a chair as though having no strength left to stand.

My father had said calmly, "No doubt he won't be long coming back. He'll have stopped at the farm."

"If he's late," my mother had added, "we'll start dinner without him. He'll catch up."

Grandmother wasn't attuned to that answer: indignantly, she had said, "You mean you're not going to go look for him?"

"Mother, we dine at eight, it's only five minutes to eight, so he's not late yet…He's twelve years old, he's quite old enough to come back on his own…Besides, where would you have me look for him, since I have no idea where he is…"

Grandmother had left the room, slamming the door, and gone to sit on a bench outside facing the driveway, to await his arrival. She was biting her thumbnail. I had come out to sit by her without saying a word. I felt that were I to talk to her or touch her he would break into pieces, perhaps faint away.

She it was who had broken the silence: "The boy will drive me crazy. Your parents treat him like some ordinary child, but I know him, he's Maurice all over again, just like him, as if the Lord had replaced him…Isn't it astonishing that the first-born of my grand-children should be born with the very same looks, the same character, the same imagination, I could say even the very same genius, as my one and only dead son?"

"Uncle Maurice?" I said. "You think Louis is like him?"

The only idea I had of Uncle Maurice came from photographs. It would never have occurred to me that Louis looked like him but, after all, Grandmother was the better judge, he was her son and he had died very young of, as the family always said without being more precise, a "grave illness"…Whenever Maurice was mentioned, my mother and grandmother wore an expression on their faces which imposed silence on us, as though the slightest inquiry would have put us all in deathly danger. In an oval frame in my mother's room, on her chest of drawers, there is a photograph of her brother and her in bathing costumes. Maurice's hair is curly, as is Louis"; his mouth is fleshy, his expression is somewhat dreamy, again like Louis"; but his eyes are light and very large, nearly round. Louis" eyes are on the small side, an almond-brown…Perhaps they had the same lofty bearing, were the same size, walked alike, the same disquiet, who knows? Louis was somewhat solitary, and often stayed in his room rather than join us in our games. He took apart watches, mechanical toys and radios and used their parts to build bizarre engines of a mysterious nature. Only Grandmother could persuade him to take part in the revels she organized for us. She was the also the only one to take his inventions seriously, or ask him to explain how they worked…

As to my father, he had given up going to his son's room altogether. The dismantling of the gold fob-watch solemnly bequeathed "To Louis, my grandson, when he reaches the age of twelve" by his own father, the disembowelling of the mahogany-cabineted radio given the boy by his godfather, had both enraged and depressed my father…His son of course had a perfect right to dispose of objects which quite certainly were his private property, so he refrained from intervening. Nonetheless he was unable to conceal his irritation…

"What exactly did Uncle Maurice die from?" I several times asked Grandmother.

"Ah, there he is," she murmured, smiling. "We can go in now. He's not late after all, we needn't have worried."

And Louis did arrive: whistling, in no hurry, a bag slung over his shoulder from within which came the clang of metal.

Grandmother had fled back to her place on a drawing-room sofa and dragged me along with her. Clearly, Louis was not to know about her anxieties.

Once again she had failed to answer my question about Uncle Maurice's illness…

A few days later I had asked her again: "How old was he when he died?"

"Twelve. The same age as Louis.

It was on my fifteenth birthday, on April 26, 1940, that I found out what had really happened to him, how Uncle Maurice had died. The war had overtaken us just as we were about to leave Soissel, our holiday house, and return to our winter quarters. My parents had decided that the wisest course was that we should remain in the country, and my father had moved mountains to get Louis admitted to the final year of the lycée in the town nearest us: "Louis needs to be properly established somewhere," he said. "For a boy, his studies are a serious matter"…He then left for the front in Alsace, telling me how deeply he regretted that "the finest years of my life should be saddened by events." As for Grandmother, she had rented an apartment next door to Louis" lycée because, she said, "I would not survive the anguish of being too far away from him…Besides, if the war brings about all sorts of restrictions, I trust no one. Louis is delicate, he should not want for anything." So she looked after his welfare. From time to time they would come by to plunder our vegetable garden, laughing and teasing one another like two lovers. Louis was then sixteen, well over six feet tall, and built so solidly that I thought Grandmother ought to feel reassured…

My mother and I were eating her only specialty, apple pudding, when suddenly, after a long, careful lick of the caramel that clung to the tip of her spoon, she said, "The day Maurice died I was fifteen, as you are today. He was boarding in a special school my parents had chosen with great care…To this day I remember the discussions they had about it, the folders and catalogues they looked at before making up their minds. One day I came across a forgotten envelope. The photographs were of a "school adapted to the particular needs of children" and they made the place look unbelievably luxurious…Why should Maurice be so privileged? Couldn't he, like you and I, go to the nearest lycée? I was envious of the ultra-careful attention always it seemed was offered to Maurice. I saw him only on holidays, and not much even then…He spent his days in a workshop, the farm workshop, where the farm-manager had cleared a part of his work-bench for him. He loved to cut, to carve, to put together and take apart. Your grandmother predicted he would become an inventor or a sculptor. It was war-time, then as now, and your grandmother and I were alone, waiting for Maurice to come back so we could sit down for dinner. It was on a very mild July evening, and it was still light at eight; the sun had only just begun to set behind the plane trees along the driveway. We heard hoof-beats and the sound of the trap as it jolted in the ruts. They drove into the courtyard. All three of them sat on the bench. The farmer pulled on the reins, and in his wife's arms lay Maurice, his head on her shoulder as if asleep, his hands, oddly inert, swaying with the horse's step. He was dead. Before the cart even came through the gate your grandmother knew it. She spoke not a word. She took Maurice in her arms, though he was bigger than she was. The farmer wanted to help her, but she refused; she wanted him all to herself; she managed and carried him to a sofa in the drawing-room. Once she had laid him down she went to get a face-cloth to clean his face and hands. At that point I saw his wrists, both wrapped in bloody rags. Your grandmother pulled on the sleeves of her sweater to hide the bandages. The farmer and his wife were crying.

"'We left for two hours to go to the doctor,' they said, sobbing. 'We had a long-standing appointment…Maurice was busy planning and filing. We had left his tea for him on the table, some junket which he loved, bread and chocolate…He was as happy as a song-bird…We should have taken away the tools…'

"Grandmother consoled them. 'He was very sick,' she said. 'It was bound to happen one day or another.'"

"What kind of a sickness is it," my mother had shouted, "that bleeds your wrists white and kills you at twelve?"

"A sickness that starts in the brain, that takes you over body and soul," Grandmother had replied. "A fatal sickness," she added taking her in her arms before sighing, "Now we'll have to tell your father."

"You have to understand," my mother had added, "that what I've just told you must remain strictly between us…Officially, Maurice died of tuberculosis."

"No, I don't really understand…"officially"? What does that mean?"

"It means that it's our business and no one else's…There are many strange ideas about this sort of sickness…Some even think it hereditary, which is ridiculous, but try and convince the malicious!"

"You think Louis is like Maurice?"

"It's hard to tell right now. At twelve they had the same hair, they were more or less the same size, and both of them, like many boys their age, were absorbed by the mechanical…Your grandmother died with Maurice. Louis was a resurrection for her…but it was also a resurrection of all the anxieties and uncertainties woven into the twelve years of their lives together. I'm not worried about Louis. He is a little eccentric, a solitary, but he's solid, I know…"

So Uncle Maurice had slit his wrists at the age of twelve… He was certainly precocious…"He was the size of a grown man," Grandmother said. "Had it not been for his migraines he would have been two or three years ahead at the Lycée."

That's about all one can get out of her about her brother. His "illness" is not talked about. She had not had to impose silence on my grandfather, her husband; the war took care of that. As for her daughter, my mother, she had inculcated in her a respect for that secret such that my mother reproached herself for having revealed it in a moment of weakness…I had sworn to tell no one, and above all not Grandmother…On the other hand, what I had further learned was that once Maurice was buried, Antoinette had shut herself up in her room for eight days. On her pillow she had left a heavy pile of her red hair gone white…She had learned of her husband's death the day after the death of her son.

"Lucky man," she had murmured. "He was spared the worst."

At fifteen, my mother had been compelled to mourn her father alone. I believe she still does, and always will, bear, somewhere within her which no one can reach, that burden. That place may be the source of her charm. Smooth and impenetrable as her face is, it conceals a wound that her violet eyes, behind her thick black lashes, have never been able to conceal. She is beautiful; this shadow makes her mysterious. Those who come near her want to penetrate that secret. From the day when, all buttoned up in his uniform as a newly-discharged officer on the 15th of February 1919, too quickly rounding a corner, he had gently bumped this tall young woman, he has been busy at that task…A week after that meeting he asked her to marry him.

We are encamped in the Occupation and its restrictions. The exodus has swept over our plains and forests; a transitory population has swollen our towns, villages, houses and barns. A wretched armistice has been signed; the wave has retreated, leaving our father in tears…But Marshall Pétain, the hero of 1914, will surely do all he can to limit the damage…We listened to the appeal of General de Gaulle on June eighteenth…What's he up to, setting the French against one another…

"He's right," Louis said calmly.

"He's right," said Grandmother.

My father remains silent. My mother had met Pétain in 1917 when she was nursing the wounded at the front: "He was a fine man," she said. "I would be inclined to trust him."

Louis said, "He's a doddering old fool."

"Let's have some respect for one of our great military leaders," said my father severely.

"Ex-," corrected Louis.

Wednesday morning…My grandmother has just called. I am doing homework for my correspondence course for the Universal School. I thank God for the interruption. My life is very solitary. Every week I have to work through a huge packet and follow the silent written instructions laid out on the wax-clothed table in the kitchen, my back to the fire that I keep going conscientiously; I hear the stove puff, and as soon as it starts to sound feeble, I get it going again; I am re-animating…avoiding suffocation…an art I have taught myself to master…I have even asked my father to put the logs next to the wood-chest, and every morning it is I who line them up by size, so that I can easily feed the fire…There is no longer time for anything, there is no one about to help…My father chops the wood, he looks after the garden; he comes home tired and doesn't want to be disturbed. My mother has never been talkative; she cleans, she cooks, and those tasks get her full attention.

Grandmother's voice is a-tremble, words tumble out, she wants to see us right away, my mother and I, but especially my mother, but I will go along, to keep her company, to avoid having to wait anxiously tonight…It's ten kilometers on our bicycles. We leave in the early afternoon, sure that we'll get back before nightfall…

The roads are full of people going home to the north, and of our defeated army's trucks on the run, still heading south. We ride on the verge, one behind the other, my mother on her old fixed-wheel black bike and I on a big man's bike. That's all we have left, our modern bikes with their gears were stolen one night we inadvertently left the garage door unlocked. It's a fine day, not too hot, we roll right along. Grandmother might as well have been at the gate…After we ring she runs down the four flights, has us climb up at full speed, we barely have time to put our bikes away.

"I must talk to you before Louis comes home…I'm very worried, I have this feeling that it's all happening over again…"

"What is?" my mother asks.

"I think Louis is not quite right, that he's *disturbed*," my grandmother says.

"What makes you say something like that?" my mother said aggressively, irritated.

"He is not as he was, he goes off…"

"What do you mean, he goes off? He skips meals, he sleeps out?…You have to get used to the idea that he's no longer a child…The most you can insist on is that he should let you know before-hand…"

"Sometimes it's that," Grandmother said. "But there are also other ways he goes off. There's an empty look about him, he often doesn't hear what I say…I recognize the symptoms…His room is full of bizarre bric-a-brac: twenty-five alarm clocks, I've counted them, heaps of dull blue stones, electric wiring…just like Maurice."

"Nothing new in that," replied my mother, softening her voice. "His room's always been full of strange objects, he is mesmerized by anything mechanical."

My grandmother was bewildered. "But what should I do?" she asked. "You know how dangerous it is to go out after dark…. All it takes is a patrol going by at the wrong moment."

"Nothing," my mother replied with calm. "Louis is a man now. Don't forget he's just turned eighteen."

"And if he doesn't come back?" Grandmother gasped, on the verge of tears. "I'll be eaten up with anxiety day and night, I'll no longer live…"

"My dear mother, that would be fate," my mother replied.

"There's nothing you can do about it…But he'll come back…some day.

My mother knows that, or wants that; he'll come back, she has nothing further to say.

Grandmother wasn't convinced, she suffers, she slips her arm onto mine and rests all her weight on it.

Looking at her watch, my mother says, "We have to get back," mother says. "My bike light is dead and I don't want to be caught out in the dark."

She hugged her mother lengthily. "Don't worry," she said. "Everything will be all right, I hope…Anyway, it's not our business to interfere. Don't harass him…feed him, love him while he's here, that's all he wants."

"He's going away?" Grandmother asked, her voice quavering.

"One day," my mother said sharply. "He's of an age to be called up."

"And his student deferment?"

"You know, these days, things have a way of not working out according to the established rules."

We were gone, Grandmother having managed a wretched smile while warning us to be prudent on the road and to call her when we got home.

"Your grandmother has to accept that Louis is ready to fly on his own wings."

"He'll leave Grandmother's?"

"One day or another, of course."

"But he'll finish his year at the lycée?"

"Perhaps."

I see Grandmother on the doorstep, overcome by this terrible menace, Louis gone; she stands bare-headed in the road, a sign of her disarray, quivering, biting her thumb-nail.

"And Grandmother? What will become of her?'

"She'll do as we do, she'll adapt to circumstances…"

Good God! What sorts of circumstances could make someone break off his studies and break the heart of the most delectable of grandmothers?

Antoinette called up from the village station to ask us to fetch her and her bundle…My father interrupted his breakfast, with complaints, to harness up the cart. He didn't look particularly worried, or even surprised…Grandmother's arrival did indicate, however, that Louis was gone.

"She might have left me time to have a couple of coffees," my father said, picking up his keys.

"I'll keep it warm for you," my mother answered. "You can have your second cup when you get back."

"Warmed-over coffee…"

The front door slammed and cut off the rest. My mother smiles. How can the two of them retain this calm of theirs? Does anyone know where Louis is?…And Grandmother, in what shape will she be when she arrives?

She had it in her hand—a brief note from Louis which she had found stuck to the mirror in her room, "Whatever you do, don't worry, I'll let you know my news as soon as possible." She handed the note to my mother who showed no surprise. Grandmother had obviously spent a sleepless night. In her other hand she had a little suitcase which my mother took in with astonishment: "That's all?"

"I don't need anything else," she replied. "Since Rip (her old dog) died, I can afford to travel light."

Thus begins our life as a quartet. Day and night Grandmother listens to footsteps that could be Louis, and the mail always disappoints. Evenings were brief and spent around the only heat in the house, the kitchen-stove, where we economize on the wood my father has fetched and chopped. Grandmother has not moved into her old room, where now my father has set up his radio and where, once he has performed his domestic tasks, he spends much of his free time…The room is an isolated one, reached by a separate and rather steep staircase; he needs, he says, to be alone from time to time, for the life he leads is tiring…It's too bad for Grandmother…Up there I've found mysterious gardening notes that make no sense…*The flowers have been cut, the leeks won't go into the soup, the baker will pick the beans…*

"Louis' room…Why his room?…He won't come back?" He

voice quavers, she is accusatory: "Where are his things? You've already got rid of them?"

My mother puts her arm around her waist and shows her Louis" new room, on the ground floor, in the former laundry room behind the kitchen, a big white room with an outside door of its own and a big cupboard full of all the things he had not taken with him.

She talks to her mother as to child: "Of course he'll come back, but he's a man now, he needs to be free to come and go."

"Come and go where?" protests Grandmother. "And to start with, where is he?"

Silence…

"Do you know where he is?"

"No my dear."

Nobody knows anything. How can Grandmother be reassured?

The moon is full, the night crisp but calm. A light breeze rustles among the leaves. It's two in the morning and despite the instructions of Home Defense she has not pulled her curtains to and her lamp is lit. Does she ever sleep at night? She comes back breathless from long walks. For some time she has been leaving in the early morning, and when we come down for breakfast her empty cup sits by the sink. It's as though it's that way on purpose, leaving before anyone can offer to accompany her…

She often drowses during the day, her nose droops to her sweater, and if my mother says to go have a nap, she protests, gets upset—she whom I've never heard say one word louder than another… Sometimes her wig slips and its fringe rests diagonally on her forehead. Yesterday she cracked her temple on the marble top of her chest of drawers…Grandmother is not well…She doesn't say much…she just nibbles at her food…If Louis doesn't come back, if he doesn't show some sign of life, she will die from his disappearance…

On another night, clear too, Grandmother's lamp burns in her window, which despite the season is half-open, as though she were listening for footsteps, you never know…Should Louis come from behind the house to go directly into his room, no one will hear him, for the wind has picked up, is not a strong wind but the whole house shakes and creaks a bit and there's no way to tell one sound from another…

My father runs down the stairs, the telephone has just rung, at midnight, my mother follows him down and I go down too with my naked feet on the tiles. Grandmother has not budged, perhaps after all she has fallen asleep, worn out by so many sleepless nights. All three of us end up in the kitchen, my father has just put the receiver back on the wall telephone, my mother's put on water to heat, we'll have an herbal tea…

"A coffee would be better, a good strong coffee."

"At midnight…?"

"We're expecting someone?"

Who knows? The coffee-pot waits in its bubbling bain-marie, it emits a long-forgotten smell, the aroma of real coffee.

The wind rises, it swells, we put our fingers in our ears.

"It was a plane," my father says.

And my mother comments, "It must have been very close."

We have sat down around the table, all three of us. No one has poured out a cup of coffee, its aroma has dissipated. They wait and I wait alongside them. They are silent and I don't dare talk to them. Nothing must disturb their listening, they are lying in wait…The wind lowers, and if someone is coming we should be able to hear his footsteps on the driveway gravel…Unless he chooses to walk across the lawn to surprise us…My father looks at his watch, he smiles nervously: "Let's be sensible, we can't hope for anything for at least a half-hour"…

"Hope for what?" I don't understand what's going on, I'm afraid, this morning I saw a German in uniform buying cigarettes in the village, that was odd, off-color, they have their own rations…I forgot to tell them that…anyway, now it's too late…Worse, the notary and he, the German, exchanged a few words…but the notary and his twelve children, everybody knows that he's for Work, Family and the Motherland…Three words that when agglutinated like that are impossible to live with whereas, standing by themselves, each one separate, they have an honorable place in our lives, indeed it is proper that heroes should die for one of them...

An hour passes, an hour-and-a-half, rain starts falling, after all it was perhaps just the wind, a big wind, a squall...

"Maia, you should go back to bed."

"Go on, darling, you have an exam to study for, you have to keep in shape...there's a month to go before the baccalaureate...We'll call you if there's any news..."

"What sort of news? Who called? What are we doing in the kitchen at two in the morning?"

They looked at one another as if trapped. My mother had let something slip. Now I know they're waiting for someone or something. If they keep this secret to themselves, I'm going to try to clear up the mystery, I'll talk about it elsewhere...

"In fact we are waiting for someone, Maia, probably Louis."

"It was he who called?"

"No, but we were led to understand he might be somewhere around here tonight."

My mother put her hands on my shoulders: "Look at me, Maia," she said. Neither her look nor her voice were joking. You may be lucky enough to see your brother, but outside of the three of us, including your grandmother, you've seen no one, you heard no telephone call, you were asleep as usual...I count on you."

I have understood...Besides, to whom would I talk, I have no one to talk to...

Soissel was the privileged home to our holidays, to our games, our childish laughter, to our Yule fires, to our Easter egg-hunts in the shrubbery, to the straw hats heaped in the front hall we grabbed on summer days; today I am imprisoned here. The plains and forests surrounding us are great, limitless walls, there's no choice about it, one sees only those who live within its enclosure, who live not too far, a bike-ride away...At times my feeling of nostalgia for the benches of the Lycée makes me weep for my loneliness. Where are they all, my friends, the teachers from whom I had thought myself happily liberated? I dream of pavements, of the push-and-shove of the street, of glances exchanged, the promiscuity of rush-hours...I even rue the loss of Sunday morning mass where I'd been wrong to be bored to death; the church had been full of people, it was warm, the organist had not held back and filled our ears with joy, the priest in surplice had propped his lace-covered belly on the rim of the pulpit and commented on the gospel of the day in a deep bass voice that thundered, threatened or caressed according to the moods of God, it was all real theater. here there's a bunch of nobodies wrapped up in Sunday grey, a harmonium vainly trying to fill out a few frail voices, and the coal stove, in the choir behind the altar with its pipe sticking through the main window, still unable to un-numb our fingers.

We have chosen to make Soissel our nest for the war: because it's in the country, because of wood that warms, of lambs-necks for meat, of milk and eggs filched from the farm...True, we die neither of hunger or cold...only from isolation...

"I want to stay with you," I say.

My mother puts a cup in front of each of us and pours out the steaming coffee, there's a little powdered sugar left, we're allowed a spoonful each, but exceptionally...

We wait, with nothing to say to each other...

He finally arrived, just as dawn was breaking. Between two downpours, we heard knocks, three soft knocks...My father was ready, he had already unlocked the door, and they came in soaked, shedding water, covered with leaves and twigs, two wet fragments of forest dripping on the tiles. Louis takes me in his arms, kisses my mother, pulls his friend by the arm: "Philip," he says. "Allow me to introduce my friend Philip."

"Is everything all right?" my father asks.

"Things are all right...Can we stay until tonight?"

"Of course. No one comes here but the mail-man...Anyway, the shutters are closed in your room, no one can see you. The only problem is your grandmother..."

Louis winks at his friend, they share a smile. "Grandmother is not a problem."

Besides which, Grandmother is there, fully-dressed in the

middle of the night: big skirt, little boots, her wig dead straight and a loving smile, reserved for Louis, lighting up her face and effacing the years: "Bravo, Grandmother, everything worked well."

"I followed the instructions, it wasn't complicated."

My mother and father held their breaths.

"What instructions?"

Louis said, "Mine."

"Conveyed just how?" barks my father. He feels beaten to the line and he doesn't like that. He had spent hours listening to the sibylline messages transmitted on the BBC. He was sure that any message his son sent out he would have recognized.

"Who telephoned?" he asked Louis.

"Someone telephoned? What did he say?"

"I don't know. Something like *the carrots are cooked*, and I re-plied, *agreed, but I don't understand a word of what you're saying*...But nonetheless I thought it was a message telling us of your visit, because we were waiting for it, we hoped for it, every day since you left..."

"Yes...but *who* telephoned, for God's sake?"

Louis looks worried.

"Perhaps some prankster," suggested Grandmother, who wanted to dispel the shadows before anxiety set it and grew, before we pan-icked.

"At midnight?...A rotten prank." Louis doesn't like that phone call, nor does Philip, who invoked the Lord after a loud "Shit!" He apologized. He had big, very pale eyes, and suddenly looked like a bewildered child.

I don't want to provoke a fit of madness, but I have to warn them:

"I saw a German buying cigarettes in the village this morn-ing."

"How do you know he was German?"

"He was in uniform."

"..."

"Could you describe him?" asked Philip.

"Average-sized, neither fat nor thin. I only saw him from the back."

"That gets us a long way…Was he wearing a kepi or a forage cap?"

"A forage cap."

Philip whispered something into Louis" ear.

"Karl maybe," they both said together.

"He spoke to the notary."

"Not a good sign," said Louis.

"Who's Karl?" asked my father.

There was no reply.

"We'll go down to the cellar until tomorrow night," Louis decided. "Enough time to see if anyone comes…Blankets and sandwiches, but apart from that you forget we exist, the bottles are long gone, there's no reason for anyone to go down there…"

My mother protested:

"I have four bottles of champagne down there that miraculously escaped plundering, and I intend to drink them as soon as the last pig leaves."

"Unto each day the evil thereof," Louis commented.

Grandmother sits silently, now she chews her thumb-nail. "Louis, you're not going to sleep in the cellar, it's cold and damp down there, you'll fall ill, I'll give you my room, no one will look for you there." Already she sees him coughing, feverish, his eyelids blinking on the verge of death.

"Don't worry, I've seen worse." She doubts it, she's afraid, she'd like to keep him while she's got him.

They left as they came, the following night. Just before noon each morning that week I drank a coffee at the village café, but I never saw another German, whether Karl or another…Grandmother looks weak again, we have no news of Louis, nor does she; she bites her thumb-nail a lot. But who knows? We already know her talent as an actress. My father still hasn't recovered from her coup, he doesn't think she can get away with it again without being caught out, he spies on her, he observes her, he thinks her anxiety is real…As is ours, who allowed them to rejoin the shadows of a mysterious and hunted-down army without understanding the first thing about it or asking any questions

Grandmother thinks about Louis, I think about Philip; I'd like him to come back, so I could talk to him, did he even notice my existence?

Grandmother showed me the clearing in a little birch-wood; it's there, nearby, that Louis and Philip were parachuted in...She made sure that they left no traces behind. Where are they now? It is said that a maquis has been formed not far from us, in the middle of the forest, a place well-chosen, for the Germans rarely come by this way, for several years the brush hasn't been cleared and the woods are thick...

Now there are two of us who don't sleep. Last night I thought I heard a shot, so did my grandmother.

"No," said my father. "I heard nothing...Did you, Jacqueline?"

"You know I sleep like lead," answered my mother.

They sleep like lead, but they look more and more tired. It's as though they've forgotten the sounds of the country: the cry of a pheasant made them jump, both of them...Grandmother is calmer, more attuned to unusual sounds. My father is the one who runs our errands in the village, for his bicycle pulls a little trailer. He listens to the rumors, he brings them faithfully home. Since "Karl" no uniform has been seen in the village, just from time to time in the station, five hundred yards beyond the village...

At five o'clock this morning—our ears were shattered, the house shook, the night was lit up not far from here—perhaps a bomb went off...No, it's the railway bridge that's been blown up...

"You think it was them?"

"Who, them?"

"Them," I repeat, still without daring name them, as though the walls *really* had ears...

"Karl," he did show up, with a dozen men. They pinned my father against a wall while they searched the house, they pushed Grandmother out of her room, they went down into the cellar and returned in triumph with the champagne bottles...It was just routine, they had no reason to suspect us...

Grandmother caught cold, she coughs, we tried to light a fire in her room but the chimney will not draw, it smokes and she coughs even more, my mother tried cupping her. A big pot simmers in the kitchen from morning to night, we eat vegetables, she drinks the stock. Her temperature rises, the doctor says it should go down within forty-eight hours, otherwise, at her age…My father and mother speak softly, I take up her bouillon, I can tell she's no longer strong enough to drink it…She is asleep and I sleep too, I don't dare leave her alone…

When I open my eyes, her bed is empty…

I find her in the kitchen, wrapped up in a shawl over her flannel nightgown, a grey wool bonnet on her head, she is busy stoking the fire.

"You see how well you looked after me?" she said. "I'm cured, I got rid of the fever"…

She warms up her barley gruel, and dips a crust in it.

"You're up bright and early, your parents are still asleep, don't wake them up, they need some rest."

"And you, Grandmother, you should be in bed, the doctor will be very angry…"

"Leave the doctor where he is, he's not needed, I'm well, I'm going out this morning…"

"I'll come with you."

"If you want, I'm going into the village."

Five minutes to get dressed and she's downstairs, hat on head, with her gloves on, brought back to life.

I'm afraid her voluminous skirt will get caught in the spokes of the wheel, but no, she does fine. It's just about daybreak, the wind isn't up yet, her hat, fixed to her chignon with two long pins, is not about to fall off. The road is empty, we pedal side by side. First stop, the church, it's half past seven and Mass is coming to an end. Grandmother takes me to a side door and into a little chapel attached to the apse where there is a painted wood statue of our local saint, Saint Roch, patron saint of hunters…A big black-and-white dog at his feet and licks his hand. The candle in Grandmother's hand is for him, I know…She hates hunting and, except for Louis, she has always like animals better than men…She joins her hands, mutters a few seconds, pushes me out the door and off we go…

The village people are beginning to open their shutters, she gets them at their rising, before they leave their houses for daily life, some of them on the threshold, some still at their windows. She's come for news, she wants to see with her own eyes, listen with her own ears, she is not all that confident in the way her son-in-law reads faces or hears words…Much as he likes to think he's at home here, this is her home territory, not his. She talks to everyone she meets, to the notary as to the rest…They feel the cold this morning, they are slow to great the pearly dawn which promises a fine day…At the baker's they seem in a greater hurry than usual.

"Don't you find their smiles a bit mechanical, yellowish?"

She doesn't like that much. She wants open hearts. She leads me to a little house set back from the road up a dead-end alleyway; she knocks on the door, puts her ear to the door, knocks again: "Marguerite, it's Antoinette."

Marguerite opens the door, she's been crying for three hours, in the dark, she hasn't opened her shutter, she doesn't want to open it…We go in anyway and Grandmother opens a few slats, just a crack of light so we don't bump up against the furniture. She embraces Marguerite, strokes her hair, we sit down on the unmade bed:

"They came through tonight, around four, I saw them, a truck with a dozen men with machine guns, they took the road that goes up through the oak-wood to the farm that used to belong to old Lanceau… I heard several salvos, I'm sure…Besides, the whole village heard them, it's not possible otherwise…Pierrot hasn't come back…"

"He bought them supplies from time to time."

"To whom?"

"I don't understand anything about it…"

Biting her lip, Marguerite looks at my grandmother, Grandmother smiles sadly, tenderly, and Marguerite says:

"They're kids, kids from the Lycées, they came from Paris. Every day they arrive…They hide up there at the farm, the Germans hunt them down, why do that? They're just children, the oldest is not even twenty…We can't let them die of hunger…"

"Have they been in touch with the maquis?"

"The maquis? What maquis?" cries Marguerite. "There are no

maquis round here, they haven't got any weapons, they're lost, just kids, they sleep in the old barn up there...Pierrot brings them a basket from time to time..."

She repeats herself, Marguerite does, always the same things, and sobs.

"Has anyone been up there to see?"

"Not yet...They may still be up there, the grey-and-greens with their machine guns..."

Grandmother ends with the question that burns on her lips:

"Do you know if Louis is with them?"

No. Marguerite knows nothing, no one in the village knows anything...From time to time they've certainly seen some young people they don't know, at the grocer's or the baker's, rarely the same place twice, nothing really out of the ordinary, you know, in a village with a main road through it.

Pierrot never came back...He had picked a bad day and a bad hour to go off with a knuckle of pork (subtracted from the Occupier's requisitions) hidden under bracken in his basket...He'd been picked up coming out of the woods a few yards from the Lanceau barn. The others were stretched out in the field, some ten or so young people lying out in the cool night, their noses down in the earth that absorbed their blood. They had lined them up with their feet in a straight furrow, one salvo, quickly done, well done, for the rest...Grandmother left me to look after Marguerite while she fetched M. Lagarde, the harness-maker, with whom she had flirted at the school-desks, from his stable. They took ten minutes to get up to the Lanceau farm. First they came across Pierrot, his nose in his basket, in which his coagulated blood lay like a brown crust on the meat...According to Lagarde, Grandmother followed the furrow to the end to make sure Louis wasn't among them...Then, helped by her old friend, she had carried Pierrot back to Marguerite, as Maurice had been carried back to her. Once laid out on the bed the two women had washed his face and hands. To hide his wound, Grandmother drapes the silk scarf she wore around her neck on his brow, and once again she entrusted them to me, Marguerite and her son who looked like a sleeping pirate...

"Call your parents," she said. "I have to go back up there."

Grandmother went through their jacket and trouser pockets, the nooks and crannies of the barn, their sleeping bags, she wants to let their parents know, to try to lessen the horror, she found nothing…clandestine they were…untraceable…

…And still no news of Louis…Grandmother keeps busy reassuring us: it's at least ten kilometers from Soissel to the Lanceau farm…Louis" very brief visit is totally unconnected, he was in contact with the Allied forces, not with a bunch of unthinking kids…And yet people in the village have their questions…Who put the bomb under the railway bridge?…If it was the young people why would they have stayed at a barn so near the scene of their "crime", at the risk of implicating the whole village and being shot themselves?…Bit by bit a conclusion is come to, it's a bunch of young people just passing through who did it, thoughtless kids dropped out of the sky, kids who left as they came, leaving others to pay the price for what they'd done…

We stay with our lips buttoned-up, we know nothing, but like everyone else we have questions, always the same questions: was the massacre a reprisal for the blowing-up of the bridge?…and *whom did blow it up?* We don't even think it through, we refuse to consider the unthinkable…My father runs his errands in the early morning, at opening time, when women are still in their kitchens, tidying up and drinking the last drops of their coffee, when everyone is in a hurry, and people barely speak…

It's raining, fitting weather, says my mother, for they are to be buried today, their graves are at the edge of the village, ten anonymous crosses and one bearing Pierrot's name in letters as golden as the precious love Marguerite bore her son, while she takes refuge in my grandmother's arms and won't leave them. People ask us for news of Louis, "He's in a business school in Clermont-Ferrand," says my father without consulting us…He picked his time, when all three of us were trying to hold up Marguerite who felt weak…Now we know what to say to cut off speculation…And Grandmother embroiders: "Absolutely, he's had superb results on his entrance exam, he always loved mathematics, and anyway anything he tries he succeeds at"…I pray that no one from the village should set foot in Clermont-Ferrand…As soon as I fall asleep, the notary is by my side, asking me impossible questions: "What is this Business School called? Is it a Paris school *moved out* for the duration?" or, "You know the name of the street it's on?"…I'm afraid to meet him.

The only one of us who allows herself neither flight nor prudence is Grandmother: "How am I supposed to know the address by heart? I noted it in my book, but it's not much use to me anyway, since I can't go and see him and barely write him"…A special pass is needed to pass from the Occupied Zone where we live and the Free Zone where we have put Louis, and from one zone to another all correspondence is limited to sets of three dots on a pre-printed form…

With its door and shutters closed, my father spends more and more time in his dovecot, my grandmother's old room, his ear glued to the radio…One morning he tells us of the allied landings in Normandy…Then the liberation of Paris…

"It would be nice to rejoice," he said. "We'll finally be able to be back *at home*." His is a half-smile, his tone is ironic and bitter.

"Nothing from Louis?" my mother asks timidly.

"Nothing…"

The mythical maquis of whom we spoke without ever having seen it suddenly emerged from the brush, a few men in our village put a human face on it, one of them had even heroically shot a German soldier who strayed from his fleeing unit with his hunting rifle…The maquis paraded on the main road behind a Cross of Lorraine, followed by all the village authorities, including the notary…But hadn't they…sometime…long ago…paraded the school children to the sound of "Marshall, here we are"? A double game, perhaps?…It is never too late, is it, to recognize one's mistakes and correct them?

I begin to realize that the solitude which has kept my sixteen-year-old self in an icy straitjacket may be at an end…The melancholia of my parents keeps me from real hope. The absence of Louis, and Marguerite, Pierrot, the graves of the unknown students, forbid any happiness. We are as though paralyzed, even as all about us is waking up.

Only my grandmother is busy, we no longer see her, she's gone in the morning, back at night, doesn't say much at dinner, goes to bed early and rises early.

"Next week the Town Council is organizing a ceremony for the young people killed at Lanceau, putting their names on the graves, their parents will come...I think we ought to invite them for a drink here...To make them welcome, give it all a little warmth..."

Grandmother never ceases to surprise us...

"A drink?" my father barks. "Apart from tap water, what am I supposed to offer them?...A drop of rot-gut the grocer will graciously allot me in return for my coupons?" Grandmother has just opened up a raw wound, our cellar emptied and indiscriminately drunk by a routed regiment. "And furthermore, I don't know these people, I have every sympathy in the world for them, but I have nothing to say to them..."

"Louis knows them."

"Louis?"

Grandmother is calm, she has things under control. As far as we're concerned, this is the best and the worst of revelations: apparently Louis is in touch with her, that means he's alive...But what's his link with the young people who were killed, what was his role, his responsibility in this desperate affair? My father stands up, sits down, gets up again, lowers himself into a chair opposite Grandmother, seizes her wrists, she winces, his grip is too tight, he's hurting her:

"No link at all," she cries out as the breaks his grip. "Are you unable to trust your own son, instead of always thinking of him in the most inextricable, the least honorable of situations?"

He said nothing. He simply took the hands of my mother who was standing behind him, she watches the anguish which makes him expect the worst from those he loves, which invades and possesses him without warning, against which he has no defense at all.

"He knows them, because he *knows*...that's his job, information, intelligence...He searches, he discovers, he analyzes, he prepares the ground...It is I who asked him to find their parents...The organizer of their network had been his math professor at the lycée..."

"What network?" interrupts my father. "How did Louis know they existed?"

There's no way to rid him of his suspicions, they overwhelm him, he is inhabited by doubt, it makes him ill…Who's going to believe that Louis had nothing to do with this horrid affair?

"Someone must have fingered them…Or at least someone with a loose tongue!…"

"Not Louis, certainly! If that's what you're insinuating," Grandmother cried out furiously. "He informed the leader of their network, the Math professor, and he informed the families…"

My father is suffocating. Once again she has check-mated him.

At the very beginning, when Louis left, my father thought he was the only one who knew that, *one way or another,* Louis had decided to evade his labor draft, which meant entering the resistance…From then on, apart from the one visit before the bridge was blown up, he had never known where Louis was, or what doing…Nor, he thought, should anyone have known, Antoinette no more than anyone else, for that was the basic rule of the clandestine life, it was the one way to survive and not compromise those around you…

I watch him crumple. His eyelids droop, his lower lip sags, revealing his pink, almost red gums against the pale, grey skin of his face.

"So he knew them…" His voice is very low, husky, resigned. "Did he have the bridge blown up when he knew the others were close by, hiding?"

Grandmother answered loudly, as if she were exasperated, "No!" She now speaks syllable by syllable as though talking to someone who is sick, who finds simple things hard to understand, or doesn't want to understand them. "He made his enquiries, I asked him to, recently. He knew who to talk to because, as I told you, that was his job in the resistance, information, intelligence…The young people were part of a student network that was dismantled after one of them was arrested, it was their misfortune that they were hiding out at Lanceau, and that someone knew…And this someone talked…Probably."

"Who?" asks my father. "Louis, who is so well-informed, he doesn't know who?"

We have set up a trestle table in front of the house under the great chestnut tree whose foliage is thick enough to protect us from sun or rain, a bed-sheet serves as a table-cloth, we have been shelling nuts all day to accompany some wretched bottles of very ordinary white wine and a few liters of cider pressed from the apples in the garden.

The ceremony was simple. Everyone here knows that it was murder, all they can do is weep. The mayor introduced the Math professor who, between sobs, tried to explain to the parents the noble dreams of their sons…de Gaulle was not mentioned, nor Leclerc, nor the glorious liberation of Paris…Our liberation is a mourning, and heroism here lies in the dignified silence of these couples who embrace the teacher "responsible" for the deaths of their sons…Marguerite too went up to embrace the professor through her tears…

They came to the house for some brief refreshments and were delicate enough to ask what had become of Louis—Who had told them about Louis?…Grandmother?

"You're bound to have news of him very soon, now that we've been liberated," they say.

"There's always the eastern front," says my father, worried.

My mother kisses the women, presses the hands the men hold out to her, she wraps them in her tenderness…

"I would like to know where Louis is," she says gently.

Grandmother is silent. She knows nothing, she says. Yesterday's verve is gone, there's no reason now to hide anything, where is Louis? His silence is useless, cruel, and there's always the eastern front, my father repeats, that's where the war is now, the real war, without respite and without mercy…

"Oh do stop!" says my grandmother in exasperation. "If he were gone there, I'd know…"

My father shrugs, his mother-in-law has always thought herself the center of Louis' life.

"Perhaps he didn't have enough time to tell you; or, more likely, he didn't *want* to tell you, no doubt so that you wouldn't worry, but also because that sort of thing, in intelligence work, you don't shout about from the roof-tops…"

The mail-man came earlier than usual, just as my mother was pouring out coffee in our breakfast cups. He handed my father a letter, of an unusual sort, a big square envelope with a simple, impressive heading, "Republique Française" below and to the left of that, "Presidency of the Provisional Government". My father took it, turned it round, his hand shakes, he doesn't dare open it but lays it down on the table; none of us moves, we stare at the big, clean, white envelope, letters of this sort, official letters, we distrust, behind the citations lies death basted with medals…like those of his two brothers, dead with fifteen days between them, in October of 1918…

Grandmother has grabbed the letter, she has slit it open cleanly with her knife and taken out three typewritten sheets attached to a hand-written letter, she coughs slightly to clear her voice and begins reading:

"Madam and dear Sir,
General de Gaulle, commander-in-chief of the army, has cited Louis P—with the military award of the Croix de Guerre by ministerial decision No.__ , dated 18.ii.45. Kindly inform him yourselves of this award first, and later I shall be happy to convey it to him personally. I ask you to pass on to him the congratulations of his brothers-in-arms. Allow us, too, to address to you, his parents, who for many long months have been worried about his fate, who have accepted the risks caused by your son's devotion to his country, and who have labored for years to form so generous a heart, our deepest and most respectful congratulations. Please accept, Madam and dear Sir, our special and respectful sympathy."

The signature was obscured by a badly-applied round stamp, and a few pale letters show through, in which we think we can read "network".

Grandmother had started her reading in a measured, controlled voice. But quickly her voice swelled, the phrases were punctuated with silences, the look she gave my father was one of triumph… "May the lesson prove profitable to you, my dear son-in-law! Perhaps now you will finally trust my grandson Louis who is, I remind you, also your son…"

The typewritten sheets are passed around, the texts of the citations… "As wily, as brave, and with an unchallengeable patriotism, despite his young age he has constantly resisted the oppression of the invader with every means at his disposal."

"'Wily'?" said my mother…She cannot recognize her son and all these talents we knew nothing about, a son who blows up trains and swims across rivers "under enemy fire"…I feel just the same, for how can I discern in this fully-grown young man, strapped with explosives, master of his fate, this hero of an adventure film, strong enough to breast the current of the Rhône, who "having been arrested…manages to escape the claws of the enemy…"

"But where is he?"

"Wait, there's a postscript: 'Louis was in Lyon on 15.xii.45 and his arrival in Clermont has been signalled today 27.xii.45'…What could be more natural," Grandmother said, looking to her son-in-law. "After all, wasn't it in Clermont-Ferrand that you found him a Business School?"

My father fails to appreciate the irony, he's never set foot in Clermont, how is he supposed to find Louis in this labyrinth, his silence is not normal, and this letter, for all its praise, is hardly reassuring…"signalled"?…By whom and to whom?

"I had hoped he'd be here for the New Year," sighed my mother.

And Christmas?…Truth to tell, we've forgotten all about Christmas, it slipped through our fingers untouched…Three days ago we had made plans to go to midnight Mass…and then the snow fell, the temperature tumbled, we weren't about to risk ourselves at night on the icy roads, we couldn't harness up the trap. We had grouped ourselves around the fire in the kitchen, we didn't look at the calendar, my father tried to teach me to play bridge, I have little talent for it, my father is annoyed.

We go to bed with death in our hearts. In the middle of the night we sneak down to see if by some miracle Louis is not asleep in his bed. In the morning our anxiety reaches a peak, the worse for the disappointment of the night…it dies down a bit during the day when we have things to do, and then comes back full force in the evening, even as hope dies away...

They come in full daylight, in fact I think almost exactly at noon, he rang the doorbell, we heard him talking and laughing, she is as tall as he is, her face half hidden by great waves of golden hair with flows over her shoulders and breasts. They walked in like the closing image of a movie, hand in hand, smiling at the happiness that is now promised them. We were all thunderstruck—as when we read the letter and didn't recognize him in it...I no longer have a brother, this is a grown man come to visit...He has outgrown his adolescence far away from us, without us, my mother flings herself in his arms and then tenderly kisses the tall blonde, man or not, he is there, present, and there's nothing she wants more...My father hugs him and kisses the girl's hand...It's my turn now and we kiss, little by little I grow used to the idea, yes, it is Louis, Louis disguised as a man, his double-breasted jacket of grey flannel, I now rediscover his almond eyes which enfold the smile of his childhood.

And Grandmother?...She stands a little away, half seated on the kitchen table and opposite the door, she doesn't move, she waits for Louis to find her out, to need her, despite this lovely new creature at his side...Too new...But she alone, Antoinette alone, who saw him born to replace Maurice, can detect what is alike and what different between the two.

Louis has walked toward her and stands there, his left arm around the girl's shoulders. He held out his hand, she put hers in his. Antoinette is tall and stands straight, her seventy years have not deprived her of an inch...The three of them now are garlanded together, turning round and round in an imaginary waltz...My father, my mother and I, we watch them live...without us.

She continued to waltz, Grandmother did, with the same high spirits...Louis" two children, a boy and a girl, have had the good fortune to take part in the whirlwind of the numberless games she continued to invent and organize; her voice, always firm and clear, has continued to offer them the rich company of fairies, of Merlin the Sorcerer, of Mowgli, of the Model Little Girls...My son, Nicolas, came into the world on her eightieth birthday, the day Louis left for Mexico with his wife and children…She began to cough, she was not to stop coughing. She has begun to subside, to give way a little, for a while she stood straight again and then she stopped trying…She no longer wears her ankle-boots, her feet hurt, she lives in her slippers…But she still bites her thumb-nail when she worries, she never misses an opportunity to stand good-humoredly apart from all conformity, in short she is still herself, Antoinette, Grandmother, independent and generous, when she is betrayed by a sudden, irremediable weakness, which stills her wings and her breath. She shows a sort of astonished resignation and offers a smile to beg our pardon for such dependence…It happens that sometimes Nicolas offers her his shoulder and matches his walk to hers…

—translated by K.B.

Melvin Lasky, 1951

Melvin J. Lasky

The Eminence Rouge

I. THE COMMISSAR (I)

It must have been in the winter of 1946–7 that I first glimpsed the eminence rouge of Soviet power in Germany—Colonel Sergei Tulpanov.
The Red Army commanders and famous war heroes, Marshal Zhukov
and Marshal Sokolovsky, were nominally in charge of policy and they
were, to be sure, highly ideological officers. Still, Stalin's political
commissars, although they were no longer in formal authority over
military units (since Stalin's 'reform' of 1940), exerted an ubiquitous
influence and, in places, it was decisive by dint of ideological strength
and personal dominance in party circles. As the "Great Fatherland
War" drew to a close, and the fighting moved rapidly forward to
Polish and German battlefields, in every regiment, division, and army
corps along the Red Army front, political priorities began to displace
the primacy of strategy. Commissar mind was to have its day again,
drawing on pure old waters of dogma and revolutionary drive.

Tulpanov, for the four years of the Soviet occupation of Germany between 1945 and 1949 dominated the scene in the Eastern march much as one of Caesar's commanders in Sicily or an Augustan imperial consul in North Africa. He seemed to be at every political meeting from Leipzig and Dresden to Chemnitz and Rostock; and the official Red Army newspaper, the *Tägliche Rundschau*, reported what he had said on the next day (and a complete text across a full page followed a few days later). He explained why Marxism was an irrefutable science; how Lenin and Stalin were destined to enrichen political theory; where the German people could find peace and security (in opting for a Communist alliance with the USSR); when they would be genuinely free and reunited (the day the revolutionary mass pressure would get the Americans out of Europe). He was a tribune for Stalin's victory, and a man to be deferred to and feared in his own right.

He was standing at a kind of a bar in the Russian Club, *Die Möwe*. Named after Chekhov's "Seagull", the ramshackle reconstruction in the Wilhelmstraße had been built in the heart of East Berlin to win over the German intelligentsia to the "progressive cause". Artists, writers, actors and their friends flowed in. Beer and vodka were cheap (and, above all, available); the *Borschtsuppe* was thick and tasty; the hot dogs were almost of pre-War *Würstchen* quality. The whole affair was a reception for Carl Zuckmayer, the famous Weimar playwright who had returned from his Vermont exile in the USA "to look around". Zuck was delighted with the way the Russians received him and had invited many of his old friends from all parts of the city as well as the cultural officers of the Western Allies. It was a high-spirited evening at which much was imbibed. Zuck said, many years later, "Could you imagine that evening, with just about everybody there, that it would all split into two halves?" I said I could.

Tulpanov was a large man with an absolutely bald head that shone brilliantly even in the dim lights of the club room. He spoke German fluently, if with a somewhat harsh Eastern accent. This time he was in uniform with colored ribbons holding down bronze and silver medals; but very often he would surprise by turning up in civvies, and the East Berlin journalists would dutifully report, as if it had a deeper social significance: "*Der Oberst erschien im hellgrauen Anzug* (the Colonel arrived in a light-grey suit)…"

On the most memorable occasion to which I was a witness he was actually in a brown-colored suit, although even out of uniform he was to flash the full authority of his absolute command. I was taken again to the club, *Die Möwe*, in the still ruined Wilhemstraße, by an actor friend of mine, Wolfgang Lukschy, who had been a romantic-musical matinée idol in German films before the War but thought it was time for him, after everything had collapsed, to become somewhat 'political'. He was subsequently to get into a bewildering agit-prop cross-fire; for he was given a starring role in the East, and it happened to be in Konstantin Simonov's ill-fated *The Russian Question (Die russische Frage)*, which had its première in the Deutsches Theater, May 1947. Its savage anti-Americanism alarmed Western opinion and caused a frightened and bewildered Wolfgang Lukschy to "defect to the West" (and, thereafter, to return to rather more glamorous roles in the movies).

Lukschy and I sat together, sipping borscht along with O.E. Hasse and Kurt Meisel, and as the hour grew late the conversation grew more serious and even more organized. I thought I recognized this accelerated earnestness from scenes in Turgenev and Dostoyevsky. But to Russian intensity at midnight was added a heavy German concern to come away with a 'message', or at least, something to think about. Lesser Russian film- and theatre-officers began to move chairs and tables, for the Colonel was evidently in fine and full voice and everybody was straining an ear to catch what was being said.

Tulpanov, who had a touch of Stanislavski about him, kept talking at his table, carefully modulating his voice for the moment to come. With him were his close friends from the days when he stalked the Communist emigrés in the German colony of Moscow, Wolfgang Langhoff and Willi Bredel.

When that moment did come, what emerged was one of the most extraordinary brief pieces of oratory I have ever heard, a mixture of his own Russian *hauteur* and German deference to the voice of command. Some say that the beer and vodka (not to mention the music) heightened the occasion. We may have heard Volga notes that weren't there; he may have uttered Neva tones that were not quite intended.

But the Colonel was a man of such consistent ideological fastness that not even a lapse into *in vino veritas* could induce truths out of him that were not somehow part of the disciplined Party-line.

As a matter of fact a year later the speech he tried out on us after midnight was re-worked into a major State-of-the-Class-Struggle message. It then caused a nation-wide sensation for it was, at some higher level, cut, revised, bowdlerized, censored, and marked the low-point of his four-year reign as the whip of the revolution in Germany.

When the music stopped and they ceased serving drinks the Colonel turned to the subject that was on his mind. What was on his mind was obvious from the tortuous difficulties he had been having in the Sovieting of the German province. Explanations were many—among them being how could Stalin ease them back to a totalitarian harness when the wounds of Hitler's controls were so fresh. Excuses were ready to hand—the devastation had been so extensive that no real results, even with the application of vaunted German efficiency, could be managed within the short term.

One other factor remained, and historians have often maintained that this was the basic reason why in the duel for power in Central Europe the Russians could not make headway—the shock of the Red Army in the conquest of the Eastern German territories.

All military defeat is cruel and humiliating. But the rapine and the looting in this case was felt to be beyond the call of comprehension and forgiveness. I, and innumerable others, heard the dismal stories a hundred times: of the *Vergewaltigung*, the rape of women, young and old, from seven-to-seventy; the stripping of every household article from door-knobs to toilet-seats and bowls, etc.... If this were so, and it was, the deep resentment would cause a barrier which two or three generations would not be able to forget. Re-organize political parties as you will; go in for police intimidation on the chance that people will be terrorized into polite conformity; tinker with the economic system and the planning thereof. Would it all prove to be any avail? No, it would not. That smart the Colonel was.

As best as I can recall the gist of his remarks (and later, as I mentioned above, he tried to put some of it on the record), he said:

All wars are full of hatred and murderous feelings. Our war, between our two peoples, was probably the worst in history. Some wounds will never be healed. Many memories of horror will never be forgotten. On both sides we experienced the ferocity, the shame, the excess. I know—and acknowledge it openly—that you and probably all of your compatriots, recall the cry '*Uhri, Uhri!*'[1] and of '*Frau, komm mit!*' when our victorious Red Army, so long deprived of all material and intimate things, finally arrived at the end of the killing. I don't have to remind you how shameful and excessive some human behaviour can be in a life-and-death struggle.... But it is over! And it is useless to make scorecard of old points of regret and recrimination. We are trying to start anew, to build together a different society. Let's not remain stuck in the past, and keep nursing old wounds. This is a time of healing. Let us make a revolution for a better world...[2]

There was a hush, and there was no further talk. All the guests shuffled out and homewards. And I felt at the time that he had done it, had hit the right note; that he might have found the point to stand—between "Russian soul" and "German sentimentalism"—to bring together the battered and embittered psyches of the two powers that could easily dominate Europe. Even in perspective it appears to me that he had almost captured the tone of the tragedy and could possibly have used it to reverse the fortunes of his hard-pressed cause.

Rhetoric need not be mere empty words. Colonel Sergei Tulpanov, the soldier-intellectual, might have turned the trick. If he went on like this, and from this, there would be nothing that could stop the onset of a new order, still marked by deceit and deception, poverty and persecution, but embraced with a tear in the eye and the warm beginnings of a small friendly smile.

Ruined antagonists and cynical collaborators had come together before, making common cause in the surprising Rapallo Treaty of 1922 and in the melodramatic Hitler-Stalin Pact of 1939. Now the Germans, still shell-shocked by the *Katastrophe* wherein civilized time appeared to sink back to the Year Zero, were again groping, learning to count again on their fingers, still uncertain (in the stock Goethe phrase) which of the two souls that dwelt in their breast would make a Faustian deal. Underneath the formal mechanical ideology which bored the already alienated millions, Tulpanov may well have sensed a shared trauma and a last hope for his cause which lay in a break-through to a more natural language used by common men.

The Colonel made, as I have said, an attempt to make it all official, if tentatively and hesitantly as befits an imaginative *appa-ratchik*. In a formal speech a year later—in May 1948, on the eve of the Blockade of Berlin—he tried to break into the same aria, going on about the horrors of Berlin's house-to-house fighting, the corpses rotting in the streets, and (in his words) "consequently the embitterment and the excesses of some of our soldiers in those days. These were offenses of men who went through four years of war full of atrocities, committed against their families.... Only reactionaries and war-mongers, attacking the Soviet Union, can still talk of '*Uhri! Uhri!*' etc."

I heard these words on Radio Berlin which broadcast Col. Tulpanov's message, but the *Tägliche Rundschau* (presumbly on orders from the highest echelon in Karlshorst or the Kremlin) edited the text. The most unusual passage, with its rare touch of self-criticism, hitting an almost humane note systematically missing in the *ukase* tone of all Russian pronouncements, failed to appear the next morning in his own official Red Army newspaper. The chief censor was censored, and the consul was counseled not to go that far, too far. His experiment in rhetoric had failed. A handful of "mere words" are not enough, especially when they don't even get to be printed.

Erik Reger[3], the authoritative editor of the West Berlin *Der Tagesspiegel* in those days, rubbed it in by publishing the discrepancies in the two versions of Colonel Tulpanov's remarks.[4]

But when I discussed it all with Erik Reger he did not seem to be aware that in the whole incident lay "a road not taken", and that it could have been a fatal turning-point in the struggle for "the minds and hearts" of the Germans if the Russians had not taken a mindless and heartless approach to the problems of maintaining their Empire in Central Europe. Reger took a formalistic approach, and seemed oblivious to the propaganda dangers; he wanted to concentrate on the everyday here-and-now and not with the phantoms of what he called "the Tauroggen complex". (He was referring to the treaty between the Prussians and the Russians in 1812 which induced the German forces, now declared "neutral", to defect from the Napoleonic alliance. "Tauroggen" and "Rapallo" were the twin ghosts that have always haunted a German foreign policy which was tempted to stay loyal and true to a Western alliance.)

> "I agree with Tulpanov, of course I do, about the war crimes of the German troops on the Eastern front—but I cannot agree that justifies their imitation against us. Weren't they, as we've so often been told, disciplined troops? Where will we end when we all start justifying one injustice by the injustices of others?.... No, I find Col. Tulpanov's speech utterly regrettable!"

Well, that made three of us. The lines of the struggle had been established, the basic Cold War positions embattled, and no single desperate inspiration by the belated dialectics of a Leningrad Commissar could alter the sandbox. The dream of a second Soviet victory in Berlin came to an end in 1949, when Stalin's blockade failed and the technical feat of the Air Lift gave the West a first and decisive victory in the Cold War.

Tulpanov escaped being purged by a hair, and he returned to take up a University chair in political theory. Academic speculation was safer, and he was a Professor for another twenty-five years, dying in the Brezhnev era of comfortable stagnation, unperturbed in his own bed. A few years later he might have been denounced, in the Gorbachov period of *glasnost*, as a Stalinist blunderer who adventurously over-estimated the historical opportunity—and clumsily created an alarmed powerful and united West which would rush to contain a previously unresisted revolutionary expansionism.

I do not intend to suggest more than that, within the manifest limits of conventional discipline, Tulpanov was impulsive, contradictory, adventurous. Some of the German journalists who served in East Berlin under his régime in the first year of the Soviet occupation were (so they told me) surprised, if not bewildered. Eager as they were to toe some clear and consistent line, they became out-of-sorts in trying to accommodate themselves to unpredictable Russian improvisation.

The first copies of the Red Army newspaper were printed during the summer of 1945 in the old Nazi Franz-Eher-Verlag, and looked chillingly like Goebbels *Völkische Beobachter.* Under the distasteful Gothic masthead, as if one propaganda machine had displaced another, there worked a hand-picked Tulpanov team of Soviet control officers who were...mostly Jews. To be sure there were technical reasons: command of the language among the sons of Volga-German families, familiarity with Berlin among some Muscovite emigrés, and the like. Still, it was an astonishing line-up in the *Tägliche Rundschau* editorial offices, featuring (as one German editor ruefully recorded) "the Gimselbergs, Epsteins, Rosenfelds, Weisspapiers, Neudorfs *und so fort....*" I heard from the same journalist later on—after Tulpanov's transfer out of Berlin, and with Stalin going into his last phase of paranoic anti-semitism—that one fine day (in 1950) the *Rundschau* staff was suddenly depleted. "The Jewish officers had been taken out of their billets during the previous night and transported to a destination unknown...."

Of such dark and bitter ironies was the legendary reputation of Sergei Tulpanov made. Tulpanov by now was back in Leningrad, still alive and in good graces; but no word of protest or even of private sadness was ever recorded coming from any member of the old Stalinist establishment. Like Schiller's Mohr, Tulpanov's Jews did what they had to do and were brusquely discarded.

> *"Der Mohr hat seine Schuldigkeit getan,*
> *der Mohr kann gehen...."*

2. A BISMARCKIAN CONVERT

The Colonel's personal background, with all of its normal autobiographical details, is lost in the bland, banal anonymity of most heroes of the Party and the secretive régime. Even in his book of memoirs he let slip no word of any intimacy, of his private life and thoughts. He seemed to spring full-blown from the brow of Bolshevism. He learned his Marxism-Leninism with bookish thoroughness, and passed it on pedantically to his students in the military academy; and when the War broke out in 1941 he was active on many fronts as a senior political commissar. It might have been coincidence, or perhaps an unwitting persistence on my part to bring the conversation around to the shadowy figure of Sergei Ivanovich Tulpanov, but his name turned up as a central figure in life-stories as I heard them from Count Heinrich von Einsiedel in Berlin, Wolfgang Leonhard in Cologne and, later, from Lev Kopelew in Moscow.[5]

Einsiedel was a young ace in the German Luftwaffe, had downed some thirty-five Soviet aircraft in the first year of the war, and was accordingly given high Hitler decorations. In August 1942, with the disastrous battle of Stalingrad still raging, he was shot down in his Messerschmitt F-109 but was lucky enough to be able to walk away from the crash. His first serious talk with a Russian officer in the prisoner-of-war camp was with a Colonel Tulpanov.

Einsiedel gave me some pages of his Russian diary to read, and he talked much, indeed somewhat obsessively, about the Commissar who had changed his life and mind. As he described him to me at the time of their first encounter, he was already stout, already completely bald, and radiated that "monastic concentration" which made him by turns admired, liked, feared and respected.

"When I got to know him better," Einsiedel once told me, "the monk that I thought him to be resembled more the strange figures that one finds on the labels of Bavarian beer bottles—hands folded over their belly, twinkling squinting eyes, and looking out into the world with a divine self-satisfaction...."

Tulpanov knew that Einsiedel was the great-grandson of Otto von Bismarck, the "Iron Chancellor", and his strategy was to handle him with a cultural carrot as well as a military stick. After a few perfunctory threats that "a few years in the salt-mines of Siberia" might change his mind about a lot of matters, Tulpanov turned surprisingly to literary subjects—in the middle of the war and with a twenty-one-year-old blond Prussian militarist!—and asked him about books he had read (and, mostly, about books he had not read). Einsiedel had leafed through bits of conventional German favourites: Rilke, Hermann Hesse, Ernst Jünger. No, he had not read anything by Karl Marx, but had heard that he was a Jew and a Communist. Russian literature? A bit of Pushkin and Lermontov and, oh yes, Taras Bulba.

"I am astonished," Tulpanov concluded after a brief *tour d'horizon* of life and letters, of men and ideas, "how little you have read, and how little you know!...." Tulpanov went on to talk about Weltliteratur, and it suggested a world to win.

This was a brilliant opening move on the chess-board. The Russian commissar had succeeded in giving the young German ace a sense of intellectual inferiority, of cultural inadequacy—embarassingly and shamefully so, in the face of a representative of a backward, primitive race. With the result that a mental vacuum had been created into which rushed the agit-prop classics of political education and a new ideological conviction. Within the year Heinrich Graf von Einsiedel emerged as one of the charismatic names in the "Free Germany" committee which Stalin had given a measure of fool's freedom all along the Western front against Hitler's armies. Tulpanov's poetic touch in ideological matters became notoriously well-known later on when he was in control of German politics in the Soviet zone of the post-War Occupation. For now, for whatever it was worth (and, as it turned out, it was not worth much) German generals like Seydlitz vied with Field-Marshals like Paulus in interlarding their anti-Nazi speeches to the German POWs in the Stalingrad camps with apt quotations from Goethe and Schiller and Hölderlin. (A stanza from the latter, Einsiedel reported, was censored because it had a bit too much about *"Sieg"*, and the very word "victory" in German poetry had to be expunged.) They were all encouraged not to be ashamed of tradition; for there were always "the best Germans (*die besten Deutschen*)" to be proud of, like von Stein, Arndt, Clausewitz, Yorck, *et al.*

I used to tease Einsiedel about the slip-shod haste with which he had rushed to become a convert. Within the year he said he became a full-fledged Communist. "From Messerschmitt to Marx, at faster than the speed of light," I said; but he always protested his honest motivation, indeed his innocence. I believed him when he insisted that in becoming a Stalinist he was being utterly sincere, and the turn from loyalty to Hitler to devotion to Stalin had nothing to do with the opportunism which often overwhelms desperate POWs in cold, famished, and brutalized prison camps. But it was something of a wonder to me that "a magical attractiveness" was still to be found in an ideology intoned by the likes of such shabby dogmatists as Walther Ulbricht, Wilhelm Pieck, and the rest of the Muscovite *"Anti-Faschistische Front."*

A year or so later Colonel Tulpanov welcomed Lt. Einsiedel as "a German comrade" to Marshal Tolbuchin's 4th Ukrainian front. The "German comrades" would do their usual round of leaflets, loudspeaker appeals, and radio broadcasts, all of which resulted in disappointingly few defections from Hitler's battered but obedient troops. German military morale might have been low and the despair deep, especially after the home-front news of the devastating Anglo-American bombing that their families were suffering. But few were prepared to break with that complex of loyalty which represented a sworn oath, an ingrained sense of duty, and an historic reluctance to go down in the books as a deserter or a traitor. In addition the over-blown Soviet propaganda generally flew in the face of the stark reality of misery and backwardness which the *Wehrmacht* troops disdainfully identified with the "noble experiment" of the Russian Revolution.

As Einsiedel could tell me, not even a Tulpanov with his penchant for a "more subtle" approach could avoid the simple, costly, errors which the Soviet system made compulsory. Einsiedel, not your ordinary defector but one in a million, was the subject of a special seductive leaflet, featuring his record as an ace and his Bismarckian genealogy; but it was impossible, just out of the question, to credit him with the thirty-five Russian planes which alone would have made credible his prominence and his battle honors. The leaflet safely reduced it to five, which wouldn't reflect so invidiously on the Red

Air Force; and the whole exercise became unpersuasive. Tulpanov had made a coup but could not break free to capitalize on it.

In our talks about the Eastern front, Count Einsiedel assured me that men like Tulpanov knew the difference between reality and propaganda, even his own. The Commissar once conceded, without either puzzlement or open problematic concern, that more Russians were deserting to the Germans than the other way round, which drove the German comrades into a private rage. When, for example, Friedrich Wolf [ideologue and playwright (*Professor Mamlock,* etc.)] heard of the heretical remark, he was furious, for after all, the USSR was a socially superior system; and according to Marxist-Leninist precepts, it was indubitably in command of indestructible, irreversible loyalties. Nothing less than the basic laws of motion in history would be seeing to it that fascists collapsed and communists persevered to the heroic end.

On other military sectors the "Tulpanovs on the front" had—as the Red Army moved from victory to victory into battlefields on the very soil of the *Reich,* at first, of course, in East Prussia—even more serious problems that could not be resolved in the fateful framework of Leninist ideology and Stalinist military pride. But it could be that all armies in great wars, East and West, ancient and modern, tend to degenerate under the pressures of long and murderous campaigns, and come to lose control, deviate from discipline, go in for what are euphemistically called excesses.

In the last merciless year of the War two great death-dealing machines were locked in combat on the European plain between Moscow and Berlin. After the carnage of the German offensive (and of the retreat, which was worse, if possible), Soviet troops were victoriously counter-attacking and meting out retributive justice; revenge may be sweet, but it is no less deadly. One army was desperate to escape falling into the hands of implacable enemies, to save what it could at any price (including scorching their earth and massacring villagers in its path). Another army hurtled forward to total victory (and its passing advantages of loot, rape, and other retaliative malefactions).

Even party-line Communists, whether Russian or German,

were horrified by the front-line "orgies of destruction" that went far beyond the ruthless violence which thrusting armies on-the-march conventionally inflict. The Red Army's hatred for everything German grew boundless in the last year of the war, and even the "German comrades" felt the full force of the mounting antipathy.

"We're no comrades of yours!" Einsiedel was told (and he had always had an anxiety about the charged political atmosphere when the fighting would reach the East Prussian capital city of Königsberg). "Haven't you read the article in *Pravda* by Ilya Ehrenburg? The only innocent creatures in Germany are dogs and unborn children!...."

Total guilt called for total devastation, and where in the wake of the last horrific winter offensive would there be a chance for that "free Germany" which was at the heart of Einsiedel's naive dream of all Communist powers living side-by-side in a new, revolutionized Europe? Hard-pressed apologists mumbled defensive explanations either to the effect that revenge was historic justice or that the lurid reports amounted to wild Nazi atrocity-stories. But they knew that the political ground—the hope that the Movement would be able to have a mass base in the post-War world—was being cut away from under them: in Poland no less than in Prussia, all the atrocious way from Brest to Berlin. Who could speak of liberation and a new order of freedom when crime and punishment were so total and indivisible?

Historians record that the first Soviet political statement—in the first month of the Soviet military administration which was to be dominated by Colonel Tulpanov—rescinded what was known as "the Ilya Ehrenburg line", that the only good German was a dead German. In its place was a pithy adage by Joseph Stalin—"The Hitlers come and go, but the German people and the German State remain!" There were several thousand placards, pasted on walls, mounted on telephone posts, set up on every street-crossing, when I first came to Berlin in the summer of 1945.

In front of the main building of the Soviet headquarters on Unter den Linden there was also a huge black-and-white portrait of Stalin, a slight smile creasing his colored cheeks, which had been re-touched by red paint. I thought of the telling lines by Tacitus on the unspeakable Domitian, "...and not a pale cheek of all that company

107

escaped those brutal eyes, that crimson face which flushed continually lest shame should unawares surprise it."

When Heinrich Graf von Einsiedel returned to Germany he was assigned to an editorial post on the Red Army's official newspaper, *Tägliche Rundschau.* There he met Colonel Tulpanov again; they embraced; and the Colonel thought it might be better to talk at home, in his Karlshorst villa in the Soviet military compound. The Colonel explained to the other editors that "We marched together from Stalingrad to Berlin!"

But marching together in war was easier than in peace. Einsiedel touched on the political consequences of the Red Army's drive to victory and now the Red Army's civil régime of hunger, terror and despair. This could only serve further to alienate the masses and end all hope of any kind of popular base for German communism. Did he really believe, Einsiedel asked Tulpanov, "that Stalin was personally aware of what had really happened, and what was going on?...." He thought he detected that the Colonel was himself shocked and depressed.

They had been speaking German, and when his wife and daughter wanted to know what news the visitor had brought from the outside, Tulpanov told them that the news was only that "the Germans are still fascists and that's why they hate us still...." Knowing Russian, Einsiedel wanted to correct the erratic impression that he gave; but, as he has recorded, a glance from the Colonel silenced him.

He also discouraged Einsiedel from writing anything about what had upset him. "It's all of no use (*Es ist ja doch alles sinnlos*)...."[6]

The Colonel gave Einsiedel his car and chauffeur to be driven back to the American sector of Berlin (where many Muscovite veterans preferred to live); and they never saw each other again. Three years later, after having painfully unlearned his Marxism-Leninism and unwillingly shed his last illusions about the soul of man under communism—Heinrich Graf von Einsiedel defected again, this time to the West.[7]

3. TULPANOV & DYMSCHYTZ

Nowhere was the Commissar's whip-lash more effective in aligning the new forces in post-War German politics than in the "forced marriage" between the Communists and the Social Democrats to prepare for a national victory of "a Workers' and Farmers' State" in a calculable future. Colonel Tulpanov drafted in 1945 the *Befehl Nr. 1* and *Nr. 2*, licensing the two "working-class political parties" whose deepest Marxist wish, as he read it, was to be united. And one way or another the unification would take place.

Once again the Commissar's psychological feeling for the tactics of power and intimidation was shrewd and forceful. Otto Grotewohl, a leading Social Democrat, was introduced to the Commandant of Berlin, General Bersarin; and Tulpanov reported what "a great impression (*welch großen Eindruck*)" the meeting left behind; and, on top of it, being introduced to the even more illustrious conqueror, Marshall Sokolovsky. The Germans of the anti-Nazi Left were, at first, a bit reserved and wary, even cool. But, as Tulpanov elatedly recorded, at the end there were the "most friendly of handshakes"—fingers clasped and sometimes even intertwined became the most favored of his political symbols. More than that, his showmanship (*Regie*) elicited expressions of national surprise at the discovery: "This is a Russian officer? (*Unwahrscheinlich! Das ist ein Russischer Offizier*)" Tulpanov, with his Marxist quotations from Bebel and Kautsky always at hand, was evidently impressive and persuasive.

At this time (1945–46) our American and British generals, their Western counterparts, would have nothing to do with any German political figures, even anti-Nazi Social Democrats. For they were "mere politicians" and not official, elected spokesmen of a duly constituted electorate (as Anglo-Saxon political-science professors, with their formal textbook guide-lines for proper Military Government, advised). The Russian-German *rapprochement* proceeded apace, at its most "intimate" with the old-timers of the KPD (Pieck, Ulbricht, Bredel, Weinert, and the sons of Friedrich Wolf, Markus and Konrad).

Said Tulpanov, "The encounters between Soviet men and German Communists were encounters between comrades, fellow-veterans who were not separated by the War but, on the contrary, brought closer together…in an indestructible friendship."

The Colonel was putting it on a bit much; but then he had to cover up the tracks of the NKVD liquidations of hundreds of tried-and-true German Communists in Stalin's Moscow which nobody (at least for the next four decades) had the reckless courage to mention.

There was to be no pluralism on the Left. If you can't destroy them—as the Bolsheviks did the Mensheviks—then amalgamate them; and Tulpanov described his excitement at the progress of the Moscow policy of "unification" towards a Socialist Unity Party. He had approved the thousands of placards which were to be printed for the hundreds of meetings in which the Stalinists would embrace the Social Democrats (whom, in the decisive years of Hitler's rise to power, they had denounced in a fatal divisiveness as "social fascists"). A quarter-of-a-century later, in a memoir of 1970, Tulpanov recorded how moved he himself had been by the placards—two strong hands, interclasped in a firm handshake—to which a chorus always sang the song, *"Brüder in eins nun die Hände* (Brothers, our hands in unity)…" He also said, looking back, that this was the historic precondition for the establishment of a rump *Reich,* the East-German Communist Republic, in 1949; but at the time he was hoping for very much more—victory in all of Berlin, and the "mass-organizational" inter-zonal domination of the small socio-political rootlets which the slow and stolid Western occupation powers were cautiously putting down in their areas.

By December 1945 the new totalitarian party was practically in place. Tulpanov was very careful, and the negotiations were sensitively supervised—"otherwise the cry would go up from the enemies of unity about alleged Soviet interference…" I found it always passing strange how, at the same time, the actual practice was alive to every nuance of danger and opportunity—but the theory was formulated in a language that was numbing and stupefying. Tulpanov reports of one of his great historic successes:

> The attempts of the Imperialist propaganda to discredit
> the Soviet Union failed because the broad masses of the

workers properly understood the form of international support that the Soviet Union was giving to the German people… (*Die Versuche der imperialistichen Propaganda, die Sowjetunion zu diskreditieren, scheiterten, weil von den breiten Massen der Arbeiter die Form der internationalen Unterstützung, die die Sowjetunion im nationalen und sozialen Interesse des deutschen Volkes gewährte, verstanden wurde…*)

Ideological gobbledygook? Skillfully camouflaged traditional Machiavellian power-politics? Whatever it was, the maneuver was loud and clear even if the message was in a fog-ridden code, with hypocritical signals and comradely formalities.

"We learned so much from our German friends," Tulpanov assures his German friends. And they, in turn, understood—accepted? forgave?—the Russians' use of force and violence (*Gewaltmassnahmen*) to deal with the reactionary enemies of unity and the Potsdam Treaty on behalf of German imperialists and their allies. This meant: midnight arrests, and incarceration (often fatal) in Buchenwald or Bautzen. After all, as Tulpanov himself says, "Not to have used force [*Gewalt*, violence] in this case…would itself have amounted to a crime." ("*Ein Nichtgebrauchen der Gewalt in diesem Falle…an ein Verbrechen gegrenzt.*")

Kurt Schumacher, the Social Democratic leader across the Soviet-zonal border in Hannover some 150 miles away, proved to be the untouchable enemy. He resisted 'unity' implacably, and saved most of his party from the take-over by the Russian and German Communists.

In response, Tulpanov once rushed his faction of loyal comrades to an audience with the Hero of the Soviet Union, Marshal Zhukov. After all, it was proving difficult "to break the Schumacher faction with the Western forces giving it every support" (a figment of the Muscovite imagination, not remotely true). Present were Wilhelm Pieck, Otto Grotewohl, and nobody else—"interpreters were excluded, because I translated" ("*Dolmetscher waren nicht zugelassen, ich übersetzte*"), Tulpanov records. Pieck mouthed his usual bromides about working-class unity—this meant only the alliance of narrow ideological élites who had arrogated to themselves the exclusive right to speak in the name of 'the proletariat' and its struggle for socialism. Grotewohl confessed how soul-searing it was to 'break' with old friends in the movement—this suggested he was very sincere, and not simply opportunistic. Marshal Zhukov reassured them that despite the fact that he was a soldier and not a diplomat he recognized their contribution to the making of a new and democratic Germany—a strong Germany, as he emphatically repeated, his medals on his uniform waving as his shoulders thrust forward. All this signified, more importantly, and he spelled it out: "Your enemies are my enemies!…"

Tulpanov was a shade embarrassed that Zhukov got the actual names of the Schumacher faction wrong. "The Marshal", in the excuse he offered, had "included all our enemies in all the hostile parties". But he felt that everything came out all right in the end when the Marshal called them "Comrades" and comforted them with the thought that "If something special turns up, just call me…" (*"Aber falls irgend etwas Ausserordentliches auftritt, rufen Sie sofort an…"*). The sense of the meeting was reported, as Tulpanov notes, that very evening to Moscow. But we do not know to whom the Colonel was actually reporting.…

Not everything went smoothly, especially in the Western sectors of Berlin; and I attended a few stormy political meetings.

Intimidation raged in the East, and understandable counter-emotions exploded in the West. There were physical clashes in the proletarian sections of Wedding. Tulpanov was incensed, especially when his omnipresent Soviet officers were prevented (as he tells it) from driving the assaulted "German comrades" to the local hospital. This, he queried bitterly, is "discussion"? and free speech for "honest opinions"? (Diskussion…*Überzeugung*)? No, he pronounced it to be worse than the usual style of anti-Communism and anti-Sovietism on behalf of old-time German imperialism and militarism. There was something new, and added to, namely: Neo-Fascism and *Revanche*-politics!

The Commissars were beginning to worry, and under such pressure and distress there is always the comforting last resort of

Lenin. Leninism would be the saving grace, even if in the surreptitious Leninist strategy of the day it could not be openly acknowledged. I have always treasured Tulpanov's dialectical explanation, slyly intended but, inevitably, stone-heavy:

> ...Even if there is in the official documents of the Party [the new amalgamated SED] nothing that would indicate that the Leninist theory of revolution belongs to its ideological first principles, all future successes of the SED could be attributed to the fact that the former Communists and the former Social Democrats both accepted with increasing resolution Lenin's principles, Lenin's theory of democratic and socialist revolution....[8]

To prove his point the Commissar quoted Walter Ulbricht, SED Party boss and faithful German lieutenant, whose Muscovite catechism was only slightly enriched by remnants of Berlin philosophical traditions (which, after all, included Professor Hegel and Dr. Marx himself). Tulpanov praised Ulbricht's "energetic stubbornness" (*Energie und Hartnäckigkeit*). Others, even in their own Party circles, would come to despise it openly as a life-narrowing monolithism:

> ...There is only one Socialist Unity party needed; for there is only *one* Scientific Socialism, one teaching of Karl Marx and Friedrich Engels.... There is only one path forward to the common great goals of socialism.

Even if he could command a few more resonantly baritone notes, Tulpanov sang the same song—and said he was proud to have helped write the libretto—when he returned in the 1960s and 1970s to inspect the DDR's embodiment of real-existing East-German socialism.

This was, I am afraid, the whole of the man, a loyal satrap of an overstretched, overblown empire, pragmatically surgical in his political operations, spiritually trapped in a dogmatical vocabulary which insulated him from the necessity of finding meaningful words to match historic deeds; but then that is the whole function of ideology in a decadent and deceitful time.

Although what the Germans call *Kulturpolitik* is always a matter of high policy and strategy, the Commissar was content to leave most of the cultural details, from realism in modern art to relevance in current literature, to his trusted aide and deputy Commissar, Major Alexander Lvovich Dymschytz.

Dymschytz was, at once, a more dogmatic and more finely-strung character. Where Tulpanov summarily disposed of Ehrenburg to put an end to the disastrous consequences of his wartime propaganda for peacetime Party politics, Dymschytz worried about the problem, returned to it nervously again and again, tried to "reconcile opposites" (or, maybe, "synthesize the anti-thesis") in order to accommodate a famous Russian writer in the pantheon of an unflawed Kulturpolitik.

I once heard Dymschytz, in an East Berlin literary discussion during the bitter winter of 1946–7 (when everybody went to meetings just to keep warm), attempt to defend Ilya Ehrenburg, who enjoyed an ineradicable unpopularity as the wartime keynoter of hate, as the broadcaster of the line of "total-death-to-the-German enemy". His name had evidently become a beloved battle-cry of the advancing Red Army troops only a few years before. But as the dialectic would have it—so Dymschytz tried to reassure his German audience—Ehrenburg's writings once served to save a German life!

The cautionary tale was one of Fritz Rasp, a well-known actor and writer in these parts. On spotting the first Soviet soldiers coming out of the East, he dug out his personally-signed copies of Ehrenburg's old novels of the 1920s and ran forward flourishing them as a kind of literary white flag of friendly welcome. The Russian lieutenant, as befitted the civilized officers of a great socialist culture, respected reading matter; he could not but be impressed by the bookish bravery of the man and called for an interpreter so they could exchange ideas. The case for German-Russian friendship was clear. Fritz Rasp was given a good meal from army rations, and a Cyrillic sign was put on Fritz's front door: "Here lives a friend of Ilya Ehrenburg, and so this house is under the protection of Soviet troops."[9]

I don't know how much of this patently contrived story was true, or to what extent Major Dymschytz, who was one of nature's "true believers", truly believed it; but this ration of processed pabulum proved indigestible, even in the early hungry years when defeated civilians were like beaten dogs, famished for a crumb, or for a kind and hopeful word.

This blockage was often taken to be a mere Russian "failure of communication", and pronounced in Western circles to be the sales pitch that couldn't sell, which were only superficial ways of describing the Kremlin's ineffective public relations or advertising. (Krushchev's agents were a bit cleverer; Gorbachov's salesmen were superb.)[10] I have always felt that there was an additional and more characteristic feature than the insincerity, and even duplicity, which the conventional tactics of making propaganda induce. Ideological imperatives of Party-line loyalty to a monolithic régime fashion a paradoxical form of obvious self-deception in which the ideologue completely believes.

The difference between the two Colonels—Dymschytz and Tulpanov, the Talmudic man of letters and the Pan-Slavist man of politics—was that one was a soft-spoken and simple-minded man for whom the approved printed word was a heartfelt matter of ideological life-and-death; and the other was a devious cynic who was driven by a desperate cunning, a frustrated casuistry that could run no course but the straight-and-narrow path of dogma.

Dymschytz often told this life-saving story—with, I am convinced, no discernible effect—to post-War German audiences; and he repeated it in various articles and memoirs.[11] There was no stopping him, and he went on to record how he told the Fritz Rasp story to Ilya Ehrenburg when he visited him in Moscow. Ilya was touched, and so much so that he gave Dymschytz a good bottle of wine and a box of Havana cigars to bring back, with an appreciative note to *"Lieber Fritz!"*. This, moreover, showed his especially heart-warming magnanimity because everyone knew how, in the coruscating Wartime broadcasts, Ehrenburg had called every Hitler-fascist *"Fritz"*! What this was supposed to prove defies understanding, except that authentic petit-bourgeois sentimentalism is obviously an untrustworthy propaganda technique.

Undoubtedly Dymschytz was grateful to Ilya Ehrenburg for providing a colourful human-interest story. It humanized somewhat an abstract message of comradely Stalinist rectitude which came through only to the *nomenklatura* of the Ulbricht régime whose stalwarts had been imported from the German emigré colony in Moscow. They, in turn, were unforgettably grateful to him and published a remarkable *Festschrift* some ten years after his death which paid lachrymose tribute to the cultural commissar who laid the foundations for the single-minded totalitarianized intellectual life that existed in East Germany.[12]

As to the steadfast loyalty to Ilya Ehrenburg, that became problematical. Dymschytz was troubled by "The Thaw" and other small signs of a springtime in the 1950s which challenged his icy certainties; and his German protegés remained similarly troubled by any departures, whether initiated by a Khrushchev or a Gorbachov, from the "old Party line" which sustained them in Stalin's time. Dymschytz described, in his larmoyant way, his relationship with Ehrenburg as "a difficult romance" (*eine schwierige Liebe*); and he guardedly expressed his painful disappointment with the deviations that marked the man's early life in avant-garde Paris—and now, in post-Stalinist Moscow, his descent indeed into something shocking called "subjectivism".

To the end of his days—and, presumably, beyond: if his adulated Lenin in Red Square was any kind of augur—Colonel Alexander Lvovich Dymschytz remained stiff and frozen in the doctrines of an old believer.

4. OF TRAITORS & COMRADES

In the heart of all the various Marxian tenets that formed and framed the Commissar's mind there was, happily enough, always the central dialectic of "the unity of theory and practice".

It was an undulating dualism, flexible to the point of casuistry. In essence a magical concept, it pretended to be philosophical or even scientific; but, whatever it was, the incantation was endowed with great pragmatic worth: for it worked. It has in fact functioned well for whole generations in post-October Russia and among pro-Soviet sympathizers in the West who had been periodically troubled by difficulties, doubts, dissensions. Its elastic strength keeps a safe tension between hopeful expectations and bitter disappointments; for it leads usefully on occasion to a denial of practical realities or, sometimes, to a minor adjustment of theoretical guide-lines. Tulpanov served to hold faith intact, stabilize confidence, and keep ideology sturdy and aggressive.

In extreme cases, where the will to believe is desperately emotional or (among some wily intellectuals, e.g. Lukács, Brecht, Kopelev) cunningly casuistical, the rationalization of the tragic amounts to accepting the fatal adage, "Evil, be thou my good...." Brecht's dialectic makes him confident that the more innocent the victims are, the more they need to be sacrificed for the revolutionary good; Lukács surmises that both Lucifer and Prometheus can be comrades; Kopelev persuades himself that lies, if they are strongly motivated enough for a noble cause, will lead to truth.

In more normal cases, where the casual believer accepts that in life there's many a slip between the cup and the lip, the conventional ruses of simple prevarication and obvious self-deception are sufficient. Put another way, where the theory is monolithic, small reparations, usually more rhetorical than real, can make understandable amends. Whatever untoward consequences may have issued, they can, provided the attachment to utopia or to revolution (or, usually, to both) is deep enough, be positively re-interpreted and painlessly absorbed.

What if there are two theories? Surely one might prove to be more justified in practice than the other, and then the cause is rightfully won, come what may.

The Commissar's instructions from Stalin were to destroy the enemy in all his hateful forms. Ilya Ehrenburg supplied the words, and the Red Army fought by them: the Germans were to be smashed, Germany was to be utterly ruined in proper retaliation for the criminal assault on the Soviet Fatherland in June of 1941.

But the Commissar was also instructed in a parallel action

to use the Germans wherever possible to weaken the Nazi cause; to "divide and rule"; to persuade the officers and men in the prisoner-of-war camps to collaborate in order to save their country from further devastations. The net effect would be to involve a deeper German patriotism in an anti-Nazi strategy which might disorient and even disintegrate the *Wehrmacht* and prepare the way not only for a Soviet victory but a new *Reich,* perhaps amputated at the edges, but a spiritual and cultural entity for all that.

Such were the gambles a *Vozhd* was free to take, for the only free man in such a régime is the tyrant himself. And how could you lose if you bet on both horses in a two-horse race?

Colonel Sergei Tulpanov, a political commissar of senior rank, had to ride the two horses in the field. On the one hand, he could not show himself to be in any way divergent from the prevailing doctrine of total destruction which was inflaming the troops to final victory in Berlin. Another political officer on the embattled front, Major Kopelev, was imprudent enough to mutter some quiet criticism of "senseless" rapine and loot and was stripped of his rank, expelled from the Party, and sentenced to a dozen years in a labour camp for "pro-German" sentiments and hence near-treason.

On the other hand, the Colonel was officially assigned to cooperate with the idealism of the German anti-Nazis in Moscow. He was to exploit the opportunism of the Generals and even Field-Marshals of the Hitler armies who were persuaded in captivity to opt for collaboration. Last but not least, he was to encourage the ideological conversion to the Communist cause of all, like young Heinrich Graf von Einsiedel, who could be susceptible to his blandishments. It was Colonel Tulpanov who set Count Einsiedel on his meteoric path to Marxism-Leninism. It was Lt. Col. Milja Sabachansky who took over the personal control of the anti-Nazi activities of Einsiedel and others in the "National Committee for a Free Germany", pledged to a new democratic humanism in the spirit of Goethe. And it was Lt. Col. Sabachansky who organized the court-martial of Major Lev Kopelev on charges of "bourgeois humanism" and favoritism to the enemy.

Propaganda was a high-risk profession; in Stalin's *manège* it was trapeze work on a thin wire without a safety net.

The Commissars might well have asked: where did we go wrong?

Stalin's high policy was two-handed and, for ambidextrous masters of statecraft, inevitably so. Nobody less than Goebbels praised him for maintaining the morale of the Soviet soldier who was, also, like the German *Landser,* "extraordinarily war-weary" but who was "inspired with an infernal hatred of everything German which must be ascribed to sophisticated Bolshevist propaganda...."

Yet the whole complex of military hatred and political guile— and I have simplified it because of my selective contact with certain representative figures in a story that must have had hundreds of such individual dramas—was fraught with contradictions. The ambivalent strategy was crude enough to give Stalin, in wartime, the smashing victory he wanted, and in peace-time the booty of a third of the old German *Reich* to control, exploit, incorporate in his dream of a European empire. But it was not sound or subtle enough to establish his imperial design with the popular support of "the masses" which was always the revolutionary's ambition since Marx and Engels. Failing that, how could the Commissar ever provide an enthusiastic enough spirit to fuel the historic expansion into the whole of Europe, which the vaunted theory predicted?

The military victory, with its unprecedented carnage and ac-companying orgies of excess, could not but undermine the prospect of ideal political victory. The national triumph of the Fatherland's patriotic offensive subverted the international cause with its promise of fraternity and solidarity across the frontiers. Even the most pro-Soviet of the German collaborators looked askance at the civic ruins and the smoldering civilian ressentiments,* and wrote off any hopes of popular support for a generation.

Stalin could not have cared less. When the time would come Ilya Ehrenburg would be put in his place, and a new *ukase* would be pronounced to the effect that "the Hitlers come and go, but the German people remain...." In the final year of the War—and this time-span shaped in all ways the future of Central Europe for half-

---

* There was, I might add, nothing on the Western front to compare with it (except in a few Swabian villages where French colonial troops passed through in the spring of 1945).

a-century—a regiment of Red Army battle-scarred troops rushing forward, burning everything in its path from Koenigsberg to Danzig to Berlin, was worth an army of political propagandists, armed to the teeth with leaflets, loudspeakers, and radio transmissions. True, Stalin had consented to the organization of a "National Committee for a Free Germany". With a minimum of ideological illusion and a maximum of guileful statecraft, he welcomed to the common cause Hitler's defectors including Generals and Field-Marschals in full (be-ribboned, be-medalled) uniform. He had shown the same insouciant Machiavellianism in 1939, when it also served his interests, by shaking hands warmly with Hitler's foreign minister, Joachim von Ribbentrop, and so sealing a pact "with blood."

Now the German Communists—whose ranks he had decimated in the purges of the 1930s, some of whose leaders he had even extra-dited to the Gestapo during the era of the Hitler-Stalin pact—were to be given a chance to redeem themselves, to make an impression after they had failed to make a revolution. Neither Roosevelt nor Churchill (and certainly not de Gaulle) had the reserves of cynicism to allow any species of untrustworthy Germans to play a role in the defeat of Hitler. Even if they might have helped, such proposals for a propaganda offensive on behalf of a real or spurious "other Germany" (flying counterfeit unreal flags for Beethoven and Bach and Kant, et al.) would have been, and indeed were, dismissed out of hand: rejected, in the operative Western phrase of the day, "unconditionally".

Goebbels was clever enough to record in his diary (5 March 1945), "Stalin is now completely in the grip of victory hysteria. He is holding the Seydlitz ["Free Germany"] Committee ready so that he can perhaps install it as a provisional German government provided a psychological opportunity presents itself and he can risk so open a provocation of the British and the Americans...."[13]

A word more from the sinister but incisive *Reichspropaganda-Minister*, for despite the devastation (and defeat) that stared in on him in his office in Berlin's Wilhelmstraße, Goebbels was calm enough to write about the "main anxiety" in the West (more *Angst,* I would say, on the realistic British side, far less so than on our bemused American side):

"...the main anxiety is lest Moscow install a Soviet satellite government, at any rate in the Russian-occupied part of Germany (the cry is a Seydlitz government), and so a communistic Germany allied to Moscow should emerge; not only would this form a bridge to the communisation of France and Belgium but it would govern the political ideological development of all Europe." (6 March 1945)

Still, Stalin was ideologically shrewd enough to sense that in all probability—given the teutonic factors of traditional national character and neo-nationalist indoctrination—the actual psychology on Germany's Eastern front was not ripe for psychological warfare.

I am tempted to ask: Was it any more ripe on the Western front? In those years I was intellectually (and, even more, emotionally) convinced, against most of the informed diplomatic and expert military opinion available, that it was. For my own part I thought at the time that at least a few Germans, some in decisive positions in the *Reich* and tactical places abroad, could be effectively called upon to act or to activate—with the result that the War with its horrific daily losses (especially in the death-camps) might have been shortened, even by a month or a week....

The failures of the anti-Nazi Germans in Moscow—from the Party-liners like Ulbricht and Becher to the new military defectors like von Paulus and von Einsiedel—have usually been attributed to the fatal fact that "the German soldier saw Soviet Russia". He had seen with his own eyes its poverty and primitivism (and this, decades after the radiant Revolution). He could hardly be expected to be easily persuaded to change sides.

Yet I knew German prisoners-of-war in 1944 in a State-side POW-camp which was set in lush green Virginia hills near prosperous American villages. They were no more accommodating. *Stur* was the official word for them, and their recalcitrance ranged from insipid issues of staple diet to terrifying incidents of patriotic ideology. I was a newly-commissioned lieutenant in the Quartermaster Corps at Camp Lee, St. Petersburg; and after a brief crisis involving a hunger strike in the nearby POW-camp our headquarters agreeably arranged for a deal. They would transfer their dinner rations of golden corn (which the German soldier despised as "pig feed" [*Schweinefutter*]) in exchange for our daily dish of green peas of which we were thoroughly sick.

I was distressed to hear at the time (and it was more than kitchen-door gossip) of the uncontrollable political terror which reigned in our Virginia camp, and not only there. Young Hitlerian officers, still unbroken in their devotion—what did they know, across the Atlantic, of the devastation of their homeland and the despair of their families?—took their "barracks revenge" against any sign of dissidence or disloyalty. Those of us in the neighboring Virginia barracks who were interested in politics (or, in the phrase of the day, "war aims") were plunged into dejection. The Third Reich would doubtless be crushed—but what could one do with the German mind if it persisted in its traditional stubbornness, in its blind national integrity, in its narrow patriotic unenlightenment?

Thus it seemed to me that neither school of East-West ideology, whether representing poverty-stricken Russian communism or liberal-affluent American capitalism, could make any significant inroads on a German steadfastness—which, lo and behold! in May 1945, the hour of *die Katastrophe* and of *der Zusammenbruch* in the Year Zero, disappeared inscrutably without a trace.

In this light, it is scarcely surprising that political commissars like Tulpanov—and Kopelev, too, before he was purged—merely came up with paltry results. It was frustrating and dispiriting for them and for all the others who were involved with them in the propaganda campaign to convince the harassed and battered *Wehrmacht* to turn its guns the other way and save what was left of the *Vaterland* from the *Führer's* mad plunge into a *Götterdämmerung* (and here I am just summarizing dozens of such vain appeals across the front-lines). I had chilling descriptions from Einsiedel and others about their attempts to address the troops in their Siberian prisoner-of-war barracks after the Stalingrad disaster. The troops, stolid in their loyalty, merely turned their backs on the "traitors".

Melvin J. Lasky

5. THE MONOLITHIC TACTICS OF DECEPTION

As I write, in the days of the dramatic attempt of Hungary and Poland to shake loose from the tentacular hold of the totalitarian post-war system, both in Budapest and Warsaw it is quite clear that the liberal reformation in its peaceful gradualism can have little chance of progress if three fortresses of the old established system are not substantially subverted. A Solidarity spokesman (in June 1989) referred to them as "the Information monopoly, the Organization monopoly, and the Administration monopoly." These were the Leninist-Stalinist principles of classical Soviet practice, and were harshly translated into "satellite reality" in the years after 1945.

For almost half-a-century they had wallowed in failure (and worse)—they had to be, as in Marx's famous remark about Hegel's ideas, "stood on their head." Oh, not a "counter-revolution" of insidious repute, but a revolving, a rotation, a changing in the wheel of fortune, a true revolution as it was originally understood by Copernicus and Hobbes (and indeed by that first revolutionary, Cromwell): a new turn to a full circle.[14]

If press and radio (not to mention television) could disseminate uncensored information, if political and cultural organizations (not to mention independent trade-unionism) could function free of state control, if the government apparatus could be significantly detached from the *nomenklatura* of the hitherto all-powerful all-dominant Party *apparatchiks*—then a post-Communist, i.e. an open, pluralistic, democratic society would at long last be in the making.

But the previous closed, monolithic, authoritarian society did not simply grow, it was superimposed. It was a breathtaking exercise in the relations between theory and power that was, in its totalitarian way, singular in European history. Neither Napoleon's conquests (possibly because he felt he had to fight on, in yet another country) nor even Hitler's occupation (he had, fortunately, so little time) translated their revolutionary principles into reality with such efficacious finality. Stalin's empire from the Urals to the Elbe may have taken on different names—tags like People's Democracies, and Soviet or Democratic Republics, among them—and were embellished with strange features, reminiscent of the old bourgeois world, such as Constitutions, Christian and Liberal parties, sometimes a Peasant movement: but the power structure, to the extent that it could be hammered securely into place, served the total ambitions of a man and his factions. He was known as the *Vozhd* (the boss, the leader) and his cadres constituted a deferential ideological élite.

In Germany it was the achievement of Colonel Sergei Tulpanov. The "only begetter" above him was, of course, Stalin (and those who carried his instructions forward: Molotov, Zhdanov, Vishinsky, et al.). And above him, too, in the truncated area of the conquered *Reich* were Marshalls Zhukov and Sokolovsky, celebrated war heroes who never appeared without their ten inches of shining medals and coloured decorations covering their uniformed left breast. Which is to say they were heavily weighed down by their formal responsibilities as governors, satraps, consuls, grand viziers, along the outer imperial frontier. To adapt the Russian formula of Sir Isaiah Berlin, they were the hedgehogs, Tulpanov was the fox. He ran from meeting to meeting, giving guideliness to the mass organizations of the teachers and the trade-unionists, instructions to the politicians, basic targets to the managers of the collectivized factories, and farms. His articles in the press formulated the Party line (and at a signal from above any drastic changes thereto). Like the Scarlet Pimpernel in another revolutionary era, he was to be found here, there, everywhere.

Although many found it hard to believe, and nowhere was there an inter-office memorandum or an *aide-mémoire* of a telephone conversation to substantiate it in terms of hard historiographical evidence, Tulpanov was the *praeceptor Germaniae* for Walter Ulbricht and Wilhelm Pieck.[15] He spoke in German, but the message was Russian. Would they move precipitously towards the establishment of a separatist Soviet Germany? Not a few observers expected it. But Stalin, in high post-War spirits, would no longer be satisfied with "building socialism" in one Occupation Zone, in only one third of a country. The line of a 'Sovietized' Eastern Germany was rejected, at least for now; there were bigger greater-German all-national prizes at stake, and Tulpanov kept his eye on them. Accordingly they could not, and would not, dispense with the old bourgeois-decadent contraceptions of Christians, Liberals, Peasants, Nationalists and other features of a relatively credible camouflage. They had to be seen to be representing all of the people, even if it was a Potemkin-populism.

Walther Ulbricht, for all his unsmiling *hauteur* of cold command, had at least the merit of clarity and candor in presenting advantages of cunning compromise. Some of his followers whom I came to know had expected the glorious decisiveness of the revolutionary militance. A youthful Muscovite like Wolfgang Leonhard wanted a clean utopian sweep of all historical entanglements and forward thrust to a long-awaited German version of the promised land, as prophesied by Marx and Engels. A late convert to Marxist-Leninist dialectics like Heinrich von Einsiedel was upset and troubled by the 'deals' which the Party, under the Kremlin's opportunistic instructions, made with the figure-heads of the old reactionary ruling class· Hitler's generals (and their taste in military clothes and Prussian parade-step); fuzzy-minded traditional Weimar politicians waffling on in outdated rhetoric, even unreconstructed Nazi voters who could be persuaded to turn up and add to the 99.9% result of required Stalinist elections. An incorrigible enthusiast like Dieter Borkowski,[16] late of the Hitler-Jugend and its last-ditch *Volksturm* of the Berlin suburbs and later the pride of Comrade Erich Honecker's new Free German Youth, slowly sensed yet another betrayal of pure principle and an onsetting disillusionment. What price youthful ideals and enthusiasm when old men proved so imperfect?

If Stalin made the policy, Tulpanov formulated the strategy and Ulbricht explained the tactics.

I was once told of the shock that obtained at the first Berlin meeting of the Party faithful; it was very early days, in the chaotic months after the end of the War. Ulbricht announced (25 June 1945) that there was to be no revival of the old organization of Communist youth as had prevailed in the Weimar days. There had to be one mass organization, and not diverse competing elements appealing to separate ideas and values. The cadres of the Party could be relied upon to control the whole movement. Thus, as in other areas of the entire civil society, the Party monopoly of power would be maintained without unduly alarming the non-Communist—mostly grouped under the name of *"nützliche Idioten"*, useful idiots—from innocent and decorative collaboration. As Ulbricht put it:

> We have to put together a sound administrative apparatus. We don't want Communists to be the Mayors of towns and cities, maybe only in our heavily red working-class districts. Let the Social Democrats be the first men, especially in the petty-bourgeois areas; also middle-class characters that belonged to the old Zentrum or the Volkspartei. It would be best if they had a *Doktor-Titel*...We can work well with these people. We need as many bourgeois types that we can find with an anti-fascist record...

Ulbricht hastened to reassure his disoriented followers who were not quite familiar with the tactics of exploiting popular fronts:

> If tomorrow morning you can find among the people you already know a bourgeois leader, then our people can come forward and take the secondary positions. We must be the deputies. Our comrades must be in charge of personnel and administration, and in every district command the post that has to do with the organization and recruitment of the police...

Many old Communists who now live in the West remember that historic meeting where Stalin, Tulpanov, and Ulbricht unveiled the Muscovite line that would consolidate the East European Empire and establish a basis in Germany for the possible re-orientation of the whole *Reich*. Some say the Party's turn to an expedient accomodation to 'real-existing' (and hence reactionary) masses was a shock, and the whole atmosphere was dispiriting. Still, the discussion, for all the Party-discipline, we said to be "lively, agitated". And the discussion was ended, as one of my friends recorded it, with a peremptory

Kremlin command, in equal parts Stalin's foxiness, Tulpanov's sharp practice, and Ulbricht's Saxon accent:

> ...Well, everything is now completely clear—it's all got to be seen as completely democratic—but we must have everything in our hands. (...*Es ist doch ganz klar: Es muß demokratisch aussehen, aber wir müssen alles in der Hand haben.*) *Mundus vult decepi, ergo decipiatur.* (The world wants deception, and so it is deceived.)[17]

Or, put another way (echoing Lord Acton), all politics dissemble, but absolutist politics dissimulate absolutely.

6. 'TULPANOLOGY'

For a number of years in the late 1940s I devoted myself to the study, such as it was in those days of intuition and surmise, of Colonel Tulpanov. I was, to be sure, a very amateur student of "Tulpanology", having had no access to Allied secret intelligence research nor even to the CIC (counter-intelligence) occasional confidential report from Karlshorst in which a 'spy' or an 'informer' passed on a few rumors and a snatch or two of Russian headquarters conversation. I simply read the Eastern daily and periodical press very closely, talked with Soviet-zone politicians (like Jakob Kaiser, Ernst Lemmer, et al.), and attended the odd public lecture by Tulpanov or Dymschytz, or by their Karlshorst staff officers.

It was astonishing what kind of portrait of a man and an intricate interpretation of a grand strategy one could build up out of the circumstantial fragments to which no professional historian would lend substantial credence. On a steady if irregular basis I would turn up in the offices of the U.S. military government commanders (from Messrs. Clay and McClure to Textor, Heimlich and Panuch) and try to reinforce their growing familiarity with the strange, recondite, and hitherto unknown body of thought known as Marxism-Leninism as authentically promulgated by Marshal Stalin. For all their mental alertness they did not, I am afraid, learn very quickly; but sufficient unto the day was the insight thereof.

I remember one day in the spring of 1948 when Professor Sidney Hook, the distinguished American authority on Marxist philosophy, visited Berlin and had an appointment to talk with General Frank Howley, the vibrant and irrepressible U.S. commandant of West Berlin. Howley (who was later to become Chancellor of New York University where Hook was still chairman of the Philosophy Department) had, of course, never heard of Sidney Hook; but I whetted his appetite for the meeting by suggesting that the philosopher would explain that every East-West argument in Berlin over a municipal water works or postal district demarcation on the Soviet-American sector border—and on these fronts Howley was superb—was, philosophically considered, of world-political significance. I gave him a thumbnail sketch of Hook's ideas, lent him my copies of *From Hegel to Marx* and *Towards the Understanding of Karl Marx*, and awaited the encounter with some trepidation.

The General, trained to read maps and deal with buck-slips, did not disappoint, and in fact elated his visitor. He began by using his pointer to indicate where exactly the Brandenburg *Tor* divided Berlin streets and bisected world-historic metaphysical conceptions of society and politics.

"You see, Professor Hook," General Howley explained, whirling his pointer about the large-scale map from East to West and back (touching Kreuzberg, scratching Tegel), "dialectical materialism is based on three elements, each devoted to a negation of a negation in both theory and practice, but reconciled in its contradictions by the following synthesis…" I remained slumped in my chair for a full twenty minutes. Sidney Hook had a bemused smile on his lips which, as he generously explained to me later, only suggested his happy surprise that American military commanders managed to interest themselves in such recondite things.

The study of Tulpanov was of a different order, for it meant all the difference if one got the dialectics of the synthesis right or wrong. On one occasion General Clay put to me a question about the Stalinist purges of 1936–38, and whether the man in the Kremlin would keep on a man with whom he sharply disagreed. Evidently the Dahlem headquarters was full of rumours about yet another disappearance of Colonel Tulpanov. How account for the presence of a mysterious Kremlin emissary known as "General Georgieff"? Otherwise reliable agents in the East reported him actually to be Lt. Gen. Mikhail Malinin who was about to make (or had already made) an offer to Robert Murphy for "President Truman's eyes only" about a comprehensive settlement between Washington and Moscow in the Cold War. This was beyond me; I knew no more than the next Kremlinologist. My rule of thumb was patience…for a few days, or weeks. If Tulpanov is never heard of again, then (as the old Union Square song had it) the Party Line has changed again. But, over the next weekend, Tulpanov returned to Karlshorst from routine consultations in the Kremlin, and all was the same track once more. I moved on to the next problem of what was known in the American Press Club on Sven Hedin Straße as "the petals of the tulip" (the putative source of Tulpanov's name).

What determined the zig-zag course of theories of Soviet behaviour in the first-half-dozen years of post-War European history was a dramatic conflict between the intellectuals who were divided into (in the German phrase of the influential Franz Borkenau[18]) the Kremlin-Astrologers and the Kremlin-Astronomers.

Astrology was a game anyone could play, and most Europeans and Americans played it. Sun-spots, or lunar conjunctions, or the stars above the Georgian heavens when the Djugashvilis had a son Joseph in Gori just before Christmas in December 1879, could reveal the pattern of what Stalin had in mind by excluding the Free-Pole leader Mikalocyk from Poland, shooting Petkov in Rumania, liquidating Rajk and Kostov and other leading Communists in Hungary or Bulgaria, in decimating the Mihailovich movement in Yugoslavia, or encouraging Tulpanov to put the sqeeze on the unsure Allied military presence in West Berlin.

But there were also astronomers, *Kreml-Astronomen*—they often disagreed amongst each other, dividing into 'Ptolemaic' and

'Copernican' factions—but were proud of their careful reading of global evidence and their astral rigor in coming to scientific conclusions. David Dallin agreed with Boris Nicolaevsky, but both had differences with Boris Souvarine; and all, including our local star-gazers (among them: Richard Lowenthal, F.R. Allemann, Boris Meissner, Ernst J. Salter, Wolfgang Leonhard), had a falling-out with the undeniable genius in the sidereal guild, Franz Borkenau. Borkenau's serious, documented, severely empirical studies of Soviet strategy and tactics I frequently published in *Der Monat*; his intuitive, sensitive, imaginative and speculative efforts were published in the newspapers (among them *Die Weltwoche* of Zurich) and regularly broadcast by Radio Free Europe in Munich (then run by William E. Griffiths). Borkenau's most famous *coup* was his conclusion, in the last week of February 1953, that Stalin was dying, or had died, or was about to be done away with. In the days before the official announcement of his death (5 March 1953) Borkenau had been studying the fine print in *Pravda, Izvestia,* and the various official communiqués that emerged in peculiar and suspect phraseology out of a strangely disquieted Kremlin. He concluded that a great black obituary was imminent.

I once asked him what method in the school of Kremlin astronomy he had used—"the Ptolemaic or the Copernican?" Anti-Marxist dialectician that he was, trained in negation of negations, he snorted, "My guiding star is the Bard! Not epistemology is the key, *mein Junge,* but dramaturgy! If you know your late Shakespeare tragedies, you remember that no play ends without at least one corpse on the stage, sometimes a whole stage-full of cadavers when the Bard brings the curtain down!"

It was at times a grisly game, predicting the victims, counting the dead. Since Borkenau had so many old friends, comrades from the old Comintern days, who were involved in the Slánský trial in Prague, he followed the official accounts of that last Stalinist show trial (1952) for "treason, espionage, sabotage" with macabre intensity. But I always detected the same wondrous keen-eyed attention he had been giving—wearing his other hat, that of a recondite scholar—to the wall-paintings in a Byzantine church or to the figures of medieval knights on the Bayeux tapestry.

Borkenau was convinced, of course, that despite their abject confessions the accused were all innocent ("even a scoundrel like André Simone" [Otto Katz]); that they would all be found guilty; and that they would all be put to death. He was not far from being completely right. There were fourteen major Czech figures including Slánský, the former Communist Party chief and deputy Premier under President Klement Gottwald—the majority of whom were described as being "of Jewish origin" (and hence "Zionists", the worst expletive in Stalin's demented old age). All were sentenced to be hanged and summarily dispatched. All were, some fourteen years later, fully "rehabilitated" during the Prague Spring of '68 when the short-lived Dubcek régime allowed the court and police archives to be opened and bitter truths to be told. Borkenau's uncanny grasp of tragic Stalinist events and of the Commissar mind never ceased to astonish. He knew, as if he had dreamed it in a Poe nightmare, the sinister place where folly conspired with fantasy, and met up with murder.

And once, after some Kremlinological small talk in our *Monat* office in Berlin-Dahlem, he added one of the most remarkable predictions that ever this kind of political science, deprived of all humdrum access to documentation and hard evidence, could triumphally list to its credit.

"And when Stalin is no more, then the leader of Chinese Revolution, Mao-Tse-Tung, will put in his own claim to world ideological leadership, defying Moscow, asserting the supremacy of Mao as the Marxist prophet...!" And it came to pass.

My friends in London at the time say he predicted the Hitler-Stalin Pact of 1939, and also the eventual falling-out of the two dictators. I copied out into my debater's notebook the following passage from Borkenau's study of 1938, and the page was dog-eared from citation during the long argumentative pro-Stalin decade (wherein such mundane common sense was rare): "...Stalin, the man who could not allow a single one of his old companions to live, is the last man to believe in the possiblity of sincere collaboration in the international field. A man such as Stalin cannot be brought to reason by argument. There is, however, just a small chance that events will teach him..."[19]

And teach him they did, and (more to the point) taught his

successors over the next decades. All, to one extent or another, were contained and deterred, and in their frustration and failure found new arguments for more reasonable behavior.

When Franz Borkenau died suddenly at the age of fifty-six in Zurich—he wrote regularly for *Die Weltwoche*, the local and much-respected political weekly which made headlines out of his prognoses—none of his friends were able to make it on time for the funeral. I was told by a Swiss journalist that "speed" had been insisted upon for mysterious reasons of "security". So Franz Borkenau, subtle student of world history and civilization, incisive commentator on contemporary affairs, was hastily buried with a perfunctory service in a near-empty hall, attended mostly by secret security agents of East and West. These were easily spotted by the obligatory trench-coat of the day, and had been keen to obtain a clue as to how (and in whose interests) a lone writer and researcher had been able to divine the obscure course of events in the Cold War. They were even prepared to search for micro-dots in certain special editions of William Shakespeare.

Indeed I am sure at the time I believed that a re-reading of *Hamlet* and *Macbeth* would have been of real service when (as the 2nd Witch said) "the hurly-burly's done/When the battle's lost or won…" (*Macbeth*, I.i.3) Or when, and if

> …you can look into the seeds of time,
> And say which grain will grow and which will not.
>
> (I.iii.58)

Among the "seeds of time", in Borkenau's subtle and cultivated vision, were the experiences of grand viziers in the Ottoman Empire; of GPU commissars in Barcelona during the Spanish Civil War; of Jesuit dialecticians preparing the counter-Reformation to the Lutheran heresies (not to mention powerful generals in the 30-Years-War who doubled in theology and astrology); of Imperial Roman pro-consuls when the ancient empire was torn between Greek philosophizing and Judaeo-Christian challenges.

And so in this spirit Tulpanology flowered. We were convinced we understood the Soviet Commissar and confidently prognosticated his strategy of battle in the hurly-burly that was called the Cold War. But in the course of the didacticism I almost lost one of my best friends.

I have already paid tribute to James Preston O'Donnell, one of the most perceptive of American foreign correspondents who, in the run-up to the Russian blockade of Berlin in 1947–1948, had warned what a disaster might be in the store for the West—and in so prophesying had altered the pattern of events. I felt at the time, and my conviction has been reinforced in the perspective of eventful decades in between, that he had earned a creditable footnote in history.

But in May 1949, when the blockade was done and the battle was won, we almost came to blows over Colonel Sergei Tulpanov and our respective schools of Tulpanology. I had just picked up my copy of the *Saturday Evening Post* at the mail room of the U.S. Press Center on Argentinische Allee, and flicking through it was increasingly agitated by Jimmy O'Donnell's latest article in the *Post* which at that time was a major force in American journalism. By the time I had reached the Sven Hedin Straße, where we regularly lunched, I was livid, outraged, explosive. In every reasonable man there is a *furor theologicus* struggling to get out. Why, the man understood nothing of *Kreml-Astronomie!* nothing of its Ptolemaic roots, nothing of its Copernican refinements! His article in the *Post* on Tulpanov could be setting us back four years to Truman's naivete in Potsdam, thirty years to Woodrow Wilson's arrogance in Paris, a hundred years to Tocqueville's remarks about a rivalry with Russia which to Americans was always a faraway country they knew nothing about...[20]

Re-reading the near-fateful article forty years on, I can still sense why Freddy the Press Club barman, who knew well all types of journalistic altercations from his pre-war days in the Hotel Adlon on Unter den Linden, was frightened we might come to physical blows. "And over what?" as he tried to calm us down, "another article, another theory..."

Well, in those days a theory, if it was sound and roughly commensurate with realities, could conceivably save the day (and its daily anxieties over precarious peace and liberty). The article was entitled: "THE STUPIDEST RUSSIAN IN EUROPE." And its subtitle across the whole broad page of the *Post* read:

"The bonehead plays of Sergei Tulpanov are endless and hilarious. What's holding him up, in a government which usually liquidates blunderers? Will Moscow ever do anything about its stooge in Berlin?"

In its invidious rhetoric and its puerile approach to politics this was, I spluttered, a retrograde step for those of us in Europe who were participating in, and welcoming, a maturing of American leadership in foreign policy and a growth of thoughtfulness in a dangerous ill-understood struggle for global power. With my second martini in my hand at Freddy's bar I could have hit Jimmy on the head with the stem. (When we recalled the incident later, with delicately iced martinis at Boston's old Union Oyster Bar, we usually said, in chorus, "But the stem's the best part of the drink!")

There was much of permanent interest in the profile which I happened to pass over. O'Donnell had seen Soviet foreign policy-makers from Molotov to Vishinsky at much closer quarters than I, and his sketch of Tulpanov deserves to be quoted, even if it is tinged with the topical jargon of the day:

> ...In physical appearance Sergei Ivanovitch is almost Hollywood caricature of the political commissar, a Slavic Eric von Stroheim. He is as outrageously bald as some of his own statements, flat faced, with an extremely broad nose, large ears, drooping eyelids and a bullet-shaped cranium. He has the glazed eyes of a methodical zealot, the face of a man who can smile, but never laughs...

Long after Tulpanov's (and O'Donnell's) retirement they happened by sheer accident to meet in Weimar, during one or another of the unending Goethe/Schiller celebrations; and the wild, argumentative, and altogether raucous evening they spent together prompted the thought that at least one paragraph (as O'Donnell wrote me) had to be revised in the light of subsequent evidence:

.... And yet in social intercourse he can be polite, cultivated, speak in a well-modulated voice, and with an air
of only slightly enforced charm and graciousness. He
prides himself on always being nattily clad, in or out of
uniform. He is abstemious in his taste for liquor, food,
cigarettes, every minor luxury....

I am, in retrospect, very contrite. It was almost as if one had developed
a vested interest in the *dramatis personae* of the East-West conflict,
and nobody could be permitted to pay anything but the most earnest
attention to the historic issues involved, their unfolding, their high
points, their idiosyncratic personal embodiments, their gravity. What
means "bonehead plays"? Where do 'stooges' come on in the fateful
denouéments of solemn Imperial conflicts?

We were, in the end, reconciled. O'Donnell told me he could
be held responsible only for the text of his article; the headlines and
subtitles were not of his doing but the page-proof inspiration of his
Saturday Evening Post editor, Ben Hibbs, who liked to think that
every article he published had his personal "touch." Author and editor have always lived on the verge of civil war in America; and this
editor in Philadelphia, Pennsylvania, could not be dissuaded from
explaining to his great American readership (five million copies sold,
from coast to coast) that foreign affairs on the final scoreboard were
mostly to be accounted for by hits, runs, and errors, with the turning points being turned by big bone-head blunders on the part of
balding players of the game.

7. CULTURE OF POLITICS

I have spoken of the "misery factor" which plagued Soviet ambitions for
power in post-war Europe, and especially the Tulpanov assignment in
Berlin but it would be misleading to leave the impression that the cause
of it was merely Eastern backwardness and Russian rapacity, or even
(as some would have it) the obtuseness of the Commissar mind.

Russian efforts in the economic and political spheres were unavoidably frustrated—and to some extent this was also true for the Western policies in the three other occupied zones—by an internal contradiction. If the Germans were collectively and criminally responsible for the entire wartime tragedy, why should they be helpfully encouraged to work and produce and become prosperous again? And if every last man of them was actually tainted by collaboration with an evil régime, what politicians, young or old, in the new political parties could truly be trusted?

On the cultural front, however, there was a certain clarity and coherence from the first. Hitler was a fascist fiend; Goethe and Schiller, Bach and Kant were great Germans. Here was a tradition which the Russians could respect and the Germans, struggling to find a revised identity, could fall back on—"humanist writers...progressive poets...enlightened thinkers...forward-looking intellectuals."

In this spirit the Russians could prepare for the German cultural future in the "superstructure" in a way that was impossible for them in the basic other fields where, despite the need for sensible and coherent Occupation policies, the day was dominated by first, rapacious dismantling of factories in a wasteful and useless reparation program; and secondly, harrowing midnight arrests numbering in the thousands by the NKVD to cripple any suspected (or imagined) political opponents.

Men of letters had an easier time of it. In the wasteland between Moscow and East Berlin they came and went, speaking of Heine and Heinrich Mann, a little later of his brother Thomas Mann too. Problems were mostly confined to what might be called aesthetical tactics. I was once told by an East-German publisher (who later fled from the East to become the senior director of a reconstituted Ullstein-Verlag in the West) that Tulpanov had once asked him about the merits of a new edition of Johann Wolfgang von Goethe. He threw up his hands, aghast at the prospect of wasting so much rationed paper and scarce printer's ink on *Faust*, *Ur-Faust*, (and the like) when, despite the general destruction, millions of copies had survived and were still around on people's shelves. Tulpanov went ahead anyway; the German comrades wanted it very much as a kind of symbolic recruitment of Goethe to the cause. And thus, in the otherwise barren winter of 1946 I was able to buy for pennies in Leipzig, a stone's throw from Auerbach's *Keller* where Mephisto was supposed to have seduced Faust over a mug of beer, a handsome newly-printed, finely-bound ten-volume *Goethe: Gesammelte Werke*.

As a matter of fact, in wartime Moscow meticulous plans had been laid. Obviously the matrices for the re-issue of all the Marx, Engels, and Lenin works (Stalin was represented too, although his name is usually omitted in current histories) were given high priority for shipment with the first freight trains to Berlin after capitulation on VE Day. Aufbau-Verlag was quickly able to produce its first titles—they included Ehrenburg, Hans Fallada, Lion Feuchtwanger, Maxim Gorky, Heinrich Mann, Friedrich Wolf. This was in the summer of 1945 when the Anglo-Americans in the West were still debating whether the nasty book-burning Germans deserved anything new, or old, to read at all. And who in Heidelberg or Hamburg could be again entrusted with the power to publish? Again, the Russians had their "organizational weapon" to hand, and gave licenses not to "bourgeois-capitalist entrepreneurs" but to the "democratic mass organizations" (all of which were under their totalitarian control).

The Party came first, and it was awarded the Verlag Neue Weg; Becher's *Kulturbund* came next, and with its Aufbau list led by 1947 in all of Germany with 100 publications and two-and-a-half million copies in circulation. They were all in a thrusting competitive mood, and were elated (for the first and last time) that they were leading the league in cultural vitality. Literary critics like Hans Mayer reinforced their confidence by reports from the West that there was nothing there but old, old-fashioned, and backward-looking writers (like Hans Carossa, Werner Bergengruen, Elisabeth Langgässer). Their "proletarian" avant-garde in the triumphant forward march of real European culture led with Anna Seghers and Bert Brecht and (odd man out) Hermann Hesse.

The Commissars had their little tactical problems, as I say; and they were troubled in the first years whether they should, for example, allow productions of Richard Wagner's operas. Ultimately they relaxed and did, although no page of Nietzsche saw the light of day for some thirty years and the first little edition of Max Weber's essays only appeared in 1989! Nevertheless, the knee-jerk ideology was always usefully tempered by targets of opportunity, the opportunism of capturing "a star." In 1945, Tulpanov visited aged Gerhart Hauptmann in Agnetendorf and (despite political doubts over his record in the *Reich*) "won him over." In 1947 the Colonel beguilingly entertained Thomas Mann in Weimar and convinced him that, among other petty deceptions, "we in the USSR are brought up on writers like Ibsen…" As Tulpanov reported: "Thomas Mann was very satisfied that in the Soviet Union one was so familiar with Western culture."

There was no other evidence that the Commissar was, in any sensitive way, interested in Ibsen, or Mann, or Hauptmann, or any other man of letters. Culture was politics, and in power-politics (as local German politicians often reported to me, with chagrin) he was not above using that most gritty of all of Lenin's formulation: *Ktvo-kovo*, "Who/whom?" or, in a German, *Wer/wen*. He thus cut through the time-consuming waffle of even the Party politicians whom he found tiresome. The jargon was contemptuously called *"Partei-Chinesisch,"* but these were the years before Mao came to full power in China.

In any case, in the Commissar's mind culture might be the cunning passage to power. An innovative Italian Marxist of the '20s, Gramsci, formulated it as an orthodox Communist alternative to fading hopes for the prospect of any kind of violent seizure of the state apparatus; and in time, when Lenin-style insurrections never happened, his strategy of capturing the "commanding heights of culture" became popular. Among the primordial myths of the revolutionary rising is (as we know it from 1789 and 1917) the storming of a prison or a palace; the bare-chested climbing of a barricade; the capture of a newspaper or radio station or, even more decisively, the electricity central or the metropolitan airport. Sometimes victory came after a "long march;" but, more devoutly to be desired, was a short sharp attack which would convert a spark into a fire. Yet, when difficulties mount, frail hopes inflate themselves into desperate dreams. Could, in the end, the spoken or written word be an arbiter of fate? Slogans—about peace or land or bread or liberty—have been known to transform an atmosphere. In the end there might be the word that would save. Could the Commissar's mind come up with a plan as a last resort, an inspired word that would rescue the cause?

8. THE COMMISSAR (II)

"The Russian film about 'a Commissar of the Revolution' has had as many ups-and-downs as the tragic story of many a real Commissar in Soviet political life.

"It was originally made by the young Moscow director, Alexander Askoldov, in the 1960s, inspired by 'the Thaw' of the Kruschchev era. It was never shown, and was totally banned—with the usual censor's stamp, "For All Time!"—after the Party's cultural commissars denounced the portrayal of the Commissars during the Civil War of the 1920s as 'tendentious...untrue...uncharacteristic...counter-revolutionary'. The film, based on a story by Vasilii Grossman (whose major novel *Life and Destiny* had been confiscated by the KGB), was also accused of being at once 'anti-semitic' and 'pro-Zionist'. The fact is that for the first time since 1917 a Jewish family had been portrayed in the Soviet cinema as singing Yiddish songs and reciting Hebrew prayers. The very sounds were unprecedented.

"Although Askoldov was expelled from the Party and officially banned, a copy of *The Commissar*—in Russian *Komissar*, in German *Die Kommissarin* (since the leading character is a woman)—was preserved. When it was shown, twenty years later, in International Film Festivals (including Cannes and Berlin), it won prizes.

"In Eastern-Germany it was banned by the Communist censors for several months in 1988. In Western-Germany, and throughout Europe, it was exhibited successfully. Askoldov, in various interviews, told the story of Grossman's (and his own) persecution by the latter-day Commissars. They had 'liquidated' his father (a Red Army officer) in the 1937 purge, and imprisoned his mother for seventeen years. The Chief Ideologist of the Party, Suslov, told Askoldov that Grossman's works would be banned 'for the next hundred years'.

"In connection with the survival of one copy of *The Commissar*, a Moscow archivist has also rescued a copy of the minutes of a Party discussion in 1965 in which the total-ban-for-all-eternity was pronounced. The charges included: a Commissar could not be responsible for murder; a Commissar would not use bad or obscene language; a Commissar would never have had hesitations about leaving her child and returning to the revolutionary cause. The cultural commissars denounced the work to be 'nihilist...counter-revolutionary...a charade...and a travesty...'.

"Commissars were heroes and heroines of history and their roles in the annals of revolution should not be distorted."

News-Items & Interviews in: Der Tagesspiegel (Berlin), *Süddeutsche Zeitung* (Munich), and *Zoom* (Zurich), 1988–89.

9. PREPARING AN HISTORIC CONGRESS

There is no more principled hope for a greater miracle, in the hearts and minds of those who are or were true believers in the secular religion of communism, than that their utopian ideals become reality in the final act of proletarian revolution. Still, some minor miracles need to be held in reserve in the event that the apocalyptic climax does not quite follow its prescribed course.

There was no emancipatory uprising to inaugurate the new and good society in Germany (nor anywhere in Soviet-liberated Eastern Europe, except for Tito's Yugoslavia). And, in the grievous absence of the stormy spirit of October, myth-enhancing in its romanticism, therefore the new economics and new politics had to carry the burden of flowering virtue. All landed estates were confiscated; every factory was expropriated, and even the little corner-shops nationalized; brand-new political organizations were created. Still the difficulties mounted, and the problem of re-fashioning society on the basis of socialist dream seemed insuperable. The economics were producing no welfare, the politics were proving divisive. Could the ready and easy solution possibly lie in the super-structure, in the sphere of culture and intellectual life?

It was always part of the miraculous scenario for artists and men of letters, with their old-world talents and frustrations, to opt for the new utopian world by joining the forces of revolutionary progress and thus give a lead. In the summer of 1947 the Commissars were desperate for a resurgence of German hope. Some of them were cultivated enough to fondle the memories of Pushkin speaking out for the Decembrists in the rebellion of 1825; of Alexander Herzen hailing the revolutionary year of 1848; of the idealism of Russian writers from Tolstoy to Maxim Gorky which prepared the climate of opinion for Lenin, himself an aristocratic defector from the old to the new class, to change the course of history.

As for 'the German comrades' who were closer to the memory of Willi Münzenberg, that cunning Comintern manipulator of the European intelligentsia in the ideologized 1930s, they knew that such things as Writers Congresses were harbingers of the radiant future. All were warmed by the reminiscence of Paris 1935, when André Malraux and André Gide and Henri Barbusse, together with Boris Pasternak and Isaac Babel and Ilya Ehrenburg, fraternized in a single progressive cause; and a word went out to the world, a powerful message, on behalf of all the ideals which Moscow had pronounced congenial. (The young Dénis de Rougemont was also there and he once told me, in a mood of melancholy reminiscence, "Never did one lie so badly, never with more enthusiasm...")

It was only some twelve years before, and could it be done again?

A few German writers (like Ludwig Renn, Anna Seghers and Heinrich Mann) remembered it well: Paris in the springtime of revolutionary enthusiasm. It had to be done again, and this time the mobilization of the intelligentsia would help make good all the setbacks that had been incurred in the East-West struggle for Germany. This was the pall of pessimism that had to be counter-balanced: the "planned poverty" of a socialist economy which could not win over the masses—the dark machinations of "the NKVD state" which was refilling the cells of nearby Buchenwald (and Sachsenhausen) with other political prisoners—the old European traditions which still sustained too many pluralizing elements, too many old-fashioned individualists with stubborn notions of bourgeois liberties—the headstrong workers who wanted to run their own trade-unions in their own way—the quiet Christians who opted for their own churches and confessional politicians—the unruly Social Democrats who insisted on organizational independence—last but not least, the pedantic Allied bureaucrats in the Four-Power Control Council in Berlin who were becoming increasingly fussy and sticklers for the fine print of such old wartime agreements that still had sticking-points that made sense.

The new society which, in the Marxian metaphor of natural birth, was supposed to issue "from the womb of the old", was suffering embryonic complications and needed forceps. Could the reserve miracle of what was later to be called a "cultural revolution" tilt the balance in Germany?

I have been reading the official historical account[21] of the preparation of the First All-National Writers Congress in 1947, and it opens in this very spirit of pious optimism—"*auch Schriftsteller Kongresse könnten zu Kampfplätzen der Geschichte werden* (also Writers Congresses can become battle-fields of history)…" It even mentioned at the outset Paris 1935, and "the lessons" it offered for what they were pleased to think of as the activation and integration of the intellectual class in the revolutionary struggle.

For what did Ernst Toller prophetically say in Moscow at the 1934 Writers Congress? The quote was at hand: "I have attended many literary conferences, and I remember only the purposeless debates and empty gestures which impressed only the literati. But here—what a richness of strength and work, marked the alliance of the writers with the masses, and the masses with literature! In this land lives the ideal reader…and growing out of the ground of new material conditions (namely, socialism) is a great and wide and all-encompassing culture."[22]

If they could still believe that, they could believe anything; and they did. In their post-War winter of discontent all doubts and differences were dismissed by a useful phrase: this was "a new historical situation" wherein the USSR, previously isolated, was aligned with the young socialist societies in Eastern Europe, and all were united

to put fascist barbarism—and a possibility of a new "imperalist re-
lapse"—utterly behind them.

Johannes R. Becher, the President of the so-called Cultural
Society for the Democratic Renewal of Germany, the "front organization" which promised a "democratic renewal of Germany",
was initiated—as the official narrative tells it—at the inspiration of
Günter Weisenborn. (I subsequently asked my friend Weisenborn
whether this was true, that he was the "only begetter" of the whole
extravaganza; and he, with due modesty, acknowledged it…the man
was naive enough to know no shame.) A Max Schröder who was
an emigrant in Paris 1935 and had "collected valuable experience" at
the Malraux-Pasternak affair was co-opted into the organizing committee. A delegation, headed by Becher, was dispatched to Zurich
where Thomas Mann was talking about Nietzsche and his meaning
nowadays.[23] There was reason to believe that the greatest living
German man-of-letters, who had long ago left his "unpolitical" youth
behind him, would not be unsympathetic to the effort.

"The literary movement of allied anti-fascist-democratic writers should become an organized part of the revolutionary change in
all of Germany." But, beyond the German national task, there was
the international duty to disappoint the ruling imperialist circles by
mobilizing progressive public opinion against all the skullduggery
of World Reaction.

I was in Zurich at the time, attending the same P.E.N. Club
conference, and listened to the speech by Johannes R. Becher which
carefully avoided suggesting any of this; I suppose it was too early
for him to expose his "secret agenda." Nevertheless, no one entertained the thought that invitations to the forthcoming Berlin Writers
Congress would exclude world politics and be confined to those
who were pre-occupied with "merely cultural and artistic matters."
As Becher frankly stated, "It will be a political, highly political affair, without any doubt. (*Eine politische, eine hochpolitische Aufgabe
zweifellos*)…" They were not ready in July, and it was postponed
until October. Some said this was due simply to "organizational difficulties", and one can sympathize with those who were trying to
cope in the ruins of Berlin with meals, and rooms, and transport for

hundreds of guests. But others said it was buying time in order to get Thomas Mann back over the Atlantic, to import Arnold Zweig from Haifa, to move Ernst Bloch from Cambridge. (None of them in fact showed up.)

The official historian hinted at another element, a conspiratorial touch perhaps characteristic of an earlier day but surely not of the time, 1979, when she was writing, namely, that "enemies" (as is their wont) would be "penetrating"—and then, once "inspirated", they might get themselves up to doing (as is their style) infernal "manipulation".

At least this was the interpretive gloss put on a recorded "cynical" remark to the exasperated effect that "the Russians will provide all the food and the Americans will contribute the ideology!" Presumably the whole summer was to be devoted to preventing just this pernicious plot.[24]

I have long since stopped speculating whether the German Communists and the Russian Bolsheviks whom I knew, talked with, listened to, and studied like cases on a couch, actually believed in the reality of the plots and conspiracies they bandied about in rhetorical outbursts or in fits of outrage. Up to a point they did believe; and gave the impression they would have done in the plotters and conspirators with their own hands. Beyond that point they did not; and suspecting (or knowing better) the fiction for what it was, they were filled with fear, or shame, or other feelings of repressive self-denial.

In that summer of 1947 Colonel Tulpanov joined Becher and the others to reflect upon the postponement and, possibly, a revised strategy to meet any maneuver the enemy might initiate. Tulpanov recognized that Germany was "provisionally split" but at least some nation-wide victory could be won, even if only on the cultural front. His own language of the day was full of such words and metaphors as "battle-readiness", "test of fire", and the like.

They all met at a pleasant Baltic sea resort called Ahrenshoop, a tiny but famed "artist's colony". A firm date had been set for the Congress but, as Tulpanov put it, "it had to be postponed at any price." The warning signal they had received was serious. It came not from a cynic at all but from a "progressive" friend whose identity still had to be protected. The Colonel talked about him only as *"der Schriftsteller W.;"* it was he that signalled the danger of a sneaky kind of Western take-over. Tulpanov evidently believed it, to the extent that (as I have said) sincerity matters in such a wilful and neurotic decision-making process. When he once reminisced about the mood at Ahrenshoop he indicated that Writer W. may have used a "coquettish formulation"—*"Das Fressen geben die Russen und die Ideologie die Amerikaner"*—but Tulpanov's conclusion was that it was a *"Schlager"*, a hit phrase that was enthusing certain pro-American intellectuals whose only "positive idea" was just such a defense of "the interests of German monopolists and imperialists."

Twenty years later, in more mellow and certainly less tense reminiscence of that weekend in Ahrenshoop, Tulpanov genially recalled the tale of an insult when one of the Becher group (not a Communist but "a Social Democratic sympathizer") discovered his intrusive presence in the sea-side resort.

"What is the Russian doing here?"

Becher explained that the Russian was a supporter of culture and altogether a *Kulturmensch*.

As Tulpanov tells the story, obviously at second-hand and without the fury he must have felt at the time, the German retaliated, "But this is a Mongol—one just has to look at him!—and he has a measure of education but not real culture…"[25]

It is altogether unlikely that a nasty personal objection to one of the most powerful Soviet officers in the land (a telephone call to the NKVD would in those years have disposed of the matter) actually proceeded in this manner. But if the Major-General deliberately recalled it then it must have constituted one of the elements of the sudden suspicion and sense of mounting alien hostility that had given cause for alarm.

When the vaunted event finally took place, to which I will come in a moment, Sergei Tulpanov was not there, at least I didn't see him; and when I asked around nobody else had either. In one of those jocular outbursts of self-critical irony which gave a certain measure of humanity to his otherwise stalwart officiousness, he played on that embarassing incident during the weekend at Ahrenshoop. According to what I was told he said, "I'll stay away—my large Mongol face may frighten the horses." He meant the knavish pro-Americans riding in from the West.

So he left the management to Major Dymschytz, presumably on the theory that a small Jewish face could command more intellectual sympathy and, accordingly, keep the things in better control and on track. He couldn't afford another failure on yet another front. Then the struggle for the whole of divided Berlin and Germany would have no other option but a naked confrontation of power. It would not necessarily be overtly military but—as in a Blockade, which cut off West Berlin eight months later—directly designed to effect the physical ejection of the bourgeois-capitalist enemy by one means or another. Yet, for the time being, there was a chance for something that was to be called, vaguely and ambiguously, a Kulturrevolution (a cultural revolution).[26]

Agreed, then—and the German committee confirmed that the Congress would be subject to a little postponement. Becher passes the good news on to Tulpanov who playfully remarks he had driven out to the same sea resort just "to relax a bit (*ich war für ein paar Tage hierher gekommen, um mich zu 'erholen'*)."

They took nice walks in the nearby Rostock woods. They felt certain that more time would give them the chance to tighten up ideological security. How they thought this was to be done I have not the faintest idea; and whatever it was it certainly did not succeed. Possibly the program was to be made more taut and muscular ("heavyweights" were invited and awaited from Moscow); and just to be on the safe side, the concluding unanimous resolutions could be prepared in advance (which they were). I would not put it beyond them also to have given a thought to money, funds, expenses—for more drink, better food, white table-cloths on all the candle-lit dinner tables. For were they both not convinced (as Becher said, and Tulpanov repeated) that "the representatives of the American ideology often love comfort more than their own ideas...?"[27]

It could be that this pride of the Commissars in their own sterling austerity, often belied by their own privileged ways of life, that this specious show of moral and intellectual superiority, contributed to their own undoing. So far as I know neither Becher nor Tulpanov ever admitted publicly that their historically strategic Congress proved to be a failure. In a memoir of 1965, when the East-German *nomenklatura* had occasion to mourn Becher's death, Tulpanov was still proclaiming it officially a Marxist-Leninist success. True, "its ideas still haven't been embraced in all of Germany, but we still know that the last chapter in the history of Germany has yet to be written..." In the chronicles of the new and better Germany the great event has been duly recorded and celebrated, and it was for Tulpanov at the same time a monument to the poet and to the nation and, if he had cared to go on, to the Revolution.

But had it not been halted, stopped, contained?

The Colonel—he was by now being addressed as "*Generalmajor Professor Dr. Dr. Tulpanov*"—considered that he had said enough on the subject. After all, the full record of the Congress has been published ("*das Stenogramm ist ja veröffentlicht worden*").

This, of course, was not true by a long shot. Since he went away, all the lesser commissars whom he left in charge of information and propaganda had been sitting on the *Protokoll* which they had announced for Aufbau-Verlag publication in 1948. It had not seen the light of day in 1965, when he assumed it was ancient history, nor even in 1984, the year of Tulpanov's death. Forty years on, it is once again included in the Aufbau publishers' list of forthcoming publications. I have met scholars and researchers in the Berlin universities who have gone down to the offices in the Französische Straße, Berlin-Mitte, a few blocks from the East–West Wall and confirmed that the whole record, neatly typed, 800 pages long, a pale third carbon copy and slightly frayed at the edges, does in fact exist and can be inspected since "publication is imminent."[28] I have been assured that whatever I contributed to that occasion has been included, verbatim.

Yet what record of an historic success has ever been suppressed for almost half-a-century? I like to think that Major-General Tulpanov lowered his voice, as if speaking discreetly about a death in the family, when he summed up: the only dissenter was an American who happened to be present.[29]

I was that lone dissenting American, and how I happened to be present was as follows.

10. A THEATRICAL SCENE

I have already sketched in the background of the world-political conflict which involved, with surprise and shock, the Western allies in increasingly desperate argumentation with their recent ally, the Soviet Union.

Berlin was the last station of the way. The die had already been cast in Potsdam (and before that, perhaps, in the preludes of Tehran and Yalta); but in the ruins of the *Reichshauptstadt* a certain facade of formal unity still obtained in the Four-Power *Kontrollrat* and *Kommandatura*. The administration of the city had already been broken into an Eastern and Western sector, but for the Western powers—the naive inexperienced Americans, the war-weary and world-weary British, the aloof and cynical French—it was only taken to be "a little local difficulty."

At least this was the best public face that was put on events that were irresistibly leading to an open break in the Four-Power unity which was supposed amicably to settle "the German question." After the frostiness of the Moscow Conference in March 1947, U.S. Secretary of State George Marshall had to admit that the Kremlin's proposals "would have established in Germany a centralized government adapted to the seizure of absolute control…".

General Clay[30] once told me that it was indeed in Moscow— where he attended the meetings (and always carried a small automatic pistol in his bag, "just in case")—that "Secretary Marshall recognized the necessity of stopping the Communist advance in Europe before the German problem could be settled…" Still, he hesitated and still had hope, because in his talk with Stalin the Generalissimo (God knows what the interpreters made of the original remarks!) had said that "these were only the first skirmishes and brushes..." Stalin presumably meant to suggest that the battle would become more severe. Generals Marshall and Clay wanted to understand merely that all could still be reconciled, that peace might break out if they only would pretend that a Cold War was not raging.

Thus, in West Berlin and throughout Western Germany, the directives to the press included a prohibition, in effect, of criticism of Soviet policy and practices. The Americans—and the British and the French as well, at a somewhat lower level of aberration—were completely oblivious to the contradiction involved in their own 'watch-dog' restrictions and their bemoaning of the traditional Germanic habits of thought-control. I once tried to argue this point, quietly, politely, with General Clay. He only said, in conventional doubt and even resignation over the future of German democracy (events proved him wrong), "I wonder whether they'll ever, despite our efforts, grasp the idea of liberty and of a truly free press..." On the contrary, I reported that I found among Berlin's editors and journalists a yearning to try and tell things "the way they actually are", and a chafing-at-the-bit over formalistic Allied inhibitions. Whenever I met with Berlin's newspaper publishers—like Erik Reger of the *Tagesspiegel*, Arno Scholz of the *Telegraf*, Paul Bourdin of the *Kurier*—we lamented the *Maulkorb*, the official muzzle and its disorienting influence on the state of emerging German public opinion on international questions. Only Erik Reger devised an ingenious way out.

On certain issues where he dared not be specific in his *Leitartikel*, or even abstract and philosophical in his *feuilleton*, I was encouraged to write a piece: nominally in English for the *New Leader* in New York. And he would thereupon translate it and "quote" it in entirety in the *Tagesspiegel*—not as an insidious Germanic attempt to subvert the unity of the victorious Allied powers but only as an informed contribution to the general understanding of Western currents of opinion. In this way I was able even to argue the case for democratic impatience with censorship no matter where it occurred and under what bureaucratic excuse. Our brief, especially, was to explore the meaning of the new word "totalitarianism" and the similarities (also the differences) between the Nazi and Soviet varieties of police-state dictatorships. It was, for both of us, an exercise not without its personal dangers.

"I could be summarily removed," Reger said with strained light-heartedness. "Just as you were almost court-martialled…"

This was a reference to an incident he knew about during the first-post-War winter when, as a young American war-historian stationed in the I.G. Farben building in Frankfurt-am-Main, I was given an assignment to lecture to the Occupation troops on "the historic meaning of the great Allied victory over Hitler's Germany." I proposed an outline of a lecture, but I had refused to insert the obligatory reference to Stalin's Russia as one of "the four Great Democracies" that were destined to guarantee peace in our time. I narrowly escaped being put on military trial on charges, presumably, of having "dangerous thoughts."

A second narrow escape, put somewhat melodramatically by Reger when the affair was all over, was on the occasion of the first German Writers Congress, organized by Colonel Tulpanov and Major Dymschytz in October 1947 with the ideological élan and desperate optimism on the part of the Commissars which I have been describing. Erik Reger and his cultural co-editor, Walther Karsch, asked me to write about it: in the event that the East-West encounter needed the extra dimension of "journalistic license" that the German *Lizenzträger* found beyond their ken. I did not suspect that I would not be writing the story but providing it.

I had come back to the Press Club in Zehlendorf-West, just off the Argentinische Allee, after having done a *West-Zonale* literary report-age for the New York *Partisan Review*, taking up the themes in the interviews I had just had with Karl Jaspers in Heidelberg, Ernst Jünger in Hannover, and Martin Heidegger in his Black-Forest *Ski-hütte*.

The note from Reger and Karsch reported that a call had been made in the name of those great worthies of German letters, Ricarda Huch and Heinrich Mann—it originated, of course, in Karlshorst in the *Kultur-Abteilung* of Tulpanov and Dymschytz, with the poet Becher polishing the prose—to convene the "*Erste Deutsche Schriftsteller-Kongress*". And its opening "all-German (*gesamtdeutsche*)" opening ceremony was indeed to be held in the U.S. sector (actually in the Hebbel-Theater where Karl-Heinz Martin had been putting on brilliant stage productions of Sartre and Giradoux). All was sweetness and light.

But the next day—for some, a shock and surprise; for others, in the logic of events—an ideological offensive was launched. Wearing three rows of ribbons and decorations on the lapel of his double-breasted tweed suit, the Moscow ideologue Vyacheslov Vishnevsky (a famous and powerful man in his day) appealed to the German writers, in East and West, to "fight shoulder-to-shoulder" with the Soviets against the American imperialists. He thundered that "reactionary forces in Washington and London are trying to create an Iron Curtain.... Brothers, comrades, we know how to answer—if you need us, call for our help and we will fight together!..."

There was the usual rhythmic applause from the pro-Communist literati, and a stunned silence from the Westerners in the audience. The next meetings were to be held in the *Kammerspiele*, the newly-decorated annex to the Max Reinhardt Theater (which happened to be, I note in passing, just around the corner from the Luisenstraße headquarters of the Soviet political police). The dismay among the non-Communists writers at the Congress led to a determined, if frantic, attempt to restore some kind of East-West balance by somehow snatching time from the next day's agenda for a Western point of view.

I will not go into the details of the tragi-comic attempt of Gunther Birkenfeld, the next day's chairman in the Kammerspiele, to find a representative and "most eloquent" American writer. I suggested that England was closer and they should think of Bertrand Russell (little did we know that the famous pacifist was having one of his little zig-zags and was contemplating "dropping the Bomb on Moscow" at the time); or that they should consider asking the Labour Government's Royal Air Force to fly in George Orwell for the occasion. No, with a fine intuition for world-political power, they cried out for a transatlantic poet or novelist.

Birkenfeld's little group of dissenters tried to get in touch with John Steinbeck (who happened to be in Moscow at that time), with

Ernest Hemingway (who was in Cuba), with Upton Sinclair (who was in Hollywood). Shortly after midnight, desperate and empty-handed, the Western contingent settled on "a young American writer, born in New York City," namely me, quickly available in Zehlendorf-West.

And in the early hours of the morning I wrote a short speech which was intended to be, if not tentative, then carefully ambiguous and not at all a polemical salvo. In the event, as the next day would show, the Russian Commissars, Tulpanov and Dymschytz, had ears finer than my pen.

The manuscript of my remarks on that Tuesday, October 1947, were lost or misplaced for a long time, some 40 years in fact, until I found it—typed on the same typewriter I am using now—hidden in one of the secret flaps of the morgue-envelopes in Erik Reger's *Tagesspiegel* archives. It was the original English version of the talk I held in German—in the City College accents I learned from Professor Kinkledey and Dr. Liptzin—from the Max Reinhardt stage on which a stormy, and indeed frightening, drama was being played.

My defense of the rights of all writers against censorship was conventional and, at first, couched in rather provincial terms; and so long as it was confined to the criticism of "small-minded American bureaucrats exercising unofficial control" or "narrow-minded middle-class moralists" (as in the cases mounted against the disagreeable novels of James Joyce and James T. Farrell), it was approved and applauded. I also mentioned some States-side difficulties of John Steinbeck and William Faulkner, John Dos Passos and Richard Wright, and this was even taken as a kudo for progressive "social realism." A friend in the audience later said that if I had stopped then and there I would have received an ovation from the Soviet writers and the German communists, and reaffirmed the Commissar's confidence in the universality of the common struggle.

But I went on to mention, by way of a passing detail, the American wartime censorship of Leon Trotsky's biography of Stalin, and a slight chill set in. Anna Seghers thought it prudent to leave her seat and proceed quickly to the foyer; she returned a minute later with Major Dymschytz who took a seat in the front row. He sat beside Valentin Katayev who, for a famous humourist, sat stone-faced thoughout, especially during the post-Trotsky remarks which compared the fate of German authors (Freud, Einstein, Thomas Mann) with the writers under all police-state tyrannies everywhere.

I ventured to touch on the comparable difficulties of Soviet writers—

"…They, too, have their problem of pressure and censorship. They, too, are having their struggle for cultural freedom. To their difficulties, I think, all of us must bring a certain measure of open-hearted sympathy."

At this point I must have been carried away by my own rhetoric, not infrequently the case when one is speaking a foreign language and in anxiety over a misplaced *umlaut* or an agglutinative slur, one exaggerates tones and inflections. I looked squarely at Dymschytz and Vishnevsky, Boris Gorbatov and Valentin Katayev, the solid phalanx in the front row, and cried out:

"We know how soul-crushing it is to work and write when behind us stands a political censor and behind him stand the police."

According to the *Wochenschau* cameramen who were filming the event, I actually pointed backward to the stage curtain, to the spectral censor and policeman. I thought of Pasternak, Babel, Mandelshtam.

Then all hell broke loose. Major Dymschytz rose and walked out, taking Katayev with him. Two or three German communists followed. A leading Eastern *Regisseur*, Gustav von Wangenheim, demanded to know how this happened to be the main speech of the day. (I had been "smuggled" in, and my name was nowhere on the Congress program.) There were shouts, protests, ominous rumblings.

I tried to ignore the interruptions and went on, calling attention to the Russian philosophers—now that Stalin had ordered them to cease and desist from "slavish adulation of Western thought"— "who hesitated to bring to their lips the names of Bacon, Descartes, Spinoza, Kant, Fichte, Hegel—"

"*Kriegshetzer!*" yelled a heckler ("war-monger" was a standard slogan of the day).

I paused for a moment, then repeated deliberately, "Kant, Fichte, Hegel—"

"What about the Eisler case?" von Wangenheim shouted.

I must have liked that pseudo-theatrical moment (worthy almost of Max Reinhardt, and I confess it crossed my mind at the time). For again I repeated "—Kant, Fichte, Hegel...for fear of committing some cardinal ideological sin." Piteous ideological sinners were also Zoshchenko and Akhmatova who failed to devote themselves to composing odes to the new Five-Year-Plan or to the old *Vozhd*, Stalin.

More commotion. Shouts. "Throw him out!" "*Genug!*" "*Kriegshetzer!*"

When I concluded and moved to leave the stages I half-expected to be detained, seized, arrested, by burly figures coming in from the wings. But I found my seat peaceably, and in a moment the temperature was cooled by a dry and funny speech. The satirist Katayev—and I had admired him since seeing a "proletarian" production in Manhattan of his play *Squaring the Circle* (1934)—expressed joy at "having finally met a flesh-and-blood war-monger face to face...." He confessed that he was roughly familiar with American writers, with Edgar Allan Poe, with Mark Twain and Steinbeck and Hemingway. But I, even at twenty-seven, was completely unknown to him.

"I believe that if Lasky should ever be immortalized through a monument, the grateful Americans will mark it with the inscription: 'Tomb of the Unknown Writer'...."

I smiled for a moment, but then winced when, in the standard Soviet ploy, Katayev felt he had to compare me with Dr. Goebbels, "inciting against the Soviet Union, telling lies from beginning to end...." I wonder whether he lived long enough to learn of the historic Khrushchev speech, saying much the same things ten years later that I had adumbrated about Stalin; or what he would have said about Gorbachov's glasnost recriminations against the 70-year record of Soviet misdemeanours in cultural mendacity.

But, as Sakharov (with Biblical concision) once said to me in Moscow: for us Russians there is a time for lying, and there will be a time for telling the truth.

II. A POETESS SUMS UP

Ricarda Huch[31] was the honorary president of the whole affair, and I had been eagerly awaiting to meet her; but she was fragile and ailing, and the eighty-three-year-old *Nestorin* of German letters was absent for most of the conference, only dragging herself to the final ceremonial reception and farewell. I had read enough in her various histories and biographies to appreciate her reputation as the great poetess among German scholars, and had still in my ears the echo of Golo Mann singing her praises as a *"königliche Frau."*

Golo was perhaps the most important Ciceronian guide apart from *die Herren* Kinkeldey and Liptzin to my learning about things German, beginning with our meeting in Manhattan in 1942 when Klaus Mann, his elder brother, was editing with Weimar vivacity a most lively intellectual review entitled *Decision* and invited me to write for it. In 1945 I met Golo again when he was still in American uniform and we were both attached to the U.S. Army headquarters in Frankfurt's I.G. Farben building. With respect to Ricarda Huch I can remember Golo exploding when another emigré, a young Hungarian who spoke good German, referred to, "Oh yes, *die Huch.*" Golo hated the use of the feminine article to signalize the talent of creative women, and I often saw him wince when reference was made to *"die Dorsch"* or *"die Arendt."*

Still, as the twists of the learning process dictate, one assimilates the bad with the good. In blue-eyed eagerness I asked to meet *"die Huch,"* confounding colloquialism with deference; and Gunther Birkenfeld, the West Berlin writer who had presided over my stormy morning session the day before, hurriedly rushed me to the table where she sat, grey and ashen and hunched, her high lace-collar crumpled around her neck, her lowered lids not quite hiding feverish eyes: but a queenly presence for all that.

We were joined by a young German poet, Rudolph Hagelstange[32] who had supported me in the noisy debates. She said to us, quietly, "Well roared, young lions (*gut gebrüllt, junge Löwen*)!"[33] Whether her hoarsely whispered conversation was medical or methodical, her message elated me. She had been present that morning at the debate, confided that she was wholly on my side, and that her situation in the *Ostzone* was so grave that she could hold out no longer and would be leaving Jena via Weimar for the West as soon as she could pack a few things. Looking over her shoulder she requested *sotto voce* that we keep this *"unter uns"*. Naturally I didn't breathe a word of it (not even to her distinguished son-in-law, Dr. Franz Böhm, that indefatigable libertarian, who must have already been organizing her flight westwards).

But the burden of the confidence grew with the days and, with a touch of guilt, over the years. For Ricarda Huch did leave for the West, caught pneumonia in that bitter winter of 1947, and died in a Taunus village near Frankfurt am Main only a few weeks later (11 November 1947). I tried to convince myself that the decision to "choose freedom" was her own historic one. Surely it was untouched by the abstract polemic she had heard from an argumentative transatlantic youth uninvolved in the post-war Eastern miseries, both public and private, which had then prevailed in the Thuringia of Goethe and Schiller.

Actually she was dissembling a little, in order to cover her tracks. She was not to return to the Soviet zone but left on a British military train from West Berlin that very night. Curiously enough, she felt impelled to write a polite letter to the Russian commanding general, apologizing for her "sudden departure"—and an unauthorized one at that—and daring to express the hope that she might soon return for a visit. This may well have been the old-fashioned custom between civilian victims and military conquerors in the Wilhelmian time of her youth. But, as she explained to me, she had always been "pro-Russian." She had once done a book about Bakunin and another on the revolution of 1848, even planned a history of the Russian Revolution; and indeed she once confessed that she was "a born Protestant and partial to revolution and rebellion (*ich war ein geborener Protestant, mit Vorliebe für Revolution und Rebellion*)."

And so it was that when others, in the spring of 1945, were deciding to flee to the West from the advancing Red Army troops, she had decided to remain in her house in Jena's Philosophenweg to welcome the conquerors from the East over the hated Hitler régime. At first it had been part of the American military zone, and when the

U.S. forces (in General Eisenhower's misguided gallantry) offered to
retreat, the Soviet occupation power moved in. Ricarda Huch, just
another little old lady to the Yanks, was immediately given special
treatment by the Moscow commissars. On the personal orders of
Col. Tulpanov fresh from his triumph of "winning over" old Gerhard
Hauptmann, the local commandant dispended extra coal and food
rations to one of the heroines of "the other Germany."

The difficulties accumulated slowly, leading to a quick disenchantment. She told me of a small incident when, in a *feuilleton* about
her diary as a six-year-old child (some 75 years earlier) she recalled
that she had played with her brother's tin soldiers—and the Soviet
censor proscribed it as "militaristic".

When the physical terror of the Stalin police-state came to
mount, with kidnappings, deportations, and indiscriminate arrests,
she knew it was time for her to leave. The *Schriftstellerkongress* in
East Berlin was to be used as a station along the way. She needed
no convincing, but her melancholy calm suggested that her age and
frailty put her quite beyond hope.

The next day I read in a book of Ricarda Huch's verses (given
to me by the poet Hagelstange, who also was to go West):

> *War, wofür du entbrannt,*
> *Kampfes wert?*

And it ended:

> *Geh schlafen, mein Herz, es ist Zeit,*
> *Kühl weht die Ewigkeit.*[34]

Dying poets can remain cool, living ideologues remain enraged.
Some time thereafter a leading member of Ulbricht's Politbüro,
Bruno Leuschner, said that "Dymschytz or Tulpanov should have
had the swine arrested on the spot!" As far as he was concerned, if
he had his own way, I would have been (in his phrase) "boiled in
oil." Given the Eastern oil shortages, then and now, I imagine I was
in no particular danger.

Still in those days they used to have their steely ideological imperatives; and in the lurid, exaggerated fashions of the day the Soviet daily newspaper in Berlin, *Die Tägliche Rundschau,* referred to this incident at the Writers Congress as (quite unhistorically) "the beginning of the East-West conflict in Berlin" and referred to me (quite undeservedly) as "the father of the Cold War."

But a final irony remains.

Not only did the Soviet Colonel Tulpanov consider my intervention in East-West affairs "a provocation", for it presaged a possible Anglo-American turn to anti-Communism and to a full and consistent Western policy of resistance to Stalin's expansionism. So did the American commander, General Lucius Clay. It ended in its way his simple American hope, sustained over years by Roosevelt and Hopkins, Byrnes and Marshall, that the German battle-ground for power would be, or could be, excepted (*ausgeklammert*) from Stalin's imperial designs, archly called by the sardonic Kremlin master "first skirmishes and brushes." Lucius Clay, fastidious general-staff officer that he was, was incensed at an outrageous outsider's intrusion into matters that were the customary province of authorized high policy makers. My performance was considered a disruption of the routine governmental agenda, an unauthorized intervention on behalf of such most irregular matters as cultural freedom and human rights: a proper scandal.

Many years later when we had become fast friends, General Clay admitted to me, with a touch of shamefaced embarrassment, that he had wanted on the very next day—after the headlines had announced that I had initiated a Cold War—to have me summarily expelled from West Berlin and Germany.

12. AN IDEOLOGICAL NEUROSIS & ITS COMPLICATIONS

I have already described the ideological neurosis which blocked the mind of the Commissars when it came to remembering, recording, or reviewing the days of October 1947. Col. Tulpanov, promoted to Major-General and assigned to control and expand Marxist-Leninist studies at Leningrad University, supposed mistakenly/erratically that the full official *Protokoll* had long since been published. But I saw the still unpublished typescript in 1989 at the Aufbau-Verlag offices; and it lay there like a neglected corpse in a morgue, already showing signs of decay as if it had been ready for the embalmer for decades. And when one East-German Marxian historian set out in the 1970s to chronicle what she called the upheaval (*Umbruch*) of the intellectual rally to prepare and carry through the First Writers Congress of 1947—it remains for some unfathomable reason a charismatic event which has special magnetic powers of attraction and repulsion—a curious thing happened on the way to the printing press.

Umbruch can also mean the last-minute proof-reading before the publication deadline, and certainly Dr. Sigrid Bock's official narrative for the East Berlin Academy of Science was subjected to intense scrutiny and even, it seems, the censor's panicky second (and possibly third) thoughts. On page 142 of the scholarly disquisition the typesetting suddenly sinks into a tiny six-point type, only to normalize again at nine-point on page 144. It was as if the historian could speak of one notoriously disagreeable event only in hushed tones, in a typographical whisper. Since the passage concerns me I may be forgiven for suggesting such a romantic or melodramatic hypothesis. Actually the students of Marxist-Leninist censorship of those days offer a more technical explanation. For they know of a number of cases of similar tinkering with texts and type-sizes when the Party bosses hesitated, and came up with conflicting authorizations for a very short and then a rather longer passage to be inserted, both rewritten and combined at the last moment and, thus, ill-fitting for the allotted space at the bottom of one page and ending overleaf.

What Dr. Bock had originally intended to say—or whether I had been, as an un-person, definitively consigned to the memory-hole—I cannot find a way of knowing; in any case, what was written was less interesting than the way it was printed. In a hectic last moment I was identified—who had time for careful proof-reading? and, anyway in German, misprints are ascribed to the Devil—as a correspondent for *The New Reader* and thus the spokesman for the spirit of the Cold War; of McCarthyism (years before the senator emerged into the limelight); of the Truman Doctrine and Totalitarianism-Theory (also years before it had been formulated); and, in general, of the Imperialist strategy against peace and progress.

One can sense that the book was being thrown at me, retrospectively, as if on that October day long ago I had happened to hurt them mortally or, at least, in some unhealing way. And if they could not omit the distasteful altercation altogether, then they had to squeeze the full indictment into the available page-and-a-bit with smaller type.

On page 144 the Marxist-Leninist historian stretches herself to normal linotyped size and pronounces that the existing consensus, nay unanimity, of the 1947 Congress could never be "wrecked." It was all an utter and complete success—"at least for the area of the Soviet Occupied Zone (*zumindest für den Bereich der sowjetisch besetzten Zone*)." In the other zones, Dr. Bock grudgingly concluded, "the Western gazettes sensationalized differences of opinions among writers and pronounced Lasky to be the Hero of the Day...."[35] Dr. Bock's official account for the Academy of Science ended with a tepid quotation from DDR-President Wilhelm Pieck as to how it all helped the "revolutionary party of the working-class" to prepare "our Five-Year-Plan" and which they also never conceded to be a failure.

Even deep into the 1980s[36] the scab on the wound—like the incurable and agonizingly spasmodic abscess of Philoctetes[37]—had not yet healed, still itched, still irritated. The 10th *Schriftstellerkongress* of that ilk was convened in East Berlin in November 1987. The keynote speaker was Stephan Hermlin who had been present as a *"junger Dichter,"* and I remember him at the 1st Congress forty years earlier as the very image of the tall, handsome, blond young poet. He was now a greying, aging, senior Commissar of letters who had been the loyal functionary all through the eras of Stalin, Krushchev, and Brezhnev. Understandably he could not resist the temptation to recall when "Lasky...a protagonist of the Cold War...used the opportunity to...etc., etc." A poet and not an historian, Hermlin claimed that those were "the McCarthy years" and "small wonder that Lasky also found some Germans who would echo him…. And even today, here and there, such echoes still reach us." What still has not reached them that the democratic indictment of the system they served for long illiberal lifetimes was to echo from Budapest, Warsaw, and Moscow.

Two years later, when the editors in East Berlin of the cultural weekly paper *Sonntag*[38] had their attention called to the fact that I was still around, in point of fact again residing in West Berlin and engaged in writing this memoir of those years, the old, warped, short-playing gramophone record was put under the scratchy needle again. It was the same troubled, flawed, self-indulgent version of events as set down by Colonels Tulpanov and Dymschytz, Dr. Sigrid Bock and Stephan Hermlin. Once, long ago, an admirable Eastern 'openness' had been darkly overshadowed. Yet progressive men of letters were slowly, but surely, recovering from the onslaughts of the Cold War. And one dissident survivor, even if he had the improbably sinister qualities of being "as flexible as he was rigid (*ebenso flexible wie starre*)," could only wallow in nostalgia….

As Hermlin noted, "Of those who were present at the time only a few are still alive (*Von den damals Anwesenden leben nur noch wenige*)…" They could take, as he did, consolation from Rosa Luxemburg: "Patience is the virtue of the revolutionary (*Geduld ist die Tugend des Revolutionärs*)." Their own Stalinist patience had stood the test of time, and even if the Commissars could not change history they could continue to make the sullen effort to rewrite it.

In the Commissar's mind there are not very many variables, and in whatever combination they may emerge there are intellectually narrow limits. In the history of the Commissariat the decisions were always taken by a small ideological faction or, most of the time, its all-dominant leader in the power structure. In the era of Stalin the range of personal motivations may have extended from unpredictable personal whims to sudden world-embracing changes of Party Line. What, if only we could see into the convoluted depths of his personality, moved Stalin to strike at friends, rivals, and relatives alike? Where did the penchant for "murder, most foul" come from? And why, in those same wildly destructive years, were vulnerable lives spared, a poet here, a diplomat there?

Even the most earnest devotion to military security (of the Revolution) and the national interest (of Mother Russia and all of the USSR) was restricted to the confines of a personally formulated dogmatism. Stalin, like Lenin before him, was taken to be an infallible exponent of the scientific method of Marxist explication.

Once, in the Hotel am Zoo on Berlin's Kurfürstendamm, I arrived early and chatted with one of the Eastern delegates to our occasional East-West discussions. He was Dr. Robert Havemann, a distinguished physicist and something of a Marxist philosopher (years later, as a dissident, he wrote courageous articles and interesting books). It was shortly before Christmas and the East Berlin press were publishing no end of fulsome birthday tributes to the genius of J.V. Stalin. I was imprudent to suggest that nobody could ever really believe that Comrade Stalin, whatever his civic virtues might be, was "the greatest scientific genius of the modern age." Havemann turned pale with surprise at the rudeness, and then livid with rage at the enormity of the insult. He packed his notes and papers into his battered pre-war briefcase, and walked out. I still have a photograph of the conference table with Havemann's name-plate in front of an empty chair.

This was in the late '40s, and the *Zeitgeist* was still replicating certain forms of abject ideological surrender which were more familiar in the 1930s. I once heard a leading Czech Communist, Artur London—he would later expiate his naiveté with a long prison-term after a humiliating show-trial in which he confessed to heinous crimes—say about Stalin: "…My heart beat faster when I saw him, and I was ecstatic when he appeared briefly at the Seventh Comintern Congress [in 1934]. When he gave interviews I thought the simple way he answered yes or no were marks of genius. Like the whole of the International Communist movement I fervently cultivated his personality…."[39]

In the ranks of the true believers all comrades were interchangeable. They accepted Stalin's views on the new Constitution for Soviet society (no matter how crassly it was contradicted by illegalities in every corner of life); on the "vile and criminal" character of the Old Bolsheviks whom Stalin had purged (no matter how unlikely it was they were all paid agents of Hitler); on the sturdiness of the Hitler-Stalin Pact (ample warnings of a Hitler invasion were dismissed as insidious tricks from London); on the wondrous successes of one unrealistic Five-Year-Plan after another (each failed, and compounded the structural errors of the wasteful and stagnant system of bureaucratic collectivism"; all were accepted by the faithful. Would-be commissars were true to an international orthodoxy as inflexibly defended in New York as in Moscow; and after the War in all the capital cities of Stalin's satellite empire.

In the régime zig-zags of policy errors were never conceded, and thus a whole society never learnt from any mistakes inevitable in the course of public life. There was only that strange phenomenon known as "Bolshevik self-criticism," which had nothing to do with a reasoned effective self-evaluation such as a normal and indeed crying need for any growing, groping society. Locked into the Bolshevik tradition of "democratic centralism"—which, in effect, meant compulsory unanimity—the Commissars faced their errors or wayward practices with a formally prescribed remorse. Mistakes became crimes, and both were the personal and free-willed responsibility of the delinquent sinner. And who was there to dare to offer a Marxist historical-materialist explanation of such widespread deviation and disaffection? Thus, failure or even serious difficulties could only be accounted for by culpable individual eccentricities. In the worst of times these entailed as well criminal acts of sabotage in the corrupt cause of the class enemy of national foe.

The political commissar and his literary counterpart—I am thinking now of our two Colonels, Tulpanov and Dymschytz, trying to do their best to win all of Berlin and, therewith, possibly all of Germany for their Master in the Kremlin—could only at great risk think of anything but treading the straight and narrow path. Move a step to the left or to the right, in loyal but thoughtful dedication to one's duty, and one might find oneself in the dire danger-zone where the assumption of heresy is automatic and a self-abasing confession was to be had on demand.[40] The price for facing reality and referring to it in some knowledgeable way, if with hesitation and prudence, can be very high. Kopelev paid for it with a dozen years in the Gulag, and Tulpanov who knew the case of Major Kopelev on the Stalingrad front "intimately" was not likely to make the same mistake.

Even some of the leading German Communists in the Soviet zone—where their political work was mortally handicapped by the phenomenon of "psychic denial," the refusal to confront what one knows, what one has heard and seen—broke through to a measure of candour.

In a story that Wolfgang Leonhard once told me, he had been pressing "one of the highest functionaries in the East" for an explanation of how Moscow could ignore the obvious problems that were upsetting them. It was a private talk some time in 1947, and this particular Party leader had been to the Kremlin on ideological business several times: "But nobody listens to us there…"

"But why can't we speak openly and frankly about things? The Party would be in a position to explain and thereby to distance itself from 'errors…incidents…difficulties…' Otherwise we'll be bruised beyond recognition!"

The high functionary hinted that he had made such an attempt, and directly with Stalin.

"Stalin answered with an old Russian proverb: 'There is a black sheep in every family.'…And then when we pressed on and emphasized the consequences, Stalin interrupted: 'I will not allow the Red Army's honor to be dragged through the mud!' and that ended the meeting…"

The unnamed functionary was Anton Ackerman,[41] a *Politbüro* member in the Ulbricht-Pieck centre of cadres. He was forced to make a public spectacle of his erratic ways in 1948, in a famous example of "Bolshevik self-criticism"; he was subsequently demoted, disgraced, pensioned off. But before he died (and he was lucky to have had a natural death) he was, in the new post-Khrushchev critique of Stalin's irresponsible ways, "rehabilitated."

Looking back I feel more than ever convinced how unprepared we in the West were for every move that Stalin made in the Cold War for power in Europe. His absolute authority had already established itself in the so-called 'People's Democracies,' a concept which doubly emphasized the people in a pleonasm that was revealing in its very philological fraudulence. Actually, the masses were being everywhere disenfranchised; and the local Parties responding with fulsome gratitude to Kremlin leadership, consolidated their power. The February 1948 *putsch* in Czechoslovakia, defenestrating Jan Masaryk (and liquidating whatever hopes for a liberal democracy his father, President Thomas Masaryk, had helped establish), completed the pattern of control by which Stalin's eastern empire was being extended.

The Soviet-occupied zone of Germany was, in this context, anomalous. For some three years one had to operate, to a certain formal extent, within the Allied framework of the Four-Power agreements. In 1946 by short-sightedly allowing genuine all-city free elections the Soviet military administration (and its political agency, the SED party) had suffered an embarrassing popular defeat. In 1947 the various "front" organizations they had created for more effective mass-control—puppet non-Communist parties to hold in check the Liberals and Christian Democrats in the post-War political community—were proving troublesome as men like Jakob Kaiser, a strong-willed Christian socialist who had been in a Nazi concentration camp, emerged as a recalcitrant leader who could not be persuaded, intimidated, or corrupted.

I have never been able to discover precisely how Soviet policy was made, and how new guide-lines were formulated for Germany. For this "decision-making-process" historians have few documents, and almost no first-hand memoirs. We know in the West who picked up the hot-line transatlantic telephone, who dictated urgent messages to the scrambler in Washington, who initiated major memos in London, why a Rooseveltian or Churchillian directive had been rescinded, whether an Allied recommendation was made "in the field" or a peremptory order had come down from on high. Colonel Tulpanov's great historic moment, at once a high point and a turning point, came in the spring of 1948.

Spring in 1948 was a mysterious season, and neither then or now do we know whether Stalin issued a *ukase*, or Molotov, or perhaps Zhdanov formulated a resolution, or whether that man for all seasons, Colonel Sergei Tulpanov was pleased to find himself implementing his own recommended "change of line" which, as a good Bolshevik, he knew could only advance the momentous struggle.

On one occasion he spoke for six hours, in fluent German and for the most part extemporaneously, to an assembly of Party functionaries. He spoke after Ulbricht who had already hinted, in his allotted five hours, that changes were about to be made. The Party would assume effective complete State power, even if a couple of extra parties would be created. (He mentioned, with a touch of sarcasm, a new Peasants *Bund*, although every acre of land had been expropriated—and a shocking new party to win over "old Nazis", the National-Democratic party; and both would serve to undermine the popular support for the two existing "bourgeois" parties.) Obviously the time was not yet ripe for the establishment, in accordance with the logic of history, of a One-Party State.

I listened to Ulbricht's speech carefully (and it was, as ever, a trying experience because he had an ear-grating Saxon accent, at once nasal and throaty and, to boot, pronunciation-twisting). I never thought much of the self-advertised Marxist-Leninist training of Ulbricht and his cadres, and here again they seemed to be responding to (and being battered by) "practical difficulties." Sergei Tulpanov was the back-up to supply the theory.

I would dearly love to look at the *Protokoll*—perhaps it is in his "personal archive" of which Tulpanov later revealed himself to be so proud—but I have it from Wolfgang Leonhard who attended the six-hour briefing that he had a manuscript in his hand but mostly "spoke freely" and extemporaneously. The comrades were reassured. The "people's democratic revolution" had a "double character" (i.e. national and democratic), and one fine day, ineluctably, inevitably, in the final analysis, it would issue in the ultimate socialist revolution.

I have been poring over the texts of the day, and such dialectical gobbledy-gook preponderates. If it had all been spoken in medieval

Latin, it would have been as effective, its aim being to bless yet another change in the party line, which would duly be greeted (except for restless, unhappy young Leonhard) by unanimous enthusiasm from the faithful. The new theory was that the dictatorship of the proletariat need not be the result of a revolutionary act but could come about by the systematic extension of the People's Democracy. The revised practical implication behind the facade of ideology and metaphysics was to prepare for the Blockade of Berlin.

The whole of Eastern Europe—and Tulpanov ran through the Stalinist progress-report in Yugoslavia, Bulgaria, Czechoslovakia, Romania and Hungary—would be looking forward to a victory in Germany, for energetic and vivacious Berlin always exercised a magnetic attraction for European revolutionaries. With its Prussian efficiency, its hard-work ethos, its science and technology, the prospect of its becoming the Marxist-Leninist heartland would raise the hopes of building a truly scientific socialism: not backwardly "in one country" but universally in a triumphant world-revolution.

If the Blockade forced the retreat of the Western Occupation powers—and what other purpose could the Blockade have except to fulfil this devoutly-to-be-wished ejection of the hegemony of U.S. monopoly-capitalism?—the Empire would be solidly ensconced in the heart of *Mittel-Europa*. If the risings of the militant forces on the Left in both France and Italy were to enjoy similar victories, who would not be (in Stalin's classic phrase) "dizzy with success?" There would be no further nonsense of a *Sonderweg*, of different paths to socialism in various countries. It was a favourite idea of a few romantic German dissenters who saw in Moscow the inadequacies of the Russian Revolution and were convinced that from Berlin a new and better path would emerge. The Colonel put it bluntly: they were all in this together, a unified bloc under Soviet Russian leadership, and there was no place for national vanities or egoisms.

At the end of Tulpanov's rhetorical efforts there was the conventional and deferential vote-of-thanks of the Germans to their Russian mentors. But, as in all great self-confident empires, deference and genuflection sat easily on the imperial satraps. Comrade

Leonhard recorded at the time Colonel Tulpanov's "off-the-record" reply to Comrade Wilhelm Pieck (soon to be the President of the East-German Republic):

> Comrades, it is an honor for me to learn from Comrade Pieck that he has such a high opinion of the Soviet Occupation power. But I still would like to say that the Soviet occupying power has committed unbelievably many and serious errors which can, alas, be made good only with difficulty. As a single excuse I can only say that we have not previously had any experience with a socialist occupation. This was something entirely new for us. Perhaps I could say this to you here, the assurance that if in the future one of our enemies forces us yet again to be an occupation force, we will have learned from the German experience and do it all better....[42]

Was he being serious in his peroration, or was he putting on a touch of sarcasm, trying out a bit of humor, always a good sign of high-spirited sovereignty? As Krupskaya once warned Vladimir Ilyich Lenin, "a Bolshevik doesn't tell political jokes!"

What, then, had he been thinking of? An occupation of West Berlin, of indeed of Western Germany, when the Anglo-Americans were pressured to retreat in panic and disarray? Would the French and the Italian Communist parties, under Comrades Thorez and Duclos and Togliatti, still have to call on—as their Eastern counterparts had—the support of Red Army bayonets?

Such catastrophic stategical conceptions, promptly repressed by all except for those few on high, were such stuff as nightmares are made of. There was grimness enough to be getting on with in the little local difficulties which would cut off, in a few months' time, all Allied traffic and supply routes leading to Berlin by road, rail, and waterway.

Wolfgang Leonhard was quick to find the answer to Tulpanov in a little-known pronouncement of Friedrich Engels, to the effect that the victorious proletariat can never impose itself on a foreign people without subverting thereby its own victory.... How could this bit of socialist morality counter the forward march of communist imperialism? The Colonel would not have been impressed.

What did impress him—indeed astonished and distressed him—was the answer General Clay found: a massive and unprecedented "Air Lift" through the three acknowledged military corridors originally assigned to the three Western powers in 1945. It brought him to bay.

13. AN ENDANGERED SPECIES

Tulpanov lived on. As in the credo of a famous French revolutionary veteran of the 1790s (Abbé Sièyes: "*J'ai vecu*," I have lived on), he was a survivor. He was a witness to the death of Stalin, to the rise and fall of Krushchev's brief adventure into truth-telling, to the stolid consolidation under Brezhnev of the régime he knew and loved. Only once did he venture into the West, nearly forty years after his student days in Heidelberg. Did he sense, during his visit, in the heady atmosphere of the youthful rebelliousness of '68 some late soteriological signs of mass movement that might compensate for the defeats of the past? Marxists at the Free University in West Berlin sent out a call to the Marxists of the Leningrad Academy, and he came: with no medals, no uniform (although he had a Major-General's rank), but in a natty summer-style suit, and a dull manuscript which encapsulated all the routine compromises with truthful analyses, with *glasnost*, that were required of even old and privileged men of that day. It scarcely made a difference to the '68 rebels, for their rebellion was against their own Western establishment and the West's enemies were, presumably, their friends.

The atmosphere of the Free University had deeply changed from the libertarianism in the founding year 1948—when student victims of the Tulpanov-Dymschytz totalitarian line in the Humboldt University in East Berlin had appealed to General Clay to establish an alternative institution in the West. For all the celebrated new critical spirit among the young there was no one who rose to ask a challenging question of the man who symbolized Stalin's blockade of the city and the notorious attempt to starve West Berlin into political submission.

Still, the famous Russian soldier who had sought to extend Lenin's revolution to Germany at the point of the Red Army's bayonets set no young minds alight. Nobody could come away from listening to his tired, lifeless theses about the immanent evils (and hence imminent collapse) of monopoly capitalism and the doomed whole of late-bourgeois society without a sense of *déjà vu* and *déjà lu*.[43] There was no fresh phrase, nor even an ambiguous word in the spirit of the younger Tulpanov, to suggest that the heirs of October Revolution were anything but a reactionary and repressive force in Europe. Nonetheless a full auditorium applauded in the rhythmic manner to which the Commissar had been accustomed. An abstract ideologized curiosity about a central figure in "ancient Berlin history" was appeased. A few university professors were enthusiastic enough to express high hopes for further "friendship with the spirit of Leningrad."

But reigning in this time was only the spirit of 'stagnation'; and the Commissar, long since disabused of his aggressive front-line activism (at least on the frontiers of East and West Berlin), had nothing new to report. Except that, if capitalism was still achieving productive accumulation, it was only hastening its ultimate demise; and that if the situation of the prospering working-class in bourgeois societies was continuously improving, it only proved that the class struggle was having results…and heading inevitably, for final victory.

For all this soporific scenario he otherwise seemed alert, and evidently followed the Manpower statistical bulletins from Washington, the *Bundesbank* reports from Frankfurt, and the columns of the London *Economist* (although this kind of material can be, and usually is, serviced by a staff of research students). Nothing appeared to have shaken his faith, to have "contradicted" Marxism, and in a somewhat charming aside he said that he actually enjoyed the arguments from "Western prosperity" as an alleged refutation—for they clearly presaged (as the dialectic would have it, wouldn't it?) the beginning of the end.

His last words were the credo of his life: "*das kapitalistische System zu liquidieren,*" liquidate the capitalistic system.

Yet the real point of his life, with all the due dialectical ironies, was to contribute to the failures and thereby the gradual liquidation of the Stalinist system which he loyally, if with occasional colorful human eccentricities, had served.[44]

After the lecture Sergei Tulpanov and his deferential University hosts, so proud of a new "Berlin-Leningrad educational exchange program," retired into the club room for refreshments. Alas, I was not invited for the occasion and the accompanying pleasantries. But I have it from my old friend, Alexander Osacyk-Korab, that at least for a tense minute or two at the bar, over a glass of wine, one direct and thoroughly embarrassing query was put (as Korab winsomely phrased it to me) "on your behalf."

"Looking back, General, wouldn't you think that your blockade of Berlin, having been evaded by the ingenious airlift, was an utter failure?"

"Well, don't all governments make mistakes?"

"But mistakes, if they proved embarrassing or distasteful to the *Vozhd*, to Stalin, were usually paid for in the usual Stalinist way of the day. How did you, when you were summoned back to Moscow in 1949 in a time of great Kremlin fury, manage to save your own head?"

Korab, who had risked his own head as a dissident in the Soviet Union, was clearly overstepping academic "protocol" in the new comradeship between East and West which the University Revolt of '68 tried to make fashionable. General Tulpanov could have sought help and supper from his fellow-Professors all round him. He preferred to grin and bear it.

"Well, if you must know, Semyonov put in a good word for me...."

One couldn't know with him, now or ever, whether he was being playful or cynical or, in fact, admitting some things that had never been conceded before. Ambassador Semyonov had superseded him as the pro-Consul of the Soviet-German satellite when it became formally a separate state, the *Deutsche Demokratische Republik* (DDR). He was Stalin's new man, and might well have interceded on behalf of his predecessor, and saved Tulpanov's head: if only for insurance to cover his own head in case of political misfortune.

Like some ancient paleolithic monsters, fearsome in physique and short on mental resources, hence unable to cope with difficult changes in the challenging climate around them, the Commissars years became an endangered species in the post-Brezhnev, and were to survive only in a few anomalous anachronistic examples.

A Tulpanov and Dymschytz, and surely even a Becher and Hermlin, would have been consigned by the new ideologues of a Gorbachov/Sakharov era of *glasnost* to a hateful, ignominious type of scavenger in a prehistoric Russian jungle. Political evolution, bringing with it changes in antediluvian customs and mores, domesticated the primeval violence and softened the barbaric cries and noises.

I now meet and talk—in East Berlin, as well as in Warsaw, Budapest, and Moscow—with the offspring of the old species of Commissars, with the successor generations whose ancestral fathers and grandfathers are at long last becoming extinct. They seem to me to be other creatures altogether.

ENDNOTES

1. *"UHRI, UHRI!"* ("you watcher, you watcher"), was common parlance for the Russian soldier's demand to every civilian he encountered in the spring and summer of 1945 to surrender all valuables, especially their wrist-watches, forthwith.

   After the end of the War a huge black market developed, with hundreds of thousands of wrist-watches changing hands. Each time-piece brought two-to-three hundred dollars in U.S. scrip, and even more if they were "Mickey Mouse watches" with some colored decoration on the dial. The U.S. scrip payments to shrewd G.I. traders were legal tender; for the currency plates had been lent by the U.S. Secretary of the Treasury (Henry Morgenthau, full of good will) to the Soviet Military Administration in order to pay its victorious armies in Germany what was owing to them in back pay. Thus, the Red Army's payroll, laundered via the Black Market (mostly in Berlin, and the Tiergarten, became a grand, crowded, East-West bazaar!), was a deficit draft on the U.S. Treasury which was estimated to amount to tens of millions of dollars.

Next to the obsession with watches among the Red Army's front-line conquering troops, the demand was for women to "Come along!"—thus, *"Komm mit!"* became short-hand slang for rape.

2. TULPANOV'S WORDS. *"...Daher die Erbitterung, daher die Excesse einiger Soldaten und Offiziere unserer Armee in jenen Tagen. Es waren Vergehen von Menschen, die durch vier Kriegsjahre gegangen waren, die vier Jahre unter dem Eindruck der Greueltaten standen, die Deutsche an den Angehörigen dieser Soldaten auf sowjetischen Boden verübten.... [Nur] die an anti-sowjetischer Hetze interessiert sind, reden heute noch von 'Uhri, Uhri'...."* etc. Radio Berlin (Ost), 3 May 1948.

3. ERIK REGER. In his *Tagesspiegel* (Berlin), see the articles, "Oberst Tulpanov und die Eroberung Berlins" and "Salz in die Wunden", 4 May 1948.

4. I refer to him as Colonel which he then was; but some years before he died (February 1984, in Leningrad) he had been promoted to Major-General.

5. TULPANOV, JEWS, NAZIS. I am citing here Rudolph Reinhardt who has recorded his experiences in *Zeitungen und Zeiten: Journalist im Berlin der Nachkriegszeit* (1988). Among the others I refer to my friend and close collaborator (until his premature death in 1963) Henri Johansen. Under the name of Ernst J. Salter which he took on leaving the East for the West and thereby "breaking with communism", he was an important opinion-maker in post-War Berlin.

6. Which could also mean, depending on the inflection, that it was utterly senseless to pursue that line of thinking.... I surmise Tulpanov meant a bit of both notions of futility and folly.

7. EINSIEDEL. My account of his relationship with Colonel Tulpanov is based on my conversations with him, after his defection to the West, and checked against his own published diaries in his *Tagebuch der Versuchung* (1950). This "diary of a temptation" was re-published in 1985 with only minor corrections.

It also includes an argumentative afterword in which Count Einsiedel attempts to defend himself and his youthful decisions against West-German critics who have never accepted "the aristocratic adventurer's rationalization" of his "treason"—as well as the defections of Field-Marshal Paulus, General von Seydlitz, and others who joined Moscow's "National Committee for a Free Germany." (Indeed they have never been recognized by official anti-Nazi circles as honorable "resistance fighters".)

Commentators have also belabored him for his naive collaboration with Soviet plans to foist the Ulbricht régime on to East Germany—and, if Stalin had been lucky or more skillful, on to all of Berlin and the West. In his polemical reply, the former Luftwaffe ace stands his ground valiantly, but he was never as good in politics as in the air.

In one of General Tulpanov's periodic visits to East Germany, in 1967, he paid tribute to his "team", consisting of the Communist (Friedrich Wolf) and the Nazi (Lt. von Einsiedel) in the last year of the War. He confessed that although Wolf, of course, played "the 'leading' role *(die führende Rolle)*" this strategem helped to take Ulbricht's comrades out of their isolation—they were no longer *Einzelgänger* nor "Bolshevik agents" but, as he preferred to believe, apparent German patriots in a national movement.

As for Einsiedel's defection Tulpanov spoke contemptuously of the man who deserted to the West for a life in Western night-clubs, *"ein Graf aus der Nachtkneipe."* Einsiedel countered: "Being a life-long drunk on the hooch of Marxism-Leninism-Stalinism is worse than all the cases of Western alcoholism...."

See Sergei Tulpanov, "Friedrich Wolf—Soldat und Dichter des Roten Oktober" in *Neues Deutschland* (East Berlin), 3 November 1967, p. 6.

8. TULPANOV'S EXPLANATIONS. For the texts of the quotations, see Sergei Ivanovic Tjulpanow, Gedanken über den Vereinigungsparteitag der SED 1946, in the East German *Zeitschrift für Geschichtswissenschaft* (Jhrg. 18, 1970), pp. 617–625.

> *Wenn auch offiziel in den Dokumenten des Parteitages nichts davon steht, dass zu den ideologischen Grundlagen der Partei die Anerkennung der Leninschen Revolutionstheorie gehört, so waren faktisch alle Erfolge der SED damit verbunden, dass sowohl die ehemaligen Mitglieder der KPD als auch die ehemaligen Sozialdemokraten immer konsequenter die Leninschen Prinzipien verwirklichten, sich von der Leninschen Theorie der demokratischen und der sozialistischen Revolution leiten liessen.*

9. FRITZ RASP (1891–1976). The connection with Ilya Ehrenburg began when he played one of the starring roles in G.W. Pabst's *Die Liebe der Jeanne Ney* (1927) based on the novel by the Russian writer then living in "exile" in Paris. Rasp who was an actor in Max Reinhardt's theater also played leading film roles in Fritz Lang's *Metropolis* (1927); in *Emil und die Detektive* based on Erich Kästner; and in *Die Dreigroschenoper* (1931), also directed by Pabst, based on Brecht-Weill, and starring Lotte Lenya and Carola Neher.

10. GORBACHOV'S SALESMEN. For an analysis of the various Kremlin approaches to 'agit-prop' as an influence in Soviet foreign policy, see: Melvin J. Lasky, "The Cycles of Western Fantasy", in *Encounter* (London, February 1988), pp.3–16, reprinted in *On the Barricades and Off* (1989), pp. 24, pp. 438–476.

11. DYMSCHYTZ REPEATS. I refer to the posthumous anthology by Alexander Dymschytz, *Ein unvergeßlicher Frühling* (East Berlin, 1970), pp. 190ff.

12. UNFORGETTABLY GRATEFUL. The remarkable tribute of various German Communists to their Soviet control officer is in *Alexander Dymschytz: Ein Lebensbild: Wissenschaftler, Soldat, Internationalist* (hrsgb. Ziermann and Baierl, East Berlin, 1977).

What is eerie about the formalized affection which suffuses these pages is that those close and 'indestructible' bonds of socialist friendship were forged in the Stalinist years of terror between 1945 and 1949—and, if in that time, any one of these writers and politicians had disappeared, suffered arrest, been accused, or denounced, or otherwise come to harm,—as so many others in these circles had been!—no one would have uttered a word or regret or protest...not even had it been the Internationalist-Scientist-Soldier himself, Alexander Lvovich Dymschytz, possibly linked darkly to the "Plot of the Jewish Doctors" which obsessed Stalin in those years. The "glittering personality" would overnight have become an Orwellian un-person.

13. GOEBBELS. The quotations are taken from *Final Entries 1945: the Diaries of Joseph Goebbels* (ed. Trevor-Roper, 1979), pp. 62, 72, 77.

The passages in *Tagebücher 1945: Die letzten Aufzeichnungen* (Hamburg, 1977) are:

> *die Siegeshysterie hat...Stalin augen-blicklich völlig mit Beschlag belegt. Er halte das Seydlitz-Komitee bereit, um es evtl. als provisorische deutsche Regierung einzusetzen, wenn sich dazu eine psychologische Möglichkeit biete und er es wagen könnte, die Engländer und Amerikaner so offen zu provozieren. (5. März 1945, S. 123)*

> *(7. März, S. 135) ...Die Hauptsorge (Englands) ist, daß Moskau eine sow-jethörige Regierung, zum mindesten in dem von ihm besetzten Teil Deutschlands, etablieren werde (Stichwort Seydlitz-Regierung) und damit ein kommunistisches, Moskau verbundenes Deutschland entstehen könnte, das nicht nur die Brücke zum kommunistischen Frankreich und Belgien bilden, sondern die politische und weltanschauliche Richtung ganz Europas bestimmen würde.—*

> *(7. März, S. 140) ...Auch die sowjetischen Soldaten seien außerordentlich kriegsmüde; aber sie seien von einem infernalischen Haß gegen allen Deutschen erfüllt, was auf eine raffinierte bolschewistische Propaganda zurückgeleitet werden müsse....*

NB [Lasky's secretary]: I have left Goebbels' compliment to Stalin as "sophisticated", although that word is peculiar to English usage. Goebbels used "*raffinierte*"; and any of the standard dictionary translations would probably be better: "subtle...artful...cunning...crafty."

There is a discrepancy of a day between the dates of Goebbels' diary as published in the German and the Anglo-American edition. As the Editor (Peter Stadelmayer) explained, the original German edition uses the date of Goebbels' dictation; and in the translation "the dates of entries are those on which the events in question occurred..."

14. REVOLUTION AND COUNTER-REVOLUTION. See, for an historical account of this idea of "revolving...rotation...full circle" (and the notion of revolution in Cromwell's day), the chapter in Melvin J. Lasky, *Utopia and Revolution*, on "The Birth of Metaphor." In German: "Die Geburt der Metapher" in: *Utopie und Revolution*, Kap. 4/5.

15. AND PERHAPS BECAUSE OF THAT, THERE IS IN SUCH A CONVENTIONALLY MACROSCOPIC NARRATIVE *History of the Two German States since 1945* BY HENRY ASHBY TURNER (228 PP., 1987), not a single reference to Sergei Tulpanov. In the index Wilhelm Pieck has three, Grotewohl, Ulbricht some 15 references.

Official accounts also chronicle the play without the prince. There is no reference to Tulpanov, for example, in Marshall Zhukov's memoirs. (See: Georgi K. Schukow's German edition, *Erinnerungen und Gedanken* [Stuttgart, 1969]). It was not customary in those Orwellian days for soldiers or diplomats to remember any fact or figure that evoked any true and human (or indeed simply interesting) events in the era of Stalin, and for long decades thereafter. In this sense Sergei Tulpanov's personal book of memoirs has no real mention himself; it is all a fable agreed upon by non-historians. Nor is Tulpanov mentioned in Alfred Grosser's standard post-War history of Germany, *Geschichte Deutschlands seit 1945* (524 pp.)

16. DIETER BORKOWSKI. See his memoirs of his youth as a young East-German Communist—and, before that, a young Berlin Nazi—in his *Für jeden kommt der Tag...* (1983). Informative as he is prolific, Borkowski's other volumes in this series are notable: *In der Heimat, da gibt's ein Wiedersehen* (1984), and an opening autobiographical account of the Third Reich, *Wer weiß, ob wir uns wiedersehen* (1980).

I have already touched on his story in a previous chapter in ("The Cardinal"), for he was imprisoned for many years in the DDR for—among other 'crimes'—reading my Berlin magazine, *Der Monat*; and we later became friends.

MEETING OF JUNE 1945. My notes of the account I have assembled have been checked against the reports by Wolfgang Leonhard in his *Die Revolution entläßt Ihre Kinder* (1955), and especially the various writings of Dieter Borkowski, especially his biography of Erich Honecker (Bertelsmann, 1987), pp. 149–151.

N.B. The German text of Ulbricht's remarks, which should be incorporated into the text verbatim more-or-less (since in conversation the account may differ somewhat from the written version):

> *Die Bezirksverwaltungen müssen politisch richtig zusammengestellt werden. Kommunisten als Bürgermeister können wir nicht brauchen.... Sucht euch zunächst einmal den Bürgermeister. Wenn ihr erst einen Bürgerlichen oder Sozialdemokraten habt, dann werdet ihr an andere herankommen. Und nun zu unseren Genossen. Der erste stellvertretende Bürgermeister, der Dezernent für Personalfragen und der Dezernent für Volksbildung—das müssen unsere Leute sein. Dann müßt ihr noch einen ganz zuverlässigen Genossen in jedem Bezirk ausfindig machen, den wir für den Aufbau der Polizei brauchen...*

> *Ulbrichts Anweisungen gipfelten in der Direktive: "Es ist ganz klar: Es muss demokratisch aussehen, aber wir müssen alles in der Hand haben...*

17. *Die Welt will betrogen sein, daher sei sie betrogen.*

18. FRANZ BORKENAU. He was born in Vienna in 1900, and died in Zurich in 1957. A good friend and a close editorial collaborator, he was among the most brilliant European intellectuals I encountered: surprising, innovative, ebullient.

Borkenau was the author of two very influential books on "Kremlinology":

a *History of the Communist International* (1938; new ed., pref. Raymond Aron, 1962); and his sequel on the development of European Communism, *Der Europäische Kommunismus* (1952). He was, in his earliest intellectual phase, a scintillating Marxist writer, close to the Horkheimer-Adorno school of "Frankfurt sociology" (whose seminars, in its Columbia University emigration, I attended in Manhattan in 1940–42). In that period he wrote a study on the emergence of the "bourgeois world" (in German: *Der Übergang vom feudalen zum bürgerlichen Weltbild* (Stuttgart/Paris, 1934). His little wartime book on Hitler and Stalin, *The Totalitarian Enemy* (1940), is also remarkable; for, if it was not the first, it was among the earliest and most influential usages of the word "totalitarianism" to characterize both the Nazi and Bolshevik régimes. (Hannah Arendt took it as a point of departure for her own book of 1951 on *The Origins of Totalitarianism*.)

A tribute to his intellectual adventurousness was paid by Richard Lowenthal in his preface to a posthumous volume of Borkenau's neglected essays in historiography, edited by Lowenthal both in English and German: *End & Beginning: On the Generations of Cultures and the Origins of the West* (1981); *Ende und Anfang: Von den Generationen der Hochkulturen und von der Entstehung des Abendlandes* (1984).

What also contributed to the seriousness which his topical journalism commanded was a trenchant book on Pareto (1936); a study of the Spanish Civil War entitled *Spanish Cockpit* (1937) which George Orwell told me he very much admired; and a characteristically sparkling volume which was published in West Germany shortly after his return from London in the English anti-Nazi emigration: *Drei Abhandlungen zur Deutschen Geschichte* (1947).

His "Kremlinological" pieces—and his place in the history of *Kreml-Astronomie*—have, alas, never been collected or assessed. Many appeared in *Der Monat*, more in *Ost-Probleme*. The latter was also a magazine project I had proposed—for an objective, analytical review of Communist affairs—and when it was accepted by the Americans the resultant journal (*Ost-Probleme*) later became in English the Washington publication, *Problems of Communism*. I recommended to Manning Williams, the first editor, to take on Dr. Borkenau; and he served as an advisory editor for several years in Berlin, Frankfurt, and Bad Nauheim.

19. BORKENAU QUOTATION. From: *The Communist International* (1938), p. 429.
20. JAMES P. O'DONNELL. The article I cite, "The Stupidest Russian in Europe" (a profile of Col. Sergei Tulpanov) appeared in the *Saturday Evening Post* (Philadelphia, vol. 220, dated 15 October 1949). The *Post* was at the time the largest weekly magazine in the USA)
21. THE OFFICIAL HISTORICAL ACCOUNT. Sigrid Bock, "Literarische Programmbildung im Umbruch. Vorbereitung und Durchführung des I. Deutschen Schriftstellerkongresses 1947 in Berlin." In: *Jahrbuch für Volkskunde und Kunstgeschichte* (Band 22, neue Folge Band 7, Jahrgang 1979), pp. 120–148. The author was identified as a Dr. Phil. of the "Central Institute for Literary Studies" of the DDR's Academy of Sciences.
22. ERNST TOLLER. The text in original is: *"Ich habe an manchen Schriftstellerkongres-*

sen teilgenommen, sie hinterließen als Erinnerung ziellose Debatten, unverbindliche Gesten. Niemand außer einigen Literaten kümmerte sich um sie. Welche Fülle von Kraft und Arbeit hat dagegen der Erste Kongress der sowjetrussischen Schriftsteller gezeigt! Diese Verbundenheit der Schriftsteller mit den Massen, der Massen mit den Schriftstellern und ihren Werken...In diesem Land lebt der ideale Leser...auf dem Boden neuer materieller Bedingungen (nämlich des Sozialismus) wächst eine große, weite, allumfassende Kultur." (q. p. 121, Bock)

23. BECHER IN ZURICH. I wrote an account of this at the time in *The New Leader*, "Thomas Mann's Nietzsche" (1947).

24. ENEMIES, MANIPULATION. For the translator: *"Gegnern...ein leichtes gewesen... gemäß zu manipulieren...zynisch—'Das Fressen geben die Russen und die Ideologie die Amerikaner!'"*

25. INSULT IN AHRENSHOOP. Tulpanov told the story to an German interviewer in 1967. See: S.I. Tulpanov, "Vom Schweren Anfang", in *Weimarer Beiträge* (Heft 5, 1967), pp. 724–32. For the German translator –

> *"Was will dieser Russe hier?"*
> *"Das ist doch ein Mongole, man braucht ihn nur anzusehen, der verfügt zwar über eine gewisse Bildung, aber nicht über wirkliche Kultur."*

26. CULTURAL REVOLUTION. The matter is now only of minor etymological interest, but the concept of Kulturrevolution was actually an integral part of Marxismus-Leninismus as elucidated by the official *sed Institut für Marxismus-Leninismus* in the DDR. See the volume published by the Aufbau-Verlag in 1981 under the title: *"...einer neuen Zeit Beginn: Erinnerungen an die Anfänge unserer Kulturrevolution 1945–1949."*

The theoreticians of the Ulbricht-Honecker eras didn't find it necessary to make any political-historical comparison with the Chinese "cultural revolution" under Mao (who didn't, obviously, confine it to the "literary" matters of the social structure). Now neither the Chinese nor the Germans have any time for such theoretical excursions, at a moment when ideas stemming from a "cultural counter-revolution" (bourgeois-democracy, Western liberalism, etc.) threaten to shake the foundations of their régimes.

I mention this because it reinforces my interpretation of the Tulpanov-Dymschytz-Becher strategy of the Writers Congress as a vague "cultural revolution" which, at the least, would recruit a few more writers for the struggle and, at the most, could "change everything utterly."

27. BECHER SAID, AND TULPANOV REPEATED. This phrase, and all other Tulpanov quotations, are to be found in the only revealing document which he has left behind (except for a few sentences in an otherwise arid book of memoirs)—an East Berlin newspaper article written on the occasion of an anniversary of Johannes R. Becher's death in 1958. It is in *Sonntag* (East Berlin weekly), for 3 May 1965, Nr. 19: "Befreiung des Menschen...Erinnerungen an die Zusammenarbeit mit

Johannes R. Becher. Von Generalmajor Professor Dr. Dr. Sergei Tulpanov", pp. 2–4.

28. PALE, FRAYED MANUSCRIPT. I am grateful to Prof. Dr. Bernd Balzer (of the Free University, Berlin) who gave me his valuable notes made in the Aufbau-Verlag editorial offices.

29. THE ONLY DISSENTER. *"Gegen das Manifest des Kongresses, dem dieses Programm [die Idee der nationalen Einheit und der demokratischen Erneuerung der gesamten Kultur des Landes] zugrunde lag, sprach lediglich ein auf dem Kongreß anwesender Amerikaner."*

In the excitement of the occasion, and the flushed sense that one had won over "minds and hearts" I didn't realize that I was so isolated. There were indeed soft murmurs of support. But Colonel Tulpanov could very well have come away with the general impression that the national intelligentsia stood with him (and his German comrades) all the way.

It was only in the ensuing reaction of the next months, the winter of discontent of '47–'48, that the Commissars sensed that a famous defeat had been suffered.

30. MARSHALL, CLAY. My notes match General Clay's official account (which I helped, in part, to write and edit.) See: Lucius D. Clay, *Decision in Germany* (1950), p. 153.

On the subject of newspapers General Clay wrote that in this domain he had his conviction reinforced of "the German inability truly to understand democratic freedom…" (p. 287).

30. RICARDA HUCH. On her life: Marie Baum, *Leuchtende Spur, das Leben Ricarda Huchs* (1950).

The distinguished Anglo-German historian, Sebastian Haffner—in "Ricarda Huchs Nein", *Zur Zeitgeschichte* (1982), pp. 78–83—pays tribute to her vigorous rejection of the appeal by Gottfried Benn in 1933 for a pledge of loyalty to the new Nazi régime.

Marcel Reich-Ranicki emphasizes that in her 1934 book on German history (*Deutsche Geschichte*, vol. 1) she vividly chronicled the tragic story of anti-Jewish persecutions in the Middle Ages and pointed up to the angry criticism of Nazi reviewers—the "bestiality" which lay deep in the abysses of nation and people, and how in the past it called forth heroic resistance. In: "Ricarda Huch der weisse Elefant", (1955) *Ricarda Huch: Studien zu ihrem Leben und Werk aus Anlass des 120. Geburtstages* (1864–1984), pp. 1–10.

Thomas Mann once called her "the first lady of Germany" (*die erste Frau Deutschlands*), at once a conservative and a romantic radical. Although her books are still kept in print, she is today an almost forgotten figure—undeservedly so, in the light of her literary qualities and sterling political integrity. A great many post-war commentators choose to ignore, or forget, the historic fact that the first open protests against the Soviet occupation authorities came from impeccably anti-Nazi voices. A melancholy, if outraged, dissent is expressed in my critique of the "anti-Anti-Communist" tendency in the Encounter essay (Sept.-Oct. 1983), reprinted in *On the Barricades, & Off* (1988), "Living with an Insult in a Mindless Zone".

And also for the record the following remark by Else Hoppe, in her biography, *Ricarda Huch* (Stuttgart, 1951, S. 915), on the illusion that R.H.'s noble opening words could maintain the fiction of East-West unity:

> *"Es war eine holde Täuschung...denn bereits über die Frage der Gedankenfreiheit wurde der latente Zwiespalt offenbar." (It was a beautiful illusion...since the latent split was already evident on the question of intellectual freedom [Gedankenfreiheit].)*

32. RUDOLPH HAGELSTANGE. Hagelstange has recorded: *"Als dann—nach einer erregten Replik von Wangenheim* [a leading Eastern theater producer]—*Melvin Lasky, der spätere Herausgeber des 'Monat', in gelassener Unbeirrbarkeit über 'Kulturelle Freiheit' sprach und dabei die sowjetische Kulturzensur attackierte, war das Ventil endgültig geöffnet, und von nun an begegneten die beiden Welten in einer Sprache..."* ("After an excited reply by the Eastern theatrical producer Wangenheim, Melvin Lasky who was later to publish *Der Monat* spoke with impertubable calm about 'cultural freedom' and attacked Soviet censorship, thus creating an opening, and from that point on the two worlds could face each other in a common language....") Rudolph Hagelstange: *Menschen und Gesichter* (1982), "Die Dame Löwenherz (Ricarda Huch)", pp. 36–46.

Many years later, some of the East German figures who were present at the first Writers Congress in East Berlin were invited to the West to do "literary readings" from their works. Among them were Anna Seghers and Stephan Hermlin. It was considered "a thaw" which compensated for the parting of the ways in October 1947. On this occasion, a leading front-page article by Dr. Günther Zehm in *Die Welt* (2 January 1965) recalled the debates of '47, over which Ricarda Huch presided, and at which there were "heated discussions between Gunter Weisenborn and Alfred Kantorowicz, W.E. Süßkind and Axel Eggebrecht."

> *"...und auf dem jener denkwürdige Zusammenstoss zwischen Melvin Lasky und dem sowjetischen Kulturmajor Dymschytz geschah, der wie ein Trompetensignal den kalten Krieg anzeigte."*

> *"...and during which occured that memorable collision between Melvin Lasky and the Russian cultural chief Major Dymschytz, which announced the Cold War like a fanfare of trumpets."*

33. "WELL ROARED..." This is one of the many German proverbial phrases that have been adapted from Shakespeare, one of "their" most popular authors. Often they consist of bits of quotation that are rarely cited in English but for some poetical, verbal or other accidental reason, "catch on" and become "proverbial". In this case *"Gut gebrüllt, Löwe!"* arises from *A Midsummer Night's Dream,* (act v, sc. 1, lines 254 and 69): "Well roared, Lion!...Well run, Thisbe!...Well shone, Moon!...Well moused, Lion!...And so the Lion vanished." A thoughtful analysis of the fate of

Shakespeare phraseology in German quotation can be found in *Encounter*, September 1961: Friedrich Walter, "Quoting Shakespeare—in German," pp. 57–60.

34. "WAS THAT WHICH AROUSED YOU / WORTH THE STRUGGLE?...Go to sleep, my heart, it is time. / Cool is the call of eternity."

35. "WRECKED...*zerstört*"...."*die westlichen Gazetten die Meinungsverschiedenheiten der Schriftsteller sensationieren und Lasky zum Helden des Tages erklärten*"...

36. DEEP INTO THE 1980S. Stephan Hermlin, opening the tenth *Schriftstellerkongress der Deutschen Demokratischen Republik* (Berlin, 24–26 November 1987), in *Neue Deutsche Literatur*, vol. 36, Heft 423 (März 1988), pp. 5–8:

> "...*gerade um diese Zeit war der kalte Krieg eröffnet worden, und einer seiner Protagonisten, der amerikanische Publizist Lasky...nützte die Gelegenheit für eine scharfe antikommunistische Attacke.... Wir lebten damals in den McCarthy Jahren, und es war kein Wunder, dass Lasky auch einige deutsche Nachbeter fand. Auch heute noch erreicht uns hier und da das Echo....*"

37. PHILOCTETES' WOUND. It is one of the odd accidents and coincidences of a lifetime that I happened to copy out into my notebook, when I first read the essay in 1940, some passages from Edmund Wilson's "Philoctetes: The Wound and the Bow"—possibly because the idea, as Wilson said at the time, "is dreary or distasteful to the young who like to identify themselves with men of action..." Which I myself did, but at the same time excerpting, in fascination, these themes which have always haunted me.

"Philoctetes remains in our mind, and his incurable wound...recurs to us with special insistence. But what is it that it means?...Sophocles, in the plays of his we have, shows himself particularly successful with people whose natures have been poisoned by narrow fanatical hatreds...The line of Odysseus is one with which the politics of our time have made us very familiar.

'Isn't it base, then, to tell falsehoods?' Neoptolemus asks.

'Not,' Odysseus replies, 'when a falsehood will bring our salvation.'"

See: Edmund Wilson, *The Wound and the Bow* (1940), ch. VII.

38. THE ATTACK IN *SONNTAG* (1989). The *Sonntag* comment was by a Professor Günter Wirth, in the *Sonntag* issue of 25 June 1989. The author was a vice-President of Johannes R. Becher's *Kulturbund* and an intellectual who mixed and mingled in religious circles (the Eastern CDU, Protestant Church activities, etc.)

He once listed as the first among the "decisive (*bestimmende*)" experiences of his ideological life a discussion in Potsdam with Major Alexander Dymschytz. What was 'unforgettable' for him, was the Major's profound distinction "between socialist realism and magical realism" which was (as young Wirth described it) "logical as well as sensitive, polemical as well as understanding (*konsequent wie einfühlend, polemisch wie verständnisvoll*)...." That evening with Dymschytz made him into a true believer of something which he held to be a Christian form of Marxism-Leninism. "*Rational wie emotional wurde dieser Abend für mich zu einem 'Damaskus'.* (Rationally and emotionally that evening put me on the 'road to Damascus'…)" See: Dr. Günter Wirth, "Alte und neue Namen", in …*einer neuen Zeit Beginn* (1981), pp. 583–588.

Dymschytz and Tulpanov had a high conversion rate among the German careerist élite in the early years of the Soviet occupation, and the converts—when, and if, they remained stable and orthodox—appeared to be forever grateful.

39. ARTUR LONDON ON STALIN. I heard him talk in Paris in 1968 when Gallimard publishers welcomed the former political prisoner from Prague and announced the French edition of his memoirs: *'L'Aveu'* (Gallimard, 1968). The English edition is entitled *On Trial* (1972), p. 193; and the German edition: *Ich gestehe: Der Prozess um Rudolf Slanský* (Hoffmann u. Campe, 1970).

40. THE DANGER-ZONE. In the run-up investigations for the so-called Slanský purges in which so many Czech Communists were condemned to death in 1952, it was apparently reported by one of the survivors (the former Deputy Foreign Minister, Artur London) that Anna Seghers as well as Egon Erwin Kisch had been at one time 'subjects of inquiry'.

Was that how close she (and possibly even Brecht) were to falling by the wayside?

Their friend (André Simon, né Otto Katz) was tried in the show trial 'confessed', and was executed. It was he whom Brecht wanted to approach for help in getting from Zurich to Berlin via Prague. Seghers' briefing of Brecht in Paris in 1947 after the East Berlin's Writers Congress induced him to be "careful" when he finally came home. Seghers and Kisch (according to Artur London) were being "accused of associating with Trotskyist intellectuals in Paris…" See: Herbert Lottmann, *The Left Bank: Writers, Artists, and Politics from the Popular Front to the Cold War* (London, 1982), p. 89.

But I think all this is more revealing for the horrid suspiciousness of the time than actual evidence for imminent police action. For one thing, Kisch had died years before (in Prague, 1948); for another the East Germans evidently resisted, as did the Poles, a purge of 'Western-oriented Communists' which was decimating the ranks of the Party élite in Hungary, Bulgaria, Czechoslovakia. The disgraced Gomulka was doubtless destined for a 'show-trial', but the Poles saved him by delaying-tactics; Ulbricht imprisoned or demoted a small handful (Zaisser, Merker, Harich, Ackerman).

It is unlikely that heroes and heroines on the cultural front like Seghers and Brecht were in any real danger. But 'nervous', and even 'frightened', they had every reason to be. Stalin (and his henchmen) to whom they were loyal was, in his last days, absolutely incalculable.

I am grateful to Prof. Eduard Goldstücker, a veteran of the Prague Spring of '68, for discussing these points with me. See his volume of *Memoiren* (Munich, 1989).

41. A HIGH NAMELESS FUNCTIONARY. I have asked my friend Wolfgang Leonhard who was involved in this conversation for permission to identify him. It happened long ago, and in another historical epoch; and he agreed that discretion was 'no

longer on.' Still, the cautious courage exhibited by Anton Ackerman—to be sure, for a few minutes in a long life of duplicity—remains a rare and exceptional feature of German-Soviet behavior in the half-century between Stalin's hey-day (1936) and the present.

42. TULPANOV'S REPLY TO PIECK. This is recorded in Wolfgang Leonhard's classic memoir, *Die Revolution entläßt ihre Kinder* (ed. 1987, Cologne), p. 430:

> *Genossen, es ehrt mich, dass unser Genosse Pieck eine so hohe Meinung von der sowjetischen Besatzungsmacht hat, aber ich möchte doch sagen, dass die sowjetische Besatzungsmacht in Deutschland unglaublich viele und ernste Fehler gemacht hat, die leider nur schwer wiedergutzumachen sind. Als einzige Entschuldigung dafür kann ich nur sagen, dass wir uns vorher mit einer sozialistischen Okkupation noch nie beschäftigt hatten. Sozialistische Okkupation—das war für uns etwas völlig Neues. Vielleicht kann ich hier, in diesem Kreis, die Versicherung abgeben, daß, wenn wir in Zukunft vielleicht noch einmal von unseren Gegnern dazu gezwungen sein sollten, sozialistische Okkupation durchzuführen, wir dann aus unseren Erfahrungen in Deutschland gelernt haben und es besser machen werden.*

There was an English edition of this invaluable book, unfortunately abridged, entitled *Child of the Revolution* (tr. C.M. Woodhouse, 1958).

43. TIRED, LIFELESS THESES. For some newspaper accounts of Tulpanov's Free University in West Berlin, see: *Der Spiegel*, no. 50, 8 December 1969, No. 51, 15 December 1969. Ernst Lemmer, "Bittere Erinnerungen an Tulpanow," *Die Welt*, 8 December 1969. M.L. Müller, "Tulpanow und sein Heil," *Der Morgenpost* (Berlin), 28 November 1969. Alexander Korab, "Wiedersehen in Berlin mit General Sergei Tulpanow," *Der Tagesspiegel* (Berlin), 29 November 1969.

Some of the phrases—and all of the clichés—are in an essay he wrote at that time, expressing in greater detail his views on the Marxist-Leninist dogma of "monopoly capitalism" and its long-awaited disintegration, as prophesied by all the founding fathers. See the volume which he co-edited for the Karl-Marx-Universität in Leipzig, *Karl Marx "Das Kapital": Erbe und Verpflichtung* (Leipzig, 1968). His own contribution was called "Das allgemeine Gesetz der kapitalistischen Akkumulation und die Lage der Arbeiterklasse" (pp. 143–169). He was identified at that time (among "the Authors") as "Doctor of Economic Science (*Doktor der ökonomischen Wissenschaften*)" and holder of the chair of "The Economy of Modern Capitalism (*Lehrstuhl der Oekonomie des Modernen Kapitalismus*)" at the Zhdanov State-University of Leningrad.

The fearsome Andrei Zhdanov, Stalin's fanatical Commissar for Culture, has also long since been "de-habilitated".

44. LOYAL TULPANOV. It comes as no surprise to note in Tulpanov's book on *The Colonial System of Imperialism and its Disintegration* (published in Moscow in 1958, German ed. rev. 1959) that in all the key points of the presentation where, previously, a reference to Stalin would have clinched the argument, here it is

Khrushchev who is quoted a dozen times in the opening pages of the preface and introduction.

For his "respected and valued German readers (*in Hochachtung und Wertschätzung meiner deutschen Leser*)" he added an extra chapter dealing with the "development perspective" of the under-developed countries by which he referred to Afro-Asia "Third World" areas. He was not far-sighted enough to see that, 30 years hence, Chairman Gorbachov would be candid enough to include the USSR (and its Warsaw Pact socialist neighbours) as among the "weak economies" that needed true development.

The last page of the book sums up the thesis of "the inevitable transition from Capitalism to Socialism" and after the first step of revolutionary colonial independent would come "the real liberation" when "the masses would take their future into their own hands." Down with the "Reformist illusions" that there is something called "Asiatic Socialism!" Only Russian Bolshevism could lead the way to the truly radiant future...

This exercise in gobbledygook—as useless, if as exotic, as some corrupt and undecipherable Latin manuscript of the Dark Ages—can be inspected in: S. Tjulpanow, *Das Kolonialsystem des Imperialismus und sein Zerfall* (East Berlin, 1959).

Henryk Skwarczyński

Polly Maggoo

G et out of here!"

"Don't listen to him," Dermot mumbled to me. "He's just saying that. In fact, he likes people. And the more he drinks, the more he loves everybody."

"You're a bunch of blockheads," Danny scowled at us. "And the Irish Americans are the worst. They only come to hear 'When Irish eyes are smiling' and to try real Guinness. That's all they care about."

We were sitting in Polly Maggoo, an obscure but cozy bar on the edge of the Latin Quarter in Paris. I had come here after my meeting with Teacher. It was exactly one week before our next mission to London. Chuck, who arrived at the bar earlier than I, was now drinking beer and talking poilitics with two nice fellows from Éire. As usual, as instructed, Chuck and I pretended ignorance, and, in case of meeting an informer, or somebody from British intelligence, were ready to condemn terrorism and even support Ian Paislay and his ilk.

The place was filling up and there was hardly enough room at

the bar to put down a mug or a glass. We were at the table closest
to the toilet, almost under the poster of a woman with the question
Qui êtes-vous Polly Maggoo? along the bottom edge. It was Maureen's
favorite table. She liked this bar, though she didn't come here as often as Chuck and I did. And she knew Kieran, the bartender. I had
told her that we should spend this evening together, but she refused.
After my last trip to England she became strange. For the first time
she didn't want me to stay in her place overnight. I even thought
she had found somebody. This was Paris, after all, and there were a
lot of men around.

> And alien tears will fill for him
> Pity's long broken urn
> For his mourners will be outcast men
> And outcasts always mourn.

"Have you already been to Père Lachaise?" asked Chuck, quoting the
inscription on Oscar Wilde's tomb.
  "At the stroke of midnight," said Dermot.
  "But the cemetery closes before then," I remarked.
  "We had to hide in a sepulcher," explained Dermot. "This one
even wept," he pointed at his companion.
  "Was he so touched?"
  "Not at all. He cried because he couldn't drink anymore, and
we still had a bottle of whisky."
  "Rubbish," Danny was indignant. "The most we had was a
half bottle."
  Dense clouds of smoke made it difficult to make out the
features of the people sitting around us. At unvarnished oak tables
thousands of words jostled each other in the clamour of clinking mugs,
high-pitched laughter, the hiss of drowing cigarette butts.
  I thought that Danny and Dermot would be perfect students
for Teach. One day he would be lecturing people like me and them
somewhere at an Irish university, maybe even at Trinity College, teaching history, and the lecture hall would be full of real students.

I was also thinking about his tale of O'Donovan. Teacher used our meetings as an opportunity to talk about Éire, but I never knew whether he was trying to strengthen our resolve by stressing our ties to the glorious past and heroic dead, or if his talking on this subject was a part of his character.

"No matter what you say," retorted Chuck. "Jacob Epstein wouldn't have honored you with a monument."

"Who was Epstein?" asked Danny.

"He probably meant Einstein," corrected Dermot.

"The theory of quality!" said Danny triumphantly.

"Relativity! Donkey!" Dermot corrected him again.

"What did they teach you in school?" wondered Chuck.

"And what are they supposed to teach us?" Danny was still aggressive.

"You don't even know who Benvenuto Cellini was."

"You mentioned Einstein, not..."

"It's not important who I was talking about," Chuck interrupted him.

"There's nothing to argue about," I offered peacefully.

"Don't imply that we're fools because you might regret it," Danny warned Chuck.

"Maybe he never heard of the fellow you mentioned, but he could have told you about General Maxwell," Dermot hadn't finished yet.

"Who was General Maxwell?" now Chuck was surprised.

"And he told us his grandparents came from Ireland," Danny mocked him.

"Let's not talk about it," I still tried to change the direction of our discussion. "American schools are not much better, if at all."

"You came straight from the States?" Dermot swallowed the bait.

"We're on our way to Normandy," Chuck evaded the question.

"Are you going to Ireland?" asked Dermot. "There's a ferry from Cherbourg."

"Maybe to Belfast, but going there seems rather risky," Chuck was a little provoking.

"Go to Dublin," said Danny. "Go pray for the souls of your grandparents and ask for forgiveness in front of the GPO."

"I have family in Belfast," Chuck developed the skills he had mastered during hitchiking.

"How are they doing?" asked Dermot.

"Well, I think, but they complain about terrorists," continued Chuck.

"Who are you calling a terrorist?" said Danny.

"Brits don't plant bombs in Dublin," noticed Chuck.

"Don't be an ass," Dermot responded. "Eight hundred years of pillaging and killing isn't enough?"

"You're a fanatic."

"And you're talking like some of the whites in South Africa."

"That's right," agreed Chuck, enticing them further and further into his swamp. "People who live in a place for several hundred years have a right to the land."

"And hang all the blacks?" asked Dermot politely.

"England brought them civilization, as it did to Ireland."

"With the spontaneous support of the rest of the population like in 1846?" Danny laughed harshly.

"One more myth," Chuck shot back. "It's enough to look at statistics. If not for England's help, the losses would be…"

"Help? He, he!" roared Danny. "Statistics? Check the Britannica. You will find Great Falls or the Great Fire of London but not one word about the Great Famine. And we're talking about more than one million dead! Today we would call it a crime against humanity."

"Call it anything, but you can't constantly be involved in the past," objected Chuck.

"Frankie Hughes and Bobby Sands are not the past."

A fight broke out at a table between the front door and the bar. Kieran, doubling as a bouncer, quickly shoved the two combatants outside where they faded into a crowd. Peace descended on faces yellow in the light of the Chinese paper lantern over the bar.

"They were armed when they were taken, weren't they?"

"In that case we should imprison every British soldier in Belfast or Derry," Danny announced.

"And he insists he's not an extremist," Chuck directed these words to me.

"Imagine," Danny tried to convince me, "A country at the end of an occupation, when suddenly all of the former supporters of the occupier flock to the most prosperous part of the state and announce that it is now an integral part of the empire that invaded it. Then you would understand how Northern Ireland was established."

"You have a choice," said Chuck. "If a divorce from England is inevitable, then so is bloodshed."

"For all practical purposes this is a war between the British oligarchy and the people of Ireland," added Dermot. "Be sure that most people in England are fed up with the whole thing and would accept unification of Ireland without a second's hesitation."

"Brits want to solve the problem like a certain doctor," Danny turned to Chuck, "who woke his patient after an operation and said, *Listen, son. I have some good and bad news for you. Which would like first?* The patient answered, *The bad. Well,* said the doctor, *we had to amputate both legs. Now here's the good news. There's someone in the next room who wants to buy your shoes!*"

"I don't get it." Chuck didn't even crack a smile.

The two young guys were using all the arguments we could have mustered so well that we could not have done better ourselves. It was too bad we had to pretend to be other than we were, but it was nice to have proof that our efforts were supported by others.

"The British amputated our legs and now they worry about our health," said Dermot.

"Ballantine and ice," I ordered. "Ice on the side, please."

"What's the difference whether you put it in yourself or he does it for you?" Dermot was curious.

"You don't get it," I turned it into a joke. "The whiskey's for drinking, the ice—for my head."

Danny grinned, laughed, snapped his fingers, and started beating the table with his palm. He began alternating a high-pitched giggle with a deeper donkey-like bray, sweeping the bar with his eyes.

Several people at the bar eyed him suspiciously, but the corners of their mouths turned up. In the end all of Polly Maggoo's regulars were laughing uproariously.

The tankard on the tables clattered joyfully and even the most poisoned regained a kind of consciousness. Laughter went right through the haze of smoke cloaking the drinkers.

"Your champion," Chuck addressed the remark to Dermot, "doesn't understand give and take."

"Give and take? Danny laughed. "Every time the Irish had a chance to get something, somebody who believed in give and take appeared. It's a British invention. The partition of Ireland is the consequence of give and take. Till today we're paying for what happened in 1921. Compromise has always been the cause of Irish setbacks. Why don't they ask the young men in Ballymurphy what they think about give and take?"

"You have a romanticized vision of what the civilized world calls terrorism," Chuck insisted. "Criminals can't dictate right or wrong."

"*The New York Times* calls these criminals guerrillas," continued Danny. "And you can't deny the political goals of these, as you put it, criminals, can you? Criminals commit their crimes for profit, don't they?"

"Everyone who uses terror as a tool for political goals is criminal," recited Chuck.

"In this case we should call almost all revolutionaries criminals, including your Washington and our de Valera."

"Baloney," protested Chuck.

"Today—criminals, tomorrow—politicians accepted by everyone," retorted Danny.

"It's enough to look at a map to realize that the island is a single entity," Dermot finished his beer.

"Still, I think the so-called Republicans are mad," added Chuck. "They kill for the sake of killing. Like those innocent tourists slain in Holland. The funniest part is that then the killers apologized for what they did."

"That doesn't mean innocent people should be punished like those accused of the Birmingham bombing," said Dermot peevishly.

"Mistakes in the courtroom are not an exclusively English privilege," noticed Chuck.

"Don't tell me about mistakes," protested Dermot. "Six innocent people spent sixteen years in prison only because they were Irish."

"I'm not sure they were entirely innocent," Chuck shook his head skeptically. "One way or another they were involved."

"In what?" Danny asked furiously.

"In illegal activities."

"Including Judith Ward, who was diagnosed as mentally ill?" Dermot asked with an ironic laugh. "Is that the reason she stayed in prison two years longer than the other accused?"

"I don't know her case, but, believe me, the law should be respected by everybody," said Chuck. "If there is any justice in Northern Ireland it is because British soldiers protect it from plunging into chaos."

"So why are kids throwing stones at armored vehicles?" Dermot asked from behind a cloud of smoke.

"They are raised by fanatics. Kids in America don't do it."

"Maybe the soldiers are simply on the same side of the barricades?"

"Don't talk nonsense. They protect all citizens from anarchy and disorder."

"All? Really?" Danny laughed.

"As long as they respect the law," insisted Chuck.

"Tell me then—why are they fighting, why are people risking prison and torture?" Danny inquired. "Did you ever try to answer this question?"

In my opinion, we were all too emotionally involved in the conversation. I knew that both Dermot and Danny were not members of any underground group, still I was afraid that they were speaking too openly and could face problems, if by chance some undesirable overheard them.

"What kind of tortures are you talking about?" Chuck played his role, like the best actor. "Nobody is tortured in British prisons. The terrorists sometimes inflict wounds on themselves but normal people don't believe those kinds of tricks."

"Read the Amnesty International report on the subject. Published in London," remarked Dermot sardonically.

"Look how the police treat criminals in the States," said Chuck.

"That's not the point…"

"What is the point?" Chuck interrupted him.

"I told you. The point is that England is governed by an oligarchy," Dermot repeated his earlier argument. "Freedom of speech is a myth as well."

"Don't exaggerate."

"It's true that the BBC has the most informative programming in the world," agreed Dermot. "But it's not allowed to have a real discussion about Ireland. I was in America and watched your TV. Sure, you enjoy freedom of speech but never in my life had I seen such garbage. The news programs are for idiots."

"But there is no censorship," Chuck stated calmly. "And I'm not saying that America is perfect."

"Perfect?" laughed Dermot. "Your cities need martial law."

"The economy is behind it," Danny started.

"Behind what?" I asked.

"The fights in Ireland and the problem of unification."

"What do you mean?"

"We would like to unify the economically poor part of the island with the rich part."

"Say what you like, but one thing is certain—British settlers built the country; without them you would still be living in bogs," said Chuck.

"You don't feel somebody is responsible for the centuries of occupation?"

"I'm telling you the British brought order and imposed the law. Otherwise, Irish landlords would have killed each other and the peasants the same. Even faster."

"Crap!" Danny almost howled. "Explain to me why the Irish Republic still doesn't have a proper fleet, even though it's an island. Or name all the occasions through the centuries when English settlers confiscated land from the Irish. That's what's wrong with the economy."

"Without civil disobedience the economy would flourish in Northern Ireland," said Chuck.

"Disobedience?" Dermot laughed again. "You already have a full-scale war. For civil disobedience you wouldn't need armored cars, thousands of soldiers, barbed wire, helicopters, death squadrons, and God only knows what else."

"Death squadrons?"

"What do you call the killing of three defenseless people in Gibraltar?"

"You're contradicting yourself." Chuck chose his argument. "You said that we have a war and soldiers are killed when they fight wars. Those three were terrorists, weren't they?"

"You don't kill unarmed soldiers."

"We're back at the starting point," remarked Chuck perfectly cool. "They were terrorists and were treated as such."

"Only drinking is eternal," I said, trying to conciliate, because, despite the alcohol, I felt that we shouldn't continue our talk.

"Where did you read that?" asked Dermot.

"Why did I have to read it anywhere? I just know it. Isn't that enough?"

I looked again at the bar and all the thirsty fellows gathered there, and I thought about how this was one of the places that has no time for prayer, where everything looks like the peasant's wedding Bruegel's painting: mugs of beer raised high, the interested glances of women, the look of Polly Maggoo, and a poster from 1888 saying that a certain train goes to London, and I wished it would all last forever.

"There must have something wrong with the onion soup I ate today," Chuck complained, understanding my attempt to change the subject. "It didn't look good. I swear I never ate anything nastier in my life."

"What soup?" Danny's eyes looked suddenly alert.

"You drowsed through it." Chuck tore open a new pack of

cigarettes. "We're talking about a certain Aussie whose hormones went crazy and everything he ate his body distilled into alcohol. He ate a few sandwiches, and he could barely stand. He put away a cake and was instantly groggy. Finally his skin broke out in red patches. He raced to a doctor who looked at him, leaned back in his chair, and said, *Keep drinking, sir, keep drinking!*"

"Did he listen to the doctor?" asked Danny.

"Hell, no." Chuck felt around for his lighter. "Before then the fellow rarely drank, but then he had a nervous breakdown and he really started sloshing it down."

Somebody with a face like Maureen's appeared at the door and looked around. Déjà vu. When I looked again the girl, or Maureen, had disappeared. The shadow standing at the door had blended into the darkness.

"We'll call you Oliver," announced Danny suddenly. "Cromwell liked our country the same way you do, though I'm afraid you chose the wrong Ireland."

We were not doing too badly, because we were still talking. Though I had once noticed that this second wind sometimes blew me into a kind of oblivion and in New York all too often afterwards I had to put a patch on my nose, a splint on my finger, bandages on my ears, not remembering a thing. But while it was happening, I could repeat every word, every gesture, and never felt the catastrophe approaching, and even when it happened in seemed to me that it was only a coincidence. And now was not much different.

"Where's our whisky?" Danny became uneasy.

"You've had enough," Kieran warned us. "We're closing."

"I don't like that fellow," mused Danny aloud.

"We can continue in the Studio on rue du Temple," Chuck unexpectedly offered.

"We've heard about that bar," Dermot seconded.

"Forty two beers and sixteen Calva," Kieran counted them quickly. "Are you paying for everything, or...?"

"One more round," demanded Danny.

"You're leaving," Kieran informed him kindly.

"Only *Oglaigh n hÉireann* is right," mumbled Danny in response.

It seemed to me that we were all sufficiently smashed.

"We're leaving," Chuck confirmed.

"You said there's a place still open?" Danny asked with renewed interest.

"We've had enough for today," said Chuck who had finally realized that we should continue.

I grabbed my *Gitanes* as we went out and stopped in front of the bar. Regulars were disappearing down various streets of the Latin Quarter. It was a warm Parisian night.

Then we walked in silence, looking ahead, thirsty. It was two in the morning. Not many passers-by were on the streets, and the city seemed empty, almost uninhabited. We passed Kilometer Zero, and Chuck led the caravan toward Notre Dame. I was quite tired and felt as though Chuck and I were in the desert and my companions wanted to leave me, and on my face I felt the wind and the blinding power of sand.

"This is not the Sahara," Danny said and stopped. "Something has to be open in this city. It is Paris, isn't it?"

I heard him and imagined that soon I would obliterate their footprints and the night would devour them, and while I was thinking about it, I saw that they were attacking Chuck. I felt fury race through my veins. I saw their contracted faces and the fear in their eyes. I hit somebody and saw that Dermot's face was stained with blood. I was winning, I was winning, I was winning. All of a sudden, I felt like a windmill batting and pummeling the air.

"If you keep on like that, I'll kill you." It was Danny who said that, hitting my face hard with his fist, but after all that had happened I didn't even feel it. I only heard a dry crack like the sound of a splintering nut.

"You're crazy," I tried to spit out through split lips.

"Do you hear him?" Danny asked Dermot, who was standing next to him. "He says we're crazy."

"You're stupid bastards," I mumbled bending over in a bow.

"We're stupid bastards," Danny repeated and hit me with all his strength in the stomach. I sank to the ground.

"You don't remember what I told you," said Dermot. "He really likes people. And the more he drinks, the more he loves every fellow creature."

Then Danny—I saw his cowhide boots distinctly—kicked me, and for the first time I felt pain and also a sweet taste in my mouth. I knew that it wasn't the end, and in the morning I'd be tired, and a glass of Bushmill might help me sweat it out till noon, and then I'd meet Chuck and we'd laugh about everything that had happened.

Then silence prevailed, and finally I heard Chuck.

"Where am I?" he moaned.

"In Paris," I informed him kindly.

Our assailants had melted into the darkness, but I lay unmoving. Chuck was on the ground nearby. The moon was full, and it was pleasant to watch clouds drifting across its placid countenance.

"No details," he wheezed out. "What's the country?

"Totally unsuitable for a member of an underground army," I sneered as he stood up and carefully felt his face. "It's too easy to surprise you."

"I'll find them."

"Sure," I said. "They'll be waiting for you at the Studio."

"I'll find them," Chuck repeated. "Even if I have to search all of Ireland."

"You have an appointment at the Studio, so don't worry. Now at least I have a topic for a good short story: Irish life in exile! Free public reading!"

"They won't come to the Studio."

"Why not?

"They know that we won't be such pushovers a second time."

"I'm not in this," I said. "I'm fine and besides that they're nice guys."

"And that's why you're flat on the sidewalk?"

"I like to rest," I stretched comfortably. "I'm taking a moon-bath."

"Is that why your face is red?"

"It's the light of the moon."

"What are you talking about?"

"Don't worry," I calmed him down. "News of the world usually reached the Celts late, even if it happened in Ireland."

"You're really a jerk," Chuck smiled wryly. "Come to the Studio tomorrow and remember that Friday we are going to Sebastian."

"I'll drop in at the Studio rather late. I promised Teacher to arrange something."

"Take care."

He walked away. I heard his steps distinctly in the silence.

ON THE ART OF FLYING

"We touched on a few important subjects yesterday."

"I would think so too, if I could remember what they were," said Chuck, looking at the clouds drifting in from the north.

It was our third day together in the flat in Turnham Green, the place we usually stayed. Every morning I removed the cover from my portable typewriter and poked at the keys, as Chuck immersed himself in his favorite book, Desmond Seward's *The Monks of War,* but around noon we would go to the store to buy lager. That would kill the writing for another day.

Tomorrow we were going to be in the City where Teacher would give us final instructions, though we already knew all the details. We knew the area and were familiar with the routine things that took place on the street where we were supposed to carry out the operation.

On the way to the store I told Chuck that Josephine was coming to Paris the following week. She had finally put her affairs in New York in order and asked me to pick her up from the airport.

"Does she know that Maureen is in Paris?"

"Not yet, but it's just a matter of time."

"Does Maureen accept the fact that you don't want to marry her?"

"She used to ask me what was more important to me—to be with her or to write. I said, to write, but I meant my duties in the Army."

"You were honest. We have more important things to do. If you have any doubts, go to Dublin and find your birthtree, your place in the grand scheme of things. Watching the tree grow, you'll make peace with your own fate. You'll also have time to think about the origin and meaning of your mother's roots and your own. It's the only way to figure out where you come from."

"Is it part of our nature to hold a rose in our hand and then cut the hand off?" I said, thinking about my relationship with Maureen. "When I'm with Maureen I sometimes forget about adventures and want only to be with her, and sometimes I simply think that I don't know what I want."

"You have to go somewhere, otherwise, you'll never understand the reason for being in this world. Go back to Dublin."

"You think Teacher would let me go?"

"Maybe not right away, but he would. Your assignment is not for the continent, so I don't see any real obstacle to the journey."

We left the store and headed for our apartment. It was noon and still wet after the rain. The clouds gathered above London meant more bad luck for street drunks. The wind whirled sand like a propeller and scattered paper bags all over the street. Our place was a real Bed & Breakfast and had a real owner, so the neighbors were accustomed to guests. By "real" I mean that it was managed by our man. And surely nobody suspected that among the visitors were people like me and Chuck.

At the first sign that somebody was showing an interest in our presence we were supposed to leave the place and never appear there again.

The good thing was that we both spoke American English because many people became suspicious if they heard an Irish accent. The flat wasn't far. Chuck always stressed "flat" in our talks because that usually provoked other comments about the language. In our living room among the old books and other odds and ends was a painting of a woman's face distorted by madness. It was twisted in a gargantuan guffaw, as it peered in the abyss.

I imagined the painter at work. It was probably the picture of his own soul and his own hysteria. Something about it had bothered him after he thought he had finished it, like a fly buzzing around an ox's tail. One night he woke up and instinctively pained a yellow frame around the inside edge of the canvas, like Michelangelo who had leaped from his bed to remove one of his *Faun's* teeth. "Now my madness is locked in," the artist probably muttered.

"I'm not able to write one genuine sentence," I said, and it was true because my old dreams about writing and becoming a writer were nothing compared to life here and now. My situation was like a story Chuck told me and Maureen in Greenwich Village about a would-be writer who hanged himself in jail.

I had never wanted to be a politician, or an architect, or a lawyer because I thought that only an artist could be master of his life, but then somehow I got involved in politics and action, and now I wasn't sure if I liked it.

"Don't worry about it," Chuck comforted me. "Go find your birthtree."

"And then join the Crusaders? I've done that already."

"Rely on your intuition. Remember Jonathan Swift's words that when a true artist appears in the world all the dunces are in confederacy against him. The same thing happens when you fight for a 'Cause'. People never accept you while the struggle is in progress."

"Swift's saying was about an artist, not a fighter."

"One day you will become a writer and you'll have to remember everything that happened around you. You have to filter it out from the chaos. You are a barbarian, naive and psychotic. You still convulse with laughter when the Knight of the Woeful Countenance attacks his windmills. Do you remember that movie scene? A girl standing in front of the execution squad takes out her lipstick and applies it meticulously to her lips. That how it should be done. We've got to hang on to our personal dignity to the end or we will drown in the straw sea."

I remembered cigarettes. We turned back to a store managed by young Pakistanis. On the way we passed a bunch of giggling youngsters. Looking at them, I thought that it wasn't good for me to be torn up inside. Besides, I was already an angel of destruction and death.

"You screamed last night," Chuck remarked as if reading my thoughts and took the cigarettes and the change.

"I guess I woke up."

"Still the same images?"

"Yeah, but this time was nothing special. I dived into murky green water. I felt the way I did once when we were on the Hudson River. Somebody looked at the muddy water and said, 'It's a miracle there are no piranhas in it yet.' That's how I felt looking at the water in my dream and trying to get out. Then some parachuters appeared sailing in, I have no idea why, Indian canoes. They were far away but they watched me the same way Teacher did in the camp when I couldn't fix our heavy machine gun during the exercises, my hands were trembling and I was pale as proverbial death. In my dream I tried to swim as quickly as possible but I had the impression that I wasn't moving ahead even one inch."

"You snarled like a dog."

"The guy we met in New York the night I was introduced to Teacher and Kevin told a similar story about a gun that hammed. What happened to him?"

"Who, Seán?"

"I don't remember his name."

"He's in Long Kesh. He was caught but not in action. He was sneaking across the border to the Republic," said Chuck. "They couldn't prove anything, but they didn't release him either."

"Anyway. I still remember the faces of the parachuters from my dream—they had the same sort of look as the painting that hangs in our room."

"You're obsessed with faces."

"The parachuters took me out of the water and screwed me to the large copper board that lay on the riverside. But before I lost consciousness they took out blades and started to cut out my eyes. I couldn't even scream because one of them hit me in the face with a monkey wrench. I came to, spitting teeth. You see, my dreams are much calmer now."

"Yeah, the ones right after your first action were really night-mares. No one could have slept through those. You're emerging."

"I would've preferred to sleep."

"Don't be so sure," Chuck retorted. "We have visitors," he added and then finished his thought, "the art of flying relies on dreams."

I recognized them. I had met Molly at the airport when I came to Paris straight from our training camp. I liked her pixie face and her calm. The man was the middleman between Teacher and us. The first time we met Kevin had been in Greenwich Village. He was quiet and rather taciturn. We didn't greet each other but entered the house together.

In our flat we sat down at the table and started to talk. Discussing the most important things, tomorrow and the action, was forbidden. All relevant information was written on scraps of paper and given to the person for whom it was meant. The paper was then burned. Nobody expected the place to be bugged, but we followed instructions. We were allowed to speak about other things. Even if somebody was listening to us, he would be under the impression that we were having a normal conversation.

I tried to summarize the short story I was working on for Molly, while Kevin gave additional instructions to Chuck and then burned up the shreds of paper on which they had been written.

My story was about two men who lived in the same town in Éire. They were good friends, young and full of dreams. Then they both went to London. One of them started to study at the university. The other took odd jobs, but didn't last. He began to tipple and gam-ble. About then the old friends parted ways not because they wanted to, but because circumstances didn't let them see each other often. The one at the university became a lawyer and, many years later, a judge. In the meantime, his friend got involved with criminals. Finally, he killed a man who had lent him money and been his benefactor for years. The two friends met again. Thirty years had passed since their last meeting. In the beginning they didn't recognize each other, but for the judge it was enough to look into the files to know that he was dealing with his old pal. Many years ago they thought that they knew everything about one another. This time was different.

The accused didn't recognize his former friend who was now bald and round and didn't associate his name with any he had known before. The judge though came home from the first court session and couldn't fall asleep. He remembered his youth, the long strolls and conversations with his friend, their first encounter with girls and first loves. From the deep well of memory forgotten dreams and discussions emerged. When he finally fell asleep in the early hours of the morning, his mind was busy in the labyrinth of the past. The next day he had to go to court again. And again.

Finally, the day came when he was supposed to pronounce the sentence. Because the accused had committed the crime in cold blood the prosecutor demanded the highest penalty for him. Having made up his mind, the judge rose to read the sentence. But before doing it he looked at the accused realized that his old friend had recognize him. He made a desperate gesture, bent his head and all of a sudden...

Molly liked this story, asking me what came next every time I thought I had rounded it off nicely, so I kept trying to improve it, invent new endings. They provided the opportunities to talk and let me believe that maybe I was really becoming a writer. I wasn't trying to send my stories to magazines yet because they were all looking for a story with a "twist" and I hated that. I thought that the story itself was important, not the unexpected oddity at the end. But I also knew that I wasn't a writer yet and the day probably come when I would need to use twists for the edification of a public more interested in the ending of a story than its narration.

While I was talking to Molly and reading her my short story, my mind was still in Paris. I thought about the strolls I had taken to Père Lachaise with Maureen. Sitting on a bench on the hill of the cemetery, we would look at the city and listen to the whispers of Delacroix, resting not far from us. The world was beautiful without all these "great" ideas and without Teacher. I even wondered if one day I would start to hate Ireland and everything connected with it, including my present involvement in the Army. Would I become a writer? And when I was happy with Maureen I always regretted being the willing victim of my "war" that put me on pyres where I immolated myself again and again.

"Nothing's better than a glass of red wine," Maureen would laugh on such days, holding a bottle of Beaujolais. She often wore a red summer dress and matching lipstick. I would stretch out on the bench with my head in her lap.

But now I was in London with other people around me.

Kevin was a published poet, a connoisseur of Dutch painting, and an avid read of the novels of Jorge Amado. There was gossip that Kevin was involved in the action in Brighton. He knew Chuck well and met us sometimes at Polly Maggoo's.

Kevin was shorter than me, though he wasn't a small man, with straight black hair and eyes of the same color. He was Irish, more Irish than anyone I had ever met. With on exception: he didn't drink or smoke at all and was content with a glass of water or apple juice.

Our meeting lasted almost two hours, and then Kevin and the Molly left us. Through the window I saw the first drop of rain. The sound of thunder rolled in from somewhere above the city. I remembered the time Chuck had invited me to Mr. Doherty's Long Island estate. We arrived during a thunderstorm. Greyish-yellow clouds gathered. Then lightning struck with the frequency of machine-gun fire. It stripped one of the trees of its bark in front of our eyes. Doherty's gardener told us that he estimated his employer's assets at around twenty million dollars. Later, we found out that Doherty's financial adviser was the old woman who cooked his sumptuous meals. Everything was reminiscent of *The Great Gatsby*. We would sit on the shore of the stream and wonder why Old Mick discussed his financial investments with his cook. We weren't there by chance. Teacher had sent us to ask for a donation, but the mission was a failure. When we told Doherty what we were up to, he wished us luck, saying that the wonder of America is that there are a thousand different ways for an individual to make money here. He advised us to start work on it right away and not to have illusions about politics. In his excitement he even offered us jobs as gardener's helpers.

The only similarity between then and now was this damned thunderstorm which brought back visions of Doherty's glorious repasts. I wouldn't have mentioned it, but for the fact that there was no food in our flat.

"Hungry?" asked Chuck as if reading my thoughts.

"A little bit," I admitted.

The day before an action we were not allowed to eat because of possible shooting wounds in the belly.

"So, what do you think about a short trip to Dublin?" Chuck put the packs down on something pretending to be a table and coughed, as he inhaled the dust billowing around us.

The storm geared up during the night. Rain pelted the roof of the house. It was pleasant inside, as we drank beer and talked. Chuck's main topic, besides historical books, was crazy artists. He talked about the relationship between their achievements and their madness. Look at them, he said. They tried to understand where we're heading. Schumann and Maupassant. And Swift. And so many others. They were honest. And so what? They left humanity in the same jungle they had found.

We went to bed before midnight not because we were sleepy but because we were following instructions. The street noise woke me around six. Chuck was already on his feet. He was sitting at the table smoking a cigarette. I pulled on my pants and two hours later was on my way to Victoria station.

The train was a bit late. Teacher was already waiting. As we walked out of the station, I had to repeat everything I was supposed to do. It was simple. To change my clothes for a construction worker's overalls in the public toilet on the edge of Hyde Park. Then to walk to a corner where a few minutes later somebody would drive up in a small van. I was to take his seat at the wheel and go—alone—to the place where the explosives were to be detonated. The special time-detonator would be hidden under the dashboard. It would be enough to pull out the headlight knob and leave the area within minutes.

In case something unexpected happened, it would still be possible to push the knob in and thwart the explosion. If everything went all right, I was to turn left at the first corner, where I would be picked up by Chuck. In the car I would change clothes and go with him to Dover. Somehow the ferry seemed safer to us than a plane, since control of the airport was probably stricter, once all ports of departure had been alerted.

I repeated the principle to remember in case of arrest: Say nothing, sign nothing, hear nothing and see nothing.

It was drizzling when, dressed as a worker, I reached the appointed place. A lot of people were milling around. Our main goal was to create fear and havoc, not kill anyone. Teacher assured us that the new explosives would unleash pandemonium. Once again I checked my documents. They were issued to an American married to a local girl.

A beggar was standing in front of the toilets. I turned my head away, as I walked by him. I often hear how often the smallest bit of evidence put people in prison.

I thought about the artist of the painting in our flat. In the hazy lamplight I saw his yellow shirt and his pants splashed with oils. I saw his madness flying above him and remembered the two dead volunteers I had seen during my training in the camp. Their bodies lay next to one another, sticky masses of blood, bone, and coal. They had both died in an accident during exercises learning to dismantle land mines. They were nice, friendly guys, and I had known them from my first day there.

I thought then of Chuck, who had once told me in a blues club in Chicago that, at the current buying power of the dollar, the human body was worth about $80 for its mineral content. We listened to fat and sassy Coco Taylor and watched her flash her gold teeth as she crooned, *"Long way from home, can't sleep at night"*...I thought then that Coco had to be worth more because she was so plump and beautiful.

*

"Nice to see you again," said Chuck when I opened the car door and slid into the seat next to him.

"The same."

"How was it?" he asked.

"I have no idea."

"We'll find out on the evening news."

"Did you hear the blast?"

"Sure I did. I'm afraid they didn't have enough time to disarm it, though we did warn them. Anyway. Teacher has invited us to dinner in Paris. He'll provide more details. The restaurant is in Montparnasse, within walking distance of Montsouri Park. That's the right place to talk."

Chuck started the engine and was ready to go. He drove the rented car at a moderate speed, though he loves driving fast. Pretty soon we were in Dover. We joined people standing at the night ferry. There we split again. I went to the upper deck by myself and watched as we slowly shoved off. Then I went to the bar. Chuck was on the other side of the counter. I started to talk to the guy next to me. He was a soccer fan on his way to France to watch something very important to him. He looked like Donald Duck and drank his beer faster than I had ever seen anyone do it. After a while I left him and went to my cabin to rest.

I was tired and slept for a couple of hours. It was getting light when we reached the French shore. When I woke up, the café was already open and people were standing in line for coffee. I took my place behind the man I had met the evening before in the bar. He turned out to be from Manchester and his soccer team seemed invincible to him. Somewhere I caught a glimpse of Chuck's face.

In Calais we were together again. A little dry-mouthed, we wandered the streets near the quay until we found an open bar where we each ordered café noir and a small Calva. We immediately felt better and started to discuss the pleasures of life in France. Relaxed for the first time, Chuck, in a silly mood, recited a limerick laughing gleefully.

> A tutor who taught on the flute
> Tried to teach two tooters to toot
> Said the two to the tutor,
> "Is it harder to toot, or
> To tutor two tooters to toot?"

On the way to Paris we talked about people who collect things, and we both tried to understand the contradiction between our will to possess and mortality. We stopped in another bar and indulged in a couple beers.

Then we paused again and did the same thing plus Calva. I wanted to change with Chuck and take the wheel, but he didn't let me. We were worn out. At a certain point we even stopped talking. The stay in England swung and swayed under our feet like a carousel.

"I decided to go to Dublin." I was the first to break the long silence.

"Will you go with Maureen?"

"I don't know," I opened the window, breathing in fresh air. "I think that our relationship, if there is one, is doomed to die. On the other hand, she has never been to Éire either. She doesn't particularly like the Irish, though both her grandparents came from Ireland. She's a terrible Francophile."

Chuck didn't say a word. Looking at him bent over the wheel, I tried to comprehend his madness. He was right, telling me once that as long as we can feel the stone's roughness and permanence without impermanent hands, anything is possible. Even madness.

On the crowded Parisian streets we forgot about yesterday and everything that had happened in London was far removed, covered over by the new reality and new events. We both knew that in the evening we had our appointment with Teacher, so it would be better if we got some sleep. And I thought that it would be wonderful to be an independent writer in this city, without any revolutionary past.

Above us we could see the white trail of a jet.

"I'm not sure that I wouldn't prefer to be a writer rather than a professional freedom fighter," I suddenly speculated.

"Nerves," laughed Chuck. "Nerves. They'll pass."

"It's not that I regret what I'm doing, but I know that I could be something else," I insisted.

"That will pass, otherwise our souls would be like the face in that painting you loved so much in the flat in Turnham Green. They're in a plane, but not even conscious of flying," Chuck commented after the disappearing plane, as he parked the car at boulevard Voltaire within walking distance of my apartment on l'Asile Popincourt.

"Polly Maggoo" is an extract from The Straw Sea.

Yuri Buida

Chemitch

Sergey Sergeyevich Chemitch was widely regarded as an exceedingly irresolute man. Some even viewed him as a 'man in a case,' not unlike the teacher Belikov in Chekhov's story. He had barely managed to drag out his first year as a high school Chemistry teacher, and at length the principal suggested that he stop tormenting himself and the students and take charge of the lab instead. Without taking the slightest umbrage, gladly even, Sergey Sergeyevich agreed and started the next school year in a narrow room adjoining the Chemistry classroom, full of cabinets, racks, tables, beakers, stands, and burners. The teaching position was filled by Azalia Kharitonovna Kerasidi, a young and beautiful Greek, and immediately everybody fell in love with her and started referring to her familiarly as Azie. Slim and willowy, energetic, with her dusky skin, her dark eyebrows arched like scimitars, and her lustrous green eyes, she excelled at her teaching, soon making everybody forget about that dub Chemitch, with his infamous laggardness, indecisiveness, some kind of glueyness, even when it came to very ordinary, everyday problems. Even if asked what two and two would be, he would pause, then mumble musingly for a while, and finally, in a rather halting manner, produce something like "Five".

Regardless of the time of the year, he took the same, once-chosen route from home to school, even though a large section of it was terribly inconvenient: a muddy path running between garden fences, through a gully which stretched along the railroad embankment. The path led to a crossing which was an excruciating obstacle on Sergey Sergeyevich"s way to school. Checking a homemade schedule repeatedly, he would wait for the Moscow Express to pass, and after letting a river of cars pass, scurry across the railway right in front of the approaching mail train. To be late for class or to be run over: that was the dilemma he faced daily, dripping sweat, nervously working himself up until he gave himself a severe headache and painful shortness of breath. Still, the idea of changing the established route seemed never to occur to him.

Azie used to poke fun at his obsession with keeping the lab in order. For example, the beaker of hydrochloric acid bore a large square label with several titles, one under the other: 'Muriatic Acid', 'Hydrochloric Acid', 'Hydrogen Chloride—Water Solution', and 'HCl'. Whenever a lesson plan involved using Bunsen burners, Sergey Sergeyevich would grow restless: not only would he give the students exhaustive instructions on how to use the hazardous equipment but he wouldn't leave the class until the experiment had been completed.

"What if something should come of it?" Azie would tease him with a smile.

At that he would merely shrug his shoulders and turn away.

One day Azie asked him to bring something from the school attic. Sergey Sergeyevich froze and then finally muttered: "Yes…but I have never been there…I don't like going to unfamiliar basements or attics…I'm sorry, Azalia Kharitonovna."

Azie laughed and dropped it. She sent to the attic a nimble student, the envy of every boy in class, all of them dreaming of an excuse to execute one of the gorgeous Azie's orders or requests, no matter how small, even if it meant risking their necks.

That same evening she entered the lab, sat down on a chair, crossed her legs, lit a thin cigarette, and nodded in the direction of a book by Chekhov lying on a table between some beakers and test tubes:

"A man in a case reading 'The Man in a Case'?" Sorry, Sergey Sergeyevich, but I've heard many people call you that.

"The blood-sucking spider," he muttered, continuing to wash a beaker with a bottle brush in the sink.

"What? What spider?" Azie was a little lost.

"You must have not revisited that story for a while," he said.

Having shaken the last drop of water out of the beaker and put it on the drying rack, he sat down facing Azie and having adjusted his glasses continued in the same unruffled tone of voice:

"Read it again, Azalia Kharitonovna. In the story, some healthy, constantly laughing people with red cheeks and black eyebrows monstrously hound a lonely miserable man who is no better but also no worse than they are. Yes, no better but no worse. Out of sheer boredom, they try to marry him to a red-cheeked, black-eyebrowed Ukrainian, whose brother detests the *man in a case* and compares him to a spider: the bloodsucking spider'. They get into a quarrel, and shortly after the *man in a case* dies."

Sergey Sergeyevich slowly opened the book, turned several pages and nodded, "Here, please, listen to this. 'One must confess'—(these are the narrator's words, not Chekhov's),—'that to bury people like Byelikov is a great pleasure.' He glanced at her over his glasses and continued.

"'We returned from the cemetery in a good humor. But no more than a week had passed before life went on as in the past, just as gloomy, oppressive, and senseless…,' You see, the problem was not the *man in a case*. That's why…," he coughed and looked away, "That's why, or maybe that's not why, as you please, but I ask you not to call me the man in a case. And please don't try to worm your way into my confidence, even if you find yourself bored all of a sudden."

He looked straight at her.

"I don't bother you, do I? Or is it that I perform my duties inadequately? Then just say so. But please leave me alone, do you understand?"

He went into a coughing fit, pressed a kerchief to his mouth and mumbled: "Please leave…Don't…. Really, don't…I beg you!"

Azie, bewildered, sprang up, rushed to the door, never ceasing to stare in amazement at Chemitch, and, not sure where to put the extinguished cigarette, suddenly slammed the door, started running, collected herself in a dead end of the hallway and turned around sharply. The hallway was empty. She was trembling, she wanted to cry, wanted to go back to that clumsy, tongue-tied bespectacled man and explain everything…But what was there to explain? Nothing like that had ever happened to her before. It was something baffling—disagreeably so, perhaps—at the very least something ponderous. Azie ran through the hallway on tiptoe, came down into the yard and, sobbing, raced home.

In the summer Azie couldn't go to the seaside because her mother was sick, and she spent entire days out on the narrow sand beaches of the Pregol and Lava rivers, surrounded by her admirers, who were keen on demonstrating their muscles and their mastery of swimming and ice-cream fetching.

At times, she would grow weary of everybody and everything and after breakfast, she would stray far from the crowded beaches—to the lakes of the Children's Home where one could dream carelessly to the gentle murmuring of willows, keeping sleepy watch over the roughish yellow lily pads gathering together in flat herds on the water's dark, nearly black surface. The lakes stretched along the Pregol in a chain, connected to the river by narrow curved tributaries hidden from view by the same leafy willows.

Azie would stroll from one lake to the other picking small white and light-blue flowers or lying in the tall grass and staring with her wide open hazel eyes at the sky where scarce, crudely moulded white clouds sailed across its fake plane. Dragonflies swooshed above her with a tinny crackle, swarms of green-veined butterflies moved about silently.

Having reached the last lake she saw the familiar bulky figure of Sergey Sergeyevich fishing on the shore, and after a moment's hesitation—how much time had passed since that day!—she walked up and sat down next to him.

"I would never have thought you the ardent fisherman type," she said. "You have such a predatory squint when looking at the bobber…"

"I don't like fishing." Sergey Sergeyevich said with a feeble smile. "This is just a good place to lounge. Secluded, quiet, meditative. Sometimes I just lie in the grass and sleep."

"Sleep? But…" She suddenly stammered not knowing what would be an appropriate thing to say. "Well, that must be good…"

He glanced at her with interest and then fixed his eyes on the bobber once more.

"All in all, yes. The only bad thing is that dreams have too many people…some of whom are quite unpleasant and it's impossible to get rid of them because evidently such are the rules of dreams." He laughed softly. "My God, what nonsense I am talking. Please forgive me."

"Not at all, Sergey Sergeyevich!"

"You can call me Chemitch. I am used to it." He shrugged. "In dreams, one seems to become free, utterly free, but really there is no enslavement worse than dreams with their dream people…

"All that's left is to be the ruler of one's real life." Suddenly Azie was afraid that he might take her words as some kind of insinuation. "Look, isn't it biting?"

"Nope, false alarm." He took off his straw hat and tousled his straw-blonde hair. "In real life, if you don't feel like associating with some—just don't. Is it not so?"

"How about a swim?" Azie got up and dropped her little dress in a single movement, remaining in a white swimsuit. Let's go! Don't be afraid!"

"I'm not afraid," he grinned.

She waited patiently for him to take off his shirt, pants, and socks in his usual unhurried manner. He had a heavy-built stoutish white body with thick red hair on the chest, arms, and the legs. In two leaps he was at the water's edge and splashing loudly into the lake.

Azie burst into laughter.

"A seal!" She yelled, "Sergey Sergeyevich, you are a giant seal!"

Chemitch came up to the surface and started propelling his

seal-like body forward with strong strokes. Azie watched in amazement: she had never seen such a refined crawl, except on TV. The man took a turn around the lake, rolled over on his back and in a few kicks reached the shore poking his crown into the sand.

"What style!" Azie said squatting next to him. "Where did you learn to do that?"

He got out of water breathing heavily and waved his hands wearily.

"—Well, you know, I was born on the Volga River, and then attended a sport school for some years. But then—bang, and that was it." He threw hair back from his forehead and smiled at her guiltily. "My heart, you know…They wouldn't even take me in the army because of my heart."

"Good Lord! Then you shouldn't have! I am such a fool, Sergey Sergeyevich!"

He looked at her in wonderment.

"Are you serious? Come on, Azie, forget it. Let's pretend that I never told you anything. And please, don't tell anybody about this…Didn't you want to take a swim, Azie? Go in, the water is marvellous!

Suddenly she realized that for the first time, he was addressing her by her nickname instead of the formal name-and-patronymic, and nearly burst into tears.

Chemitch was standing in front of her, at a loss.

"Azie…Did something happen? Did I do something wrong again…"

She shook her head: no.

"Would you like me to teach you how to swim the right way? No? Azie…, what would you like then?"

"I don't know," She sat down on the sand and recovered her breath. "Tell me, what else do you see in your dreams?"

He wrinkled his forehead.

"I see fish. With the midriffs of beautiful women." He put his glasses on. "And a lot of unnecessary people. But what's wrong with you, Azalia Kharitonovna?" The tone of his voice was friendly but somewhat dry. "What would you like?"

She looked at him with a rueful smile.

"Kiss me, Sergey Sergeyevich. Please. Or else I'll start bawling."

She came home very late but her Mother wasn't asleep yet.

"What is it, Azie?" Mother suffered from shortness of breath. "There's such an air of freshness coming from you, as if you were happy."

"I really am happy, Ma! I fell in love today, came to love someone, and became a woman!"

Her mother looked at her—Azie guessed her gaze in the dark.

"And who might your hero be?"

"Ma! Was it not you who told me a hundred times that only fools marry heroes?"

"So you've already decided to marry?"

"Yes. He is not a hero, he is my love, Ma! Honest!"

Their wedding of course created quite a sensation in the sleepy town where everybody predicted that Azie's husband would be a General at the very least. And now, go figure: this someone not even registered for service, whose military ID reads 'fit for non-combatant duties only'. The beauty's choice smacked not of a whim even, but rather of some dark mystery and by no means of love.

As years passed, for they have lived together for nearly six years, every day Azie explored her unusual husband like some strange, mysterious planet or country, with cities and waterfalls, nightmares and boundless oceans. Like most Russians, Sergey Sergeyevich saw the world as a chaotic succession of random happenings and in order to create some order and safety for himself and his loved ones (in a year they had a daughter) Chemitch employed two methods concurrently: deliberate slowness and imagination.

He was never in a hurry to open the door, not because of fear or cowardliness but just because he tried to go over all the possible scenarios of meeting the visitor or visitors: at the door, there might be neighbors, birds, a closet-dwelling monster, Don Quixote, or a cobra withered by its many-thousand-kilometer voyage, its venom exhausted, with no desires left but to find rest at the feet of its last master.

He wouldn't rush to open the mail, trying hard to predict the content of a letter. Each of them seemed to carry some message, otherwise why would somebody waste time and ink? He himself never wrote letters, for, in his own estimation, he lacked the mastery of words necessary to help someone in misfortune, to heal a soul, to stop a villain, or to exalt a righteous man. At first, Azie found it amusing but soon, as if contracting it from her husband, she began to regard letters and words in general with the same care, her silence scaring even her own mother.

"Are you in distress, maybe?" The old Greek worried, "You have become so quiet…"

"And happy."

Mother just shook her head: silent happiness was something new in a world created in the Word and by the Word.

Sergey Sergeyevich continued to sleep a lot. He once told Azie: "In sleep it's easier to endure happiness," and added with a smile, "In addition, I lose weight when sleeping."

More and more often, he would find himself in a hospital bed: his failing heart called for attention. One day it stopped. Azie buried him with a sealed envelope stuck under his hands folded on his chest. She wrote the letter upon learning of his death. Nobody knows what message she sent to her lover into Eternity but when a colleague in the teachers room suggested under his breath that, on the brink of death Sergey Sergeyevich thought not 'Am I dying?' but rather 'Should I die?', she suddenly hit the table with her fist and yelled throwing her face up toward the ceiling and straining her voice:

"Don't you dare! Don't you dare! You didn't know him and didn't want to know! But I knew…I know him! And I can't stand your Chekhov! Can-not-stand-him! Can-not…"

Conall Ryan

Hostivar

Ladislav Repa waited in the Prague train station for the 14.16 from Munich to arrive. Combed straight back, his hair sagged towards his ears in the heat. Light trickled through the iron-and-glass cowl of the station, and the air was choked with brick dust. He hoped he would be spared from boarding another student. The last one had argued about the rate and spilled beer on his carpets. An adult tonight, he thought. Someone with a job, and manners.

He heard the bite and hiss of brakes before the train came into view. Full. Passengers streamed by, reduced in height and composure by the great heat. One family separated just as another was reuniting, strangers maintaining an odd balance between happiness and sorrow.

A beetle-shaped man walked towards Ladislav, followed by a porter wheeling a steamer trunk. Surely such an elegant gentleman would have hotel reservations. But there was no price for asking. He stepped in front of the man.

"Accommodation?"

"Who are you?"

"I have private accommodation. Not far." What was eight more miles if you had come all the way from Munich? "Nice rooms. Quiet. I show you?" Before the man could respond, Ladislav drew photographs from his jacket. He showed them to the man, then looked at them himself and smiled.

"You say it's quiet?"

Dogs barked all night—fine dogs from fine families—and old Sedivy kept chickens and rabbits, but Ladislav put these disturbances more into the category of atmosphere. He nodded. "Only the sounds you love to hear."

"And who is that charming woman in the garden?"

"That is my wife, Hana."

"I will stay a week," the man said, shifting his gaze from Hana's photograph to Ladislav's ears. "Maybe more."

Ladislav's jaw and cheekbones were prominent, almost distinguished, but the handles on either side of his face gave him the bewildered expression of a boy listening to seashells. He needed the porter's help to lift the steamer trunk into his car.

"Will it be miserably hot again tomorrow, or can we look forward to a breeze?" the man asked. When Ladislav shrugged—thinking *this trunk weighs a month, a year*—the man gripped his shoulder. "There is more to running a guesthouse than providing a bed. You must study the weather."

They agreed on a price in dollars that was ten percent below what Ladislav could exchange them for on the street. The black marketers in Old Town Square offered the best rates, but they would tuck one-thousand-dinar notes in with the bills if they thought you couldn't tell one comrade tilling the fields from another. Worse were the short-haired Czechs posing as tourists who marched across the cobblestones snapping photographs of the transactions. What was the goal of ex-surveillance specialists and break-in artists and wrist-twisters? Stabilize the currency! For dealing with these unreliable elements of the population, Ladislav deserved a small premium.

At noon the next day, he marched up and down the stairs in his garden boots to rouse the new boarder. He paused to adjust the muskets and ice boots decorating the walls, pulling his shirt cuff over the skating blades, sweeping each riser with the water-warped hockey stick Hana had given him for his fiftieth birthday, to which she had added a dense beard of broom bristles. Ladislav wiped cobwebs off the ceiling, hip-checked couches and chairs out of his way, wristed dust out of the corners. A Canadian coach had tried to lure him to Quebec when he was nineteen. Hana's father countered with a promise to make him an assistant in the housing authority. A portrait of the great Mecir hung inside the foyer to remind him of this dubious honor. Hana's advice was succinct: "Leave Prague and forget about me." Ladislav didn't relish the prospect of waking up alone every morning in a far-away hotel; the smell of baked ice that never left his body in those days his only connection to home. He glided through the house, cherishing the corner of himself that he kept frozen at the precise temperature of tender clueless youth, found a wadded up sock by the staircase, slapped it across the threshold to the kitchen.

Hana found the sock, tossed it out of the kitchen, and positioned herself in the doorway.

"I'll score again," he said.

"No."

The sock rose off his broom. Hana moved her hip to the right, deflecting the sock.

"You must be putting on weight. Normally that shot gets by you."

Hana, three pounds heavier than the day they married, patted down her dress. She had set out poppy-seed cakes and strawberries and fresh bread and minced eggs with chives. A pot of tea grew strong and cold. Ladislav drummed his feet on the landing, rattled his collection of swords in the brass umbrella bucket at the top of the stairs.

Below, language books dominated the kitchen table in three uneven columns. Ladislav listened to Hana's staccato recitations from the stairs.

"Good-a-day...You like tea or coffee...The tram is over the street...Come out, come out, wherever you are...." And now in Czech: "Will he ever wake up?"

"He's tired. He's had a long journey."

"My bread's had a long journey."

When Hana's collection of antique winding clocks chimed one, Ladislav rapped on the guest's door. "Mr. Kaup?" Excuse me, but I thought you might care for something to eat."

The door opened, and there was Kaup, sixty-eight years old according to his passport, wearing a towel that emphasized his hunched and slippery dimensions.

"First, I will have a bath in your splendid tub. Nice piece of property you have here. You must have worked in the old government. Are those rabbit pens in your neighbor's yard?"

"Yes," Ladislav said, feeling tricked. "An eccentric fellow. Many times I complain."

"Nonsense. What could be more practical?"

Kaup bathed, ate, made some phone calls, and retired to his room. Dogs barked. A rock sailed through the window and rolled to a stop near Ladislav's feet while he was napping in his favorite chair. Suspecting the neighborhood boy who occasionally snatched one of Sedivy's chickens for a free meal, he swept up the glass and carried his hockey stick out to the street. The boy deserved a good whack in the shins. But the street was empty.

When two more days had passed without incident, Ladislav slipped brochures and maps of Prague under Kaup's door. He turned the radio to an all-news station while Hana polished the silver to see if the endless overstated disasters of the world might coax their guest from his room.

"The shades are drawn, but I can hear him pacing," Hana said. "What's he doing up there?"

The pacing stopped when the phone rang. Kaup's door creaked open. He had many conversations. His first visitors were elderly, a limping man and a woman who kept her wig in place with a straw hat. They stayed for fifteen minutes, never letting go of each other. Kaup gave them a satin bag. They took turns peeking inside the bag, shook Kaup's hand, and left. The woman helped the man down the stairs.

All was quiet for a week. Then Kaup asked Ladislav if he could use the dining room for an hour. He set the table for six. The china he produced was exquisite, patterned in blue and white with gold inlays, obviously old, and not a chip or scratch in the lot. Kaup rattled a cup on its saucer while he waited. A couple even older that the satin-bag pair arrived at the appointed time, sat at the table with Kaup, listened, nodded, squeezed Kaup's scaley hands, stacked the beautiful china into a box, and left.

Another rock announced itself with a hail of glass that night, preceded by a shout from Sedivy. Ladislav rushed to the door.

"There were two of them," Sedivy said, pointing down the street. Sedivy smoked so much that his voice buzzed. "They drove up. One got out and threw the rock. Then they sped off."

"It's my fault," Kaup said. "A misunderstanding. Let me make a few phone calls."

Ladislav found the rock. It wasn't a rock. It was a gold-bottomed paperweight inscribed with the initials *VTM*. The top was glass covering a forest scene.

"Someone you know?" Ladislav asked, handing the paperweight to Kaup.

"I may have made the acquaintance of their grandparents."

"Perhaps they don't want to be reminded of the past."

"And yet here I am," Kaup said, tapping the paperweight on the table.

Ladislav watched Prague come alive that summer, teeming with words, celebrating new beginnings without forgetting that it was still a city inhabited by the missing and the dead. Skodas stalled in traffic and drivers abandoned them, creating instant monuments to corrosion. Fights broke out in U Flecku's drinking garden when German youths miscalculated their capacity for its syrupy beer and began celebrating victory over Czechoslovakia in the World Cup with a display of singing and foot-stomping that reminded their hosts of uniforms and rifles. Folk tunes echoed across Goldmaker's Alley and down the Old Castle Steps, flanked by steep walls and a drizzle of red vines. Songs that had been ground into the pavement by tank treads in 1968 were suddenly popular again—everywhere Ladislav turned there was a young man with a guitar and an amplifier singing *Purple Haze*. Classically trained vocalists lugged boom boxes to the Charles Bridge and sang arias to taped accompaniment, competing alongside vegetable growers and gypsies selling clay whistles. Chess matches dotted the first courtyard of St. Vitus, grandmasters dispatching students to move six-foot-high papier maché pieces that had been pelted repeatedly by rain. Political posters competed for space on kiosks with advertisements for acid house parties and graffiti. *You think we Czechs are very funny. Well fuck you and fuck your money.* Tourists seeped into Old Town Square from every direction like unwanted colors into an old black-and-white movie. Wenceslas Square, somber as a lump of coal, garlanded with thousands of empty candle-holders staring up from the pavement like sightless eyes, was a shrine of wax.

With the housing authority officially abolished, Ladislav found himself free to undertake the considerable amount of work that needed to be done around the house. He mixed concrete for the new patio while Hana picked roses from the garden. Together, they pressed their palms into the concrete and drank beer with their lunch and belted pillows to their knees while they scrubbed the kitchen floor. Then Hana put on the kettle for tea and rearranged her winding clocks in the dining room. There were seven in all; she would assign each a new position. She had explained this most peaceful and unhurried moment in her day to him once, but rearranging the clocks had since passed into the elevated realm of ritual, joining the dust pucks he broomed through the house. It was while sipping tea and watching her put back five minutes on a clock that would lose five more tomorrow that Ladislav forgot Kaup was in the house. The German had joined the inconspicuous living things that lodged in the rafters, the gutters, under the porch. He was there but not there. It had been four weeks since the last broken window. Ladislav felt in his pockets for his pills, kissing the small curl of silver hair that would never stay tucked behind Hana's ear. "Still three empty rooms. You have a lazy husband."

"Yesterday, a man came to see Kaup while you were at the station. Older than us. I brought them coffee. The man was playing the a bassoon. Kaup sat there, listening to him play. Then the man took his bassoon and left."

"Kaup had a man come to play the bassoon for him?"

"Kaup *gave* him the bassoon."

"Does he ever mention how long he intends to stay?"

"He speaks too fast for me to understand. And he turns my clocks over in his hands when he thinks I'm not looking."

The clocks were a gift from Hana's father. One night after they had returned home from a state function and the portrait of Mecir seemed especially luminous, Hana whispered that the ticks of the clocks reminded her of her father's shoes clicking across the cobbles of Old Town Square. Mecir's strides were so long that she had to run to keep up with him.

"I miss him, too," Ladislav lied.

Mecir had always disapproved of Ladislav, staging their public encounters as subtle tests that Ladislav invariably failed. In private, Mecir ignored him.

As he lay dying, a time when the habit of discretion surely must lose some of its appeal, Mecir had refused to speak to anyone whose ear wasn't within nibbling distance of his lips. Hana leaned over the bed for hours listening patiently. Ladislav viewed Mecir's infirmity as a pending release. Hana seemed under a spell made more powerful with each cough. With no children of their own, Ladislav would always be the failed hockey player, and Hana would always be Daddy's little girl. Shoved under the hospital bed, Mecir's shoes still gleamed with authority.

Something changed in Hana during those nights. Ladislav wasn't sure if it was letting her father go, or having to take possession of secrets he had bitten into her. Was Mecir the self-possessed patriot who helped plot the assassination of Heydrich in 1942? Or an opportunist who had identified candidates for deportation to Terezin as early as '41, appeasing the Nazis while freeing up housing stock that he could resell at higher prices? Or both? "Prague would be a bombed out pit but for men like me," he coughed in Hana's ear, convinced to the end that surrender to Germany had been an attack of beauty, the art of self-preservation.

Competition at the station was fierce. Grandmothers skulked about in trench coats with snapshots of guestrooms pinned inside. Their rates weren't better than Ladislav's, but they enjoyed mixing with foreigners. They were as welcoming as he was wary. As soon as the tourists looked at him, they knew he wanted to send them away. He suppressed the urge to shout, *It's a new world and I'm irrelevant in it.* So many respectable people were shouting these days that joining in, especially in the separation-reunification zone of the central train station, would scarcely draw attention. If he could summon the nerve, Ladislav would shout that he only pretended to be competing for boarders when he had really come to confront nothing less than the arrival of the future. *Rusty yes, but plenty of miles left. I will not be left behind!*

"Need accommodation?" he asked an attractive young woman, reaching for his pictures. "I have nice rooms. Not far."

"Some consider Hostivar a bit out of the way," she said, snatching the pictures and taking him by the elbow. "Have you registered with the Tourist Bureau?"

Ladislav waited until they were seated at a small table behind the ticket counter before saying the magic word: *Mecir.* He said it using the same tone of his interrogator, and received a prompt apology for any trouble caused, the new situation was so fluid and confusing, but Mecir, Mecir, why hadn't he said so right away?

A victory for the past! A solemn endorsement from the grave!

Ladislav returned home to find Kaup and Hana in the kitchen. Hana was removing a steaming pan from the oven. Kaup looked formidable in dress pants and a starched shirt. Hana swiped a hunk of bread in the pan and handed it to Ladislav.

"Delicious. What is it?"

"Your neighbor's rabbit, mostly," Kaup said. He gave Ladislav money for another week and went to bed.

"He scurries," Ladislav complained after Hana had convinced him to go for a swim. "And his back is rounded like a piece of armor, when it should be flat." They picked their way along the moonlit path until they reached the dam in the river. Hana unpinned her hair and slipped out of her clothes. She had a figure that could be considered vain for a woman of her age, but to Ladislav, her slimness was a natural consequence of the discipline she brought to every task. The only hint of wildness was in her hair. It was the one thing about her that wasn't economical. When her hair was hanging lose she could be argumentative, but water and darkness mediated her temper. Ladislav dove into the murky water, plunging deeper and deeper until his fingertips almost touched the spongy bottom, his lungs burning, returning noiselessly to Hana, who floated on the still, twinkling surface of the river.

"He's asked me to help him. He took some things when he was here during the war," she said. "Now he wants to give them back. He'll pay, of course."

"I don't like it."

"You've seen the things he's returning to people. They're harmless."

"A soldier collects bayonets and pistols and enemy ears as souvenirs, not fancy plates and paperweights and bassoons! What kind of lunatic have we brought into our home?"

"One who's prepared to pay us to join his little game. We need the money."

"For what? To buy glass and putty when they throw his gifts back through our windows? There's no telling what else he might have in that trunk!"

Now it was her turn to dive. She surprised him from below by ticking his legs. He recognized the Hana who wanted something as she pressed into his back and moved her hands up to his stomach. He missed that Hana and was afraid to say anything that might scare her away.

"We could use the money," she said again, softly.

"Kaup keeps asking me if I was in the old government."

A fountain of river water shot up from her mouth. "He came from Munich. He didn't pick you. You picked him."

And who is that charming woman in the garden?

That is my wife Hana, who swims like a mermaid, who misses her father, who longs to be young again.

"Just a little research." She touched his stomach. "Let's try it and see how it goes."

Kaup bought a basket of eggs from Sedivy the next day and, upon presenting them to Hana, asked if he could accompany her on her morning errands.

"The light through the stained glass at St. Vitus could be his, but he wants to learn the secrets of buying meat and tram tickets," Ladislav hissed at the portrait of Mecir. He skated into Kaup's room on his socks, picturing the glorious moment at fifteen years of age when he had wheeled on a Russian Army lieutenant and sent his winger in for a short-handed goal. The steamer truck was locked tight.

When Hana returned home, Ladislav was annoyed at the obvious care she had taken in applying her makeup and nail polish and fixing her hair. "And where is the great man now?"

"The train station."

Kaup brought back two Irish girls on holiday and an American architect. The architect came in from the rain without folding his new Obcanske Forum umbrella; the *O* embarrsingly filled in with the eyes and smile of a happy face. Good-bye communism. Hello democracy. Have a nice day. "I'm sure you will find them satisfactory," Kaup said to Ladislav, handing over a packet of bills. "Please bring me breakfast in my room tomorrow, and arrange for me to receive the German papers."

Kaup kept the house filled with boarders in return for these minor luxuries. He slaughtered chickens and rabbits with Sedivy, deflecting inquiries about his past with the humility of a knight resting between great deeds. After helping Hana clean out the attic, he climbed down the ladder with three filthy dolls that had been stuffed between the eaves for so long that Ladislav had come to think of them as insulation. Ladislav chuckled to himself when Kaup asked to keep the dolls. By all means—what could anyone possibly want with those shattered porcelain faces, those soiled clumps of rags? Ladislav could tolerate strange behavior. It was the proficiencies of the man that irritated him. Kaup worked the entrances to Old Town Square and learned how to squeeze three more crowns out of every dollar than Ladislav, himself—a once well-placed minor official in the government!—could negotiate. He instructed Hana in German and English, demonstrating in the process a curious facility for making her laugh. He wasn't just a moneychanger. He was a people-changer. He recognized a currency in Hana that eluded Ladislav. If Kaup knew it was there, he could trade it, convert it, to other forms of currency. All relationships boiled down to this gift. Kaup celebrated Germany's World Cup victory with a lecture on the tactics that could have delivered more talented teams the prize. Finally, he purchased a leather-bound book and recommended in the strongest possible terms that the Repas use it to keep a ledger of boarders' names, nationalities, passport numbers, arrival and departure dates, and comments.

Ladislav studied the book in the kitchen while Kaup gave Hana a German lesson. "Comments?" he asked. "About what?"

"Hana's food. The quality of your greeting. The texture of the towels and the blankets. Barking. You read the comments and make necessary improvements."

"But I think all of those things are fine."

"What you think isn't so important."

Hana helped Kaup reunite several families with their belongings. For the most part, they were not valuable things. But they were personal things. "You see?" she would say, holding her hand over the phone mouthpiece. "Harmless."

Two days after someone poured a bucket of red paint on the front steps, Kaup hired a part-time bodyguard, a Slovak with the shoulders of a wrestler and eyes that were barely visible beneath ridges of scar tissue. Ladislav returned from a swim to find him blocking the porch. He asked for identification.

"This is my house," Ladislav said.

"Prove it," the bodyguard answered.

Since Hana and Ladislav had agreed that they would not accept orphan items as gifts, Kaup started bestowing them on boarders: earrings and a gold tea ball to a Polish girl, a stamp collection to a Swedish boy, an Oriental throw rug to a Dutch physics professor. It was upon seeing the rug that Ladislav decided Kaup's steamer trunk came from the same dream factory as the carpetbag Mary Poppins unpacked in front of the Banks children. The bag appeared to have a fixed height, length, and width, but its actual volume was infinite. Mr. Banks had no answer for Mary Poppins because her existence was a blank check. She could pull whatever she needed out of her bag. Kaup's trunk was similarly bottomless.

"Only two names left," Hana reassured him. "Alperovitch and Goldhaber. I'll be lucky if I find anything."

A parade of strangers continued to pass through the house, adding poems and drawings to the guest book ("Wonderful time!"— "Magical week!"), brushing on makeup, throwing up beer and dumplings in the tub in the middle of the night. Ladislav inspected their rooms when they went out sightseeing, sifting through letters and diaries, jewelry, bibles, deodorants, birth-control devices, shampoos, school assignments, dietary supplements, plane tickets, and the occasional foil-wrapped lump of hashish, the largest of which apparently brought physics alive for the Dutch professor. Every day, another group of tourists arrived, expecting the streets and bridges to be trimmed in velvet, tipping their mouths back to receive the sour rain as if being in Prague would transform water into hope. The city couldn't possibly deliver on all the promises they had made themselves. Ladislav replaced the possessions exactly where he had found them.

One afternoon, Kaup boarded the tram with a long cardboard tube under his arm. Ladislav followed in his car. In six previous tries, he had lost Kaup every time, but he preferred the game to sitting at home. Kaup got off near the Vlatava, walked to a grey stone building, pulled a tarnished key chain from his pocket, and inserted a key in the padlock on the door. It didn't fit. He put the keys back in his pocket, strode to the corner, and turned right. Ladislav parked and followed on foot. Kaup met up with his bodyguard in Old Town Square. They drank coffee and read the paper. The bodyguard used the paper as a shade for surveying the plaza around them. In a side street, while the bodyguard fanned himself with the paper, Kaup tried another key on a brightly painted yellow door. When it wouldn't turn in the lock, he peered up at the tops of the buildings and inserted the key in the adjacent building. That door didn't open either. Kaup bought a green pepper from a street vendor and smuggled it into a pub where he used it to upgrade a meal of pork, dumplings and beer. The pub was adjacent to a detached brick building with an oak door that Kaup's keys couldn't open. Early evening came, and with it the slants of light that give Prague its striped, conspiratorial character.

Kaup and the bodyguard finished their meal. The beer loosened up Kaup's gait. He ambled through side streets and alleys, flipping the keys back and forth over his knuckles. The bodyguard stayed a few steps ahead. Ladislav watched them turn a corner into a square where five paths met. By the time he reached the square, they had vanished.

Hana kissed Ladislav with such ferocity at sun-up that he thought they had awakened as newlyweds. Then he noticed a bundle of money under the bed.

He asked Kaup if he would like to read his newspapers by the dam. The sun was merciless. Birds shrieked in the trees. "Your feet will feel nice in the water, Mr. Kaup."

On the way to the dam, Kaup suddenly stepped off the path into the woods. "Hana showed me a faster route."

"But we never go this way."

"Hana showed me." They walked along a narrow path until they reached a clearing. Someone had strung a wire between two trees. Shirts and trousers hung from the wire. There was a breeze, and the shirts cast billowing shadows on the path. Ladislav looked up at the clothes.

"Don't you recognize them?" The colors and shapes were un-convincing. Ladislav had to smell them before he knew they were his. He held a shirt to his face and detected the unmistakable aroma of city and forest that had been pressed into his clothes by the wind for thirty years. It was a smell he had always loved, but rather ordinary when you removed the mystery from it. He pulled a shirt from the wire, imagining Hana's arms slipping treacherously around Kaup's rounded back. If she led him here, what else might she have done while Ladislav's shirts fluttered helplessly above?

"You must leave our house. I'll return the money you gave Hana." Five stacks of bills sat in an uncovered shoebox on the win-dowsill in their room. Hana had been passing by it all morning as if attending a wake for the fortune she would never have.

Kaup plucked a sock off the wire and wiped his shoes. "My trunk is empty. But you and Hana still have some giving back to do."

Hana was waiting for them, stretching in the front yard.

"Mr. Kaup is moving out," Ladislav said.

"We'll have our last gathering tonight," Kaup said, showing his teeth. "I've bought you a new dress. I would be delighted if you could join us."

Joining them, of course, meant serving them, but Hana dutifully wore the dress—the red sash around her waist took years off her age—and gathered her newly dyed hair into a ponytail and tittered—yes, that was the word for it—not the laugh that comes from the area around a wise heart, but the nervous burning ears and cheeks titter of a girl who finds herself on a sudden miraculous adventure—*tittered* while Kaup and the bodyguard smoked and ate, letting their blunt fingers stray to her hands as they took poppy-seed cakes from the serving plate.

"Are we expecting someone?" Ladislav asked.

"Yes," Hana said.

A rap came at the front door. Ladislav ushered in a woman of indeterminate age, gray hair twisted carelessly into a bun, hands bumpy with aurthritis, nose and cheeks and chin barely concealing her bones. She wore a purple ankle-length dress and a strand of pearls.

Kaup escorted her to the kitchen, off-limits to other boarders.

"Where are they?" she asked. There was no unpleasantness in her voice, but its firmness eliminated any chance of idle conversation.

Kaup reappeared, hugging three porcelain dolls. They were the most beautiful dolls Ladislav had ever seen, with green eyes, silk dresses, and luxurious hair.

"Bring them to me," the woman said.

Kaup set the dolls down in front of her.

She picked up the first doll. Smelled the hair. Closed the green eyes. The doll's lids bobbed open again as soon as she lifted her fingers.

"So?" Kaup asked.

She took her time examining the dolls, rocking the first, singing to the second. The third doll was the loveliest of all. She cradled it in her arms and wept.

"I did my best to restore them," Hana said.

The woman reached into her pocket and brought out a small folding knife. Turning the third doll over on its stomach, she made an incision along its back and probed the doll's cottony insides with her fingers. Finding nothing, she set the doll aside, closed the knife, and composed her hands in her lap. Ladislav stood against the back door.

"I'm sorry," Kaup said.

"I'm grateful to have them back." She pinched the doll's dress closed.

Ladislav felt tightness in his chest. *What could anyone possibly want with those shattered porcelain faces, those soiled clumps of rags?* She was holding the dolls from the attic, the insulation dolls, sitting where she might have played with them as a girl while her mother stirred the evening's meal on the stove and they waited together for her father to come home. The wounded doll stared at Ladislav, demanding what couldn't be given back. Perhaps Mecir had gouged out the valuables when he confiscated the property. It was possible that they had slept unnoticed in the doll's belly until Kaup found them. Either way, they were gone.

The woman gathered her dolls and left.

Kaup moved out the next day. Sedivy had offered him a free room in exchange for the guidance that had transformed the Repas' stolen home into a profitable tourist destination. Carpenters, painters, and assorted craftsmen soon appeared to transform Sedivy's shabby dwelling into the best bed and breakfast for miles around. They painted it a brilliant yellow, a directional yellow, a false, tempting yellow. But their transplanted flowerbeds didn't take, and Sedivy refused to give up his chickens.

Ladislav spent his afternoons at the station. Trains rumbled past in both directions with such frequency that the ground never stopped shuddering. When he leaned against the wall to take the pressure off his lower back, his shirt collar worked the folds of his neck like a butter knife stuck in gristle.

"How many?" Hana asked when he returned home.

"None, as usual."

"Good, because we're filled to capacity. Four arrived today. Two Americans, an Italian, and a Swede. The Italian asked me if I would make her the poppy-seed cakes she had heard so much about. And a travel agent called from Baltimore." Hana had purchased a second phone line and a small weekly ad in the *Herald Tribune*. "I saw Kaup in the market. Sedivy has empty rooms. We almost have enough money coming in to buy new mattresses, pillows, and blankets."

Ladislav had specialized in accommodation his whole life, but it was Hana who had the true gift for it. In her presence, foreigners of all ages were transformed into rambunctious children, filling the house with food and music and endless, restless conversation. The strangers Ladislav had feared would come between them actually held them together. Missionaries from the guest book had instructed their Prague-bound friends to board with the woman who swore in three languages and the man who swept up with his hockey stick.

Archives

R.B. Cunninghame Graham

The Gold Fish

Outside the little straw-thatched café in a small courtyard trellised with vines, before a miniature table painted in red and blue, and upon which stood a dome-shaped pewter teapot and a painted glass half filled with mint, sat Amarabat, resting and smoking hemp. He was of those whom Allah in his mercy (or because man in the Blad-Allah has made no railways) has ordained to run. Set upon the road, his shoes pulled up, his waistband tightened, in his hand a staff, a palm-leaf wallet at his back, and in it bread, some hemp, a match or two (known to him as *el spiritus*), and a letter to take anywhere, crossing the plains, fording the streams, struggling along the mountain paths, sleeping but fitfully, a burning rope steeped in saltpeter fastened on his foot, he trotted day and night—untiring as a camel, faithful as a dog. In Rabat as he sat dozing, watching the greenish smoke curl upwards from his hemp pipe, word came to him from the Khalifa of the town. So Amarabat rose, paid for his tea with a handful of defaced and greasy copper coins, and took his way towards the white palace with crenelated walls, which on the cliff, hanging above the roaring tide-rip, just inside the bar of the great river, looks at Salee. Around the horseshoe archway of the gate stood soldiers, wild, fierce-eyed, armed to the teeth, descendants, most of them, of the famed warriors whom Sultan Muley Ismail (may God have pardoned him!) bred for his service, after the fashion of the Carlylean hero Frederic; and Amarabat walked through them, not aggressively, but with the staring eyes of a confirmed hemp-smoker, with the long stride of one who knows that he is born to run, and the assurance of a man who waits upon his lord. Some time he waited whilst the Khalifa dispensed what he thought justice, chaffered with Jewish pedlars for cheap European goods, gossiped with friends, looked at the antics of a dwarf, or priced a Georgian or Circassian girl brought with more care than glass by some rich merchant from the East. At last Amarabat stood in his presence, and the Khalifa, sitting upon a pile of cushions playing with a Waterbury watch, a pistol and a Koran by his side, addressed him thus:

"Amarabat, son of Bjorma, my purpose is to send thee to Tafilet, where our liege lord the Sultan lies with his camp. Look upon this glass bowl made by the Kaffir, but clear as is the crystal of the rock; see how the light falls on the water, and the shifting colors that it makes, as when the Bride of the Rain stands in the heavens, after a shower in spring. Inside are seven gold fish, each scale as bright as letters in an Indian book. The Christian from whom I bought them said originally they came from the Far East where the Djin-descended Jawi live, the little yellow people of the faith. That may be, but such as they are, they are a gift for kings. Therefore, take thou the bowl. Take it with care, and bear it as it were thy life. Stay not, but in an hour start from the town. Delay not on the road, be careful of the fish, change not their water at the muddy pool where tortoises bask in the sunshine, but at running brooks; talk not to friends, look not upon the face of woman by the way, although she were as a gazelle, or as the maiden who when she walked through the fields the sheep stopped feeding to admire. Stop not, but run through day and night, pass through the Atlas at the Glaui; beware the frost, cover the bowl with thine own haik; upon the other side shield the bowl from the Saharan sun, and drink not of the water if thou a day athirst when toiling through the sand. Break not the bowl, and see the fish arrive in Tafilet, and then present them, with this letter, to our lord. Allah be with you, and his Prophet; go, and above all things see though breakest not the bowl."

And Amarabat, after the manner of his kind, taking the bowl of gold fish, placed one hand upon his heart and said: "Inshallah, it shall be as thou hast said. God gives the feet and lungs. He also give the luck upon the road."

So he passed out under the horseshoe arch, holding the bowl almost at arm's length so as not to touch his legs, and with the palmetto string by which he carried it, bound round with rags. The soldiers looked at him, but spoke not, and their eyes seemed to see far away, and to pass over all in the middle distance, though no doubt they marked the smallest detail of his gait and dress. He passed between the horses of the guard all standing nodding under the fierce sun, the reins tied to the cantles of their high red saddles, a boy in charge of every two or three: he passed beside the camels resting beside the well, the donkeys standing dejected by the firewood they had brought: passed women, veiled white figures going to the baths; and passing underneath the lofty gateway of the town, exchanged a greeting with the half-mad, half-religious beggar just outside the walls, and then emerged upon the sandy road, between the aloe hedges, which skirts along the sea. So as he walked, little by little he fell into his stride; then got his second wind, and smoking now and then a pipe of hemp, began, as Arabs say, to eat the miles, his eyes fixed on the horizon, his stick stuck down between his shirt and back, the knob protruding over the left shoulder like the hilt of a two-handed sword. And still he held the precious bowl from Franquestan in which the golden fish swam to and fro, diving and circling in the sunlight, or flapped their tails to steady themselves as the water danced with the motion of his steps. Never before in his experience had he been charged with such a mission, never before been sent to stand before Allah's viceregent upon earth. But still the strangeness of his business was what preoccupied him most. The fish like molten gold, the water to be changed only at running streams, the fish to be preserved from frost and sun; and then the bowl: had not the Khalifa said at the last, "Beware, break not the bowl"? So it appeared to him that most undoubtedly a charm was in the fish and in the bowl, for who sends a common fish on such a journey through the land? Then he resolved at any hazard to bring them safe and keep the bowl intact, and trotting onward, smoked his hemp, and wondered why he of all men should have had the luck to bear the precious gift. He knew he kept his law, at least as far as a poor man can keep it, prayed when he thought of prayer, or was assailed by terror in the night alone upon the plains; fasted in Ramadan, although most of his life was one continual fast; drank of the shameful but seldom, and on the sly, so as to give offence to no believer, and seldom looked upon the face of the strange women, Daughters of the Illegitimate, whom Sidna Mohammed himself has said, avoid. But all these things he knew were done by many of the faithful, and so he did not set himself up as of exceeding virtue, but rather left the praise to God, who helped his slave with strength to keep his law. Then left off thinking, judging the matter was ordained, and trotted, trotted over the burning plains, the gold fish dancing in the water as the miles melted and passed away.

Duar and Kasbah, castles of the Caids, Arabs' black tents, suddra zaribas, camels grazing—antediluvian in appearance—on the little hills, the muddy streams edged all along the banks with oleanders, the solitary horsemen holding their long and brass-hooped guns like spears, the white-robed noiseless-footed travellers on the roads, the chattering storks upon the village mosques, the cow-birds sitting on the cattle in the fields—he saw, but marked not, as he trotted on. Day faded into night, no twilight intervening, and the stars shone out, Soheil and Rigel with Betelgeuse and Aldebaran, and the three bright lamps which cursed Christians known as the Three Maries—called, he supposed, after the mother of their Prophet; and still he trotted on. Then by the side of a lone palm-tree springing up from a cleft in the tall rock, an island on the plain, he stopped to pray; and sleeping, slept but fitfully, the strangeness of the business making him wonder; and he who cavils over matters in the night can never rest, for thus the jackal and the hyena pass their nights talking and reasoning about the thoughts which fill their minds when men lie with their faces covered in their haiks, and after prayer sleep. Rising after an hour or two and going to the nearest stream, he changed the water of his fish, leaving a little in the bottom of the bowl, and dipping with his brass drinking-cup into the stream for fear of accidents. He passed the Kasbah of el Daudi, passed the land of the Rahamna, accursed folk always in 'siba', saw the great snowy wall of Atlas rise, skirted Marakesh, the Kutubieh, rising first from the plain and sinking last from sight as he approached the mountains and left the great white city sleeping in the plain.

Little by little the country altered as he ran: cool streams for muddy rivers, groves of almond trees, ashes and elms, with grape-vines binding them together as the liana binds the canela and the urunday in the dark forests of Brazil and Paraguay. At mid-day, when the sun was at its height, when locusts, whirring through the air, sank in the dust as flying fish sink in the waves, when palm-trees seem to nod their heads, and lizards are abroad drinking the heat and basking in the rays, when the dry air shimmers, and sparks appear to dance before the traveller's eye, and a thin, reddish dust lies on the leaves, on clothes of men, and upon every hair of horses' coats, he reached a spring. A river springing from a rock, or issuing after running underground, had formed a little pond. Around the edge grew bulrushes, great catmace, water-soldiers, tall arums and metallic-looking sedge-grass, which gave an air as of an outpost of the tropics lost in the desert sand. Fish played beneath the rock where the stream issued, flitting to and fro, or hanging suspended for an instant in the clear stream, darted into the dark recesses of the sides; and in the middle of the pond enormous tortoises, horrid and antediluvian-looking, basked with their backs awash or raised their heads to snap at flies, and all about them hung a dark and fetid slime.

A troop of thin brown Arab girls filled their tall amphorae whilst washing in the pond. Placing his bowl of fish upon a jutting rock, the messenger drew near. "Gazelles," he said, "will one of you give me fresh water for the Sultan's golden fish?" Laughing and giggling, the girls drew near, looked at the bowl, had never seen such fish. "Allah is great; why do you not let them go in the pond and play a little with their brothers?" And Amarabat with a shiver answered, "Play, let them play! and if they come not back my life will answer for it." Fear fell upon the girls, and one advancing, holding the skirt of her long shift between her teeth to veil her face, poured water from her amphora upon the fish.

Then Amarabat, setting down his precious bowl, drew from his wallet a pomegranate and began to eat, and for a farthing buying a piece of bread from the women, was satisfied, and after smoking, slept, and dreamed he was approaching Tafilet; he saw the palm-trees rising from the sand; the gardens; all the oasis stretching beyond his sight; at the edge of the Sultan's camp, a town of canvas, with the horses, camels, and the mules picketed, all in rows, and in the midst of the great 'duar' the Sultan's tent, like a great palace all of canvas, shining in the sun. All this he saw, and he saw himself entering the camp, delivering up his fish, perhaps admitted to the sacred tent, or at least paid by a vizier, as one who has performed his duty well. The slow match blistering his foot, he woke to find himself alone, the 'gazelles' departed, and the sun shining on the bowl, making the fish appear more magical, more wondrous, brighter, and more golden than before.

And so he took his way along the winding Atlas paths, and slept at the Demnats, then, entering the mountains, met long trains of travellers going to the south. Passing through groves of chestnuts, walnut-trees, and hedges thick with blackberries and travellers' joy, he climbed through vineyards rich with black Atlas grapes, and passed flat mud-built Berber villages nestling against the rocks. Eagles flew by and moufflons gazed at him from the peaks, and from the thickets of lentiscus and dwarf arbutus wild boars appeared, grunted, and slowly walked across the path, and still he climbed, the icy wind from the snow chilling him in his cotton shirt, for his warm Tadla haik was long ago wrapped around the bowl to shield the precious fish. Crossing the Wad Ghadat, the current to his chin, his bowl of fish held in one hand, he struggled on. The Berber tribesmen at Tetsula and Zarkten, hard-featured, shaved but for a chin-tuft, and robed in their 'achnifs' with the curious eye woven in the skirt, saw he was a 'rekass', or thought the fish not worth their notice, so gave him a free road. Night caught him at the stone-built, antedeluvian-looking Kasbah of the Glaui, perched in the eye of the pass, with the small plain of Teluet two thousand feet below. Off the high snow-peaks came a whistling wind, water froze solid in all the pots and pans, earthenware jars and bottles throughout the castle, save in the bowl which Amarabat, shivering to the embers, hearing the muezzin at each call to prayers; praying himself to keep awake so that his fish might live. Dawn saw him on the trail, the bowl wrapped in a woollen rag, and the fish fed with bread-crumbs, but himself hungry and his head swimming with want of sleep, with smoking kief, and with the bitter wind which from El Tisi N'Glaui flagellates the road. Right through the valley of Teluet he still kept on, and day and night still trotting, trotting on, changing his bowl almost instinctively from hand to hand, a broad leaf floating on the top to keep the water still, he left Agurzga, with its twin castles, Ghresat and Dads, behind. Then rapidly descending, in a day reached an oasis between Todghra and Ferkla, and rested at a village for the night. Sheltered by palm-trees and hedged round with cactuses and aloes, either to keep out thieves or as a symbol of the thorniness of life, the village lay, looking back on the white Atlas gaunt and mysterious, and on the other side towards the brown Sahara, land of the palm-tree (Belad-el-Jerid), the refuge of the true Ishmaelite; for in the desert, learning, good faith, and hospitality can still be found—at least, so Arabs say.

Orange and azofaifa trees, with almonds, sweet limes and walnuts, stood up against the waning light, outlined in the clear atmosphere almost so sharply as to wound the eye. Around the well goats and sheep lay, whilst a girl led a camel round the Noria track; women sat here and there and gossiped, with their tall earthenware jars stuck by the point into the ground, and waited for their turn, just as they did in the old times, so far removed from us, but which in Arab life is but as yesterday, when Jacob cheated Esau, and the whole scheme of Arab life was photographed for us by the writers of the Pentateuch. In fact, the self-same scene which has been acted every evening for two thousand years throughout North Africa, since the adventurous ancestors of the tribesmen of today left Hadrumut or Yemen, and upon which Allah looks down approvingly, as recognizing that the traditions of his first recorded life have been well kept. Next day he trotted through the barren plain of Seddat, the Jibel Saghra making a black line on the horizon to the south. Here Berber tribes sweep in their razzias like hawks; but who would plunder a rekass carrying a bowl of fish? Crossing the dreary plain and dreaming of his entry into Tafilet, which now was almost in his reach not two days distant, the sun beating on his head, the water almost boiling in the bowl, hungry and footsore, and in the state betwixt waking and sleep into which those who smoke hemp on journeys often get, he branched away upon a trail leading towards the south. Between the oases of Todghra and Ferkla, nothing but stone and sand, black stones on yellow sand; sand, and yet more sand, and then again stretches of blackish rocks with a Sahara bush or two, and here and there a colocynth, bitter and beautiful as love or life, smiling up at the traveller from amongst the stones. Towards mid-day the path led towards a sandy tract all over-grown with sandrac bushes and crossed by trails of jackals and hyenas, then it quite disappeared, and Amarabat waking from his dream saw he was lost. Like a good shepherd, his first thought was for his fish; for he imagined the last few hours of sun had made them faint, and one of them looked heavy and swam sideways, and the rest kept rising to the surface in an uneasy way. Not for a moment was Amarabat frightened, but looked about for some known landmark, and finding none started to go back on his trail. But to his horror the wind which always sweeps across the Sahara had covered up his tracks, and on the stony paths which he had passed his feet had left no prints. Then Amarabat, the first moments of despair passed by, took a long look at the horizon, tightened his belt, pulled up his slipper heels, covered his precious bowl with a corner of his robe, and started doggedly back upon the road he thought he traversed on the deceitful path. How long he trotted, what he endured, whether the fish died first, or if he drank, or, faithful to the last, thirsting met death, no one can say. Most likely wandering in the waste of sandhills and of suddra bushes he stumbled on, smoking his hashish while it lasted, turning to Mecca at the time of prayer, and trotting on more feebly (for he was born to run), till he sat down beneath the sun-dried bushes where the Shinghiti on his Mehari found him dead beside the trail. Under a stunted sandarac tree, the head turned to the east, his body lay, swollen and distorted by the pangs of thirst, the tongue protruding rough as a parrot's, and beside him lay the seven golden fish, once bright and shining as the pure gold when the goldsmith pours it molten from its pot, but now turned black and bloated, stiff, dry and dead. Life the mysterious, the mocking, the inscrutable, unseizable, the uncomprehended essence of nothing and of everything, had fled, both from the faithful messenger and from his fish. But the Khalifa's parting caution had been well obeyed, for by the tree, unbroken, the crystal bowl still glistened beautiful as gold, in the fierce rays of the Sahara sun.

Poems

John Randolf Carter

Someone Comes Knocking

I let them in.
They tell me I'm a jerk.
I tell them to fuck off.
They go away.

I take a nap.
When I wake up I find
soldiers in my bed—
toy soldiers fighting
a miniature war.

I tell them to go away.
They become watermelons
and I carry them to my
car and drive to the
country where I sell them
at a roadside stand.

I take the proceeds and
buy a lamp to help shed
some light on my
sorry state of affairs.

The Reader

Andrew Saltarelli's *Book Against Forgetting*

T his is not the age of the masterpiece. We seem not to expect, less to demand, greatness from our artists. Perhaps, in our egalitarian trance, we no longer believe in greatness. Pity, then, the genuine article and the aggressive neglect it inspires. The masterpiece in question, *The Book Against God*, springs from the ardent pen of James Wood, the justly esteemed author of *The Broken Estate*, the finest book of literary essays since Alfred Kazin's *The Inmost Leaf.* They blow off the dust that has settled on the necropolis of literature. Woods reads Jane Austen, Knut Hamsun, Flaubert, and others as if no one has ever done so before, as if no one has even come close to describing the contours of their genius. His touch is electric. He kindles the dead into incandescence. His heresy is to hold contemporary fiction to the same exalted standards as the canonical. He discovers cloddish feet propelling our sacred cows. Readers of Pynchon, he avers, intimidated by his "indexical intelligence," "mistake bright lights for evidence of habitation." Bemoaning Updike's tendency to fall into the prose equivalent of "lyric kitsch," that "stainless quality that ensures that his books never quite agitate us (or, on the other hand, never quite console us) as great works do," Wood asks him to "be a *novelist*, abandon himself to negative capability, and depict something he does not like."

Wood's polemical fervor derives from his conviction that realism "has been the novel's insistent preoccupation since the beginning of the form." The real is "contour, aspiration, tyrant...the atlas of fiction, over which all novelists thirst." Literature is a delicate, constantly shifting interplay between the reality of fiction and the reality of what we, the readers, "fumblingly call 'true' or 'real.'" "The gentle *request* to believe," Wood argues, "is what makes fiction so moving." Unlike religion, fiction does not assert its reality. We can always close the book. The writer must earn his covenant with the reader, must appeal to our shared sense of the real. Even when we do assent to the reality of fiction, our belief is "not quite" belief: "our belief is itself metaphorical—it only *resembles* actual belief, and is never therefore wholly belief." In asking us to judge its reality, in having to compel a wavering belief through the artifice of form, literature constitutes a "special realm of freedom." Fiction may be the valley of the possible, the sanctuary for all our imaginary kingdoms, but nevertheless the kingdom it sanctions must look and feel like a real kingdom, or risk our censure, our voluntary exodus from its pastures.

Wood is especially skeptical of writers who shirk their duties to the real and "ripen [their] chimeras in a false heat." Magical realism is a tautology. In the temple of literature, the greatest priests are those who, like Virginia Woolf, can move "between the religious impulse and the novelistic impulse, to distinguish between them, and yet, miraculously, to draw on both." The use of the word *miraculously* unlocks Wood's deepest feelings about literature. A miracle, in its secular meaning as an extremely outstanding or unusual event, nevertheless gains a certain gravity from its shadow meaning as a divinely natural phenomena. Literature is not like a miracle, it is a miracle. It is something made out of nothing, a viol in the void, as Nabokov called one of his pampered children. The transcendence that a great book offers us is real, the miracle of the wrought object, but it is a partial transcendence, unable and unwilling to leap from the saving frailties of the human to the coercive absolutism of the divine. Every novel discloses, almost helplessly, a vision of reality. That vision may be, and should be, skeptical and inquisitorial, humble before the staggering complexity of experience, but in the greatest fiction that revelation of reality enacts a kind of mysticism: the fiction itself becomes an obstructing veil that points beyond its own vision to the spider of reality glinting between its web of sentences. It leads the reader back to life, but a life charged and enchanted by its magnification in fiction. In Virginia Woolf the mystical does not spring from some Platonic realm of the Good but is intrinsic to what we call reality, the realm apprehended through the senses, and can only be airily grasped at by the imagination. In Woolf the "novel acts mystically, only to show that we cannot reach the godhead, for the godhead has disappeared." Her art reenacts, or rather, attempts to reverse, the Fall. Her imagination reaches out to a reconciling vision, but just when the tableau is complete in her mind she wakes from her dream. The finished manuscript is a frieze of this tragic arc. Art is imprisoned in the very solidity it would expose as illusory. Though the work itself is condemned to the stasis of arranged sentences, the living impulse is restless, questing, forever straining beyond itself; like Lily Briscoe in *To The Lighthouse,* sitting at her easel, yearning for "the thing itself before it has been made anything." The great novels, then, draw their energies from a reality that is at once palpable and yet elusive, unstable, a mirage of appearances that seems to conceal some ultimate pattern. The "contradictory belief," Wood writes, "that truth can be looked for but not looked at, and that art is the greatest way of giving form to this contradiction is what moves us so intensely."

Fiction is like a star that can only be seen from the corner of the eye. Looked at frontally, the glow dissolves; the spark of light melts into its background. Fiction resists adult certainties, the brusque thrusts of the reportorial instinct. It prefers the rustle of the errant mind, the capers of the leaping imagination. Art is not the end but the erratic beginning of perception. When we have finished a great novel like *To The Lighthouse,* we are aware that meaning, finlike, moves on, "partially palpable, always hiding its larger invisibilities."

Art refreshes our curiosity in the radical mystery of our being, restoring us to wonder.

Wood's debut masterpiece calmly rebels against certain cliches of our literary culture. Chief among them is the dogma, propounded tirelessly by Sven Birkerts, that the proper subject of the ambitious novel is the swarming, hyper-distracted, depersonalizing organism of post-industrial society. Adam Begley, writing in *The Observer,* laments that Wood has "allowed his imagination the freedom to decorate a long, narrow scroll of fiddly detail, and to frame several handsome, small-scale portraits," inviting us to imagine "what he might accomplish with a vast canvas, a broad brush and a bold palette." This is like chastising Vermeer for not painting battle scenes. But its silliness reveals a conceptual stance than can only be ruinous to the health and survival of the novel. Human beings, runs this logic, are only compelling when they illustrate or embody larger, and typically sinister, forces of the culture. In the post-industrial era the real protaganist is the culture. There appears to be a general yearning for writers to show how much worse off we are now than we have ever been, to cooly diagnose our decline, delineate our digital thinness, that waning of the self visible in the novels of Stone, Pynchon, and Delillo. The postmodernist route, favored by hermetic academics, is to retreat completely from the world of real people and authentic incident and scribble on the class room walls self-conscious sentences that bend back on themselves, negating their own claims, cheekily confessing their own hollowness. In both routes lurks the despair of an animal fearing its own extinction. Wood, of course, has always cast a wary eye on Delillo and his less talented acolytes. Delillo is a great artist and a courageous genius, modernist in his unblinking seriousness, but the idea that his path is the only viable path for the writer mired in the contemporary maelstrom is a foolish and hampering notion. Why, when our novelists roll their mirrors down our roadways, do we so rarely see ourselves? We only see pallid hallucinations of ourselves, didactic scarecrows or nihilistic solipsists. Where, we ask, have the characters gone? Surely we have not totally disappeared into the post-human future. Surely there is more to us than our weary disaffections, our communal malaise. Surely, despite the identity-disintegrating octopus tentacles of the media, it is still possible to make human connections. More importantly, there are still individuals seeking such connections, and therefore seeking their novel. And the novel is where we, the seekers, meet.

The manly ambition to ensnare society in a linguistic spider's web has bloated the novel with information while enfeebling its beating heart. With all our obsessive concern with the unreality of contemporary life, we, the supposed guardians of the actual, have lost sight of the real. And the real is what Wood gives us on every page; in every crisp, quietly witty, melodious sentence. His characters are as slippery and evasive, endearing and exasperating as our friends and neighbors. They are not smothered under swaggering concepts. They do not tilt at trendy windmills. They do not pull double duty as apocalyptic sermons. And they are a joy to read about, a pleasure to live among. When Daniel Mendelsohn, writing in *The New York Review of Books,* chirps that "Wood has been caught with his pants down," perpetrating a novel that drips with the sins his criticism rails against, "clever symbolisms, self-consciously allegorical structure, slyly autobiographical references, and glib provincial humor," this reader can only sigh, scratch his forehead, and say, "Come now. That is not the book you have been reading. That is the book you wanted to read." The symbolism is not clever but organic: that is, the symbols emerge, as freely as leaves on a tree, from the textures of actuality and therefore deepen that actuality. The characters are never in bondage to some master idea. The novel's roomy structure could not be farther from the prison of allegory. The characters are too complicated, too contradictory, too *human,* to serve as symbolic representations of some truth about existence. They are simply intellectuals and intellectuals attempt, with often comical results, to live by their ideals. To accuse them of functioning as closet allegorical figures verges on willful delusion. Are Woods' autobiographical references sly? This reader has no way of knowing. Every writer uses his autobiography when he needs to, plucks apples from his past to hang on his imaginary boughs. Wood's criticism does not censure this almost involuntary process. Its inclusion in Mendelsohn's list must be accounted a mystery. For the condescending phrase 'glib provincial humor' substitute 'the touching stubborn quiddities of some English villagers.' Mendelsohn complains earlier that Wood "believes in the novel with the unyielding belief of the fundamentalist, rather than the gentler and more complicated passion of the true humanist." It is always easier to call someone names than truly understand their position. Wood believes in the novel, certainly, as well as the partial transcendence it offers. His unforgiving rigor is a measure of that belief. Mendelsohn, it seems, would prefer Wood to be a softer, kinder critic. But the great irony is that it is precisely the gentler and more complicated passions of the true humanist that Wood's ferocity protects and honors. Mendelsohn confuses the chicken with the egg. It is because Wood has so much reverence for the human being that he cannot abide fiction that distorts the proper subject of fiction: our lives. When a leading American journal prints such a soupy and smugly inaccurate caricature, it is not the writer, but the reader, who suffers.

One of the delights of *The Book Against God* is our immersion in an enclosed world redolent less of Queen Elizabeth's tabloid swamp than the sceptered isle of Victoria. It is not, by any means, an alternate universe, an irritating anti-terra a la *Ada*, but a walled terrace which lets in only as much light and life as it can make sense of. The novel is narrated, leisurely and yet from time-to-time with a snapping urgency, by Thomas Bunting, a ne'er do well philosopher who can't finish his Ph.D. dissertation because he is obsessed with his pet project and life's work: his BAG—Book Against God. Swollen to four large notebooks, it is a massive dialectical disquisition on matters of religion and philosophy. He is a kind of theological swashbuckler, combating the dread Kierkegaard with his jousting logic. His father, Peter, is a provincial vicar in Sundershall. Most of the book shuttles, both in memory and action, from that little village to London, where Thomas's marriage to Jane Sheridan, a concert pianist, is rapidly disintegrating. His friendship with his boyhood friend Max Thurlow, an "intellectually de-luxe columnist at the *Times*—the type who mentions Tacitus or Mill every other week," is likewise fraying. Only with his sybaritic Uncle Karl—not a real uncle, but a German refugee who was taken under the elder Bunting's wing at Durham University—does he stay in good graces. All the minor characters brim with healthy energy, and it is a relief to encounter so many vigorous souls blithely indifferent to the Zeitgeist. Roger Trelawny, the bustling impresario of an early music choir, steals every scene he's in with his exuberantly oblivious volubility, his chattering absorption in music. Colin Thurlow, Max's humorless father, is a cistern of pedantic malice, the cold fish academic incarnate. The novel itself has the spaciousness of a nineteenth century garden party. The characters circulate with splendid ease, and their exchanges, their orbital rubbings, never feel contrived or even faintly implausible. Indeed, the effect of this intricately structured novel is to convey the haphazard, meandering quality of life. Wood seems less impressed by chaos, no growling Roth he, than with the patterns and symmetries that form and dissolve at the raveled edges of memory. He glides through time like a hang-glider floating with the currents.

Reviewers have made a mountain out of the bunny hill of Thomas Bunting's odiousness. He is prodigal with other people's money yet cannot bestir himself to earn his own. He is priggish and elitist. He lies. His dishonesty is more than a tic. It is closer to a way of life. He is at his most repugnant, in fact, whenever pontificating on his habit of deceit. He derides Jane for treating every lie as an enormous betrayal of trust. He wishes she would understand that some lies are so nugatory the question of betrayal is moot. His ideal life is a mixture of edifying contemplation and elegant dissolution: "Plato by day and Alcibiades by night." He recruits Nietzsche and Camus to his cause. He blames his father for his "extravagant tastes." Peter's decision to resign his job teaching theology at Durham University and become a parish priest ensured a steady financial strain and a certain material thinness to the Buntings' domestic life. Thomas believes his pronounced aversion to the ordinary derives from these privations. His sins grow worse. He fakes an orgasm on Christmas Eve, one of Jane's optimal windows for pregnancy, and then assures her that he'd climaxed, a terrible betrayal in light of Jane's maternal yearnings. Marooned in Sundershall after separating from his wife, moping about and drinking whiskey on the sly, he tells his father, swept up in the "glorious intimacy and tenderness" of a long conversation in the car, that he is "seeking God." Lastly, at his father's funeral, he delivers an embarrassing, heated eulogy in which he quotes Schopenhauer, rambles on about his BAG and his collapsing marriage, and tactlessly asserts that his father was "no angel" before a furious Jane beckons him off the pulpit.

Thomas is immensely likeable. With what winning eloquence does he cloak his apologias! "The secularist, as I certainly consider myself, has a duty to be worldly, to take the pagan waters at spas of his own choosing." It is not simply the felicity of his prose style that endears him to us. It is the fact—and this is what makes the novel a masterpiece, this is the achieved grace of aesthetic form—that Thomas has so much affection, indeed, so much love for the world, that he scrupulously records its surfaces and echoes, its streaks and intonations. The care and attentiveness, the earned clarity, which a man lavishes on the external world exposes the depth and sensitivity of his interior one. His descriptive passages are grace notes, when the curtain, as it were, of Thomas' personality is swept away to reveal the pith and marrow of his soul. That soul, freed through the rigors of aesthetic precision from the distortions of egotism, is searching, amused, sweetly teasing, metaphysically elated, and so playfully, astonishingly observant it can think to compare the white creases in a light-brown leather coat to striations of fat in a piece of meat. How beautifully he describes Jane at the piano: "The short sleeves of her bunched and hilly dress throttled her thin upper arms, whose white skin caught the light as she lifted her hands—lifted them gently, in paddling movements, as if trying to calm the piano." When he mulls over the hands of Terry Upshaw, a lumbering rustic who does odd jobs for his father, you can hear the questioning awe of a child: "Yes, that was it, Terry worked as if eating through his jobs, with resigned hunger...I looked at Terry's hands, broad with earthy seams."

Certain reviewers seemed to regard Thomas's metaphors as expensive pieces of real estate that Wood benevolently loaned his creation, instead of redeeming emanations from Thomas himself. Morris Dickstein in *Slate* writes that "Wood has a near-fatal attraction to metaphors that call attention to themselves, like actors in mid-performance taking a bow." Dickstein's objection would be valid only if Thomas' seizures of metaphor blurred the world, smearing it with images that blunt each other by their jostling proliferation, precisely the kind of mandarin excess Wood dislikes in Nabokov. A metaphor that calls attention to itself does the opposite of what it intends, losing both objects in a haze of language. But Wood's metaphors always make us see the thing itself more clearly. They re-enchant the world, make the real more real by rendering it unfamiliar. When Thomas observes that "crowds were shuffling along the pavements as if they were chained together at the streets," he does not simply communicate his horror at the daily grind. He in fact subverts our customary way of looking at the world, nudging us to a bleak but liberating perception, startling us into wakefulness. In this one deft sentence can be heard all the howling of Dostoevsky's underground man. Reticence gives feeling elbow room, allows it to breathe. Bombast stultifies. Or take a more subtle example, quoted by Adam Begley to illustrate how "all very English" it is. Waiting for lunch, Thomas observes a traffic warden "going from car to car, pen in hand, like the waiters inside the restaurant soliciting orders." This is not merely a fanciful simile, a feat of observation. It is a profound moral insight. The waiter treats his customers as the traffic warden treats the cars, as if they were *things,* not souls. It is this routine dehumanization that Thomas later calls the "silent mutual murder" that constitutes most of ordinary life, and which causes so much suffering. But there is yet another level of poignance here. Thomas cannot, like his father, simply declare that we have immortal souls, that we are in fact not psycho-chemical constructs or souped-up computers, and be done with it. But clearly Thomas finds human beings magical, and if they are not divine they are at least flecked with a kind of mythic dust, a stellar residue, that compels our compassion and our awe. His simile clarifies the nature of his anguish. He is stirred by all that stirs the most fanatical Christian ecstatics, yet he cannot bracket the fallen world as a test, a soiled mirage. It is all there is. That so much injustice and evil mars what could be a marvelous garden is tragic, and to invent a God to redeem this tragedy is an insult to the reality of suffering. Reviewers who chuckle at Thomas' graduate student angst ignore the substance of his anguish, and the idea that somehow these questions of theology and belief should evaporate as one matures seems to me vaguely sinister, a plea for shallowness. What would they make of Tolstoy raving in his old age? Are we unable to take seriousness seriously?

Thomas's metaphors are a kind of makeshift parish he shelters in. They are agents of higher awareness. Far from repelling the reader with their gratuitous flamboyance, they disclose a hedged saintliness. His sentences honor the precepts of the Sanskrit triad at the end of *The Waste Land* that Wood quotes with approbation in his essay on T.S. Eliot. Datta. Dayadhvam. Damyata. *Give. Sympathize. Control.* The gift is the linguistic necklace. The sympathy is in the caressing glance of the tone; the empathy that inheres in humanizing observation. And the control is the sweat of the artist, determined that all his laboriously stitched and unstitched lines will seem nought but a moment's thought.

Style in *The Book Against God* is always subordinate to character. The sentences never pile up, sterile testaments to the writer's virtuosity. There are spaces between each word; echoing silences between each period. The reader is given just enough data, just enough insight, to liberate her own imagination. A textured depth of characterization accrues almost mysteriously between the characters; we form an impression of a dense web of *living* relationships of which we are permitted illuminating glimpses. The characters are always walking off the page and into each other's kitchens. We catch them on the fly, hovering above their commotion. We see, for instance, Max exchanging a puzzled look with Peter when Tom's Ph.D. is mentioned. We imagine Sarah Bunting stealing worried glances at Jane, proud of her accomplished daughter-in-law but fearful for the future of their marriage. Wood has freed them from the puppeteer's rigid strings, the fictionist's grip. He stands behind them, a benevolent magician, loving his characters, as Chekhov said a writer ought to, from afar. Reading the novel for the third time—and this is a novel that repays rereading—one is continually reminded of Iris Murdoch's assertion that the artist "*is* the good man: the lover who, nothing himself, lets other things be through him."

One of Wood's more impressive achievements is fashioning a prose style that is at once imperially subjective and yet cannily objective. We trust Bunting's observations because they are expressed with that measured calmness, that hallowed cleanness, which is the hallmark of the disinterested observer. This permits an extraordinary subtlety. For instance, when Jane drives away from the vicarage, the driveway gravel glows with pathos. "The car bristled away over the gravel—that luxurious substance that bears no impress, retains no memory of wear." It is the grace of Wood's novel that this subdued lament deepens and deepens until it becomes the real theme. For this is, above all, a book of memory. Thomas Bunting is writing it, he tells us, in a lonely bedsit above a karate studio, where, "during the day, yelps of triumph and pain can be heard." He misses Jane, the quiet pleasures of their marriage. "At dusk, holding a drink by the window and feeling luxurious and waiting for Jane to return from work, I loved to see the streetlights going on all over town in amber hesitations." Alone and in disgrace, this memoir is Thomas's atonement. And if, at times, he seems a little too in love with his baroque posturing, who among us does not secretly cherish, and cunningly justify, the rogues we harbor in our souls. Thomas is an egotist, not an egoist. The distinction is subtle but important. The egoist makes a philosophical fetish about the motivating powers of self-interest. If Thomas were merely an egoist his memoirs would be boorishly sophomoric, a hymn of self-exculpation. Fortunately, he is only wonderfully full of himself, infatuated with his "secular maunder." The real drama of the book is his regard, his tender fondness, for the faces crowding his past. In each weighted sentence he nuzzles the memory of those he loved and betrayed. The act of writing itself sweats with poignance. We see Thomas bent over his desk, his propitiatory pen wooing Jane and his father back to life. A scribbler is nothing without his Pygmalion yearnings.

To paint the world in its true colors, loyal only to the contours of one's astonishment, makes an artist a slave to the concrete, the damaged human realm we share. This need not be a dispiriting task, rank with quotidian tedium, especially if the artist agrees with Paul Celan that there is another world, and it is this one. What are these linguistic brush-strokes but acts of love, a way of caressing a fleeting reality? Saul Bellow, whose novels Wood admires, has written that love is, or ought to be, life's vocation. Wood has clearly learned from Bellow. Here is the same spirited intellectual comedy, the same prickly vanity, the same underground glooms and haunted houses of memory. *The Book Against God* reads, at times, like a less messy, less imperial, more reticent *Herzog*. Wood himself has said that America's vitalities fly. Would it be fair to say that England's vitalities pace a stately trot? Thomas Bunting, maverick philosopher, has discovered, one feels, in the process of writing his book, that higher vocation of love. He has, at last, loosed the poet from his philosophical fetters. In the early chapters Thomas still plays the sophist, still tries to wriggle free of guilt, as when he professes not to understand the difference between lying to one's wife and lying to a corporation. Philosophically, he may be right: there is no difference. The difference is all in the heart, a distinction Thomas learns as he combs through his losses. So the philosopher's arguments fade away with a dying fall. And Thomas Bunting, almost in spite of himself, verifies Pascal's famous apothegm. That unreasonable organ indeed has reasons whereof the mind knows nothing.

Thomas, of course, knew this conceptually. There is a curious passage in which Thomas elaborates a metaphor for the human condition. "No, underneath each soul is a bowl of tears, whose level rises and rises in a lifetime." Happiness is rare and "sparkles away." Unhappiness is the norm. Thomas, surprisingly, claims that "*I* was happy, I *am* happy." It is a jarring confession. Happiness is not the word his bedsit evokes. But he is happy, one realizes, because he is writing this book. He is happy because he is reliving his life. He is happy because as long as he *is* writing this book his father is still alive, Jane has not left him, and his BAG is not an estranging catastrophe but a feat of genius that will garner him laurels. The book is his second orchard. When he finishes it he will suffer a second exile. Appropriately, then, the novel ends on a swell of feeling.

Jane invites him to supper at her flat. She puts on a record, a live performance of Richter playing Beethoven 109. Thomas listens intently: "There was something about that first chord which made everything following it less exciting. That first chord was pristine, and pushed its successors out into an ordinary exile." He hears childhood, of course. The melody that supplants those first "simple and hymn-like" chords is "very stable, neither joyful nor melancholy; instead it seemed to be the gold of truth, constant behind our stormy extremes as the sun is behind clouds." He hears another sound, like a "man sniffling." It is the pianist breathing. "It was the sound of hard work, but it was also the sound of existence itself—a man's ordinary breath, the give and take of the organism, our colorless wind of survival, the zephyr of it all." Thomas cries. Jane is touched. We expect a dramatic reconciliation. The scene that follows is heartbreaking in its stubborn humanness, its quiet fidelity to the ways we misunderstand each other: the ways we miss each other. Thomas, truthful at last, tells her it's the pianist's breathing that moves him. Jane is taken aback. She wanted him to hear the tune's simplicity. When questioned, he fails to recognize it is the same tune she played at the concert when they were first introduced. It is a curious moment, a pregnant lull, and one can almost feel Jane draw back, crushed and mystified by his obtuseness. He has become a stranger to her.

What Jane does not see, cannot see, is that Thomas's nostalgia for the lost orchards of his childhood is more powerful than his nostalgia for their sundered union, their broken estate. And what, precisely, is this nostalgia? It is not a longing for the faith of the religion he has lost, but the faith of the parish he was exiled from: the faith of childhood. In a sense, Thomas suffered a double exile. The crippling self-consciousness of adolescence tore him not only from the warm hearth but also from the church. The adolescent turns violently away from his childhood because the loss of it is too painful to endure. Thomas's rebuke took the form of a long intellectual crusade, a perpetual shadowboxing with the father whose faith made his lonely, happy childhood possible. That linkage of adjectives is not an oxymoron. For an only child left alone with his fleeting dreams in the solid adult world, loneliness *is* a kind of happiness, an enchanted realm where a dreamy vagueness gilds the commonest object with mystery's lacquer. Thomas the child does not strike one as having many playmates. He was alone with his imagination and his sensitivity. Nothing diffused the looming power of his parents. Nothing broke up their dominion. That Peter was to Thomas as God is to a troubled believer is not a facile analogy. For are we not lonely in His kingdom? Has He not given us a green earth poisoned by our rage and desperation at our aloneness? And does He not answer our questions with a father's adult shrug? Thomas' anger towards his father is our anger towards a God who banished us from the garden He himself had created.

The swell of feeling climaxes shortly after Jane and Tom fail to reconcile. The next morning Tom has a peculiar epiphany, linking something that happened at his father's funeral with a troubling incident buried in the past. After his ignominious eulogy his mother takes his hand and holds it throughout the service. "I was grateful to her. It felt oddly familiar; the touch of her hand reminded me of something I could not quite recall." The morning after he sees Jane, the morning, that is, after his heart has been awakened to its grief, he recalls this something. One of Thomas's central memories, which haunts him with bleak frequency, is an incident that happened long ago during his grandmother's funeral. Thomas was only a boy then, standing awkwardly with the mourners. Confused and frightened, he runs away from the crowd towards the hearse. He trips over a tree stump and twists his ankle. His father strides towards him in a black cassock "with a furious look on his face." He has never forgot that "stern face," the face of a wrathful God. He has a recurrent nightmare in which his father, robed in his black cassock, strides toward him while his grandmother, wakened from the sleep of the dead, whistles a creepy hymn. But now, his father gone, his chance for a reconciliation with Jane failed, a curious thing happens. He connects his mother's hand with his father's hand. His father, he realizes, had held his hand throughout his grandmother's service, comforting the distraught boy. While his father is alive Thomas clings to this image of a wrathful father. He needs it to fuel his rebellion. Because he doesn't want to merely not believe in God; he wants to hate God, to punish God for his botched creation. But his father was blessed, and it is the luminous halo that seems to hover over him that the adult Thomas cannot stomach. For however happy he was in his secular maunder he never moved with his father's serene assurance; he never felt himself graced with a halcyon equanimity. He is jealous of the peace his father has made with doubt and loss. But now, his father dead, he can see him as he truly was: a man touched by a rare grace, whose absence is nearly unendurable. Disputation gives way to elegy. Self-justification surrenders to searing grief. Kafka's ax falls: the frozen seas within shatter.

"All my adult years I only held his hand to shake it, to say hello or goodbye. I would like to put my hand out now, and actually touch his.

"Oh Father, there were days so exciting when I was a little boy that each morning was a delicious surprise, a joy adults can only mimic when they are fortunate enough to make a long journey by night and rise in an undiscovered place in the morning and see it in the first light."

How moving that Thomas Bunting suffers from the most common ailment of them all: homesickness. His is the universal lament for those with happy childhoods, for those who knew the earth as a place of enchantment: you can't go home again. Or, you can go home again, but only as an exile, a refugee of the spirit, condemned to the nagging aches and cares of the quotidian while that other world, the child's bright kingdom, hums in the hallways like a music box in a distant room, whose melody can only be inferred.

In Wood's Virginia Woolf essay, he writes that "her work is full of the sense that art is an 'incessant unmethodical pacing' around meaning rather than toward it, and that this continuous circling is art's straightest metaphysical path. It is all art can do, it is everything that art can do." And what is this everything? It is a live action film of the interior, an intricate layering of moods, tones, and auras spattered with the grit of the world. Art is the medium through which the soul defines itself; makes itself manifest, visible. The soul, though, does not live in a vacuum. An imperturbable autonomy is not possible. It defines itself through its chafing relations with people and its negotiations with the past. It is involved, therefore, in a continuous dialectic, the inner and outer worlds commingling in complicated ways. Wood is not haunted like Virginia Woolf by the reality of a reality behind reality. He is not, like her, a metaphysician of impressions. His "incessant unmethodical pacing" roams through the corridors of time, not the whispering spaces between people. He is haunted by the presence of absence; the strange palpability of the absent. The pathos of Wood's art is to show that we are never alone, even when we think we are most alone. We are always surrounded by, held hostage by, ghosts. The past is always pressing in, seeping into the present like chimes carried by the wind. To lose contact with that past is to lose contact with the profoundest sources of our being.

Dwelling on the past is a disparaging phrase in our culture. We prefer the eternal present to the knotty past. But to dwell on the past, to cultivate memory, is, on the contrary, the only way to resist the infantalizing forces of this culture. Identity depends on the archeological resources of our inwardness. Identity depends, therefore, on serious reading. In his quiet way, Wood may be hinting to us that the so-called crisis of mediation does not have to overwhelm us. It need not drown out the higher, finer activities. Thomas is a true hero of this resistance. The tone and harmony of his prose grows a garden in the reader's soul. The fruit that springs forth in this soil must be our sustenance on the hard path of our resistance. But Wood offers us neither the rotten apple of paranoid anger nor the sour grapes of the black humorist. No, it is the rarest persimmon of the heart he's plucked from his orchard. And it is the savor of this harvest that may be as close as we come to a savior.

The Book Against God is narrated by a philosopher more comfortable with abstractions than feeling, but, miraculously, his fidelity to the felt reality and matter of life, to what is enduring and essential, "renders," to borrow Conrad's memorable phrase, "the highest kind of justice to the visible universe." Woods makes us hear, he makes us see, but, above all, he makes us *feel*. This emphasis on feeling must not be confused with the sloppy effusions of the confessional school, especially glaring in the memoir of late. It is earned feeling, winnowed of false notes, purged of self-indulgence. Wood's polemic against the rancorous vision that warps Delillo's *Underworld* is really a plea for vulnerability. The problem with *Underworld* is that "one can read, unmoved at the deepest levels, more than eight hundred pages." We have come to the heart of the matter, and for that matter, to the heart of the human condition. What are these deepest levels? Critics usually shy away from such vague phrases: they seem contaminated by mysticism. I must speak here as an individual reader. To me these deepest levels are the very marrow of literature. We speak of reading as secular prayer for good reason. The communion that transpires between reader and writer is a miracle of empathy. When we read we awaken to the reality of another human soul. "The subtle but invincible conviction of solidarity that knits together the loneliness of innumerable hearts," as Conrad gorgeously put it, is renewed and affirmed. If a novel dissolves our critical faculties, if a novel compels our belief in its living reality, then we are in a position to be stirred at the deepest levels. Those deepest levels, of course, like all mystical experiences, elude the nets of language. It is a state of emotional fullness, a welling effervescence of the heart. We apprehend the limitations of rational thought when, with Hamlet, we tell Horatio there is more in heaven and earth than is dreamt of in his philosophy. A description of this state, need it be said, will not stand up to the epistemological scrutiny of a logical positivist. One can only say, "When I am in this state, I *know:* I *know* that I have a soul passionately and strangely involved with the universe; I *know* that my life, our lives, have meaning, signify something, promise something." No one has ever come closer than Nathaniel Hawthorne to capturing these moments when we flame and awaken: "Indeed, we are but shadows; we are not endowed with real life, and all that seems most real about us is but the thinnest substance of a dream, till the heart be touched. That touch creates us, then we begin to be, thereby we are beings of reality and inheritors of eternity." It is a state of being that dissolves dualities. That is why it deserves our reverence. It is our wholeness.

Thomas Bunting cannot believe in God. But he is no mere nihilist. He believes, though he might blanch at so bald a statement, in the dignity of the human spirit. That is why his last sorrowful words console us. They affirm the sphere of our freedom. We are the creature that asks questions. We are the creature that quarrels with its fate. In doing so we uncover laws that can only be called transcendent, for they seem to come, as Proust famously said, from "some other world...based on goodness, scrupulousness, sacrifice...laws which we have obeyed because we carried their precepts within us without knowing who inscribed them there." At the end of his magnificent novel Wood ushers us before the tabernacle of the greatest mystery: the compulsion of the artist, who may, like Thomas, be an objectionable character, to requite with unswerving fidelity the sacrament of the real. And when he has done that, when he has traced his shifting impressions of reality and fired them in the kiln of human language, he is free to stand back from both creations, his own and the one it fondly mirrors, and calmly wonder why. "When anyone asks me, I say that my childhood was happy, and for once, for once, I am not lying. Wasn't it an orchard, my childhood? But why, then, the worm? Why the worm? Tell me." Thomas Bunting has descended into himself and returned with an olive branch. He takes the reader's hand, as we, like him, prepare to leave his meadow of sentences and resume our search for our own lost orchards.

New Fiction

Dan Sleigh, *Islands*, orig. *Eilande* (1992) (tr. J.M. Coetze, London, Secker & Warburg, £17.99)

Henry Green: *Pack My Bag: A Self-Portrait* (New Directions, $14.95)

Josip Novakovich, *April Fool's Day* (Harper Collins, $23.95)

Gert Hofmann, *Lichtenberg and the Little Flower Girl*, orig. Dic klcinc Stechardin (1999) tr. Michael Hofmann (New Directions, $23.95)

To start with the disconcertingly best, I urge all Readers to get themselves a copy of Dan Sleigh's *Islands*. The author's offhand name (not his fault), the novel's provenance (it is translated from the original Afrikaans), the few and lazy critics who may have noticed it, its rivetingly documentary base (Sleigh is a not-at-all young historian who is a researcher in the National Archives, and this is his only book), the period of its setting (at the opening up of the Dutch colony on the Cape), its being a South African book, with all that implies of moanings about the evils of Apartheid, all militate against it.

I imagine a U.S. edition is in the works, but don't wait. It is a brilliant book in human terms, technically dazzling—the narrator tells seven tales before fully revealing himself as the clerk de Grevenbroek—and a compelling read, one of those books that make you slow down and savor a prose of almost documentary sobriety, richness and flexibility. It transports you in time to the second half of the seventeenth century, here especially unfamiliar because it deals as equally with the mentality of the pre-colonial, the aboriginal Hottentot tribes, as it does the enterprising, cruel, beleaguered world of the mercantile empire created by the Dutch.

In fact, it is the clash between these two cultures, between the paradise lost and the heavy hand of capital and its enslavements, which forms the basic structure of the book. To portray this alone would be a remarkable achievement, but to do so with a density of detail and a style that, without borrowing archaisms, is as solid as a treatise in Roman-Dutch law and as plain as a document, is the work of solitary genius beyond any literary genre, outside of any school. The 'stories' told describe this transition in terms of two women: Eva (born Krotoa), a Goringhaicona ('watermen'), daughter of their ruined chief's sister and raised as a companion to the daughter of Van Riebeeck, the first chief of the new colony, and her daughter Pieternella by the soldier Peter Havgaard. Eva is tainted by the new language and new religion and progressively dispossessed of her original culture by the colonizers for whom she is an intermediary. She may be a Goringhaicona, but her heart has become Dutch. Thus she (like the native culture) dies first spiritually and then, through vicissitude and solitude, cut off from her people, dies physically through alcohol and prostitution.

If redemption is at all possible for a mixed-blood, Pieternella embodies it. When her father is murdered in Madagascar—on an expedition to extract 'wealth' from a new territory—she finds protection with a fisherman called Bart; with a callow German soldier involved in the dreadful Lowland wars; with the legalizing Deneyn, a Puritan of the nastier, lecherous, grasping sort; and finally with a humble cooper, Daniel Zaaijman, with whom she seemingly recovers her mother's lost paradise in Mauritius—only to find that, too, a mirage, when the Dutch abandon the island as 'unprofitable'.

These are the bare bones. One is transported in time, but in material time, not abstract. The deities that preside over the book, whether the gods of the natives or the Lords Seventeen of the Dutch East India Company, are material gods. The structure that holds all this together is powerful. Perhaps its most striking character is that it rests on a physical universe and the death or ever-imperilled survival of the absolutely ordinary. To these people cattle, fish, timber, rope, the land, the sea (a dominating presence) are all that really counts. The dreams of wealth, the speculations of the Dutch East India Company, both commercial and metaphysical (all its officials are led by a myth of the untold wealth of the East, for which the Cape is a mere victualling station), turn out to be an illusion for the Dutch as for Pieternella, her men and her children. The reality—that of 'ordinary' people leading normal daily lives—is one to which most readers are unaccustomed. This book is no romance.

If it is a 'historical' novel, it has to be said that it is one not calculated to make the past more exciting or enticing. It is 'solid' history, so that the detail (lovingly described) dominates over the broad sweep. History, in which these people are caught up and whirled about and destroyed is, in fact, a sort of secondary player throughout. De Grevenbroek is its archivist. Because otherwise nobody will notice it. 'Seven of us,' writes the narrator on the first page, 'carried in our hearts the same woman…We were soldiers, a herdsman, sailors, a clerk, people with little emotion in our speech and very, very little emotion in our lives, apart from fear and rage.' On the last, he reflects back on the stories he has told: 'This is how history repeats itself: the first time as tragedy, the second time as farce. One circle merges into the next, nobody notices it. The great ocean moves on and never changes.'

Though I can read Dutch, I have never tried Afrikaans. It remains hard to believe that any stylist, and Sleigh is one, of a seventeenth-century temper could be better served than by the devoted work done here by the South African novelist André Brink with these

271

extraordinary 758 pages. What you get from reading *Islands*, besides living characters, compelling stories, and a venture into a millennial past, is a book with the *gravitas* and thoughtfulness of W.G. Sebald and a style that is neither ironical nor detached, nor even sentimental or 'humanitarian'. Something you might get from Herman Melville, whose presence (wittingly or not) broods over the book. The Melville of *Omoo* and *Typee*, but also of the customs-inspector that Melville was, the Melville of *Bartleby*, but also the far more cruel and self-consistent Melville of *Moby Dick*.

*

There can be few more odd or redolent autobiographies than Henry Green's *Pack My Bag*, written in fear of death (which was not to come for another thirty-odd years) and first published in 1940. We should all be grateful for its re-issue as one of New Directions' 'Classics', a series as enterprising as *The New York Review of Books*. (A parallel New Directions series, called 'Bibelots' brings us a hugely welcome reprint of the warm, quirky stories of Delmore Schwartz as well as his poems, under the title *Screeno*. Schwartz, too, was an odd man out, like his contemporary Nathaniel West, the pair being the infrastructure on which the modern American Jewish novel was built, and whose ultimate American language Saul Bellow so commands.)

Henry Green was (as was Delmore Schwartz) a particular passion of many in my group of literary friends in the late 'Forties and early 'Fifties. I think we were much engaged with style and there were few writers then who seemed so idiosyncratic about words, their order, their relation to speech and syntax (not to speak of his terse titles, *Living*, etc.), as Green. I did not take to him then, but I was wrong; and having re-read several of his novels, I think he needs a fresh look—as do so many of the so-called 'lesser' English writers of the period between the two world wars, Garnett, de la Mare, Benson, Gerhardie and many others. They all had common phantasms caused by the Great War of 1914–1918 and the destruction of a once-stable society—a period we may be entering ourselves.

When I say 'idiosyncratic' I don't mean eccentric (though Green clearly in some ways was), I mean consistently himself and at odds with convention. He was a rich and lonely child, a worker, once a 'bright young thing', a fire-warden, and had (at least after Oxford)—rather than a life of privilege—a life that intermingled peculiarly, in fact uniquely, with the lives, halting speech and abrupt, devious manners of the less well-off. This led him, in his examination of himself and others, into a strange, bluff grammar which makes the reader work to discern his real meaning. In that diction there is guilt, a sort of mental and moral stammer, that is often disconcerting, especially over the long run. The passage following will indicate what I mean:

> Now on an evening when I stayed to dinner my dark friend said in front of a large party she wished I would act with them. I said I could not really. Then turning on that remembered look which was so much of all I could call to mind of what I had ever read, she said, 'Henry, if you do I shall let you kiss me.' I blushed and, it was rare enough, could find nothing to say, to express how false I thought she had been to let me in for this in front of all these people and yet how extraordinarily generous it was of her to let me put my mouth on what I then felt to be all the race of women laughing.

I rest my case, and hate to think what an MLA editor (the bane of culture) would do to this passage, in un-Greening it, adjusting its punctuation, asking curtly who or what the 'it' is that was 'rare enough'. Reading this autobiography is to be confronted by a portly young man who is both an aesthete and an idler, who is bluff but also sensual and self-spending, who must have puzzled the girls he lusted after and even more the 'ordinary' people he favored and whose voices, much like E.H. Carr, he so carefully listened to. It is writing out loud, with a blush. It is both advancing and retreating, both telling and concealing.

Green's son (Green was his nom de plume—he was really Henry Yorke) Sebastian detects traces of haste, of fleeing before the expected doom of the London bombings, in the latter part of this short, delicious book. I don't agree. Green is as at home with the precision of billiards, the nastiness of school athletes, as with the literary condition (his first novel was published as he went up to Oxford), as he is with his responsibility for being who he is in the English society that was:

> One is always caught up, one inevitably has to take a hand but what I miss now is the reluctance I had then. It is not that one was ever afraid to die. One may resent being killed, but most of us are quite ready. What is despairing in my case is that I should acquiesce, in the old days I should never have done so, and that is my farewell to youth in this absolute bewilderment of July 1939, that I should be so little unwilling to fight and yet likely enough to die by fighting for something which, as I am now, for the life of me I cannot understand.

Or it may be that having had a not dissimilar childhood, that in 1938–1939, I remember the railings being dismantled for salvage and re-use that girded the parks into which I was led by the hand, or the issuance of rubbery and heavy gas-masks the need for which I, then ten, could no more understand than Henry Green. But I think it a wonderful book, to be read and savored as slowly as it was perhaps writ.

*

I shared a table for two days, judging the applicants for grants for the Massachusetts Council for the Arts, with three bright well-trained ladies, and a man of slouching demeanor, a certain looseness of flesh (no jogger he!) and pronounced Slavic features. He thought the manuscripts he had read and was presenting were all good enough but perhaps not all that good, and said so with an easy diffidence that was hard to contest. It was obvious he had very different ideas about literature than those held by the writers we were judging, but was always charitable. We made a few joint dashes downstairs (he for fresh air and I for a smoke) and found a certain liking for one another.

Which is a roundabout way of introducing Josip Novakovich, whose novel, *April Fool's Day*, is a wonder. And a good portent, for I have noticed a powerful and long-overdue revival of the narrative base of the novel, of a sense that fiction is addressed to a reader and that the reader can be expected to appreciate a good story well-told. In an earlier book (*Yolk*, Graywolf, 1995), the matter of the opening story, 'The Burning Clog', this Croat writer from the eastern provinces, tells us that,

> My father's assistant Nenad used to tell me stories while hammering nails into the wood to pinch the leather so no water could leak into the clogs he was making. The hammer punctuated his story like a gusle—the instrument of singers of tales—but more sharply, less melodiously.

Novakovich wants to know more: how does one tell stories, where do they spring from? He is an awkward interviewer, Nenad a practiced prevaricator—is that not what story-tellers are? He tells his would-be interviewer, 'Why are you so stuck on this? It's easy to tell a story. You start right here, and lead the listener farther and farther away, or start from far away and get us here.' That is both quite true, and disingenuous. As all the masters have known (though, alas! as the grant process showed, not many graduates of writers' workshops) there has to be a story that requires to be told, people about whom the reader wants to hear, voices which resonate, beginnings, middles and ends, and, if possible, marvels. Good stories involve both hammering nails and sharpness over melody.

April Fool's Day takes Ivan Dolinar from his birth on the 1st of April 1948 through Yugoslavia's history, which may seem complicated from the outside but from inside is based on a ludicrously simple formula: power is profitable and lack of power can be fatal. Ivan seems to have absorbed this with his mother's milk, which he absorbed for a year: 'From early on, Ivan wanted to distinguish himself, as though he knew he suffered a handicap. He fell in love with power as soon as he learned to crawl.' He is by turn brute, bully, coward.

As a child, 'adoring power, Ivan was ready to love the army, the state, and the president himself.' The latter being Josip Broz, Tito. The trouble with this, as with so many love affairs, is that it may not be reciprocated, especially if the means to arrive at distinction and recognition are phony and fraudulent. Thus, when he writes to praise the president ('Hallowed be thy name, thy will be done abroad as at home, give us daily bread and soccer balls of leather'), it's taken as an insult. Everything this distinction-lusting Candide (who is far from innocent) does indeed turns against him—indeed, the only tangible reward he has is a gilt fan handed him by Mme. Gandhi as he sweats in a labor camp.

I would not wish to spoil your pleasure by recounting Ivan's many adventures. A sort of turncoat Good Soldier Schweik they are too many, too funny, too cynically troublesome, too beautifully crafted to be enjoyed outside of his own words. Let it be said that this is a fantastical and rich writer, and that his stories are not just romps for our delectation, that they are not 'exotic' for taking place in that part of Novakovich's mind that still lives in the Croatia of yore, but have a hard edge and a pungency, and an economy of style and narrative, that all good readers, saying 'Yes, that's true', will relish. And yes, he and I voted for the best story-teller among the applicants. By the way, *this* April Fool is the best 'explanation' I have ever read (at least since the essays of Hubert Butler) of the peculiar fatality of the Balkan states. It contains everything you need to know about the stubborn fatality, the bizarre deviations of religion, the self-hatred that is masked by puny nationalism, the bragadoccio of underdevelopment, the pleasures and ills of sex in the antique manner, the ordinary, everyday farmyard brutality, the intellectual pretensions of the Yugoslav comity. That is, until we stepped in and broke it all up somewhat irreparably, leaving little in its place.

*

Gert Hofmann's brief, aphoristic book, loosely based on the real Georg Christoph Lichtenberg (1742–1799), whom the author's son, Michael, who translated the book with extraordinary freshness of language, described as a 'card of the Enlightenment', is the most purely beguiling book I've read in many a year, being a traditional eighteenth-century love story which is actually about love and not about sex, seduction and society. Hofmann's Lichtenberg stands here for the Enlightenment project, a redistribution of human speculation from religion to science. Machines fascinate him, as does the electricity of frogs and the vast learning of this brave new world in which Lichtenberg is just a cog, not rising much higher than his kite or farther afield than a survey of Osnabrück on behalf of his Hanoverian majesty of England.

He is a dwarf, a hunch-back, a bewigged fop, an eccentric professor, a student of mysteries, and therefore a throwback to the physical gargoyles of the Middle Ages. Herein lies the irony of a clean Enlightenment mind encased in a Bosch-like body. That this body should triumph over mind thanks to an uneducated thirteen-year-old flower-girl of deplorable parentage is a great feat of Hofmann's imagination and one of the truest love stories I have read: down to the very details of intimate human cohabitation, for the flower-girl simply accepts that Lichtenberg, mentor, master, gentleman, is lovable for his unique qualities, and because he loves her. The deformity becomes invisible, the preciosity part of her fun, her domain splendidly domesticated and bedded.

To pull all this off and make us believe that it is so and had to be so, required of Hofmann, a man who never wrote a novel until his last years, in which he wrote twelve, dying as he finished the last, prodigies of style and structure. The real Lichtenberg is known—if he is known at all (he was just a name I had heard)—for his Sudelbücher, or 'Waste Books', notebooks in which he wrote incessantly his observations and conclusions. This imposed on Hofmann—or perhaps suggested itself to him—the form of this novel, in which brief, pungent paragraphs, each one in itself an aphorism of a mood, a part of a day, a stage in love, succeed one another with barely a connection except that they follow the imposing order of the time that lies between childhood and death.

Her name was Marie Stechard, or 'the Stechardin', *die kleine Stechardin*, and she is shy, open, willing, grateful, generous, caring, and independent in her own domain. She is as wonderful a creation as the triple-her-age heteroginist with whom she takes up life as she finds it. The exchanges between them—I will only cite one of many, all moving, all bright and fresh as flowers—are a pure delight: one takes what one gets, they have an understanding that goes beyond his learning and her true candor, her unsolipsistic belief in herself. Here she is as she leaves home for Lichtenberg's house:

> Then she was sitting with him again in his grotto in the Gottmarstraße. He was wearing his wig. He could feel her warmth through her thin skirt.
>
> Did she want to feel his as well?
>
> With his slightly bent gouty fingers, he could pick up a pen and paper at a moment's notice. He was about to write something again, but just didn't know what.
>
> In the evening, when they had eaten, 'this day as well was coming to an end.' The Stechardess cleared the table. She folded up the white tablecloth. She fetched first his chair, then hers, and stood them side by side.
>
> Now their supper table had reverted to being a desk. She went and got a couple of cushions for him. They sat there side by side, and 'plunged into the floods of knowledge.' 'I have made it my rule that the rising sun is never to find me abed,' Lichtenberg once wrote. Or: 'In the course of a morning's reading, the head will find no end of material!' Then he said: There! and the little Stechard embarked on her reading and writing. Every second or third word he had to help her with. The moon, he said.
>
> That shines, she read.

Anyone not transfixed by writing at this level of purity is deaf to real literature. And I could cite many dozen such miniature joys. Recalling his teachers as a boy, when 'their names were all listed under a gallows,' Lichtenberg, going 'back into his head' where he 'ran into this and that', realizes they are 'all gone now -- peacefully, deceasefully—to their graves.' Or his description of 'the pretty back of her head which was where, as she said, she was to be found.' Or how she was 'brutal, like all beautiful women, even if they are still children.' But as Lichtenberg would say, 'Stop! I've said this already.'

*

I would also like to bring to our readers' attention: the debut collection of short stories by our contributor, Naama Goldstein, *The Place Will Comfort You* (Scribner's, $23.00); the latest book of poems by Harvey Shapiro, *How Charlie Shavers Died and Other Poems* (Wesleyan University Press, $13.95)—Shapiro being a poet I have always liked for his conflation of ordinary speech with high diction, here speaking of a visit to David Ignatow in hospital (…I say to the nurse, his color is good. / And she says, that's because we're giving / him blood, pointing to the tubing. Count / Dracula was right, she says, it / makes you look good. / But it's not for real.); and to Jean Echenoz's two excellent novels, *Piano* (New Press, $21.95) and *Chopin's Move* (Dalkey Archive, p/b $12.95)—Echenoz is by a long chalk the best current French novelist in that disconcerting world where literature meets crime, doubt, anxiety, fear and chance.

—K.B.

Pierre Bayle's Notebook

Averitable Last Call appeared in a recent advertisement, and I think it only right to pass it on to our readers. It comes from the reputable house of Heinemann and reads as follows:

> Are you the author of an African Writers Series title published by Heinemann between 1962 and 2002? If so, Heinemann Educational Publishers would like to speak to you about an exciting new initiative in partnership with ProQuest Information and Learning. Please contact us with your current contact details, so that we can send you further information.

I like of course, the whole idea of a 'new' initiative, since I am pretty sick of the old ones. But what really attracted me to the ad was the 'Quest' theme. Heinemann did in fact publish a series devoted to African writers, and some of them were well worth publishing. Only somehow, in the forty years intervening, they have misplaced them.

A pity, since African writers are now good for business. Otherwise ProQuest (listed on the New York Stock Exchange as PQE) would not be promoting this exciting initiative. Quest, and its subsidiary, the infamous Chadwick-Healey, are eager outright purchasers of texts which they then sell at a mark-up of several thousand percent. Caveat vendor! And Heinemann, send out one of those fearless explorers of old!

*

The presidential election has come and gone. Here is my two cents on the subject.

I hear that a lady walking her dog on New York's West Side felt fortunate, in the wake of the election, that she lived 'in an Island off Europe' and not among the unwashed to the west of Manhattan, those people 'out there' who were so simple-minded as to vote for George Bush. Alas for her, 'out there' was still, at last reckoning anyway, part of the United States, though it is *terra incognita* to *The New York Times* and much of the American intelligentsia, not to speak of those Europeans who thought it fitting to tell me how to vote. These illiberal 'liberals' simply cannot understand that anyone would disagree with them. Hence the much weeping and gnashing of teeth at yet another loss to the 'morons', to people who don't eat soufflés, don't value the departed Jacques Derrida, and are baffled by the common agricultural policy! To the propagandists of the Enlightenment project, why would anyone vote for a man who, in James Bowman's utterly 'straight' words, is 'just an ordinary guy trying to do what is best for his country'? Maybe what we need is cheap package tours to Kansas, Oklahoma, Texas, Tennessee and the like.

The Counter-Revolution, however, is *not* the reason why John Kerry lost the election or why George W. Bush won it. Nor was it entirely won by the Republicans. It was lost by the Democrats. In our national elections, it is perceptions that count, 'gut feelings', intuitions, a sense of one's place in the world, what psephologists and the pitch-men of the monstrous advertising industry call one's 'comfort level'. These inner convictions and (often) unstated feelings are rich, complex and almost impossible to fathom, and artists are far more likely to get them right (intuitively) than scientists armed with measuring sticks, surveys and charts.

Let me offer a single, hypothetical example. If you, dear Reader, are the political 'analyst', your guesswork appears in brackets.

Harold B. is black (therefore a Democrat) and lives and works in Tennessee (Republican). He works as a gang foreman for the electricity company, a lower-management job he's held for twelve years (Republican?). He is now thirty-eight (swing-voter). Had he been college-educated, he now knows, he would be on the management side; instead, he is unionized and on an hourly wage (Democrat). His take-home wage is roughly $35,000 a year (Democrat), but his company has recently been merged with another and he is insecure about his job (Democrat). He has been married twice, the first time to a black woman who works for the city government (Democrat) and has two children he sees only intermittently (Republican, because he is bitter about the treatment he received in the courts from an elected Democratic judge). Nor does he think much of the way his children are being educated by unionized teachers (Republican). He knows several co-workers who have been to Iraq and have told him that the war, which he considered unavoidable (Republican) is going badly (Democrat). His second wife is feisty, young, Hispanic and hard-working (Democrat), but has liberal attitudes (likely to make him vote Republican) and generally despises politics and politicians (Democrat). He is indifferent to religion (Democrat) but believes himself to be a responsible working-class citizen (Republican). He did not vote in the last election (swing vote) but if he had, he would not have voted for Al Gore (Republican) because he thinks Gore would have taken him for granted (Republican). In his eyes, the same applies to Kerry (Republican). He knows no homosexuals (Republican), and certainly can't quite understand why they should want to marry one another (Republican). His co-workers and buddies, many of whom do not vote, wouldn't dream of voting Republican, because that's the big money party (Democrat), but he himself thinks of himself as an 'independent' (Republican).

I could go on about the intimate details that might influence his choice, but that is enough to show that there is *no way* a journalist, a social scientist, or a political activist can be sure which way Harold B., or anyone else, is going to vote. Indeed, poor Harold has no sure conviction himself. Those who seek his vote, therefore, must somehow wrest it from him. Huge amounts of money were spent to that end, great forces were mobilized.

But if there is one thing I am sure about in the recent election, it is that this largesse, this insistent scream, this electoral Blitzkrieg, is something the millions of Harold B.'s, even in New York, do *not* like. Because he (and those other millions) thinks 'independently', he doesn't like to be sold a bill of goods. In fact, over his whole adult life, he has become increasingly resistant to anyone who seeks to seduce him or sell him anything. For him (and them) journalists, ad-men, the CEO's of big companies (including his own), lawyers and politicians are all cut of the same cloth. They are not only useless and idle and too big for their boots, they represent a sort of insidious evil which he cannot identify rationally but understands is destructive of the often painful but idealistic America his mother and grandmother have told him about.

If it costs a billion dollars to win an election and those running for president have to be millionaires, or take money from millionaires, who *gets* those millions? Advertisers, TV, newspaper, lawyers, that's who. Why should an election cost billions when voting is such a simple matter?

In other words, it is the very *excess* of politics and of the money it involves, the superfoetation of opinion and pundits and talking heads who think they know how he is going to vote, that actually revolts him. Neither money nor stridency, neither bullying nor patronizing, make it any easier for the average American to choose whom to vote for. In fact, it makes it a lot more difficult.

What do most of us do when the messages we receive are hugely contradictory, divisive, murky, confused? I suggest that we move into some quiet, internal space in which we know, regardless of what others tell us, what the worth or non-worth of persons X, Y and Z really is. We say to ourselves, 'Do I want him sitting next to me at the bar? How would I react if I ran across him in the street? Would I tell him anything about how my life really is?'

Do I know any better than anyone else what happened on November 2? Probably not. The movement of opinion in any mass is fickle. Am I saying this is an irrational process? Yes. Democracy is. Money and morals simply make it more irrational.

Of one thing I am fairly sure, and that is that the whole Enlightenment project has been hi-jacked by the intolerant. I know that, whatever their personal merits, neither Al Gore, in 2000 nor John Kerry in 2004, are representative of anything particularly *American*. And if a president does not represent the whole people, how can he lead his people? Bill Clinton, whatever his faults, and they were many, *was* a representative American—perhaps more in his faults than his virtues. So were all the electable Democratic candidates in my lifetime. And I voted for them, though I did not for Clinton. The historical compromises involved in the Electoral College guarantee that.

The forefathers saw to it that the differences between Americans would be mitigated by the several states, that the will of the Majority would not *necessarily* triumph over the individual rights and traditions of the Minority. That is, that a president could only be elected when a sufficient number of that minority felt comfortable with majority opinion.

Since the Second World War (I first voted for Harry Truman of Blessed Memory) and with the single exception of John Kennedy (by the narrowest of margins), the Democratic presidents in my time have been from what was once a broad party of Consensus. I grew up believing, like most Americans, that the Republicans represented Money, Business and the Booboisie. It was the party of the vast Middle West, of the *Volk*, of Progress and Optimism and the Rotary Club, of Boosters and Chambers of Commerce. In a profoundly and fortunately centrist nation, the Democratic party was our 'left' and the Republicans were our 'right'. This, of course, was a misunderstanding on our part. We were right about the Republicans of the day (Eisenhower and Reagan were its icons) but wrong about the Democrats.

The Democratic party of Truman (from a conservative border state), of Lyndon Johnson (from the South) and Jimmy Carter (likewise), was a party with two constituencies: the solid, conservative South and the heteroclite industrial belt, sustained ideologically by an immigrant intelligentsia. To put it at its simplest, the Democrats ceased to be the 'natural' majority party when they threw away (or alienated) their southern, states' rights, base. The gurus of the cities, inflamed by issues of civil liberties, captured the party. Thus they lost the long-range war. The South, and a startling proportion of the newer immigrant vote, is now Republican. In terms of the Electoral College, that leaves the Democrats with population, but not votes.

Yet this is a total contradiction of the natural order of things. The great leap forward of the United States—of involvement with the world, of civil liberties, of economic prosperity, of educational equality—is a product of Franklin Delano Roosevelt and Lyndon B. Johnson who, to add to his luster, also extricated the nation from Kennedy's war in Viet Nam. They won because of their party's natural base in the southern states. Yet can anyone imagine the present Democratic party nominating either man? Roosevelt, Truman and Johnson all believed that the government should act for all the people; it was they who enfranchised the poor; yet they were part of and dependent on retaining that minority of states (and electoral votes) that wished for none of the reforms that took place. Nonetheless, they in their wisdom finally accepted that the changes were inevitable, and perhaps even desirable.

That the most recent Democratic candidates were not for all the people is, I think, self-evident. They were anthropophagously virulent about Bush and his kind of people. Like Hollywood darlings, Bruce Springsteen, or the *Guardian* of England they weren't simply against Bush; they wanted him for lunch. They perfectly reflected the lady walking her dog on Central Park West: those who voted for Bush were 'morons'. Necessarily so, because they don't agree with Us.

Since all political analysis is essentially personal, I will tell you why and when this life-long Democratic voter did not vote for Kerry. Quite apart from the issues of war or the environment my epiphany came with the arrival in my mail-box of *The New Yorker,* the East Coast middlebrow weekly to which a million people subscribe because if you don't, six or seven times a year (and ever more rarely) you may miss something really good. And half way through the magazine was a full page photographic portrait of Act Up, a homosexual activist group. Ten bodies are portrayed with stencils saying 'STOP AIDS' across their pectorals and dugs, with trousers (yes, the women too) around their feet, and four of them in the front row with everything else, including pubes and genitals, showing, dead center being a quiescent black penis. This, the magazine was saying, is what you should be voting for.

I chose not to and I think many Americans felt as I do. The portrait, the magazine, the harassment, liberal money, the Smart set, the failure to understand the nature of offensiveness, did not sit well in the America I prefer, the America of my inner space. If more of that was what Kerry had to offer America, I wanted no part of it. The tastes of the few have become the agenda of a party adrift in a sea of solipsism, hedonism and seething hatred. Thus does a self-styled intelligentsia commit public suicide. Unless it recovers its base, I see nothing to indicate that it will not repeat its own disembowelment in 2008.

*

A recent review by Michael Gorra deals with Orhan Pamuk and a subject I think bears a close look, the development of an 'international' style, one that 'travels well from one country to another.' Gorra lists its avatars: Grass's *Tin Drum*, Gabriel Garcia Marquez's *One Hundred Years of Solitude*, Rushdie's *Midnight's Children*. Easy enough to think of others: Peter Esterhazy in Hungary, Kundera, displaced in France, Julian Marias in Spain, Paul Auster, somewhere. Its characteristics Gorra defines as (1) having 'a political edge', grappling with 'terror, atrocity and tyranny'; (2) 'grimly comic'; (3) 'not above trading on the charms of the exotic'; (4) in style, 'flamboyant' and 'prolix'; (5) sometimes 'fantastic' and often referring to the 'folk tale' and the 'oral tradition'; (6) in characterization 'broad' and 'at times over-determined' or 'verging on caricature and therefore coming 'to stand...as the embodiment of an entire national literature, as though one story could indeed do the job of many.' Wryly, Gorra goes on to argue, that for writers in these un-English literatures, the international style has become 'the choice of those who expect to be read in translation.'

This is meaty stuff—a search for universals, for events and processes that are particular to a single culture but must be perceptible to another. I don't think this works. Literature is firmly based in language, and thereby horribly dependent on translation. There is no such thing as an 'universal' literature, any more than there is a world-wide language, or can ever be 'universal' jurisdictions or law. We are products of a particular place and particular customs. Those who seek to transcend their own cultures for the sake of 'general' ideas sacrifice the only readers likely to see their messages as relevant to themselves.

*

I have been playing and listening to a lot of Janáček piano music lately. He didn't write much. It is quiet, reflective music: 'emotion recollected in tranquillity' describes it perfectly. He had a troubled life; women agitated him, as they do most artists. He wrote much of it in the country, an idealized place which artists often seek out (see Martial) but where in most cases they spend their days chopping logs. The result is serene, sometimes foggy, seldom bright, mainly autumnal. It is where he explored what might be called 'private' harmonies, the ones he would use later in noisier, more open compositions.

I happen to like that quietist approach to music, which is why I went down to Hampden-Sydney College in Virginia just as summer was about to break on us. Hampden-Sydney is a small private college founded in 1776, and it annually offers a very attractive chamber music festival. The countryside is lovely, the campus clean, the auditorium modest but pleasant, the audience (largely but not exclusively drawn from Washington) is cultivated, the musicians friendly and available. As does Gidon Kremer at Lockenhaus, its directors, the clarinetist Ethan Sloane and the pianist James C. Kidd, keep its proportions reasonable. Though there are young and talented artists around, the festival is neither a show-case, nor just an assembly of seasoned musicians seeking extra summer honoraria by offering the public lollipops. It is not as earnest as Marlboro (nor indeed as faintly pretentious) nor as dumbed-down as the modern Tanglewood can sometimes be. Its programs are neither over-long nor skimpy, and seek neither to shock nor to bore. In short, it's rather close to what I truly want from a festival, and it is devoted to chamber music of the sort with which we are all familiar, but know insufficiently, largely drawn from the nineteenth century.

This sort of chamber music repertory is far more taxing than it seems, though every instrumentalist of caliber has probably 'been through' it. Its special quality, of course, is that it brings out the best in those whose instrumental careers have not led them to the purely grandiose. Chamber music is ever intimate and requires that the players interrelate and blend, that they submerge their big moments into the whole, and that they pay every attention to detail while retaining the over-all flow of the music. This does not exclude virtuosity, as was amply proven in the two concerts I attended.

The first program included Mozart's E-flat major trio for piano, clarinet and viola, the latter not being the most ingratiating of parts. Ethan Sloane, Gilbert Kalish and Auturo Delmoni performed it in a sprightly, melodic and clean-as-a-whistle style. If I say that this was followed by two works, Fauré's Elégie and Saint-Saëns' Allegro appassionato, both for cello and piano, both played with mastery and great lyricism by Messrs. Rosen and Kidd, you will have an idea that the Hampden-Sydney Festival does explore even the remoter parts of the repertory. Both were revealing as music and nicely romantic in performance. The center-piece was Dvořák's Dumky trio, which I have never heard played with more verve, a greater drive in the parts where drive is required, and a lyrical subtlety and expressiveness in the haunting lentos and adagios that are the heartland of this piece. Here Delmoni showed his prowess with the bow, Gilbert Kalish his fine understanding of how this great melodist's rhythms need to be observed but not thumped, and Rosen on the cello just had himself one of those utterly memorable performances that congenial group-playing sometimes produces.

The same could be said of the second concert. A Glinka trio pathétique was nothing great as music, but sympathetically played proved to have plenty of musical ideas, especially for the clarinet, where Sloane had a seamless sense of melody and showed no signs of strain, sustaining even the longest lines. There followed a medley of quite spectacular show-pieces (by Kreisler, Chopin, Sibelius and Fauré) that showed to advantage Delmoni's Paganini side (which is considerable both as to musicianship and technique) and Kidd's delicacy of touch. Here again we ended with a formidable, brooding, many-colored trio, Schubert's in B-flat major. And once again, a trio (itself a formidable challenge to a composer) that is, in so many celebrated hands, a war-horse to be played for effect, came completely alive. Would that Delmoni-Rosen-Kalisch were a permanent trio! And recorded!

—K.B.

Back issue contents

NUMBER 1

TEXTS
Saul Bellow: View from Intensive Care
Emilio Lascano Tegui: Of Elegance While One Sleeps
Arturo Loria: The Sirens
John Auerbach: Requiem for a Dog
NICANOR PARRA: FOUR POEMS

BOOKS
Bohumil Hrabal a Tribute
Sean Jackson on Flann O'Brien
Chris Walsh on Amis and Johnson

MUSIC
Keith Botsford: Four Pianists

PB'S NOTEBOOK

NUMBER 2

TEXTS
Louis Guilloux: Salido
Christopher Ricks and *William Empson:* A Correspondence

ARIAS
Saul Bellow: Graven Images
Philip O'Connor: Last Journal?; Or, Philippics
James Wood: Real Life
Raymond Tallis: A Dark Mirror, Reflections on Dementia
Saul Bellow: On the Floor

ARCHIVES
Samuel Butler: Quis Desiderio…?
Cesare Lombroso: Crazies Literary, Political, and Religious

BOOKS
Janis Freedman Bellow on Philip Roth
Chris Walsh on Yeechh

Bette Howland on Studs Lonigan's Neighborhood

ART

Keith Botsford on Vermeer

PB'S NOTEBOOK

NUMBER 3

TEXTS

W.G. Sebald: From *Saturn's Rings*

Karl Logher: My Father in the Mirror

B.H. Friedman: Swimming

ARIAS

Martin Amis: Cars and the Man

Saul Bellow: Ralph Ellison in Tivoli

George Walden: Christ Goes to Golyvood

LIVES

Samuel Lipman: Musicians Wrestle Everywhere

ARCHIVES

Leopardi: Dialogue with the Dead

ART

Sarah Walden: Whistler's Mother

MUSIC

Chris Walsh on a Certain Philharmonia

POEMS

Rudaki

Marcia Karp

PB'S NOTEBOOK

NUMBER 4

Bette Howland: Trial (A Reportage)

TEXTS

Saul Bellow: All Marbles Still Accounted For

Roberto Arlt: The Hidden Springs

Ken Kalfus: Budyonnovsk

ARIAS
Marguerite Duras: The Fly on the Wall
Melvin J. Lasky: Odd Poets Laureate
Richard G. Stern: From Van Meegeren to Van Blederen

ARCHIVES
Victor Hugo: The Interment of Napoleon

BOOKS
Janis Freedman Bellow on *Night Train*
Chris Walsh on *Resurrection*

POEMS
Michael Hulse

PB'S NOTEBOOK

NUMBER 5
Jack Miles: A Parable
Ripostes by *Saul Bellow* and a Taoist Surfer

TEXTS
Annie Dillard: Encounters
Claire Messud: Leaving Algiers
Mark Harris: Her Career at True Blue Car
Murray Bail: The Seduction of My Sister

BOOKS
Chris Walsh on *Already Dead*
Jonathan Vogels on *The Material Ghost*

POEMS
Marcia Karp
Alane Rollings

LIVES
Philip O'Connor
David Rousset

PB'S NOTEBOOK

NUMBER 6

INSERT

G. V. Desani: A.D. 1952

TEXTS

Salvatore Sciona: Prairie

Mark Greenberg: In the Dark

ARIAS

Murray Bail: Killing an Elephant

Raymond Tallis: On Ted Hughes

CORRESPONDENCE

Jack Miles: The Parable Pinned

LIVES

Rudolf Kessner: Abbé Galiani

Alan Govenar and *Leonard St. Clair:* Life as a Tattoo Artist

BOOKS

Chrish Walsh on Jane Smiley

POEMS

Marcia Karp

Gary Roberts

POLITICS

Regis Debray on Kosovo

PB'S NOTEBOOK

NUMBER 7

INSERT

Joshua Barkan: Before Hiroshima

TEXTS

W.G. Sebald: Beyle, or Love is a Madness Most Discreet

Keith Botsford: The Mothers

ARIA

Julia Copeland: Sex and Musicians

LIVES

Saul Bellow: Saul Steinberg

ARCHIVES
John Aubrey: Thomas Hobbes

POEMS
Arthur Johnston
Michael Hulse

PB's NOTEBOOK

NUMBER 8

TEXTS
Saul Bellow: From *Ravelstein*
Naama Goldstein: Mr. Durchschlag's Medal
Bette Howland: The Lost Daughter
Julia Copeland: Terra Incognita

ARIA
Richard Stern: Where the Chips Fall

ARCHIVES
Francois De Chateaubriand: Daily Life in Combourg

LIVES
Herbert Gold: King of the Cleveland Beatniks

POEMS
Adam Kirsch

PB's NOTEBOOK

NUMBER 9

INSERT
Keith Botsford: Skip to My Lou

TEXT
Herbert Gold: Afterword: Haiti 2000

ARIAS
William A. Simpson: R. I. non P.: The Deposition of the Social
    Sciences
Keith Botsford: On Being Written

LIVES
Stephen Miller: Eric Hoffer Revisited

The Republic of Letters

POEMS
Sassan Tabatabai
Adam Seelig
Bernhard Frank
Cevat Capan

BOOKS
James Wood on Sartre and Camus
Bette Howland on Sister Carrie

PB'S NOTEBOOK

NUMBER 10

INSERT
Chantal Loiseau Hunt: Joseph

TEXTS
Federigo Tozzi: The Clocks
W.G. Sebald: From *Austerlitz*
Chaim Lapid: From *The Crime of Writing*

LIVES
Kenneth H. Brown: Krim's Way
Richard Stern: An Old Writer Looks at Himself

POEMS
Shafi-Kadkani
Jessica Hornick
Nora Seton

THE READER

PB'S NOTEBOOK

NUMBER 11
W.G. "Max" Sebald: 1944–2001

TEXTS
John Auerbach: Endgame in Kiryat-Gat
Dolores Moyano Martin: The Nazi and the Knights
Melvin J. Lasky: The Banalization of the Concept of Culture

ARIAS
Jacques Julliard: Of French Intellectuals and Anti-Americanism
James Wood: The American Novel after September 11
Sassan Tabatabai: Requiem for a Prayer

LIVES
Victor Serge: Notebooks
Marcella Olschki: Sixth Form, 1939

POEMS
Penelope Shuttle
Bernhard Frank
John Kinsella

PB's NOTEBOOK

NUMBER 12

ARIAS
Herbert Gold: The Soup Dossier

TEXTS
Alfred Andersch: The Oath
John Auerbach: The Black Madonna
Herbert Gold: When Love Dies, Where is it Buried?
Yesi T. Mills: La Rosa y un Favor / Rosa and a Favor
Leon Rooke: Son of Light
David Hart: All Saints Elegies

POEMS
Bernhard Frank
Michael Hulse
Sassan Tabatabai

ARCHIVES
Charles Morgan: The Independence of Landor
Walter Savage Landor: Alfierei & Metastasio

PB's NOTEBOOK

The Republic of Letters

NUMBER 13

ARIAS
Prudence Crowther: Cellini at the Met

TEXTS
Yesi T. Mills: Cracks in the Sidewalk, Paint on the Wall
Keith Botsford: Saturday
Herbert Gold: The Tragedy You Can Dance To: Haiti 2003
David Green: Lost Soul
Gustaw Herling: The Tower

ARCHIVES
Xavier De Maistre: The Leper of Aosta
Alberto Rangel: Xavier the Leper

POETRY
Susan Hamlyn
George Kalogeris
Katia Kapovich

LIVES
Aharon Appelfeld: Budapest

THE READER
On William Trevor, New Fiction
PB'S NOTEBOOK

The Republic of Letters
Back Issues

A small number of back issues is available.

Issues 1 through 5 cost $19.95 each
Issues 6 through 13 cost $9.95 each

Please mail check or credit card details, and we will be pleased
to mail these to you. Please add $5 for postage and handling.

The Toby Press LLC
POB 8531
New Milford, CT 06776-8531
USA